Not what you think

MELISSA HILL

arrow books

Published in 2005 by Arrow Books

9 10

Copyright © Melissa Hill 2004

Melissa Hill has asserted her right under the Copyright, Designs
and Patents Act, 1988 to be identified as the author of this work

First published in 2004 by Poolbeg Press Ltd

Arrow Books
Random House, 20 Vauxhall Bridge Road,
London SW1V 2SA

www.rbooks.co.uk

Addresses for companies within The Random House Group
Limited can be found at: www.randomhouse.co.uk/offices.htm

The Random House Group Limited Reg. No. 954009

A CIP catalogue record for this book
is available from the British Library

ISBN 9780099486923

The Random House Group Limited supports The Forest Stewardship
Council (FSC), the leading international forest certification organisation.
All our titles that are printed on Greenpeace approved FSC certified paper
carry the FSC logo. Our paper procurement policy can be found at:
www.rbooks.co.uk/environment

Printed and bound in Great Britain by
CPI Antony Rowe, Chippenham, Wiltshire

To Mam & Dad
With lots of love and thanks

Acknowledgements

Firstly, much love and thanks to Kevin for your wonderful support, advice and good humour, and mostly for keeping me sane when things get hectic – I really couldn't do this without you. Also, to Homer, whose clever antics gave me the inspiration for Barney!

To my family, Mam, Dad and especially Sharon, who – through phenomenal effort last summer – must have been single-handedly responsible for the majority of my book sales! To Amanda, who got away lightly last time, but who I know was with me in spirit.

This novel relates to the ups and downs of female friendship, and I'm lucky to have some great ones – thank you Maria, Fiona, Lisa, Breda and Aine for being so supportive through it all.

Once again, thanks to Ger Nichol, for guidance and endless encouragement. To Poolbeg – especially Paula, Brona and Lynda for making my first time out such an enjoyable experience, Sarah for Herculean publicity efforts, and Gaye for insightful editing and enthusiasm – working with you all is such a pleasure.

Many thanks to booksellers throughout the country for promotion, wonderful displays and great welcomes, and to my local bookshops – Bridge St Books, Wicklow; Eason, Clonmel; and particularly the Book Nook, Cashel, for tremendous support throughout the summer. Also, massive thanks to John and Carmel Dolan and all the staff of SuperValu, Cahir for promoting the book so enthusiastically – you have no idea how much I appreciate it. To friends and neighbours in both Tipp and Wicklow for lovely comments, good wishes and great support.

To all the journalists who were kind enough to give me and the book a mention, particularly Tony Butler in Tipp, and Lynne Glanville in Wicklow, and to the reviewers who said such nice things – thank you so much. Also, to Carol and Denis at Tipp FM for letting me natter away and take up so much airtime!

To fellow writers Clare Dowling and Mary Hosty for lovely dinners, all the Irish Girls for helpful chats and good craic, but particularly to Sarah Webb for invaluable advice and for being so welcoming to a first-timer.

To all those who shared their stories and provided me with the special insights that made this story possible. I am immensely grateful and hope I have done you justice.

Finally, a colossal thanks to everyone who has bought and read the book. With lots of fantastic books on the shelves, I'm amazed that so many people took a chance on an author they'd never heard of, and I very much appreciate it. Also, many thanks to those who sent lovely emails telling me how much they enjoyed it – I hope I managed to reply to you all. Hearing from readers is one of the most rewarding parts of being a writer, so please, drop me a line any time.

www.melissahill.info

Not what you think

Prologue

April

Chloe knew she should be concentrating on her driving, but she couldn't help it. She just *couldn't* look away. There it was, glistening attractively in the afternoon sunshine, newly polished and extraordinary, adorning the third finger of her left hand. Was there anything in the whole wide world more exhilarating than an engagement ring – *your own* engagement ring?

Chloe didn't think so.

"So what do you think I should wear on Sunday?" her best friend Lynne asked.

Chloe groaned inwardly. Lynne had been chattering down the phone about her latest shopping trip for the last twenty minutes. Chloe loved a good natter about what to wear as much as the next girl, but she just wasn't in the right frame of mind for discussing the merits of see-through strap bras as opposed to strapless ones – not today. She was just too excited.

"Lynne, I really have to hang up – there's a garda

patrol car ahead," she said, deciding she'd better pay more attention to the road.

"Oh, OK." The other girl sounded disappointed. "I suppose I'll see you at Alison's barbecue – you and Dan *are* going, I presume?"

"Should be," Chloe replied. "I'll talk to you later – wish me luck!"

"Oh, yes, I forgot you were going down there today. Good luck!"

After they had said their goodbyes, Chloe hung up and tossed her mobile onto the passenger seat. *Of course* she and Dan would be at the barbecue on Sunday. Chloe had picked up an amazing Gharani Strok beaded top to go with her cropped Karen Millen trousers especially for the occasion, and she would be damned if she was going to miss the opportunity to show it off.

She shivered with excitement as she approached Wicklow town. It was a pity that Dan couldn't come with her today, but he had simply laughed when she suggested that he take the morning off to drive down here with her.

Sometimes Dan didn't understand how much all of this meant to her.

Chloe weaved through the busy main street – she hadn't expected the town to be so thronged. Then, attempting to negotiate a narrow stretch of road between cars parked on each side of the street, Chloe was horrified to find that not only had she clipped her own wing mirror, but her Rav4 had actually shattered the mirror of the Astra parked on her right.

Yikes! Heart pounding, Chloe drove on as if nothing had happened. There was no one in the car, and she didn't

2

think anyone had seen her, so if she could get away with it . . . Anyway, it was the driver's fault for parking on double yellow lines, she reassured herself. What else could he expect? She was no Michael Schumacher after all. Anyway, she was in a hurry – she just didn't have time to wait around and discuss broken mirrors today. She could always pop back later and leave a note and her mobile number on the windscreen or something. Maybe. Oh dear, why did this have to happen today – and a broken mirror of all things! If Lynne were here, no doubt she'd start going on about seven years' bad luck and all that. Lynne was unbelievably superstitious and, on an important day like today, Chloe did not want to even *think* about the possibility of bad luck.

Finally finding a parking space just off the main street, Chloe removed her sunglasses and checked her reflection in the rear-view mirror. She applied a fresh coat of Mac 'Siss' lipstick and touched up her foundation. Eventually pleased with what she saw, she got out and locked her Jeep, but couldn't help checking her reflection once more in the driver's window. Using her sunglasses to tuck her blonde bob behind her ears, she straightened her skirt and began walking purposefully down the street. She smiled when a gang of teenagers loitering outside a video store wolf-whistled as she passed them by. Probably admiring her long legs. Well, Chloe thought with a self-satisfied grin, they were worth admiring.

Minutes later, she approached the store. She pushed open the door of Amazing Days Design and walked directly to the sales counter.

"Hello, I'm looking for Debbie, please. I spoke with

3

her on the telephone yesterday," she said in a business-like tone.

The teenage sales assistant regarded her with a bored look. "She's on her lunch," she said rudely, without looking up from her magazine.

Chloe's eyes widened when she noticed that the girl was reading an article entitled *Oral Sex – To Give Is More Blessed Than To Receive?*. Hardly a good first impression in a place like this, she thought. And what sort of a way was that to treat a customer?

"Well, I'm sure you can help me then," she said. "I'm here to see some designs –"

"Hi, Chloe!" The aforementioned Debbie arrived in the door, apparently back from her lunch break. "Sorry to keep you waiting, but I didn't think you'd be here until after two o'clock."

Chloe said nothing. According to her watch it was *already* after two. Still, she supposed she'd better not be too uptight about it. "I know I'm a little early, but I'm dying to take a look," she said then, with as much cordiality as she could muster but secretly hoping they didn't apply this laissez-faire attitude to every aspect of their business.

"Well, I came up with a few designs that I think might be suitable. Come in the back and I'll show them to you."

Chloe eagerly followed Debbie towards the rear of the store.

"You said on the phone that a friend recommended me?" Debbie probed.

"Alison Caffrey – well, she's Alison Kelly now," Chloe explained. "Everyone was raving about her invitations a few months back and when I began planning my own wedding I asked her for your details." It had absolutely *killed* Chloe to have to ask stuck-up Alison for the Amazing Days Design number, but if she and Dan wanted the best she had to bite the bullet and admit to their friend that she had loved her invites.

"Ah, yes, Alison," Debbie recalled. "She chose the gold-inscribed linen, if I remember correctly. But you said you were looking for something a little less traditional?"

Chloe nodded. Actually, something a *lot* unlike Alison's. She couldn't have people saying that she was stealing her friend's idea. Not in a million years. These designs had better be good.

"Well, take a look at these and see what you think," Debbie said pleasantly. "I used the details you gave me on the phone last week, and came up with a few personalised samples."

Chloe gasped when she saw the assortment of cards on the table.

"These are gorgeous!" she said, examining a white hammer-effect card with a picture of a cute smiling flowerpot 'couple' on the front, and tied with a scarlet ribbon – the colour of Chloe's bridesmaids' dresses. It was pretty but perhaps a little bit tacky – she had been hoping for something a little classier. Then, a second card caught her eye: this one was plain white with an embossed silver stained-glass-effect border, and elevated silver hearts in the centre.

She opened the second card, and felt her heart leap with pride as there, inscribed in silver foil, were the words she had been waiting to see:

Mr John & Mrs Rita Fallon,
Request the pleasure of the company of

. . . .

On the occasion of the marriage of their daughter
Chloe Maria,

to

Mr Daniel Ignatius Hunt
at St Anthony's Church,
Donnybrook,
On Friday, September 25th
and afterwards at the reception in
The Four Seasons Hotel, Ballsbridge, Dublin 4.,

∽∾∽

"Oh, they're really beautiful!" she exclaimed, putting a hand to her mouth.

She was getting married. She was really getting married. Chloe had been dreaming about her own wedding for most of her twenty-eight years, yet she didn't think that it had really hit her, not until then – not until she'd seen the words written down like that.

Of course, she'd done all the other things – reserved the Sharon Hoey dress, ordered the flowers, booked the hotel – but the dress was just a design, it wasn't yet hers, and the flowers were just a 'concept' in the florist's artistic little head. But here *now*, Chloe was holding in her hand tangible evidence of her forthcoming wedding, and she didn't think she had ever felt so exhilarated in her entire life.

"Are you all right?" she heard Debbie ask kindly.

Chloe turned to her, blinking back tears.

"You know, it's lovely to see a reaction like yours," Debbie continued, when Chloe didn't respond. "I've always thought that the wedding invitations should be chosen with as much, if not more, thought as the wedding dress. After all, the invitations herald the entire showpiece. Your guests get to see those before they get to see the dress, the flowers and the rest of it."

"No, it's nothing – I'm just being silly," Chloe said, collecting herself. She really shouldn't have let Debbie see her react like that. Now the woman would probably charge them a fortune.

"It's all right, dear," Debbie said, obviously mistaking Chloe's change of expression for embarrassment. "You don't need to explain anything to me. Now do you want a cuppa while you pick out the design you want, or will I just leave you to it?"

"I think the design chose me," Chloe said, unable to let go of the silver-embossed card she grasped in her left hand.

"You're sure? You don't need to OK it with himself, or anything?"

"No, it's my decision and he'll be happy to go along with my choice. Anyway," Chloe added dismissively, "you know what men are like."

How *dare* that woman undermine her relationship like that? As if she would have to 'OK' it with anyone!

"I do indeed," Debbie agreed, seemingly unaware of her customer's affronted feelings, "but you'd be surprised. I had a couple in here last weekend, and your man was calling all the shots and wouldn't let the girlfriend get a word in edgeways. I tell you, he was one of the fussiest divils I've ever come across, enquiring about the origins of the paper we use, and the environmental friendliness of the ink and all that. And the same fella was wearing a leather jacket! The misfortunate wife-to-be was mortified by the time they left the place."

Chloe said nothing. How unprofessional! In her eyes, the customer was always right, and she wasn't too impressed to hear Debbie gossiping merrily about one Amazing Days Design client to another. Still, she supposed Debbie couldn't help it. Idle chitchat was no doubt a way of life down here in the country. Chloe would have preferred to employ a wedding-stationery design company from Dublin, but nothing in the city had come close to Amazing Days Design. Such unprofessional conduct was obviously the price you had to pay for dealing with a company down in the sticks.

She chuckled inwardly. Dan would murder her if she said something like that in front of him. Her fiancé had been born and bred in Longford and was proud of it. Still, being well-educated as he was, his roots didn't show, and to Chloe that was the main thing. Not that Mr & Mrs Hunt were farmers or anything like that – nothing of the sort actually. Although semi-retired, Dan's father owned a construction company and Mrs Hunt had 'supported him' throughout his working years. Something Chloe wouldn't mind doing for Dan once they got married. She hated her job as legal secretary to one of her father's partners in his solicitor's practice. Although, she supposed there were *some* perks. Like taking time off on a Friday afternoon to choose wedding invitations, for example.

Chloe sighed as she studied the invite. She wouldn't

mind Dan getting just a teeny bit more involved in the wedding plans, but it wasn't really his thing. Anyway, he was just too busy – especially at this time of the year. Most of the companies on the books of O'Leary & Hunt Chartered Certified Accountants had their accounts year-end in March, which meant that by the middle of April Dan was up to his eyes preparing profit and loss accounts and balance sheets. Chloe could hardly expect him to traipse around after her at the weekends, or take afternoons off just to choose their wedding stationery. Anyway, he would probably only be in the way.

"Embossed Silver Hearts it is then," Debbie said, writing the details in her order book, which Chloe noted seemed to be full of bookings. She wasn't surprised. The company had really created a name for itself, and it wasn't difficult to see why. It was a pity though that so many people seemed to have heard of them. Was she doing the right thing here? Would Amazing Days Design invites be two-a-penny by the time their wedding came around, and would everyone poke fun at Chloe's lack of originality?

"The wedding is when – September?" Debbie said, a pen in her mouth. "And you said you want matching place-cards and evening invites too?"

Chloe nodded.

"OK," Debbie said, studying the order book, "I should have them ready for about the first week in July – how does that sound?"

"Well, I'd actually prefer earlier," Chloe said quickly. "We'll need them well before then."

First week in July indeed! That was four months away – how long did it take to run off a few invites?

Debbie looked apologetic. "The card you've chosen is one of our newer designs for this year and, unfortunately, stock for the full set won't be available until early June. And, of course, I'll need a few weeks from then to work on the inscriptions."

"Of course," Chloe resisted the urge to roll her eyes. Well, she thought, at least now she knew that her chosen design *would* be original.

"And because you're ordering so far ahead," Debbie went on, "I would always suggest that my customers leave it as close as they can to the wedding itself before deciding on the final particulars, just in case anything needs to be changed in the meantime."

Chloe couldn't help feeling affronted. "I should think I know the details of my own wedding! What would I need to change, for goodness sake?"

Debbie spoke kindly. "Well, I'm just speaking from experience, Ms Fallon. You just never know. If anyone is ill, or things don't go according to plan, or perhaps the date needs changing –"

"Look, can we have them in June, or not? If not, I'll have to go somewhere else." She was desperately hoping that the designer might make allowances.

Debbie looked taken aback. "All right then, I'll do my best."

"Fine. Give me a call when they're ready for collection."

With a curt goodbye, Chloe lowered her sunglasses and breezed out of the store – her sample invitation clutched in her hand.

Debbie came out front and exchanged glances with the shop assistant, who looked up momentarily from her magazine. The stationery designer raised an eyebrow as the door shut behind her latest client with a flourish.

That one was a madam if ever she saw one.

And in this business, Debbie thought with a sigh, she had seen plenty.

Chapter 1

Nicola Peters finished getting dressed, tied her fair curls in a ponytail, and sat patiently in her chair awaiting Jack Collins' return. It was a mild June day, but despite the warm temperatures, she couldn't help but shiver.

She heard him knock softly on the door. "Are you OK in there?"

"Sure, I'm dressed now. You can come back in." Dr Collins was such a sweetheart, Nicola thought. She had been seeing him for a long time and, at this stage, there was little point in trying to preserve her modesty.

With her medical chart in hand, the doctor came back into the room and sat down beside her.

"Well, Nicola, I'm pleased to advise that you're in pretty good shape."

She beamed up at him. "Really?"

"Yes. The back pain and tiredness you've been experiencing recently are probably down to stress and overwork but –"

"I had suspected that," she interrupted, nodding sagely, "but I thought I'd get it checked out – just to be sure."

"Well, you're absolutely right. Now, your blood pressure has dropped a little from your last reading – which is good news – although I do feel that you could benefit from some more exercise."

Nicola glanced downwards, and grimaced. "Doctor, you don't have to tell *me* that. And, at my age, things can only get worse."

"Will you listen to yourself? I wish I could still see the world through the eyes of a thirty-year-old. But, for your own sake, we should try and do something about that weight. Go out and about, do some shopping, out with the dog – anything to get the blood moving."

She groaned. "OK, I promise I'll make the effort. Thanks, doctor."

Nicola left the surgery, and made her way out front towards her car. It was quarter past eleven, and she was due back at work for twelve – not a lot of time to spare. The rumbling in her tummy reminded her that she had skipped breakfast, and she resolved to stop off somewhere on her way to work.

The traffic from town to Rathfarnham was crazy, and she was quickly running out of time to stop off anywhere for lunch. It was times like this, she thought irritably, that she really missed her bicycle. When she cycled, she used to zip around the city in no time – not to mention the fact that the exercise was good for the figure. But these days, unfortunately, she was stuck with the blasted car.

Up ahead, Nicola spied a sign for the Nutgrove Shopping Centre. Perfect! She could pop in, grab a salad

Melissa Hill

roll (and, despite Dr Collins' advice, some chocolate) and be in and out of there in no time. The carpark looked busy, and there didn't seem to be any spaces up front near the entrance. Nicola looked impatiently from left to right. She really didn't have the time to go searching for a space further down and . . . oh, blast it, one of the mother and baby ones would have to do – there were a few of them vacant and she wouldn't be more than a minute in the shop. Anyway, she thought to herself, you didn't get dirty looks when you parked in these spaces, unlike the disabled ones, which often drew menacing stares from all around.

She made it back to the office just before twelve.

"The boss-man's gone out to lunch," Sally, the receptionist, told her. "He said to tell you he'd speak to you later."

"Thanks, Sally. I'm just going to grab a bite at my desk now but if you need anything give me a shout."

Just after two o'clock, Nicola put her hands behind her head, and yawned. Despite the sunshine earlier, the day had now turned wet and dreary – typical Irish summer – and she just wasn't in the mood for all this paperwork. Unfortunately, as it was once again the end of the month, invoices needed paying and the accounts needing updating. She couldn't wait until Motiv8 Leisure Club was doing well enough to employ an accountant full-time to look after this stuff. Then she could concentrate on actually running the place.

Nicola moved across to the window and adjusted the lateral blinds to let some much-needed light into the room. She stared idly at the River Dodder below for a few moments, until the telephone startled her out of her reverie.

The receptionist sounded out of breath with excitement.

"Nicola, you will never guess who's on the line! One of the features editors from that new *Mode* magazine!"

Nicola tightened her ponytail and smiled. Sally could be so juvenile sometimes. Irish features and fashion magazine, *Mode*, had recently been launched, amid much hype and furore, upon the unsuspecting public. Starstruck Sally had obviously been lapping up the coverage.

"Well, look, if she's enquiring about membership, just give her the information and –"

"No, no!" Nicola could mentally picture Sally waving her arms excitedly in the air. "They want to do a feature on us!"

"A feature – on the club?"

"Yes! Her name is Fidelma Corrigan and she's on line two. Will you take it?"

"Of course." Nicola was intrigued. A feature on Motiv8 Leisure Club! What had they done to deserve this?

The features writer was polite and charming, and explained to Nicola that the magazine would be running an extensive Health and Leisure supplement in a forthcoming issue. Would Motiv8 like to participate? They really would be mad to miss this type of exposure at such a competitive advertising rate . . . blah-de-blah, blah. Nicola rolled her eyes. Quit the sales jingle and cut to the bottom line, she urged silently.

When the woman eventually quoted a rate, Nicola discovered that it really *was* too good an opportunity to pass up.

"We'd love to do it," she told her warmly. If the club signed only three new members as a result of this feature, then the advertising would have paid for itself.

"We'd like to concentrate specifically on the club's Alternative Therapies, Ms Peters. I understand your new Hydrotherapy Unit has resulted in a surge of membership? And of course you carry the usual – aromatherapy massage, health spa, Jacuzzi etc, etc . . ."

Nicola listened absently. The exposure would mean fantastic publicity for the centre, which would hopefully translate into a rush for membership. *Which* in turn might translate into an actual pat on the back from Ken – for once.

When Ken Harris – her manager from a previous job in another leisure facility – had contacted her a year ago and offered her an executive post in his new leisure centre, Nicola didn't have to think twice. After almost two years, she'd had enough of life in London. She'd worked with Ken in The Metamorph Club, one of Dublin's most popular city fitness centres, and knew it would be a good move. Ken knew the business inside out, having worked in the leisure industry from an early age.

Still, it had been a difficult first year for the club. While he and his partners had spared no expense in converting what had once been an old mill in Rathfarnham into a state-of-the-art leisure club, initial registrations had been slow, and their membership figures were well under target.

Nicola had been surprised by the size of the place once the builders had finished with it. From the outside, it looked nondescript but once inside clients never failed to be taken aback by the spacious and airy reception area which had been decorated in soothing cream and purple. Huge banana-plants, palms and fiscus trees created a tropical and luxurious feel, as did the vivid modernist prints hanging on the cream-coloured walls.

A relaxation and meditation room was situated just off the main reception, and the glass-fronted gym enabled staff to keep an eye on any overenthusiastic fitness fanatics. A twenty-metre, mosaic-tiled swimming-pool and Jacuzzi had been installed, on what had once been the site of an extensive grain silo. The centre also featured the essential steam room and sauna, but the most popular, and most utilised area by far, was the alternative therapies area. Nicola's first mission had been to employ a qualified aromatherapist, but her *coup de maître* had been her insistence on the hydrotherapy unit – having experienced first-hand the popularity and benefits of hydrotherapy treatments in London.

Luckily, Ken didn't object too much to her ambitious managerial plans, and had given her a loose rein on things. However, he wouldn't budge on the staff issue and Nicola, instead of using her sales abilities and promotional aptitude to recruit more members, had been forced to look after the more mundane, everyday administration of the club.

"Just until we find our feet," he had said, when Nicola had complained about her growing pile of paperwork for about the umpteenth time.

"But we won't find our feet unless I have more time to get the brand out there. Ken, we don't even have a website – let alone any kind of profile."

But he had been insistent, and Nicola had had to relent – for the time being. Maybe this feature would be just the thing to give the entire project a lift, and justify that she had what it took to really manage the place, if only he'd let her.

The *Mode* features writer was still talking on the other end of the telephone.

"I'm just getting participants finalised at the moment," Fidelma was saying, "and we'll also need some background info on the centre. So could I contact you again at a later date to arrange the interview? And just so we won't take up too much of your time, we should probably do the photoshoot then too."

"Sure, just give me plenty of notice. Things can get a little hectic around here," Nicola said, not particularly looking forward to the photo shoot.

"Okay, I'll talk to you in a couple of weeks, and we'll arrange a date between us. Thanks again."

"Thank you too." Nicola rang off, and sat back in her seat and smiled. The day was beginning to improve.

She was just about to try Ken's office extension to let him know about the feature, when he appeared in the doorway.

"Ms Peters, all these half-days just aren't good enough, I'm afraid," he said, without preamble.

"Well, I'm very sorry, Mr Harris, but I do recall telling you that I had an important appointment this morning."

"That's not the point, Ms Peters. We need you here – I need you here."

"Oh, really?" she said, brazenly. "I thought you were more than capable of running things when I'm not around, *Mr* Harris."

"Well, you thought wrong."

Nicola grinned as he came round her desk and planted

a kiss lightly on her forehead. "I can't cope without you."

"Saddo," she teased, wrapping her arms around him.

"So, how did it go with Dr Collins?" he asked, crouching down alongside her chair.

"Fine."

Ken's eyes widened and he sat back on his haunches. "Just fine? Did you tell him about the tiredness?"

She shrugged. "He reckons it's nothing to worry about, but my blood pressure is still too high, and I need to get more exercise."

"Well, didn't I tell you should give the swimming a go?" he said gently. "You couldn't be in a better place for exercise, after all." He stood up. "Oh, and now that I think of it, the Wheelchair Association were enquiring about the Hydrotherapy Unit. Can you contact them about it? Organise some kind of a discount, maybe?"

"Sounds promising," she said thoughtfully, straight back in business-mode. "I'll give them a ring later."

"And I wondered what your thoughts might be on a Mother and Baby swimming morning?"

Nicola grimaced. "Not so sure. It could be disadvantageous if we're trying for exclusivity – what with the carry-on of some of them." Some members brought their toddlers along to the swimming-pool, and didn't pay as much attention to the children's behaviour as the management and staff would have liked.

"Well, we have to do something, Nicola. The numbers aren't coming through these last few months."

Nicola studied him. Lately, Ken was looking jaded and more than a little dishevelled. The other partners were probably giving him grief, she thought, although Ken would never admit to worrying about things like that. His dark hair, normally closely cropped, was beginning to curl just above his ears, and his chocolate-brown eyes – arguably his best feature – were today devoid of their trademark sparkle.

"Well, I might have just the thing for that," she said, trying to put his mind at ease by outlining the upcoming advertising feature and how it should benefit the Motiv8 profile.

"Great!" As expected, Ken was pleased. "I knew I hired you for more than your looks!"

"Ha!"

When she and Ken had got together some months back, Nicola wasn't sure at first whether or not she should continue working at the club. The two had known one other professionally for some time and had enjoyed an amiable, while not altogether friendly, association over the years. Nicola was only a few months into her manager's job at Motiv8 when she and Ken had begun getting to know one another on a more intimate basis. She had always thought him a bit of a workaholic, but as the months went by she began to view her old colleague in a brand-new light. Soon, Nicola had inadvertently fallen in love with Ken Harris, and when he eventually admitted he felt the same way, they had never looked back. He was everything Nicola had ever wanted in a man: honest, selfless, uncomplicated and, she supposed, attractive in an easy-going kind of way.

From the very beginning, she and Ken were determined that they would make a success of Motiv8 Leisure Club, but decided that if they ever found that working together was damaging their relationship, they would have no hesitation in doing something about it. So far, that hadn't happened, and the two were blissfully content in both aspects.

"Oh, another thing," Ken said, remembering, "Laura was on the phone for you earlier." He smiled. "She sounded kind of harassed, actually – all this wedding business must be getting to her."

Laura, Nicola's closest friend, was getting married in a few months' time.

"I'd better give her a call then," she said, grateful for any excuse to avoid her paperwork.

Just then her extension buzzed.

"Is Ken with you?" the receptionist asked over the intercom. "The accountant is looking for him." The staff were fully aware of Nicola and Ken's relationship, but because they kept things professional at work, it didn't bother them.

"I'll send him down to you, Sally."

Ken groaned. "That blasted accountant is the last person I want to see. I know he'll have nothing but bad news for me." He gave her another quick kiss. "Are you sure you don't want me to call over to your place later?"

Nicola shook her head. "Nah, you enjoy your golf in peace – I'm baby-sitting Kerry tonight. Anyway," she added, grinning mischievously "I could do with a night off from you – you can be a bit of a handful sometimes."

"I'll remember that," Ken teased, his brown eyes twinkling, "the next time you get a hankering for Ben & Jerry's and old muggins here has to drive halfway across Dublin to get it for you!"

"Well, at least you're good for something!"

"Oh yeah?" He began to tickle her. "And what about last night, eh? You didn't have too many complaints then!"

"OK, OK, I'm sorry!" she said, giggling. "You're a man of many talents – really!"

"That's more like it." Ken stood up, and straightened his tie. "Now, no more skiving, please, Ms Peters," he said, feigning a bossy tone. "It looks to me as though you have plenty of work to do."

"I *was* working before I was so rudely interrupted!" Nicola countered, wide-eyed.

He was no sooner out the door than her extension buzzed again and this time it was Laura.

"Listen, is there any chance I could come over to your place tonight?" Nicola's best friend asked. "I need to talk to you about something."

"Of course you can . . . no, hold on – I'm baby-sitting and I told Kerry that I'd bring her to the cinema. So unless you want to come along –"

"No, thanks, I'll leave you to it," Laura said quickly. "I'm not really in the mood for the latest all-singing, all-dancing Disney extravaganza."

"What's wrong? You seem very down in yourself." She remembered what Ken had said about Laura sounding harassed.

Her friend grunted. "It's this blasted wedding – my mother is really getting on my nerves about it. *Now* she's not happy with the photographer I've booked because he's" – she affected a sing-song tone – "'supposed to be a bit of a letch'! Nicola, I went to school with Kieran Molloy

22

and he's as gay as Christmas! As far as I'm concerned he can letch all he wants!"

Nicola smiled, but she could understand her friend's frustration. Laura and her partner Neil had become engaged at Christmas, and had promptly set the wedding date for the coming September. They wanted a simple no-frills, fuss-free wedding, something that Maureen Fanning (who Nicola thought could make J-Lo look laid-back) couldn't tolerate. Not when she'd been dreaming about orchestrating her eldest daughter's Big Day for most of her life.

But there was a good reason for the couple's no-fuss approach. Neil's mother had recently discovered a malignant lump in her breast, and was about to undergo hospital treatment. Neil was anxious for his mother to have something to concentrate on other than her illness and wanted the wedding to happen sooner rather than later – just in case.

"Well, you could take off and get married yourselves, just the two of you," said Nicola. *Like I did*, she added silently.

"Are you mad? My mother would have a heart attack! She's bad enough as it is."

Nicola frowned. It wasn't like Laura to be so down in the dumps.

"Well, look, don't let her get to you. As long as you and Neil are happy with the wedding plans, then what else matters?"

"Yes, but you know my mother!" Laura groaned. "And, unfortunately, Neil isn't much help."

"He'd probably just prefer to keep out of it." Neil Connolly was as easy-going as they came, and one of the few people who could actually handle Maureen Fanning without resorting to extreme violence.

"To be honest, he's just too busy with the agency. At this very moment he's off on some fact-finding trip to Mauritius – lucky git."

Neil was a partner in his family's travel agency, and the business was currently attempting to break into the more exclusive faraway-shores market.

"Anyway, the wedding isn't the real reason I wanted to talk to you," Laura said cryptically.

"Oh?" Her tone piqued Nicola's interest. "I'm intrigued."

"Well, if I can't see you tonight, I'm afraid you'll just have to wait." There was a slight smile in her voice.

"That's not fair! What's going on, Laura?"

"Nope – I'd prefer to tell you face to face."

"Now I'm dying to know!" Nicola thought quickly. "OK – why don't you call over tomorrow night? Helen's coming over anyway, so you might as well join us." Nicola, Laura and Helen had been friends for many years but lately, Nicola thought, hadn't had many opportunities to get together. It would be nice for the three of them to have a bit of a natter.

But Laura hesitated, and for a moment Nicola wondered if she had said the wrong thing. "Unless you'd prefer to leave it for another night – just the two of us," she offered.

"No, no, it's fine. I'll bring a bottle of wine, will I?"

"Do. We'll have a bit of chat, get the latest on Helen's new man and, oh – I'll be able to show you *my* new wheels!"

"Not again!" Laura teased. "What did you get this

time – a coupé, roadster, something along the lines of a Ferrari, maybe?"

"I *wish*. Look, I'd better go – I've another call coming in. See you tomorrow, round about eight?

"Great, I'm looking forward to it!" Laura rang off, already sounding in much better form.

Nicola hit the other line. Was she *ever* going to get anything done today?

"Can you come down to the pool?" Sally sounded worried. "It's Mrs Murphy-Ryan and her twins again. You won't believe what they've done this time."

* * *

Laura replaced the receiver and smiled. As always, she felt a lot better after speaking to Nicola – it was a pity really that they couldn't meet up tonight.

But, tomorrow night would do just as well, and she hadn't seen Helen in ages. Nicola had mentioned that their friend had a new man but, where Helen was concerned, that was hardly surprising. Helen went through men like Bewleys went through coffee, and most men adored her – the deliciously attractive combination of blonde hair, olive skin and dark, ochre eyes almost impossible to resist. Helen Jackson was everything Laura wanted to be – glamorous, effortlessly thin, successful and supremely confident.

Of course, the men Helen attracted were always equally glamorous, if you could use that term for a man. Laura picked up the framed picture of her fiancé. Poor old Neil – glamorous he wasn't.

Laura had met him in Penney's in O'Connell Street, on

an unexpectedly showery Friday morning (goodness knows why unexpected, she thought now – in Ireland showery days were almost mandatory!) – when they both tried to buy the last available umbrella.

She shook her head. If Helen had a new man, it wouldn't last a wet or even a *dry* week. Relationships just didn't seem to be Helen's thing – not these days anyway – and no matter how good-looking he might be, there was very little chance that she would commit. Laura smiled ruefully. At home in Glengarrah when they were teenagers, Helen always attracted the guys with film-star looks while Laura got the ones who looked like extras from *Emmerdale*.

Not that Neil was all that bad. Dressed in his dark suits and brightly coloured ties, he was attractive in his own kind of way, but her fiancé was unlikely to be asked to one day drop everything and star in the Diet Coke ad. An ad for Mr Muscle bathroom-cleaner, maybe, but with his slight frame, definitely *not* Diet Coke.

Still, the thought of Helen being at Nicola's tomorrow night didn't exactly fill her with excitement. Although she and Helen had been friends for as long as Laura could remember, they no longer had that much in common, and their friendship was now based more on past association than any real closeness. It was a terrible pity but, Laura thought, if it weren't for Nicola, she was certain that she and Helen would have drifted apart long ago – and she didn't think her old friend would be all that bothered.

She glanced at the clock. It was almost three – she'd better ring the stationery company about their wedding invitations, having promised the designer she'd let her know their choice of design before the end of this week.

When one of her mother's friends had recommended her stationery designer niece for their wedding invitations, Laura had despaired. Knowing her taste, the cards would be all doves, ribbons and Holy Marys, but thankfully that hadn't been the case at all.

Amazing Day Designs were indeed amazing. She and Neil had enjoyed their recent visit to the store in Wicklow, more than Laura had expected. The designer had produced some beautiful sample invitations, having already personalised some of them with Laura and Neil's wedding details. To Laura's artistic eye, the originality and quality of the work was excellent.

Her call was answered on the second ring. "Amazing Days, Debbie speaking."

"Hi Debbie, Laura Fanning here. I just wanted to let you know our choice for the invites."

"Laura, hi!" Debbie said warmly. "Thanks for getting back to me. Well, what have you decided?"

After much indecision, Laura and Neil had settled upon a traditional ivory and gold parchment design with separate RSVP cards, both of which Laura had to admit were utterly stunning. After double-checking the details, Debbie advised that Laura's choice was in stock, and the invites would be ready within a couple of weeks.

"Just give me a quick call before you come down to collect them, just to be sure," she said pleasantly, before ringing off and leaving Laura thinking what an absolute pleasure it had been dealing with Amazing Days.

It was such a pity that the rest of the wedding preparations were turning out to be a lot more hassle than she'd expected. Her mother was driving her absolutely demented and couldn't accept the fact that she wasn't inviting the whole of County Carlow to the wedding.

When Laura had announced that it would be a small wedding – close friends and family only – in her home village of Glengarrah, and that in no circumstances would any of Maureen's fourteen free-loading siblings be invited, her mother had been appalled.

"But it's a big family day!" Maureen had moaned, mentally fretting over what all the relations would say about her.

Still, there was no point in worrying about it now. Laura had a lot more on her mind. Her boss would be leaving the office for the afternoon soon so she'd better get going. Laura shut down the spreadsheet program on her PC, opened her word processor and began to type, feeling a tiny tingle of anticipation as she did.

Then she paused, thinking again about tomorrow night. What would they make of her news? Would they be pleased, supportive, enthusiastic – or would her friends think she had gone completely mad? Laura hoped not. She was sure; no, she was *certain* that she was making the right decision.

She had known all along that Neil would support her. He didn't need any convincing – he'd been all for it and his blatant enthusiasm had given Laura the courage to think very seriously about what she was about to do. She was certain she could do this; in fact, she knew she should have done it a long time ago.

Although it was a scary prospect, Laura didn't want to put it off any longer. She *couldn't* put it off any longer. The timing was important. She had all the groundwork done, knew exactly what would be expected of her, and what sacrifices she would have to make. And she was more than prepared to make those sacrifices. Ideally, she should maybe wait until after the wedding, but she knew that she couldn't wait that long. She had waited long enough.

Anyway, there was no time like the present.

She spellchecked her document before printing it out, then reread it, signed it, and after a few nervous moments put it into an envelope.

Then Laura stood up from her desk, took a deep breath and – letter in hand – walked resolutely towards her manager's office.

Chapter 2

What colour clutch-bag to take? Helen Jackson held one black and one silver against her plum-coloured satin Maria Grachvogel dress. She adjusted the plunging neckline to ensure it didn't expose quite so much of her chest. She didn't want Richard gaping at her cleavage all night – or did she?

Helen smiled at her reflection.

Tonight was definitely the night. She and Richard Moore had been seeing one another for quite some time now, and she was certain that it was time to take their relationship further. The thought of it all made her more nervous than she would normally allow herself to be.

This, she thought, was probably due to the fact that she liked Richard a lot – actually, *more* than a lot –and definitely *much* more than any of the others she had been out with in recent years. Richard was intelligent, good-humoured and *very* sexy. Helen worked as business consultant manager for XL Business Software in Sandymount, and had met Richard after his recruitment company had sought their advice. Throughout their first meeting, Helen had been as she always was with a client – brisk, professional but unashamedly flirtatious. As she had so often told her sales staff, feminism didn't earn anyone enough bonuses to keep them in two-bedroom seafront apartments in Monkstown.

But Helen didn't have to force herself all that much to flirt with a man who looked like Richard Moore. Shortly after their first meeting, and a few equally coquettish phone consultations, the company had upgraded their office network, and Richard had asked her out.

Helen had enjoyed herself immensely each time they went out together, and although there had been more than a few passionate encounters, so far they hadn't slept together. Helen took this as a positive sign. It meant that he wasn't just after her thirty-year-old body, and was just as interested in her as a person.

Yes, tonight would be the night, Helen decided.

Maybe finally she would have someone to take the place of the empty chair that positioned itself permanently opposite her, whenever there were any formal get-togethers. Her friends all sat across from their respective partners, as did her colleagues, whereas Helen always got stuck with the empty chair. In fairness, she and the chair were by now way beyond first-name terms, and indeed over the last few years had become best buddies.

She smiled ruefully, and once again concentrated on the task in hand.

Deciding that with this dress the silver bag looked infinitely more glamorous than the black one, Helen rummaged through her wardrobe, and seconds later emerged with a pair of spaghetti-strap mules that were ridiculously high-heeled. OK, they were only *imitation* Manolos but, more importantly, they matched the bag perfectly. For every hand, clutch, and shoulder-bag she possessed, Helen *always* had a matching pair of shoes. When the supermarkets stopped giving out free plastic bags, her friends joked that they would soon be seeing Helen shopping in Superquinn wearing a pair of shoes that matched her 'Bag for Life'.

Anyway, Helen thought, everyone knew that it was bad luck to wear mismatched accessories. God only knew how Laura got away with wearing those silver and gold jewellery combos she put together in her spare time.

Helen ran a brush through her freshly blow-dried locks, and checked her watch. It was almost seven, and she was meeting Richard in town at half past. She'd better get a move on – who knew how long it would take to get a taxi into town on a Friday night? She picked up her bag and coat, tottered downstairs, and slammed the front door behind her – the impact shuddering through the large, empty apartment.

* * *

"You look amazing!" Richard smiled appreciatively, as Helen wobbled unsteadily to where he stood waiting outside the restaurant.

Her heart soared as he leant forward and kissed her

softly on the lips. Those silver heels certainly hadn't been designed with Dublin's unevenly cobbled footpaths in mind, she thought, following him inside, but it had been worth the discomfort. Thank God she hadn't worn her precious Jimmy Choos. Although it was a possibility that one of these days she might actually have to wear them *outside* of the apartment.

"You don't look so bad yourself, considering you've come straight from the office." Helen nudged him playfully, trying to dispel the rising butterflies in her stomach. Richard *did* look good. His short dark hair had been recently cropped, and to her delight, Helen noticed there was a slight covering of stubble on his tanned chin. In her opinion, there was nothing sexier than a stubbled chin. Not a beard, mind, Helen drew the line at beards, and she really *hated* that freshly-shaven Mummy's-boy look. Stubble was just perfect.

"What time are we eating?" she asked, glancing around the packed restaurant.

Richard raised an eyebrow. "Hopefully soon. I haven't eaten anything since midday."

As if on cue, a waitress approached and called them to their table, which fortunately, Helen noted, was situated towards the rear of the room in a dark, quiet corner.

All the better for intimacy.

Helen's gaze raked over the menu, but she found that she was so nervous she could barely see what was written on it. She watched Richard out of the corner of her eye. He was studying the wine list intently – probably trying to decide between his personal favourites: Australian or

South African Cabernet. It was a little scary actually: they had only been together for a short time, but yet Helen could read him like the *Cosmo* fashion pages. It had been the same with her previous partner, Jamie, who was as open and transparent as any man could get. Too transparent, probably. Jamie had been so open that he had one day informed Helen that he felt tied down, was bored with the rat race, and was taking off for a while to South Africa to 'find himself'.

That was almost four years ago, and since then Jamie had not only found himself, but – handily enough for him, Helen thought – someone else. OK, she decided, seeing Richard close the wine list, if he orders Australian it's a good omen, and South African is *definitely* a bad one.

"Ready to order?" the waitress asked pleasantly.

"Yes, thanks. Helen?" Ever the gentleman, Richard waited while she deliberated over lamb or pork. She eventually decided upon the lamb and Richard ordered medium-rare fillet steak.

"Wine?" the waitress enquired.

Helen smiled at Richard. "I'd better let the sommelier decide," she said, knowing that Richard considered himself a bit of a wine expert.

Please, please, pick the Australian! Despite herself, Helen's heart began to pound as she waited for his response. Richard waved the menu away and smiled at the waitress. "Thanks, but I think I'll just throw caution to the winds tonight. Can you recommend anything?"

The girl paused for a moment. "Well, considering your choice of main course, I would definitely say the South African Guardian Peak Cabernet. It's one of the most popular wines on our list, and it's the perfect accompaniment to red meat dishes – lamb in particular," she added, smiling at Helen.

Shit, shit, shit!

Richard beamed at her. "Perfect, we'll have that then – thank you."

The waitress collected their menus and left the table, Helen berating herself for being so foolish as to think that the bloody wine she and Richard were having for their meal should affect their relationship. She'd really have to try and stop with all this signs and omens nonsense. That was the kind of game only a child would play.

Another butterfly (there's always a latecomer) rose up inside Helen's stomach.

"So what have you been up to this week?" Richard reached across the table, and took her hand in his.

"Not much. Got the Carver Property and the Tip-Top Distribution contracts finalised and countersigned yesterday." She feigned a shrug, and hid a smile. "A quiet week, really."

"You did not!" Richard gave a disbelieving guffaw. "Bloody hell, you're something else, Helen Jackson, do you know that?"

Helen had told him previously that XL had been chasing both contracts for some time, and there was a real danger that Carver's in particular would opt for a rival consultancy. At the very last minute, and following an especially persuasive meeting with Helen, Ronnie Carver had changed his mind and signed a five-year contract with XL. Which meant that Helen could look forward to what could only be described as an obese bonus cheque at the end of the month. She filled him in on the story, while they made inroads on their starters.

"Wow," Richard smiled and clinked her glass, "I think I'll keep you. The ultimate career woman, huh?"

The little voice inside her brain was deafening. *Tell him. Tell him now!*

Helen took a deep breath. *Relax,* said the voice. *You two get on well together and he really likes you. What difference could it make?*

She gulped a mouthful of wine, and set her glass back down on the table.

"Richard?" she asked softly and the words were out before she could stop herself. "How do you feel about children?"

Shit, shit, shit, the voice berated her. *It wasn't supposed to come out so quickly – you were supposed to ease it into the conversation. Typical you, and your bloody size four-an'-a-halves!*

Richard looked as though she had just asked him to eat a bull's testicle.

"Children?" he repeated warily. "What kind of a question is that?"

Helen felt completely deflated. It was going to happen again – she just knew it.

"I mean, do you like children?" She tried to lighten the tone. "I mean, by any chance do you have some of your own or . . . or would you *like* some of your own?"

Oh God, this was getting worse by the minute, she thought.

Richard now looked as though he had been presented with a *plate* of bulls' testicles.

"Helen, what the hell are you talking about? You know that I've never been married . . ." Before she could reply, his face changed. "Hang on a second . . . are you up the pole?" he hissed at her. "Because if you are, and you think you can trap *me* into fatherhood, then I think you've forgotten something. I don't know what the hell *you've* been doing but, for the record, we haven't even shagged properly, so it couldn't be me! For Chrissake, Helen –"

"Forget it, Richard!" Helen reached for her bag, red-faced and in shock. How dare he? If he would behave like this over a mention of children, how the hell would he behave when he knew the truth? What had happened to the perfect gentleman?

Richard softened when he saw her expression. "Look, I'm sorry, I didn't mean it to come out like that . . . it's just I know I couldn't have –"

"It's not what you think, Richard – I'm not pregnant," Helen interjected. "Not any longer, anyway."

He looked at her with a bemused expression.

What the hell, she might as well put him out of his misery. "I have a three-and-a-half-year-old daughter that I haven't told you about. As you and I were getting to know one another better, and becoming – *I* thought – more serious, I felt that you should know."

"Helen . . . I . . . I'm sorry . . ." His voice trailed off, but by his expression, Helen knew all there was to know.

They were finished.

The usual story.

At that moment, the waitress appeared with their main course.

"I think I should go," Helen stood up.

"No, stay – please. Tell me about your – your daughter." The way he said it, it was as though Helen had just told him she had a severe case of leprosy.

She wasn't about to stay just for the sake of it, not this time – not ever again. She'd played out this scenario too many times for one lifetime.

"No, I think I *will* go, actually. Thanks anyway – for dinner."

Richard nodded slowly. "You're welcome." Suddenly he was being as formal as he had been that first day in her office. "I'll phone you?" he added, almost automatically and certainly, Helen knew, untruthfully.

"Sure."

Her feet must have been feeling sorry for her, because Helen didn't feel them once as she walked dazedly up Grafton Street and towards the taxi rank. She tried to bite back tears as she got into the cab she had hailed with surprising ease. Then again, it was only nine o'clock. No one out enjoying themselves in Dublin on a Friday night came home early. No one but sad, spinster, single mothers like Helen.

A while later, the cab pulled up outside Nicola's house in Stepaside, and Helen asked the driver to wait.

Soon after, she reappeared accompanied by a drowsy-eyed three-year-old version of herself, the little girl's hair tossed, and her face red from pillow-marks. Helen knew Nicola had been surprised to see her home so early, but thankfully her friend knew better than to ask any questions.

Helen put her still half-asleep daughter in the back seat of the cab, closed the door and sat in the front passenger seat.

Tonight, she thought, staring straight ahead, and making it plain to the taxi-driver that she wasn't interested in idle conversation, she couldn't tolerate having that child anywhere near her.

Chapter 3

"That's it?" Nicola asked, surprised. The following evening, she and Helen were sharing a bottle of wine in her living-room – Helen's daughter Kerry lying on the carpet in front of them and tickling Nicola's dog. "You're not seeing him again?"

Helen shrugged nonchalantly. "I guess not."

"But why? I mean . . . I thought you really liked this Richard?"

"Well, I did at first, but as time went by I realised that we weren't really suited."

"Oh."

"Come on, Kerry. It's time for bed," Helen announced firmly – conveniently changing the subject. Kerry looked up disappointed, as did the Labrador Barney who seemed to be enjoying the attention.

Nicola was amazed. She had baby-sat Kerry a number of times in the last few months to allow Helen go out with this Richard Moore. Now her friend had casually announced that she wouldn't be seeing him any more! It was weird the way Helen could go off a man for no particular reason.

But she knew by Helen's tone (and the swiftness with which she swept her daughter off to Nicola's spare bedroom) that she wasn't prepared to discuss it any further.

Shortly after Helen arrived back to the living-room, Barney jumped up and raced eagerly towards the front door, a sure sign to Nicola that another visitor was imminent.

Laura stood in the doorway, anxiously brushing her dark hair away from her pretty face and looking a little ill at ease. Then again, Nicola thought wryly, Laura nearly always looked ill at ease.

Barney, who adored Laura, jumped up and almost knocked her to the ground.

Laura laughed. "Hey, relax," she said easily, bending down and ruffling his ears.

"You're early," Nicola ushered her inside. "Helen's already here, but Kerry's just gone to bed, so we have to be quiet for a while at least."

Barney jumped up and, with his paws, closed the front door behind them.

Laura looked at him, her eyes widening. "Wow! You know, I sometimes forget just how intelligent that dog can be!" she laughed.

"Good boy!" Nicola patted him on the head and Barney followed them into the living-room, tongue out and long tail wagging excitedly.

"Hi, Helen," Laura said, with a smile. "How are things?"

"Hi." Helen barely looked away from the television, causing Laura to throw Nicola a 'she's obviously in one of her moods' look.

Nicola nodded. "OK!" she said cheerfully, trying to lighten the mood, "Laura, you sit down there and I'll get you a glass."

"I'll get it." Helen got up and went out to the kitchen.

"What's eating her?"

"Don't ask. She's barely said two words since she and Kerry arrived here nearly an hour ago. Poor child – she seemed to sense that Mummy wasn't in the best of form and kept offering her some M&Ms." She frowned. "Helen was quite short with her, actually."

"Man trouble?"

"Undoubtedly." Nicola rolled her eyes.

"Oh, I wonder should I wait for another time, then?" Laura looked thoughtful

"Another time for what?" Helen came back into the room with a freshly uncorked bottle, and a third wineglass.

Laura sat down and began nervously caressing Barney's silky coat. She looked hesitant. "Well, as I was telling Nicola on the phone yesterday . . . I have a bit of news."

"News?" Helen repeated. "Oh, don't tell me – you're pregnant."

Nicola watched Laura carefully. She had suspected the same thing.

"No, nothing like that." Laura swallowed hard. "It's just . . . well, yesterday afternoon . . . I handed in my resignation."

Nicola looked at her. Laura had sounded strange on

the phone yesterday, but she hadn't expected *this*. "You're leaving? You never said anything about another job – what's going on?"

"I'm thinking of starting my own business," Laura said timidly. "Well, not thinking actually, I've already *decided* to start my own business."

"Doing what?" Helen asked.

"Designing and selling my jewellery."

"What? That's fantastic news, Laura!" Nicola was thrilled for her. "And about bloody time too!"

Laura had studied at Art College but, when a job didn't materialise after her diploma, for financial reasons (or more likely, Nicola believed, because of her lack of self-confidence) she had taken a succession of office jobs, rather than continue with her life-long passion for design. Lately though, Laura had resumed her interest and had taken to creating distinctive and elaborate one-off pieces of contemporary jewellery for herself, her family and friends.

Nicola had no doubts that Laura was favourably equipped to do well with her designs, having excelled in her metal and jewellery studies at college, and possessing a great eye for artistic form. She adored the glass-beaded and liquid silver bracelet Laura had designed for her thirtieth birthday a few months earlier. It was so 'her' and exactly what she would have chosen for herself. She remembered being completely taken aback when Laura had eventually admitted that she designed the piece herself.

"I've been doing a few bits and pieces at home," she had said shyly. "Neil sourced the materials for me."

Since meeting her fiancé, Laura had become a different girl. Neil Connolly had brought out the very best in her, and had recognised Laura's love for working with her hands, duly encouraging it. He had obviously provided sufficient encouragement to give her the confidence to offer her designs for sale. Good for her.

"You don't think I'm mad? For giving up my job and everything?" Laura bit her lip, and looked warily at Helen, who was busily lighting a cigarette.

"Don't be silly," Nicola answered, when Helen didn't respond. "It's a fantastic idea and I think you'll do extremely well. I'm sure there's a market for your work and these days everyone wants something different and original – something they can show off."

"You really think so?"

"Absolutely! It's terrific news!" Nicola reached across and gave her a hug. "Is Neil thrilled you're finally going for it?"

Laura nodded. "Well, yes, he's very much behind me on it and so supportive."

Of course Neil would be supportive of Laura's dreams, Nicola thought. He absolutely adored her, notwithstanding the fact that he knew first-hand what it was like to be self-employed, working as he did in the family travel agency.

"Well, like I do, he knows how talented and hardworking you are. Any regrets about leaving Morley's?" She knew that Laura had never been happy with her job in the accounts office of the popular Dublin department store. In fact, she couldn't remember Laura *ever* being completely happy in any job. Obviously her friend had finally decided that she should exploit her creative talents, and that nine-to-five was not her thing.

"No, none at all. I'd been working up to resigning for months and now – well, now I'm free to work on pursuing my dream!" She grinned excitedly. "Oh, I'm so pleased you're behind me on this. I wasn't sure what kind of a reaction I'd get. I haven't yet told that many people."

"Well, anyone who sees your jewellery will know as well as I do that you can make a real go of this. You already have a business plan?"

Laura nodded seriously. "I've already begun the groundwork. The bank has agreed to finance on the basis of my business plan, and Neil and I are going to use some of our savings. I've registered with the Crafts Council and the Enterprise Board – they've seen my designs and, believe it or not, they sound really positive about it, so maybe I might get some kind of a grant. I'm not sure yet. I'll just have to wait and see . . ."

Laura's pretty face glowed with enthusiasm and her dark, almost black eyes shone with passion. If anyone could do this, Nicola thought, Laura could. She was delighted for her friend; she obviously wanted to make a real go of it, and her designs were excellent. Given time, this business could definitely take off.

She just wished Helen would say something.

Apparently oblivious to Helen's silence, Laura outlined the remainder of her plans. "The Craft Council have already given me lots of help getting started with the accounting and the paperwork, so I hope to be open for business within the next couple of weeks and *well* before the wedding. It's now June, so I'll have a few months to find my feet, and then we'll do a full-on promotional drive in November, just in time for Christmas. With all that, and hopefully with a bit of word of mouth, I'll get the name out and about in no time." She grinned happily.

"Well, I'll be telling everyone all about you!" Nicola said. "And I'll make sure that I wear that fab bracelet you designed for me. People admire it every time I wear it – now I can tell them where they can get one for themselves!" Nicola squeezed her friend's hand. "Oh, it's really fantastic news. I'm so proud of you. Speaking of proud – what did your mother say? She must be over the moon about it!" She inwardly urged Helen to say something – *anything*.

Laura shook her head, and glanced again towards Helen. "I haven't told them about it yet – they'll just worry about my resigning, what with the wedding coming up. Anyway, I want to get everything up and running before I tell them."

"They'll be thrilled, Laura. Who wouldn't? Imagine their daughter – an entrepreneur!"

"I know." Laura smiled bashfully. Then she drained her glass and stood up. "Back in a minute, nature calls!"

When she was safely out of earshot, Nicola glared at Helen. "Why the hell didn't you say something? Didn't you see her watching for your reaction?"

Helen frowned and exhaled a cloud of cigarette smoke. "I didn't say anything because I couldn't trust myself to speak," she said evenly. "Personally, I think she's stone mad. What does someone like Laura know about running a business?"

Nicola sighed. She wished sometimes that Helen could see past their friend's timidity, and in this case realise that Laura was incredibly brave for doing what she was about to do. But Helen seemed to have a knack for making her feel inferior.

It had been that way for as long as Nicola had known the two of them. They had been friends since childhood, both coming from the same Carlow village, but Helen had always been the confident and independent one, Laura the shy awkward one in her friend's shadow.

Nicola had met Helen many years ago when she had been going out briefly with Nicola's older brother Jack. The two women had hit it off immediately, and had stayed friends long after the relationship ended. She had got to know Laura through Helen, and soon discovered that in Laura Fanning one couldn't find a more loyal or generous friend. More often than once, and especially in recent years, Laura had been her rock.

Now she was prepared to return the favour, and give Laura every ounce of support and encouragement possible. It was the very least her friend deserved. Nicola wished that Helen was prepared to do the same.

"I mean, why give up a perfectly good job to play arts and crafts in your front room?" Helen shook her head. "I just don't know."

"Well, can't you just *pretend* that you're happy, then – for her sake? She's really excited about this."

"Maybe, but you and I know that Laura doesn't have the killer instinct."

Nicola made a face. "Killer instinct? Like you, you mean? Come on, Helen. Give the girl a break."

"Seriously, Nic. What does Laura know about selling anything? She's too emotional, too *nice* to survive in the cut and thrust of the business world. It's dog eat dog out there. You know that."

"I'm sure Laura knows that too. Look, it'll be hard

enough getting started without hearing negatives from us. Could you just keep your opinions to yourself for once, and show the girl some support? She'd do it for you."

Helen nodded. "OK, but this will only end in tears, I'm sure of it."

"Sssh, she's coming back," Nicola whispered, hearing footsteps outside the door.

Laura rejoined them on the sofa, still full of obvious excitement.

"So what do *you* think, Helen?" she asked directly, her face eager.

Helen stubbed out her cigarette. "Look, are you absolutely sure that you've thought this through properly?" she said, and Nicola's heart sank even further than Laura's expression. "I mean, I know that you've always been into that kind of thing, but realistically, Laura, will it pay your mortgage for you?"

Laura looked away. "I'm not going into this blind, you know," she said quietly. "Neil and I have discussed it. We have some savings to use as working capital and he's sure that we can make it work. I told you that I signed up with the Crafts Council and they think –"

"Look, I'm sorry but I've never heard of anyone making millions selling hand-made trinkets – not someone like yourself anyway."

"Helen!" Nicola was shocked at her bluntness.

Laura looked duly wounded.

"Oh, look, I'm not being nasty – you know exactly what I mean." She turned to Laura. "In business, you need a thick skin. You need to be pushy and confident and, Laura, you're not like that."

"I'm sure she'll learn, Helen," Nicola said shortly, unable to hide her annoyance.

Helen took the hint and her tone softened. "Look, all I'm saying is that it won't be easy. You and Neil are getting married soon and I'm sure that's drained your savings a little?"

Laura nodded.

"And what about the mortgage? How will the two of you cope on just one salary? Laura, are you absolutely certain that you've thought it through?"

"Of course I have! Believe me, I kept it to myself but I've thought of nothing else for the past year and a half," Laura answered hoarsely. "I've done the market research, I've got a business plan and Neil thinks – Neil thinks it's a great idea, that there's a market, that I would be *good* at it."

"Well, what's your target market then?"

"Sorry?"

Helen sat forward. "Your target market – are you going to sell directly to the general public, or are you hoping to be stocked by gift stores, accessory stores, etc?"

"Well, both, I think."

"You *think*? Laura, you should know."

Laura looked doubtful. "I *do* know – it's just, I need to find my feet to begin with and . . ."

Her voice trailed off and Nicola knew that Helen's reaction was now making Laura doubt herself. Typical bloody Helen. What the hell was wrong with her? She was in really bad form today. Obviously things hadn't gone well on her date last night but she didn't have to take it out on Laura.

She sat forward in her chair and touched Laura's arm. "Again, I think it's a fantastic idea," she said pleasantly. "Don't mind that one, you know what she's like – she just has a bee in her bonnet about something or other." She made a face at Helen, hoping to lighten the mood.

Helen sighed and sat back in her chair. "Oh, she's right, you know," she said, topping up Laura's wineglass. "Sorry, Laura, I *am* being unfair. I'm just worried, that's all. Look, don't mind me – if you'd come in here and told me you'd won the Lotto I'd still probably challenge you about it."

"It's OK," Laura smiled graciously at her. "When I walked in I knew you were in a bad mood. I wasn't going to say anything, but then I couldn't help myself." She gleefully rubbed her hands together again. "I've kept it to myself for long enough and I'm just so excited!"

Nicola saw Helen arrange her features into something resembling a smile, and raised a silent prayer of thanks. She would eventually come round, and any fool alive could see that Laura had real talent. OK, Nicola too was worried about how someone as timid as Laura would survive in an often ruthless and unforgiving business world, but she was sure that with good advice and plenty of support, Laura would be fine. Either way, it was certainly worth taking the chance. Didn't she know only too well that life was what you made it?

And in fairness, with all that Laura was about to undertake, if she couldn't rely upon the support of the people closest to her, then who *could* she rely upon?

Chapter 4

Frustrated, Dan Hunt snatched up the telephone receiver.

"What?" he barked down the line at yet another anonymous office junior. Jesus, he thought. What was the bloody point of bringing in these school-leavers at the end of June to make things harder for everyone else? They weren't running a bloody crèche here after all.

"Um," Dan heard the girl swallow hard, "Mr Dooley from Dooley Interiors is on line two asking to speak to you."

Bloody Lorcan Dooley again! The same Lorcan Dooley that had been tormenting Dan for the past two weeks, because his office had somehow lost the majority of their staff Tax Deduction cards, and couldn't Dan have a word in the Revenue's ear? As if the Revenue was a living breathing person, instead of a crowd of bored civil servants well used to hearing the same tired excuses over and over again . . . ? Well, Lorcan Dooley could go jump, if he thought that Dan was going to spend the next three hours on hold trying to sort it out. He could already feel a knot of tension form in his brain as he hit line two.

"Lorcan, how are you?" Dan said cordially, trying his best not to sound like he felt. Despite everything, Dooley Interiors were still very good customers, and in fairness Lorcan had recommended Dan's accountancy practice to all and sundry in the Bray area.

"Dan, still no joy with those tax cards. Is there any chance you could sort it out for us?"

Dan bristled. "Lorcan, like I said already, there's not a lot I can do about it. You must have *some* records available. I know there's little point in saying it now, but as I've told you before, a company your size should really think about getting your wages system computerised."

A long telephone conversation later, a highly pissed-off Dan hung up. He was just about to dial the Revenue's number when his extension buzzed again.

"Yes?" he hissed through gritted teeth.

"That's a nice way to greet your fiancée," a female voice said huffily.

Dan sighed. The last thing he needed now was Chloe in one of her moods.

"Sorry, love, I'm just having a bummer of a day. How are you?"

"Fine. Listen, I need a favour."

"Go on." Dan groaned inwardly, while kneading his aching brain. Couldn't *anyone* do anything for themselves these days?

"I know you're up to your eyes, but I just got a call from Debbie."

"Debbie?"

"About the wedding invitations!" she exclaimed, knowing full well that he hadn't the first clue as to who Debbie might be. "Dan, do you ever listen to a word I say?"

"Oh right, I forgot. What about them?"

"Well, they're *finally* ready, and I hoped that you'd pop down later to collect them – you're only about twenty minutes from there."

Dan groaned. "Do I have to, Chlo? I was really hoping to get in a game of golf with John this evening. Can't you collect them yourself – or we could pop down tomorrow?"

"I have a fitting for my wedding dress tomorrow, Dan, you know that," Chloe was petulant, "and didn't I already tell you that tonight I'm meeting Lynne for cocktails? I simply won't have the time to call all that way down to Wicklow, and we need to send them out soon."

"OK, OK," Dan conceded. Anything for a quiet life. "Where is this place, anyway?"

At five thirty, a weary Dan picked up his briefcase and walked out of the office. The last thing he wanted to do on a Friday evening was battle the traffic from Wicklow back to their place in Stillorgan. It would be a bloody nightmare. Still, he supposed he'd better do as he was told. He adored Chloe, but it really was amazing how preparations for a simple wedding could turn a normally reasonable woman into something resembling a rabid dog. And lately, as the big day drew ever closer, Chloe was behaving like the pit bull variety.

To Dan's surprise, the traffic on the N11 was light, apart from a few caravan-pulling Jeeps, no doubt on their way to the coast for the weekend. Lucky bastards, he thought. He could do with a few days off. He had been working like crazy these last few months, and all Chloe's wedding preparations were driving him demented. You'd swear they were the only ones who were ever going to get married, with all her fussing and foostering about the flowers, the cake, the dress and these blasted invitations. He supposed he should be a little more supportive, and maybe a little more enthusiastic about it all, but it just didn't feel the same.

Not this time.

Stop it, he told himself. You're getting married to a great girl in a couple of months' time. No point in thinking about the past now. And Chloe was a stunner and a half. Dan just wished she'd lay off on the wedding talk.

He found the Amazing Days store with little difficulty.

"I'm here to collect the wedding invitations – Hunt is the name," he announced to the sales assistant, who looked no older than ten, but was wearing the most hideous make-up he had ever seen. She wore purple sparkly eye-shadow, deep red lipstick, and it seemed to Dan as though every piece of exposed skin had been covered with a thick coat of some new, and obviously trendy, fluorescent orange foundation. The girl's jaws stopped chewing for a second, as she regarded Dan with an interested look. Dan was used to the attention. Over six foot tall, and often told he resembled a young Mel Gibson, he knew women found him attractive, despite the fact that he was heading for thirty-five and beginning to develop a bit of a beer-gut, which Chloe had been on at him to do something about before the wedding.

Having had a good look, the girl eventually bent down

behind the counter, exposing a non-existent cleavage, ostensibly for Dan's benefit. "When's the weddin'?"

"Sorry?"

"The weddin'," the girl repeated wearily, "when is it?"

"Oh – September 15th," Dan answered, panicking as he realised he wasn't quite sure. "No, no, it's September 25th – yes, definitely September 25th." He puffed out his chest in an attempt to appear more assertive.

"Well, there's no Hunt here for Septemba," she said, fiddling with a strand of her hair.

"Well, try Fallon then – my fiancée may have given her maiden name."

"Righ'." The girl disappeared beneath the counter again and seconds later produced an ivory cardboard box.

"Thanks, Ms Fallon told me that she's already paid for them?" Dan put the box under his arm.

The girl nodded mutely, looking disappointed as her good-looking customer quickly disappeared out the door.

A relieved Dan unlocked his Saab, and tossed the heavy cardboard box onto the passenger seat. It was well after six and the traffic was bound to be mental. Maybe he should go back to Bray and join the others for a pint until the traffic cleared. One pint wouldn't do him any harm, and he'd drink it slowly. Better than having to sit in a two-mile-long tailback just to get out of Ashford, and having nothing to entertain him but a bunch of fancy wedding invitations.

* * *

Nicola was enjoying her Saturday off. It had been a brainwave of Laura's to suggest that the two of them head to Wicklow for the day. They had spent most of the morning wandering around the local shops and, even though the day was cloudy, it was very mild. Now they were heading towards a cosy little café for lunch.

In the café, Laura looked enviously at Nicola's plate and grimaced towards her own salad. "I can't wait until *I* can get back to eating lasagne and chips again," she said ruefully.

"Keep imagining how gorgeous you'll look in your wedding dress," Nicola teased, tucking shamelessly into her food. "So tell me, how are your business plans going? Any news from the Enterprise Board?"

Laura's eyes lit up instantly at this, and Nicola smiled.

"Not yet," she said ruefully, "and I think it'll be a long wait. Still, everything else is coming along very well. I'm going to use one of the downstairs bedrooms as a mini-office until Neil organises a proper workshop for me in the garage."

"So you're going to work from the house until then?"

Laura nodded. "I've faxed some press releases to the newspapers and magazines that might be interested and I'm in the *Golden Pages*, so you'd never know . . ."

"And what about the website? Did you get someone to organise that for you?"

Laura hoped to display and sell a selection of her designs online.

"Neil's cousin. He's only fifteen but he's an absolute whiz kid on the web. You should see the logos and animations he's come up with. I'm sure he has a big future ahead of him in graphic design or something like that."

"A website will be a big help starting out, particularly if people can order from you directly."

Laura sat forward, her eyes shining with excitement. "I still can't quite get my head around the fact that I'm going out on my own. I'm almost afraid to say it out loud in case I jinx it, or something. Nicola, my very own business!"

"Just imagine – you could be the next Anita Roddick!" Nicola teased. "No, seriously, Laura, it is a brave thing that you're doing, and you should be very proud of yourself."

Laura bit her lip. "Let's just hope I don't fall flat on my face."

"And what does it matter if you do?" Nicola shrugged. "At least you're willing to make a go of it. There aren't many of us who would have the courage to do what you're doing, and that's an achievement in itself. Anyway, I can't see that happening. Your jewellery is great and it's a terrific idea. Ken was over the moon when I told him."

"Was he?" Laura smiled bashfully.

"Yep. And he said to tell you that if you need any help with finding a decent accountant or anything like that, you should give him a shout."

"He's such a sweetheart, Nicola. You're really very lucky."

"I am, aren't I?" Nicola grinned. "Anyway, you're not doing too badly yourself, with your big wedding and your big business, are you?"

"True." Laura smiled and sat back as the waiter collected their empty plates. "It's very exciting though, Nic. For the first time ever, I really feel as though I know where I'm going with my life." She giggled. "Sorry, I know I'm probably boring you to tears with all this talk, but sometimes I get so excited, I can hardly help myself!"

Nicola nodded sagely. "So you've noticed my eyes glazing over every time you open your mouth?" she teased.

Laura threw a napkin at her. "Shall we go? I need to collect my wedding invites, and I thought that on the way back to Dublin we should drop in to Mount Usher Gardens for a while – they should be really beautiful at this time of year."

Nicola gathered her things, and followed her friend out towards the busy main street.

They were in and out of Amazing Day Designs within minutes, Laura eagerly clutching the white cardboard box she had collected from the sulky counter assistant – the same one, she informed Nicola, who had been blatantly eyeing Neil throughout their first visit to the store a few weeks earlier.

"Give me a look!" Nicola urged, trying to keep up with her as they hurried along the narrow, crowded street.

"No, not until we get back to the car."

"Oh come on – please! I'm dying to see them."

"Nicola Peters, you are the most annoying, the most impatient –"

"OK, OK, I'll wait 'til we get back to the bloody car!"

When the two girls had reached the public carpark, and were safely inside Nicola's Ford Focus, Laura excitedly opened the box. Nicola reached across to take a look, and as she did, she saw Laura's expression wrinkle in confusion.

"These aren't mine," Laura said irritably. She pointed at the name on the lid. "Look, they're labelled *Fallon*."

"Oh dear, the girl obviously misheard your surname." Nicola reached for the driver's door. "Come on. We'd better go back."

She was halfway out of the car but stopped short when she saw Laura staring fixedly at the contents of the open box, her eyes wide with alarm.

"What's wrong?" she asked.

Laura looked up, her expression uneasy.

"The groom . . ." she said quietly. "It has to be . . . it's Dan – *your* Dan. Nicola . . . he's getting married again."

Chapter 5

Dan was not impressed.

"What do you mean, it was an 'easy mistake'? How could it be 'an easy mistake'? Don't tell me the bloody girl can't *read*?"

"Mr Hunt, I believe that you were in quite a hurry yesterday afternoon and –"

"That's not the bloody point!" Dan was becoming more agitated by the second. "You gave me the wrong box, and you gave *our* invitations to somebody else."

That was the terrible part, he thought. It was bad enough finding out that he had taken the wrong box, but the fact that Laura had his, well . . . that was even worse.

He hadn't noticed anything himself, not having given the invitations a second glance at the time. In fact, they were still in the car until Chloe returned to the apartment this morning. She'd stayed the previous night at Lynne's, the two of them having gone out on the town the night before. She was in great form, today's dress fitting having apparently 'gone well'. Dan wondered how a simple fitting for a dress could go any other way but he didn't bother to ask. Chloe would simply sigh, give him one of her withering looks, and tell him that he didn't understand. And she was right. Dan didn't understand, he *couldn't* understand what all the bloody fuss was about. It was strange, but he couldn't quite get it into his head that he was actually marrying Chloe, and that she was no longer just his girlfriend, but his *fiancée*.

It had all happened so quickly, he supposed. They had only been together for eight months or so, before Dan had begun literally falling over the numerous hints that Chloe had dropped about marriage proposals and engagement rings. Most of the other women in her circle of friends were married, and he knew that Chloe was determined not to be the one left behind. Dan didn't want to spend the rest of his life being single either, although it wasn't just that – he did love Chloe. She was bright, gorgeous, great fun (when she wasn't organising weddings) and Dan had to admit that the two of them were well matched.

But he just didn't feel the same enthusiasm about this wedding as Chloe did. Still, he supposed it was because he had been through the whole thing already. Although back then, things had been different.

Shortly after her return from Lynne's, Chloe had let out a screech that Dan thought would not only awaken the dead, but have them covering their ears in pain.

"These aren't ours!" she yelled, waving the box lid frantically above her head.

"What? Of course, they're ours," Dan didn't bother to

look away from the newspaper he was reading. "Who else's would they be?"

Chloe's shrill tones pierced his eardrums. "Well, *unless* you've suddenly changed your name to Neil Connolly, and you're marrying someone called . . ." She read the invitation again, "Laura *Fanning* without telling me, then, yes, they might be ours after all."

It was only then that Dan looked up from his newspaper. "What did you say?" he asked, getting up from his armchair.

"I said, unless you've changed your name to –" Chloe trailed off surprised, as Dan abruptly grabbed the invite and read it intently from beginning to end.

He couldn't believe this. What a bloody coincidence! They were finally tying the knot, then.

Dan swallowed hard. Nicola would almost certainly be one of the bridesmaids. She and Laura had been best friends for years. Then, a thought struck him, and heart pounding, he read the date of Laura and Neil's wedding: September 26th. The bloody day after his own. What if . . .?

He had driven the Saab back to Wicklow as if it was on fire, waving away Chloe's protestations.

"It can wait until Monday, Dan. I'll phone them now, give them a piece of my mind and make sure we get not only an apology, but a hefty discount."

But Dan had insisted. He *had* to make sure that Laura wouldn't find out about his wedding, not like that anyway. He had wanted to tell Nicola, had hoped to tell her that he had met someone else, but somehow he kept putting it off and putting it off. Anyway, he reassured himself, he had no way of contacting her, had he? As far as he knew, she was still in London. But she would definitely be back for Laura's wedding.

And if Laura discovered he was getting married again, it wouldn't be long before Nicola knew. He *had* to get it sorted.

But he had no sooner set foot in the stationery store than Debbie began to apologise profusely, and Dan knew that his worst fears were realised. It turned out that Laura had, only earlier that same day, collected his and Chloe's invitations.

Debbie was soothing. "Mr Hunt, I appreciate your position – really I do. But these things happen. With the surnames being similar, and the closeness of the wedding dates –"

"Oh, for goodness sake!" Dan interjected. "If you people can't be bothered to double-check names and dates, considering the business you're in . . ." he trailed off and shook his head, "I don't know."

Debbie tried a different tactic. "Well, I could offer you a small discount on the invoiced amount –"

"I don't want a bloody discount! I want an explanation as to how this could have happened! Do you have any idea how much trouble this could cause? Do you have any bloody idea?"

"Certainly a mistake has been made, Mr Hunt. But the other party identified the mix-up and returned the box immediately. While your invites are here waiting for you, Ms Fanning is still waiting for hers to be returned."

Dan knew what she was trying to say – that Laura was the one who should be standing here ranting and raving about mistakes – but Debbie didn't understand, did she?

"Can you let me have a contact number for the other lady?" he asked suddenly. "It's important that I speak with her . . . to explain."

"Mr Hunt, our client's details are private," Debbie stated firmly, "but I can assure you that I have explained the situation to Ms Fanning, and she's been quite lovely about it and –"

"Can you just give me the bloody phone number?" he bellowed impatiently.

Debbie took a step back, and Dan could tell by her demeanour that she was beginning to lose patience with him.

"No disrespect intended, Mr Hunt, but these things happen," she said, folding her arms across her chest. "The other lady was absolutely fine about it, and there's been no harm done. Now, I'm very sorry, but there's very little else I can do and –"

Dan didn't wait for her to finish; he just grabbed the invites, shook his head, and marched out the door.

These things happen, Debbie had said. No harm done.

Little did she know.

Chapter 6

"Hey, Helen, guess where I'm off to next weekend?"

On her way out the door, Helen turned and fixed twenty-one-year-old Tom Russell with a look that almost cut him in half. "*Hay* is something one generally finds under a horse, Tom."

Tom swallowed nervously, and at this, Helen grinned.

"Where *are* you off to then?" she asked easily.

He was relieved. Sometimes you just didn't know what way the wind blew with the boss. One minute she was all smiles and chat, and the next she was cold as ice. He supposed that was why some of the others on their team were more than a little afraid of her, which in turn meant that they tended to perform well, and Helen's monthly sales figures tended to be better than most.

"Anfield. Two tickets, Kop Stand, corner flag," he grinned.

"You're kidding!" Helen was definitely interested now. "For the pre-season game with Madrid? The one where our ace striker will be back to cause havoc in their defence? Should be some game!"

"The very one." Tom looked mightily pleased with himself. Football was the one thing that always got Helen Jackson's motor running. Her eyes lit up in the same way most other women's did when they stumbled across a bargain in the sales. Tom thought she was the sexiest woman alive. And even better, she was a Liverpool fan.

"How did you manage that? Those tickets are almost impossible to get!"

"Not when you have a mate who's well in with the ticket office over there."

"You never told me that."

"You never asked. Anyway, myself and my mate are going over this weekend – but if you ever fancy going sometime . . ."

Helen laughed. "I might hold you to that, Tom."

Tom had to stop himself from actually drooling as Helen eased smoothly past his desk and out the door. Even her bleedin' *walk* was erotic! He checked his watch, debating whether or not to follow her out and spend a few minutes longer chatting on the way downstairs. Maybe she might even offer him a lift home. Tom picked up his jacket and said goodbye to the others, but when he reached the lift, she was already gone.

Tom sighed. God, what he wouldn't do to take Helen Jackson to a football match. That would be a different kind of heaven altogether.

* * *

Helen turned out of the XL car park and drove towards

Cornelscourt. Tom's 'invitation', God love him, had reminded her of just how long it was since she'd been to a football match. Four years at least, she thought grimacing. Good old Kerry had put paid to that, as she'd done to most things her mother enjoyed.

When was the last time she had taken a holiday abroad? Not since Kerry was born, that was for sure. She and Jamie used to have at least two holidays a year – winter in the Canaries, and then two weeks somewhere further afield – the Caribbean, the Red Sea and one wonderful time in the Maldives. And of course the odd soccer weekend in England. She and Jamie's shared passion for football meant that they went to a game at least three times a year.

But one fateful morning had changed all that, the morning that Helen discovered the blue line on her pregnancy test.

Throughout their six-year relationship, she and Jamie had never spoken seriously about children. At their age, there was no need. Anyway, they were too busy spending their healthy salaries on impulsive weekends away, romantic meals and nights out in the pub with other equally childless couples. Nobody in their circle of friends had even discussed children. Why would they? There was too much fun to be had, they were all in their mid-twenties and enjoying life to the full. Who in their right mind would trade in all that they had for a life of dirty nappies, sleepless nights and shapeless clothes?

Not Helen, that was for sure. She had never been particularly maternal, unlike Laura and Nicola, who could stand cooing over a newborn baby for hours on end. It wasn't that she didn't *like* children, it was just that to her they represented an entirely different way of life, one that Helen wasn't partial to. Yes, babies were cute and cuddly and all the rest of it, but they were also loud, demanding and had a tendency to – without warning – projectile vomit three feet across a room. She and Jamie could start thinking about that kind of thing after they were married, long after. Luckily Jamie felt the same way.

Yet, a few months after she and Jamie bought the apartment together (and had spent one glorious week christening every piece of furniture, never mind every *room*), Helen began feeling different. She felt faint, light-headed and weak and, even worse, Jamie pointed out that she had put on weight. At work, she was uninterested, listless and couldn't make a sale to save her life. Helen then confessed to Laura that at the age of twenty-five, she worried she was heading for burn-out.

"Maybe you're pregnant," Laura had offered artlessly and Helen nearly had a stroke there and then.

As did Jamie, when Helen did a positive home-pregnancy test and soon after a doctor cheerfully informed him that his girlfriend was nearly three months gone.

"What the fuck happened?" he accused her, as they left the surgery.

"Couldn't have put it better myself," answered a distraught Helen.

And that was the beginning of the end.

Helen immediately considered abortion, but knew that she would never be able to go through with it. Anyway, she told herself, in time maybe they might get used to the idea. Maybe it might be the best thing that ever happened to them. They might even end up getting married as a result. So, Helen resolved to get on with it and hope for the best.

Jamie, however, had other ideas. There was no question of him getting used to the idea. Throughout her pregnancy he couldn't even look at Helen, let alone get close to her.

She had had a difficult pregnancy, which to her felt more like a terminal illness than a so-called 'blessing'. The last few months of her pregnancy were spent in bed able to do little else but watch Jamie become more and more resentful towards her, and what she had become.

He began to go out in the evenings, leaving her alone in the apartment, and on the evening Helen rang him in the middle of a poker game with the lads, to announce that her waters had broken, she knew by his face when he came home that he had begun to hate her.

It wasn't any better after Kerry was born. The baby had some sort of problem with her oesophagus, which meant that she couldn't keep any milk down, and spent most of the day – and night – screaming. For the first four months of her daughter's existence, Helen recalled getting only a few hours' 'real' sleep a night. By the fifth month, and just when Kerry had begun to improve, Jamie was gone.

"This isn't what I wanted for us," he said. "I feel tied down."

At the time, she hadn't had the energy to convince him to stay. Knowing Jamie as well as she did, she knew she would be fighting a losing battle

Kerry's arrival signalled the end of Helen's social life – the spontaneous nights out, the romantic evenings in, the much-anticipated holidays abroad. The only holidays

Helen had to anticipate these days were in dull, grey Glengarrah, where she and Kerry would spend the odd weekend at her dad's farm. Kerry loved the farm animals, and got a great kick out of collecting hens' eggs each morning with her grandfather.

Good for Kerry.

Helen parked outside the childminder's house, and berated herself for the thoughts she had been having lately. She hated feeling down like this, but sometimes she just couldn't help it. Things got on top of her now and again. Things like her non-existent life.

"Hi, Helen!" Kerry's childminder stood at the door, awaiting Helen's arrival. Jo was a rotund, kindly, earth-mother type, who had been looking after Kerry for almost three years now.

Uh-oh, Helen thought, realising instantly that Jo wanted to have 'a little chat'. Jo often wanted 'little chats'. Helen supposed it was a good thing that she was interested in Kerry's welfare but sometimes . . .

"Is something the matter?" she asked. "Where's Kerry?"

"No, no, nothing's wrong. She's in the garden playing with little Mark from next door." Jo stood back and ushered Helen into the hallway. "Look, Helen, tell me to mind my own business but . . ." the childminder apologetically wrung her hands together, "it's been a couple of months now and there's been little improvement. If anything, she's getting worse."

Helen looked at her. "Jo, I'm sorry, but what more do you expect me to do?"

"Look, I don't mean to sound forward but . . ."

Perish the thought, Helen thought unkindly.

"Are you still doing the exercises with her?"

"Well, I'm doing what I can, but I don't always have the time to do them with her," Helen said. "By the time I get home, have dinner and clean up, the evenings just seem to disappear."

Jo looked troubled. "Helen, I know it's none of my business, and I really wouldn't say anything if I wasn't worried. Just keep on eye on her, OK?"

Jesus! What kind of a mother does she think I am? Helen thought, her pulse quickening with anger.

"I will." Helen didn't have the energy to argue about it today. "Now, if she's ready . . .?"

"Of course."

She followed Jo into the living-room, where Kerry sat playing happily on the ground with one of the neighbour's children.

Immediately catching sight of Helen, Kerry beamed. "Mommy!"

"Hi, hon, are you ready to go home?"

"Yep!" Kerry nodded enthusiastically, racing to her mother's side.

"OK, now get your things and say goodbye to Mark and Jo."

Kerry looked from one to the other. "Bye, M-m-m-m-m . . ." The little girl reddened and glanced at her mother for support, but Helen couldn't look her in the eye.

"Take a breath, Kerry," she said.

She tried again. "Bye, M-m-m . . ."

Jo took her hand. "It's all right, pet. He knows you're going. We'll see you tomorrow, OK?"

Kerry nodded again but looked upset.

In the hallway, Helen caught Jo's 'I told you so' look, and it really annoyed her.

She was getting a little tired of the childminder's interference in Kerry's upbringing. Yes, her daughter was a slow developer, but what could Helen do about it? Didn't she do her best for Kerry, working all day every day to keep them going? They now lived in a much nicer apartment than the one she and Jamie had, she always got the best of clothes, the best of toys, the best of *everything*.

Hadn't Helen taken her to the bloody speech therapist when Jo noticed her speech blockages a while back? Hadn't she bought her that talking-book software that the speech therapist recommended? The idea was that Kerry would improve her speech through looking at pictures onscreen, and listening to the correct pronunciations of the words. The software was for her computer. Her computer! How many three-and-a-half-year-olds had their own bloody computer?

Even though Helen *had* noticed some repetitions in her daughter's speech, she wasn't overly concerned. Kerry wasn't even four years old, for goodness sake. The problem would undoubtedly sort itself out with age. What did Jo expect – that she be able to recite the entire works of Shakespeare? She had been sure that Jo was overreacting, but to get the childminder off her back she had agreed to take Kerry to a speech therapist recommended by her GP.

A very *expensive* speech therapist.

They had their first consultation a few months back and the therapist had advocated that each day Helen allot a 'selective listening' period, a relaxed time allowing Kerry to chatter away at her own comfortable pace.

"Try not to place time-burdens on her speech, Ms Jackson. All adults, especially working mothers like yourself, are on constant time-demands, and tend to speak almost as quickly as is physically possible. As Kerry is just learning how to coordinate her speech mechanisms, she needs to speak slowly."

"You're saying that *my* rate of speech can affect Kerry's progress?"

"In a way, yes. Some days you might come home from work, tired and frazzled and with possibly a pile of housework to tackle. There is an immediate demand on your time. Kerry, of course, will sense this, and may interpret it as a message that she is not interesting, or not worth listening to."

Helen shook her head. *Selective listening?* Where was she supposed to find time for that?

Their first consultation with Dr Davis had been over two hours long, the therapist almost immediately diagnosing Kerry with a 'moderate-to-severe disfluency'.

Well, which was it, Helen had thought at the time – moderate or severe?

And *of course* Kerry had a problem, Helen thought sceptically. If she didn't have a problem, how on earth would the doctor afford her next holiday in the South Pacific?

Dr Davis had droned on about how Helen would have to take time out to spend some quality conversation time with Kerry, and help her develop 'healthy and appropriate communication attitudes'.

If there was one thing Helen abhorred, it was psychobabble. There was nothing wrong with Kerry that time couldn't cure. Admittedly, Kerry was shy and nervous, and didn't nervous children always have trouble expressing themselves?

"Kerry doesn't stutter because she's nervous," Dr Davis had explained. "Rather she is nervous because she stutters. It's a vicious cycle. Even a child as young as Kerry will realise that she isn't speaking as well as everybody else, but what is most important is that she does not acquire a negative self-image, or be ashamed or embarrassed about it. If she feels badly about her speech, she is more likely to struggle in attempts to be fluent, and if this happens, the problem will almost certainly escalate. This is where you come in, Ms Jackson. As a parent, Kerry will look to you for a reaction. If you show any signs of frustration, fear or annoyance when Kerry struggles, it won't be long before she begins to show similar reactions. So, as well as increasing Kerry's concerns about her speech, these reactions may also increase the severity of her stuttering. Your own approach, and indeed your childminder's approach towards stuttering, will play a critical role in Kerry's development of a healthy attitude."

"Look, I'm really not sure that Kerry has all that much of a problem," Helen said defensively. "I mean, she doesn't stutter all the time, very rarely in fact." Rarely around me anyway, Helen thought.

"Well, a person with epilepsy doesn't have seizures all the time either, Ms Jackson. Stuttering by definition is simply a breakdown in our inbuilt speaking mechanisms, and the system does not break down all of the time. However, I would caution against taking this problem lightly – intervention at an early age is crucial."

Crucial for your bank account maybe, Helen thought uncharitably. She shook her head. "I just don't know — perhaps we should just wait and see."

The doctor looked at her. "Ms Jackson, believe me, stuttering is too awful a problem to just 'wait and see'. Your own efforts are crucial in preventing this from becoming a chronic problem."

In Helen's opinion the whole thing had been an expensive waste of time.

Jo however, had thrown herself wholeheartedly into the programme Dr Davis had advised. She was careful never to react overtly to Kerry's repetitions, and never to interrupt, or finish a sentence for her.

Helen still believed that dramatising and paying too much attention to Kerry's so-called problem was only contributing to it. Kerry usually only stuttered when she was over-excited or surprised by something. What toddler *didn't* have problems getting sentences out when they were excited?

What the hell was she supposed to do, she asked herself, as she settled Kerry in the backseat of the Golf. She could hardly force the words out of her, could she? The way Jo went on, you'd swear Kerry's problems were all Helen's fault. Couldn't she see that she was just doing her best? Anyway, Kerry had just started attending preschool, so mixing with other kids would probably sort out the so-called 'problem' once and for all. Nothing like a narky teacher to get you learning properly, she thought, remembering her own school days.

She glanced in her rear-view mirror to where Kerry was sitting in silence.

"So what did you do at Jo's today?" she asked, then idly remembered Dr Davis mentioning something about trying not to ask questions that required a lengthy response.

"We made Wice Kwispie buns," Kerry answered without stumbling.

There, Helen thought, she *knew* Jo was overreacting. The woman overreacted to everything. She could just imagine Jo trying to force Kerry to say various things throughout the day. No wonder her daughter struggled at times.

"And did Mark help with the Rice Krispie buns?" she asked.

"Yep," Kerry said quickly, "buh–buh-buh-buh . . ." She hesitated and caught her mother's eye in the rear-view mirror.

Unbeknownst to herself, Helen was frowning. "But what?" she finished for her.

Kerry looked uncomfortable. "Sometimes the w-w-w-words get s-s-s-stuck in my mouth, Mommy," she said mournfully. "Jo says it's called b-b-b-bumpy talk."

"What? There's no such thing, Kerry. You're still only a little girl, that's all."

Kerry looked away and out of the window, her mother's dismissive explanation not sitting well with her.

Helen was livid. Jo had obviously been putting ideas in her daughter's head. What kind of a thing was that to do? Now *Kerry* believed she had some kind of a problem.

That was all Helen needed!

She felt a familiar impatience rise up from the pit of her stomach. It was hard enough as it was, doing a hard day's work, without having to play up to Kerry as well. It was all right for Jo, she had a husband to share the domestics and cater for her every whim, with nothing to trouble her but what to watch on television every evening. She didn't have to face a mountain of washing and an untidy apartment to clean. She didn't have to spend the next few hours working on a presentation for a client, and then be expected to 'listen selectively' to a three-and-a-half-year-old.

Jo had really annoyed her with the suggestion that she wasn't doing enough to help Kerry with her speech. What did *she* know about raising a child?

Helen sighed. Everything seemed to be getting on top of her these days. She knew that she had been unfairly negative with Laura that time about her plans for her new business, and she was being especially impatient and impossible at work. Normally she took a hardline approach with her sales team, believing that respect and a little bit of fear would get better results than treating them all like babies. But today, one of the newer girls on her sales team had asked Helen for advice, and she had nearly bitten off the poor girl's head. How could anyone be expected to get results if Helen carried on like that?

Glancing in the rear-view mirror, she indicated right and drove towards her apartment in Monkstown.

She needed a break. Even a decent night out would do, but when was the last time she'd had one of those? As expected, the delectable Richard Moore hadn't been in contact. In the same way that all the promising men she had gone out with had never again been seen or heard from, once they learnt of Kerry's existence.

It wasn't fair. Why should she be doomed to a lifetime

of spinsterhood just because she was a single mother? She had done her best for Kerry, was always doing her best for Kerry and what thanks did she get for it all? Absolutely none. Kerry was clingy, tearful and needy and now, thanks to Jo, she was becoming increasingly aware of her speech difficulty. She always made Helen feel guilty for going out at night without her, although she loved staying at Auntie Nicola's where she could play with Barney or sometimes Auntie Laura's where she was fussed over by Neil.

But what about Helen? Who the hell would fuss over her?

Helen let herself and Kerry into the building, then checked the postbox in the hallway. There was only one envelope addressed to her and she recognised the handwriting immediately. Great – Jamie's guilt money. At least that might help pay some of these speech-therapy bills.

She put the key in the door of their modern, *expensive* ground-floor apartment. What was wrong with her lately? Why was she so down all the time? But she didn't need to look very far for an answer.

She was desperately lonely. She wanted – no, she *needed* someone – someone to share the gossip when she came home after a long hard day in the office, someone to get excited as she did over the football results. She needed intelligent, exciting conversation, something more stimulating than babbling and questions from a three-and-a-half-year-old. She needed someone to cuddle up to when she was feeling down, someone to share her problems and tell her that everything would be all right.

Someone who didn't leave a mess in the kitchen, and toys all over the living-room.

Helen just needed someone to love her, to fulfil her, to make her *happy*.

In the same way Jamie had before Kerry had come along and ruined everything.

Chapter 7

On Tuesday morning, Nicola was yawning as she approached the leisure centre. She hated opening up, especially at this hour, and sure enough there were some very early birds waiting in the doorway, ready and anxious to fit in a workout before heading off to a full day's work.

Motiv8's assistant manager, who usually opened the centre had phoned Nicola at 6am that morning, and announced that she had a throat infection and would be out for the next few days. She had arranged for Jack Duffy to cover her early-morning pool duty, but as a result of her absence and the fact that one of the gym attendants had called in sick, Nicola would need to man the reception until at least mid-morning, instead of tackling her paperwork like she had intended.

Nicola remembered with a shudder that because of Ken's idea to bring in more custom, they were now holding a Mother and Baby swimming morning on Tuesdays.

Terrific, she said to herself as she greeted the members outside the Motiv8 entrance: hours of screaming kids and fussy mothers was just what Nicola needed today. She switched on the lights and the electricity and soon a handful of members appeared from the changing rooms eager to begin a warm-up.

Although she wouldn't admit it to Laura, Nicola had been sent into a tailspin by the news of Dan's impending second marriage.

At the time, she had read the invite word for word and dismissed it with a cursory wave of her arm. "What he does these days is none of my business," she had said airily and waited in the car while Laura went to return the invites to Amazing Day Designs. According to her friend, upon her empty-handed return from the store, the wrong box had been given out to the other party a day earlier and hadn't yet been returned.

Nicola now wondered whether Dan had been aware of the mistake, whether he had seen Laura's invites. He would almost certainly recognise the name.

She shook her head. It was as if somebody somewhere wanted her to know about Dan's intentions, seeing as he hadn't bothered letting her know about it himself. She hadn't known he was even in a relationship. Then again, she thought, checking the acidity level in the swimming-pool, why would he tell her?

They had been out of one another's lives for a long time now – years in fact. But the divorce had come through only last year. Good old Dan hadn't wasted any time, had he?

Then again, *she* could hardly talk. She and Ken had got

together just before the divorce was finalised, and Nicola hadn't exactly gone running to Dan about that, had she? Although, she thought uncomfortably, that was different and, of course, Ken and Dan knew one another from when Nicola worked with Ken in town.

She wondered idly what the future Mrs Hunt was like. Judging by the get-up of the invitations and the plush hotel hosting the reception, her family must be worth a few bob. And she was probably young, definitely younger than Dan, anyway. Nicola smiled as she adjusted the pool backwash. She was almost certainly blonde. Dan *always* had a thing for blondes.

So Dan was getting on with it. Should she be really be all that surprised? Nicola wasn't sure. It's not as though she'd even thought about him since her return. Not all that much, anyway.

She sighed and shook her head. There was no point in reminiscing about it now. After all, hadn't she been the one insisting they get on with their lives? Hadn't she been the one to move away – away from the disappointment and regret that would surely have consumed her had she stayed here?

After their official separation and her move to London, she had instructed her solicitor to begin divorce proceedings, and luckily Dan hadn't objected to the terms, nor her plans to sell their home and split the proceeds.

Upon her return, Nicola had bought a small, two-bedroom cottage in Stepaside, not far from Laura's house in Ballinteer, and initially had stayed at her mother's while having some essential modifications done.

Just under a year later, her English divorce had come

through with the minimum of fuss, and Nicola and Dan hadn't spoken face to face in years. Now he was getting married again. Should she care? Should it bother her that he hadn't told her? Then again, how could he have told her, even had he wanted to? For a time, she had been living with her aunt in Fulham and he wouldn't have known how to contact her other than through her family or Laura. He would have known that Laura wouldn't be too forthcoming with any details, and he would surely have known that the hurt would still be very raw for her own family too.

Nicola sighed. She hadn't yet said anything to Ken about the mix-up with the invites, and because she hadn't told him about it at the time, she now wasn't sure how to broach the subject. She could hardly admit that it was bothering her, could she?

Her thoughts were interrupted by a loud roar coming from the gym. Great, she thought with a groan, the first treadmill casualty of the day!

* * *

Later that evening, at dinner, Laura was outlining events to her fiancé who had returned that evening from another trip abroad.

"It was awful, Neil. I didn't know what to say to her," she said, spooning mashed potatoes onto her plate. "I feel a bit guilty for asking her to come to Wicklow with me. If I had gone on my own, I would've seen the mistake and said nothing."

Neil gave her a shrewd glance. "You would have said nothing? I don't think so, love. You wouldn't be able to keep something like that from her."

"Maybe," she sighed deeply. "Still, she carried on as though it didn't affect her, but surely she must have felt *something*?"

But Nicola had said nothing about it since, nothing at all. Laura knew her friend well enough to know that the incident would have knocked her for six. And why wouldn't it? It had certainly given Laura a shock. Dan – getting married again? It just didn't seem real.

"Well, maybe it doesn't bother her," Neil said. "I mean, it's over and done with a long time ago and Dan's well out of her life now."

"Have you seen him yourself, lately?" she asked. The couples had socialised a lot together and she knew that both Dan and Neil had continued their drinking buddy friendship for a while after the separation, until the strain of trying not to mention Nicola had finally got to them both.

Neil laid down his knife and fork. "OK, I may as well admit it. I knew about the wedding."

"*What?*"

He shrugged. "I didn't say anything because it's not really any of my business."

"Neil!"

"Well, it isn't! Anyway, John O'Leary rang me up one day looking for a cheap holiday and we got talking."

Laura snorted. "Typical!" Dan's partner in the accountancy practice was as tight as a duck's backside, and would try anything for a freebie.

"We met for lunch, naturally I asked how Dan was doing and he told me he was getting married to – his exact words – 'a cute little blonde with a body to die for'."

Laura made a face. "What a sleazebag!"

Neil nodded. "I know, I never liked him myself, but what could I do?" He began to eat again.

"What else did he say?"

"Well, Dan and this other girl had been going out for a while, and apparently they got engaged shortly after the divorce came through."

"Rat!"

"Oh come on, Laura! What was Dan supposed to do? Nicola wanted the divorce."

"Hold on a second," Laura interjected. "What was *she* supposed to do? Stay married to him – after everything?"

Neil answered with his mouth full. "Depends on how you look at it, I suppose."

"Just don't start."

"What?"

"Don't start taking his side again."

"Laura, it was years ago. Don't you think that Dan has suffered enough? Doesn't he deserve some happiness too?"

"What do you mean 'too'?"

"Well, Nicola's fine now, isn't she? Her life's back on track, she has Ken and she's doing fine." Neil shrugged and continued eating, his point made as far as he was concerned.

"Will you listen to yourself – sticking up for that – that coward! Nicola is our friend, for goodness sake."

"OK, OK, you're right. I'm sorry. It's just sometimes . . ." he trailed off.

"What?"

"Well, sometimes I don't know who to feel most sorry

for. I know that Nicola had it tough, but Dan, well, he was the outcast in all of this, wasn't he?"

"With good reason!"

"Yes, but . . .oh look, let's not talk about it any more. There's no point in our fighting about it, is there?"

"No, but I can't believe you didn't tell me he was getting married again."

"What was the point? They're divorced, they've both moved on – end of story."

End of story? For Nicola's sake, Laura hoped so.

She knew that Dan and Nicola hadn't spoken since the divorce. In fact they had stopped speaking long before then, back when the hurt was still there, for Nicola anyway. But surely Dan should have had the decency to inform his ex of his plans, to let her know that he was beginning a new life, albeit a life without her. But, she thought, Dan had changed, had begun to change a long time ago.

Laura cleared the table, and as she began to wash up she let her mind drift back to the very first time she and Nicola had laid eyes on Dan Hunt.

* * *

The two had headed into town for late-night shopping, and had been sitting in an unmoving and seemingly unending line of traffic on O'Connell St for over forty-five minutes. Nicola, who hated town at the best of times, was not impressed.

"Oh, I'm so bloody sick of this!" she groaned.

"What?" Laura had said airily, rummaging in her handbag for a hairbrush.

"The blasted traffic, what do you think?" Nicola impatiently tapped the steering wheel.

"Oh that."

There had been no forward movement for twenty minutes, and the pelting rain seemed to contribute to the misery of their scenario, at least for Nicola. Then again, Laura thought, Nicola normally cycled wherever she could in order to avoid the traffic. "All that stress isn't good for my health!" she'd argue, and Laura had to agree, suspecting that the very concept of road rage had been invented with Nicola in mind. Traffic, quite literally, drove her friend crazy, but Laura couldn't really understand why she always got so worked up about it. It was hardly a surprise; these days traffic and Dublin went hand in hand, and there was little point in getting upset about something you couldn't control. After all, everybody else was in a similar jam. Laura giggled at her own unintended pun, but quickly altered her expression when Nicola glowered at her.

"I don't know why you're being so cheerful about it anyway," Nicola said smartly. "Aren't you going to be late for your hairdresser's appointment?"

Laura checked her watch. "Oh, shit! I had completely forgotten about that!" She was already fifteen minutes late and they weren't anyway near the Ilac Centre's multi-storey carpark.

"Well, you could always go on ahead without me," Nicola suggested. "If I can organise parking before the end of the next millennium, we can meet up somewhere afterwards."

"Are you sure? I shouldn't be too long; it's only a blow

dry." Laura checked her side mirror to ensure that she didn't topple some unsuspecting cyclist upon opening her passenger door as she'd done once before.

"Go ahead," Nicola sighed. "I'll text your mobile and let you know where I am, assuming that I get out of here before rigor mortis sets in."

"It's my fault – I shouldn't have dragged you all the way in here tonight. The traffic is always crazy for late-night shopping."

Nicola waved her away with a grin. "Off you go – you can make it up to me by treating me to something nice in Bewley's later."

"You're sure?"

"Yes – go on!"

Laura stepped out onto the wet tarmac and weaved in and out between the halted cars, struggling against the heavy wind and rain with her umbrella.

She felt awful about leaving her friend like that. After all, it had been *her* idea to come into town this evening and Nicola wasn't particularly enamoured of shopping. Her friend was a rare breed of female shopper in the sense that she became impatient very easily. And browsing was a dirty word as far as she was concerned. If Nicola wanted something she bought it there and then, none of this have-a-look-somewhere-else-and-then go-back-to-the-first-shop-anyway business. Which in Laura's book was half the fun.

Anyway, she thought, quickening her pace towards the hair salon, Nicola wouldn't be in the mood for any nonsense by the time she got out of that traffic. Didn't she already have a face that would trip a jackass when she left her?

She was comfortably ensconced in the salon and chatting

affably to her hairdresser, when she got a text message from Nicola: *"Meet me outside Arnotts when you're ready."*

That was quick. Laura replaced her mobile in her handbag, while at the same time trying to keep her head perfectly still. The queue of traffic must have broken up in no time at all after she left. Good – Nicola might be that bit more relaxed now.

Soon after, Laura left the salon happily coiffed, and made her way towards Arnotts Department Store. She almost immediately spied Nicola leaning casually just inside the entrance, smoking a cigarette. As she drew near, she saw that her friend wasn't alone. A tall, dark-suited man wearing an overcoat seemed to be having some kind of 'discussion' with her. Judging by the fact that his face was puce and he was waving his arms animatedly in the air, he wasn't just bemoaning the weather.

"But – but, you can't just up and *leave*!" Laura heard the man splutter.

Oh dear, what had Nicola done now, she wondered, approaching the two.

"And why not?" Nicola exhaled her cigarette smoke, and gave him a look that would flatten Lennox Lewis. "Is it *my* problem that no one in this godforsaken city has a clue how to manage the bloody traffic?"

"So your way around the problem is to just up and out of it, is it?"

"Yep," Nicola said, in a tone that bode no argument.

"But what about the rest of us?" the man cried in astonishment. "What about the likes of me who's been stuck directly behind your blasted yellow Polo for the last hour or so!"

"Blame the Corporation," Nicola said matter-of-factly. "Now, I'm sorry but I don't have time to stand around and chat about this all day long. My friend is here now and we're going shopping, aren't we, Laura?"

"What's happened, Nicola? Where's the car?" Laura asked.

"Where's the car, she asks?" the man yelled. "Where's the car? I'll tell you where the bloody car is – it's *abandoned* in the middle of bloody O'Connell St, that's where it is!"

"Oh, you didn't?" Laura regarded her with a look of absolute astonishment.

Nicola shrugged her shoulders. "I was going mad, Laura. I couldn't wait there any longer."

"So she just gets out, slings her handbag over her shoulder, slams the door and stomps off in the direction of Henry St without a care in the world!" exclaimed the attractive but so-far-unnamed man, shaking his head from side to side. "I couldn't believe my bloody eyes when I saw it happening!"

"But you'll be towed away or clamped or something!" Laura cried. Nicola would be lucky not be arrested. But not for the first time, her impatience had got the better of her and she had simply flown in the face of everyone else and had done her own thing. How embarrassing!

Nicola put a hand on her hip. "Better than waiting another hour before I could even begin looking for a parking space. Now, come on, we're wasting valuable shopping time standing around like this."

"I don't bloody believe this," the man said with another shake of his head. "I just don't bloody believe this."

Laura looked at her friend, who shrugged again and

obviously wasn't a bit put out about it. She supposed she'd better say something to the poor fellow.

"I'm really sorry, Mr . . ." Laura began.

"Hunt," he said, running a hand through his damp hair. "Dan Hunt."

"Well, Mr Hunt, I'm sure Nicola just acted on the spur of the moment. The traffic situation is pretty bad this evening and –"

"Well, if it was bloody bad before, it's a lot bloody worse now! I can't move! And *then*, then I get bloody soaked trying to run after this – this bloody woman!" Laura noticed that the 'bloody' word-count was getting higher by the second.

"OK, OK, I'll go back to the blasted car!" Nicola flung her cigarette butt on the ground and squashed it vehemently under her foot, before stomping up towards O'Connell St, Laura and the businessman struggling to keep up with her in the pouring rain.

Laura could hear the honking and horning even before they reached the top of the street and there, in exactly the same spot where she had got out, was her friend's bright yellow Polo. Except by now there was a long stretch of clear road in front of it, and the traffic in the lane alongside was moving very slowly, leaving no opportunity for the drivers in Nicola's lane to overtake.

Her friend's return was met with a resounding chorus of beeps and jeers from the drivers misfortunate enough to be marooned behind the Polo.

"Get that feckin' banger off the road!" a bus driver two cars down shouted at her.

Nicola mortified Laura even further by giving him the

finger before she casually unlocked the car and plonked herself in the driver's seat. Laura tried desperately to make herself invisible as she waited for Nicola to unlock the passenger door.

Dan Hunt tapped the driver's window.

"Thank you," he said, exasperated, rainwater dripping from his nose. "Thank you so bloody much. Not only have I missed my bloody flight but now I've probably gone and caught bloody pneumonia running around after the likes of you." He wiped his nose with the sleeve of his dripping overcoat. "Well?"

"Well, what?" Nicola made a face as another driver mouthed silent abuse at her from the other lane.

"Don't you have anything to say?" Dan Hunt's voice rose in frustration as he struggled to wipe away the incessant drops falling from his dark fringe. Laura couldn't help but stare. His alarmingly blue eyes looked striking against his drenched skin. "Or do you think all of this is funny, or something?"

"Sorry." Nicola grinned brazenly as she started the engine.

"I don't bloody believe this," he said for about the third time that day. "I just don't bloody believe this."

But as he looked away, Laura noticed that, despite himself, the corners of Dan Hunt's mouth had risen upwards with the beginnings of what, seconds later, became a breathtaking smile.

Chapter 8

"News? What kind of news?"

At the other end of the line, Laura detected a note of apprehension in her mother's tone.

"Nothing bad, Mam. Look, I shouldn't have said anything. I'll wait until we get there and then I'll tell you everything, OK?"

Maureen Fanning's miffed tone was palpable. "Suit yourself. But don't be dilly-dallying on your way down – the dinner will be on the table at seven and not a minute later."

Laura rang off having assured her mother that she and Neil would make it their business to be at her parents' house by dinnertime. She went back into the living-room, where Neil was enjoying what had lately become a rare opportunity to flop in front of the television, Eamonn the cat in his lap.

"Well, did you tell her?" he asked, lazily stroking the cat's fur.

Laura shook her head. "I told her I had some news but she seemed a bit preoccupied. I think I might leave it for a while, Neil – at least until after the wedding."

"Why do you keep putting off telling them, love? They'll be thrilled when they find out. And you said yourself that you'll be meeting so many people at the wedding it would be a shame to waste the opportunity for a little self-promotion."

"I know, but –"

"But what? Come here a second." Neil indicated the space beside him and when Laura sat down he put his arms around her. At this, Eamonn gave him the cat version of a dirty look. "Look, I know you're nervous about all of this. It's one thing to talk about it amongst ourselves, but quite another to tell the world about it, right?"

She nodded.

"But this is what being in business is all about, love. You have to let people know you exist, otherwise how will you sell anything?"

Laura grimaced. "I know. I'm being stupid. But I've put so much work into setting it up, I just hope that people won't think I'm making a big mistake."

"Who cares what people think? What is it to them? *You're* the one taking the chance, and you're the one doing all the work. Not to mention taking all the profits," he added with a grin. "Look, I know how you feel. Hold off telling the world until after the wedding if you'd prefer. But you need at least to tell your family about it. And look, with the likes of your mother on the case, you'll get as much coverage as you would with a billboard in Times Square."

Laura sat up. "I never thought of that."

Neil was right. She had been putting off telling her parents about the new business because she thought that they would worry about Neil and her having only one source of income, what with the wedding and the new mortgage. But she had forgotten how much her mother loved to boast about her family to all and sundry in the village.

When Laura's younger married sister, Cathy, had three years ago produced twin boys – the first Fanning grandchildren – Maureen had been ecstatic, and there was no one in Glengarrah that didn't know all about it, from the weight of the babies to the number of stitches her misfortunate sister had needed afterwards.

Maureen would be in her element with the news that her older daughter was entering the business world. She could just imagine her mother after Mass on a Sunday.

"Laura? She's in Dublin now. Yes, getting married to a lovely respectable fellow. Oh, you didn't know she had her own business? Yes, she's doing very well, can hardly keep up with the demand. But sure, we always knew she'd make something of herself." All said in the irritating smug tone that Laura usually hated, but could easily tolerate if Maureen was talking about *her*.

It would be nice to give her mother something to boast about – for once. She had never been particularly bright at school and her exam results (with the exception of Art, at which she excelled) were usually best kept hidden.

In her mother's eyes, the Art & Design diploma she had taken had been a complete waste of time.

"You'll never find employment drawing pictures and

making matchstick men," she had told Laura shortly after graduation. "You should go back to the Tech for a year and do a secretarial course."

Although in fairness, the one-year computer course she had taken after her diploma had certainly proved itself useful in Laura's finding employment. She had never any problems in that regard. The words that kept cropping up in her references were 'dedicated, diligent and dependable', which in her opinion translated to 'dull, dull and dull'. She found no excitement, no challenge in drawing up reports and churning out figures on some pre-programmed software package. She had thought computers would stimulate her imagination, and that accounts might be a little less humdrum than banking or sales, both of which she had tried in equal measures.

Her hobby had been her only escape from her mind-numbing working week, and it wasn't until she had met Neil, who made her feel as though she could do *anything*, that Laura began to consider putting her God-given talents to good use.

These last few weeks had been absolute bliss. She couldn't remember ever feeling so alive, so blissfully happy. For the first time ever, she felt as though she knew exactly where she was going with the rest of her life.

It would be brilliant telling the others, and seeing the pride in her parents' faces. Their daughter – a successful businesswoman, a brave entrepreneur.

Her family would be thrilled.

* * *

"What do you mean you gave up your job? Why would

you do a stupid thing like that?" Maureen Fanning trilled.

Laura and Neil had arrived at the Fanning household in Glengarrah earlier that evening, and the dishes had just been cleared away when Laura made her announcement.

She felt her heart pound. "It's not stupid, Mam. I haven't been happy with what I've been doing for a long time now. You know that."

"Sure none of us are happy with what we're doing, but don't we have to put up with it?" Maureen began to sweep the floor. "Do you think that *I* was happy stuck here day after day cleaning up after you lot for most of my life? I had no choice, Laura."

"But that's it, Mam. I *have* a choice. And I've decided . . ." she looked at Neil and he gave her a supportive wink, "I've decided to go into business on my own – selling my jewellery."

Maureen gave a curt laugh and Laura felt her insides tighten.

"Your *jewellery*? You mean the bits and pieces of plastic that you're always messing around with? Why would anyone be interested in the likes of that?"

"Because she's talented, Maureen." By his tone, Laura knew that Neil was annoyed. "Your daughter is one of the most talented and hardworking people I know."

"But it's only a hobby, Laura!" Maureen continued as if she hadn't heard him. "Your 'jewellery' is all right for the likes of us, but you don't seriously expect decent people to pay out good money for those things, do you?"

"And why not?" Laura felt the blood pulse through her veins and two spots of pink appeared on her cheeks as she raised her voice. "Those *things* were all right for you and your cronies down at the flower club when any of their daughters were getting married, or going to a debs, weren't they?"

Maureen, taken aback by her daughter's uncharacteristic outburst, pursed her lips and continued sweeping, saying nothing more.

Laura felt like she always did when Maureen tried this tactic – like an absolute heel. "Mam, I'm sorry – I didn't mean to shout at you, but this is really important and it's a big step. I had hoped you'd be happy for me."

"And what are you going to do – set up a stall in Moore Street, or something?"

Laura bit her tongue. "No, Mam, it'll be a real business."

"I see." Maureen paused and put a hand on her hip. "Look, I think that you're fooling yourself if you think you can make some kind of living out of this. We're just ordinary working people, Laura. We're not the types to be setting up businesses." At this, she glanced slyly across at Neil. "You wouldn't know the first thing about it."

Neil had to say something.

"Maureen, with all due respect, if you feel that way, then you really don't know your daughter. She's worked hands-on in accounts and retail for years, and knows possibly as much about business as any college graduate. Not to mention you're completely ignoring the fact that she's bloody good at what she does."

Maureen's head snapped up his tone and at the mention of what she considered a swear word.

Laura sighed. "Mam, I'm not going into this with my eyes closed. I've done the market research and there seems to be a definite niche there."

"But giving up your job – now of all times, with the wedding and everything," Joe Fanning said quietly.

Laura couldn't read her father's expression, so she wasn't sure whether or not he agreed with Maureen.

"You should see some of the designs she's come up with," Neil offered, hoping to turn the tide a little. "People are raving about them already."

"Oh, for goodness sake, cop on to yourselves!" Maureen said tightly. "People rave about my sponge cakes, but you don't see me going off pretending that I'm the next Delia Smith, do you?"

Laura tried to bite back the tears she knew were threatening.

"I think you're running away with yourself, Laura. And as your mother, it's my responsibility to make sure that you don't do anything stupid, and fall flat on your face. Setting up your own business, indeed!"

The others were silent, and for a long moment the air was thick with tension.

Eventually Maureen spoke again. "And what about Miss Jackson – I suppose she's all for it?" she asked with, Laura thought, a hint of sarcasm.

"Helen is very supportive, yes." She wasn't about to give her mother ammunition by admitting that in the beginning Helen had been far from enthusiastic at the prospect. Although lately, her friend *had* been making a bit of an effort, and had even offered to put Laura in touch with some of her contacts in the business world.

"Well, isn't it well for her to be supportive of some people?" Maureen said. "And her poor father living all on his own above on the farm. He hasn't seen sight nor sound of her in over a month, he says." Maureen had never made any secret of her dislike of Laura's childhood friend.

"Helen's very busy at work, Mam. She doesn't always have the time."

"Hah! I'm sure she's plenty of time for gallivanting with fellas, though. She certainly did plenty of that when she was here."

Helen's good looks had always ensured she was popular with men, but unlike some of their friends, Helen didn't sleep around. Maureen was being grossly unfair.

"And I suppose there's still no sign of the child's father?" Helen's single motherhood was another cause of Maureen's sanctimonious ire.

"No, Mam, he abandoned Helen, remember?" For some reason Laura always felt obliged to stand up for Helen. Not that her friend would need anyone to fight her corner, Helen being well used to (and more than able for) the judgmental residents of Glengarrah.

Maureen sniffed. "I'm not surprised he wouldn't marry her. That one was always too big for her own boots."

Out of the corner of her eye, Laura saw Neil smile and shake his head. Maureen's narrow-minded attitude was always a great source of entertainment to him but it annoyed Laura no end that her mother couldn't even be the tiniest bit gracious about anyone that went their own way. Helen was doing her best. What right had Maureen to criticise her way of life?

"Helen works very hard to bring up her daughter, Mam."

Maureen turned around, frowning. "Sure don't we all, Laura? But it doesn't necessarily guarantee that the child will turn out all right, does it?"

Laura tried to convince herself that her mother didn't mean anything by that last comment, that she was still talking about Helen and not about her. But why did it feel like that? Why did she feel as if she had somehow disappointed her mother, that no matter what she did she would always disappoint her? She had been so sure that her family would be proud of her for taking a risk and going out on her own. But surely, Laura thought now, surely knowing her mother as well as she did, she should have anticipated a negative reaction. Negatives were all that Maureen seemed to understand. Couldn't she see how much this meant to her? Couldn't she understand how much she wanted this, how much she had always wanted it? It wasn't success as such, Laura thought – that wasn't it – it was just finally *doing* something with your life, doing something worthwhile, in essence following a dream. Didn't that matter to Maureen at all?

No, Laura thought, those things didn't matter. All that mattered to Maureen was whether or not she succeeded.

"I'm not surprised that young one has problems, having to put up with a mother the likes of that one," Maureen continued, apparently determined to continue badmouthing Helen.

"Mam, Kerry's stutter has nothing to do with Helen," Laura said wearily. "It's just one of those things."

"One of those things? I don't think so, Laura. Didn't she cut the young one's hair long before the child had said a single word?"

"What?"

"What's that got to do with it, Maureen?" Neil asked, intrigued as to what gems of wisdom his mother-in-law would dispense next.

"Sure every fool from here to Timbucktoo will tell you that that's why children stutter in the first place," Maureen announced. "You're not supposed to cut a child's hair before they say their first words."

"I see," Neil said, biting back a smile. Maureen had an old wives' tale for everything.

"Well, Helen's trying speech therapy now, so hopefully Kerry should improve," Laura said.

Maureen was dismissive. "Speech therapy, indeed! In the old days, they used to belt the child across the mouth with a dish-cloth, but sure you if you did that in this day and age, you'd be up in court for child abuse," she said, her expression perfectly serious.

"Mam!" Laura was outraged. "It's not Kerry's fault that she has a problem and you certainly can't *beat* it out of her!"

Maureen was miffed. "I'm only telling you what worked in my day, Laura. It was either that, or walk around with a few marbles in the bottom of your mouth."

Neil sniggered, and Laura gave him a reproachful look. She knew he found it hilarious that the 'In My Day' speeches were still alive and well in Glengarrah. Coming from a rather tolerant and well-educated background, he never failed to find amusement in Maureen's colloquialisms.

"Mam, those are just old wives' tales. I really don't think –"

"Ah, your mother's not too far wrong, Laura," Joe piped

up from the corner. "Sure, old wives' tales are superstitions, and different versions of the same superstitions are found in every culture."

Laura smiled. Her father's long-standing subscription to *Reader's Digest* and the like ensured that he could always be relied upon for little pieces of (factual) trivia. Her father would read anything – newspapers, magazines, even the back of a milk carton if he could find nothing else.

"I suppose you got that from a book, Joe," Maureen sniffed, as if reading books was on a par with being drunken and disorderly on Glengarrah Main St, neither of which (as far as Laura knew anyway) she had ever done in her life. "Well, *I* don't need books to tell me things that are just common sense."

Joe shrugged, not seeming all that bothered by his wife's attitude, but Laura hated the way her mother dismissed him like that. It had always been the same, as though Maureen felt threatened by anyone claiming to know that little bit more about a topic than she did.

Then Maureen turned to look at her. "So, about this – this *business*. What will it be called? Some fancy name or another, I suppose."

Laura reddened. This was the bit she had been dreading. "Actually . . . um . . . I've decided to call it Laura . . . um . . . Connolly Designs." For a long moment, she couldn't meet her mother's eyes.

"Really? And who is Laura Connolly when she's at home?" she challenged.

"Well, I'll be changing my name after the wedding and everything, so I couldn't really change the . . ." Her voice trailed off. Laura knew there was no point in even trying to explain.

"I see."

Her expression telling Laura all she needed to know, Maureen turned to the sink and busied herself noisily with the washing-up.

Discussion over.

Chapter 9

Helen sat back on the bed, and rested her daughter's head against her chest. She turned the page. *"Then Snow White opened her eyes, and looked into seven expectant little faces."*

Kerry sat up and her eyes opened wide. "Oh! W-w-w-was Snow White . . . scaid, Mommy?" she asked fearfully.

Helen looked at her. "Why would she be scared, honey? The seven dwarfs are Snow White's friends – you know that."

"S-s-seven dwawfs her fwends?" When she could, Kerry often avoided using verbs. Helen sighed inwardly, noticing this. As much as she hated to admit it, and despite her hopes that pre-school would improve things, Helen had lately begun to accept that Jo and Dr Davis might have been correct in their earlier diagnosis of Kerry's speech disfluency. The problem had aired itself again recently, when Helen had got a call from her pre-school teacher, concerned about the child's apparent lack of communication skills.

As a result, Helen was now trying to look past her own denials and parental insecurities in order to seriously consider Jo's concerns. Yes, Jo could be an interfering old so-and-so but at the end of the day, she did have Kerry's welfare at heart. Helen supposed she had brushed the childminder's fears aside at first because Kerry had never been a particularly chatty toddler. Still, with Kerry now almost four years of age, Helen had to agree with Jo and admit that it wasn't good that Kerry was still mispronouncing her consonants, and using single words instead of sentences. Following a lengthy conversation with the pre-school teacher, she had immediately booked another appointment at the speech-therapy clinic and just last week had brought Kerry to see Dr Davis again. The speech therapist has suggested she spend more relaxed time with Kerry and recommended she read out loud to her each night – the slower rate of speech useful in helping the child become familiar with the correct pronunciation of words. Helen had done this every night since, even when sometimes all she wanted to do was slob in front of the telly. "It's friends, Kerry, not *fwends*." Helen corrected. "Now say it again."

Kerry repeated with her mother, concentrating hard. "F-f-fwends."

Helen sighed. "No, no, listen to me – it's *frrrrriends*."

Kerry screwed up her face and tried again, but still couldn't pronounce the word properly.

Too late Helen remembered to do as the speech therapist advised and tried to hide her frustration so that Kerry wouldn't feel under pressure or self-conscious. Kerry shook her head. "I g-g-go sleep now, Mommy," she said quietly.

"OK, hon." Helen kissed her softly on the forehead,

sensing that she might have been too hard on her. Kerry was tired, and her speech was always worse when she was tired or upset.

Helen plugged in the nightlight, and was about to leave the room when Kerry sat up again, as if remembering something. She looked at Helen, and pointed nervously towards her wardrobe. "Mommy, monstaw."

Helen walked across and opened the wardrobe, having been through this routine many times before. "Kerry, there's no monster in there. Look, he wouldn't fit in with all your toys. Anyway, what about the sign?" She pointed towards a sign hanging on the back of the bedroom door, one Laura had bought Kerry a while back to help curb her fears. It read: *No Monsters Allowed*.

Kerry looked from Helen to the sign, the wardrobe and then back again to Helen. She grinned and lay back down, snuggling under the covers.

"N-n-night, night," she said.

"Night, honey."

"Night, Michael," she heard Kerry whisper to her poster of the footballer Michael Owen. For some reason, Kerry seemed to share Helen's love of football – possibly because it was so often on the television when they were at home together.

Helen shut the bedroom door behind her. She couldn't understand how Kerry could be such a nervous child, sometimes. She had heard the fairytale many times before and yet she always worried that the dwarfs would hurt Snow White. In the same way she worried about monsters in her wardrobe, and that Helen would somehow forget to pick her up from the childminder every day.

Helen shook her head. If anything, she was becoming a much more clingy child as she got older. Maybe it was her stutter and the accompanying self-consciousness that triggered Kerry's almost instinctive fear of people.

It was worrying too that she still hadn't settled in at the pre-school. As well as the problems she was having with her speech, Helen had also gathered from Mrs Elliot, the pre-school teacher, that Kerry was shy around the other children and found it difficult to make friends. It was still early days but . . . Helen shook her head, knowing that if anything Kerry seemed to crave solitude. She loved the interactive books Nicola had bought her for her last birthday, and spent hours just sitting and looking at the pictures. Helen often heard her in her room trying to pronounce the words out loud when she thought no one could hear her.

Hopefully, with the combination of her exercises at home, and the help of Mrs Elliot, they would soon see a real improvement in Kerry's speech. Helen certainly hoped so; Kerry would be starting primary school in September, and the teachers there certainly wouldn't have time to give her any special treatment or extra attention. Still, there was nothing more Helen could do. She was now trying everything, had painstakingly gone through the exercises the speech therapist had recommended, and was insisting that Kerry practise her pronunciation, particularly with her R's and Th's.

Anyway, Helen thought, returning quietly to the living-room, she'd better do some exercises of her own before she ended up letting herself go altogether. And letting herself go was not an option for Helen.

Exercising always gave her plenty of adrenalin, and tonight, she thought wryly, she would certainly need that.

She warmed up, did a couple of stretches and then did her usual fifty tummy crunches and fifty hip-and-thigh bends. She missed her old three-day-a-week gym sessions – these days she was lucky if she got there even once a month. And worryingly, she thought, it was beginning to show.

Having finished her exercising, Helen poured herself a glass of Ballygowan, put a CD on low volume, and sat on the sofa to catch a breather. For a quiet few moments, she sat back and listened to the soothing tones of David Gray asking her to 'sail away'.

Helen stared at the telephone. Should she do it? She'd been so determined earlier, but now she wasn't so sure. Blast it, why not? He who hesitates and all that . . .

After all, what had she got to lose?

Helen dialled the number from memory and, despite herself, felt her heartbeat quicken as she waited for an answer.

"Hello?"

"Is that Richard?" Helen asked, using her huskiest voice, the one she used on all the male clients at work.

"Yes, it is. Who's calling please?"

Suddenly Helen felt unsure. It sounded as though she had caught him at a bad time. "Richard, it's Helen here."

A slight pause at the other end. "I'm sorry, who?"

Oh God! Helen thought she would die of mortification. Despite all the time they'd spent together, Richard Moore didn't recognise her – or even worse, he didn't remember her!

"Helen Jackson."

Another pause. "Oh, Helen, hi . . . I . . . um . . . I didn't recognise your voice."

"So I gather," Helen said coquettishly. "So, tell me, how are *you* doing? How's business?"

"Fine. Is this a business call, Helen?" Richard said, in a tone that suggested he wanted her to get to the point.

Helen suddenly felt very silly. She had been working up to this for a while now, had thought that maybe with a little time Richard might come round to the idea that she had a child. They had got on so well and he had never made any secret of his interest in her, so . . .

"No," Helen said quietly. "No, it's not. I just thought you might like to . . ."

'Go on,' her inner voice told her. 'You might as well be hung for a sheep as a lamb.'

"I thought you might like to meet up some time, you know, for a drink, or something."

Another, longer pause. "Helen, I'm sorry, but I really don't think there's any point. I mean you're a fantastic person and –"

"Richard, look, just because I have a child doesn't mean that anything has to change between us, does it? It's not as though I expect you to spend any time with her or anything . . ." Helen knew she sounded desperate, but she just couldn't help herself. She *was* desperate.

"I'm sorry, Helen," Richard said again. "I just don't think it would work. It was great fun but that kind of thing . . ." he hesitated. "Look, the whole kids thing just isn't my scene, but thanks anyway." With that, Richard disconnected.

Helen stared at the receiver, mortified. Oh God, what

had she done? It had seemed like such a good idea at the time, but now she had made a bad situation even worse. But, if Richard would just give her a chance, then surely . . ?

Helen slumped down on the sofa. Was this what she had been reduced to? One of those clingy, cringeworthy, *desperate* women that she had always detested?

She clenched her fists in frustration. What was *wrong* with her? When was the last time she had to beg a man for a date? How the hell had she ended up like this?

But, of course, there was only one answer to that. Kerry. Helen had ended up like this – sad, lonely and desperate – because of Kerry.

For the last four years, everything Helen did (or wanted to do) *had* to revolve around Kerry.

Wasn't she entitled to a life of her own? Yes, she was a mother but did that mean that she had to sacrifice everything that was important to her, everything that made her happy, just because she had a child?

Helen's face crumpled. The very fact that she felt this way made her feel worse. The guilt was sometimes crucifying. Here she was, sitting on the sofa feeling bitter and twisted, while the poor child was sleeping innocently in the next room. It wasn't Kerry's fault, God love her, that her mother just wasn't maternal.

Helen couldn't help it. The feelings had never come. Those feelings of exceptional, overpowering, unconditional love that all the magazines and the baby books were so sure existed. This had never happened to Helen. Yes, she loved Kerry, in the same way that you might love your baby sister, but that was it. A mother's love? Helen didn't understand it.

After the difficulties she had throughout the pregnancy and with Kerry's illness, Helen had been expecting – had been *waiting* for the big flash, the big realisation – this so-called burst of maternal love. At first, she had thought it was because she was still pining for Jamie, and so transferring her own misery to the child. And at the time, she hadn't been able to discuss it with anyone. Her own mother had died when Helen was in her early teens, but the two of them had had what Helen considered a relatively normal mother/daughter relationship, so no amateur psychology clues there.

Not that it was something you could really discuss with the others. What was she supposed to say to them? "Hi, girls – listen, I don't actually feel any great adoration for my child – what should I do?"

In fairness, she had lost contact with most of her and Jamie's circle after the birth, and especially during Kerry's illness. Laura had been great, of course, calling to see her, helping in any way she could, but that was Laura – Miss Reliable.

Nicola had sensed something once, a long time ago, when Helen was feeling particularly sorry for herself, but she hadn't pursued it.

"It takes time," she had said. "You've had some huge upheavals in your life lately – the birth and the end of a long relationship. You just need time to get back on track. Then everything will fall into place." Helen had been almost ashamed at the time, because back then Nicola was dealing with a huge upheaval of her own and coping admirably.

So, Helen had said nothing and just waited. Waited

for it to happen, waited for the big bang, waited for things to 'fall into place'.

But by the time Kerry's first birthday came around and there was *still* nothing, Helen had decided that maybe she just wasn't like that. Maybe she just wasn't the maternal kind.

Surely she couldn't be the *only* mother out there who didn't feel this so-called 'overwhelming passion' for her child? Weren't all people different in the way they felt, in the way they loved? Wasn't it possible that some women just weren't made that way?

To her absolute amazement, Helen felt warm tears streak across her face. She hated the way she was feeling, hated what she had become. What kind of a person was she? Why couldn't she just be normal?

But what was normal?

Helen remembered watching some wildlife programme on TV a while back. There was some animal – some kind of rodent (appropriately enough, she thought wryly) that didn't suckle its young after birth. The babies were simply born and left to find their own way in the world, the mother going about her business as normal. If it could happen with animals, then why not with humans?

Helen exhaled deeply. Not that she would ever leave Kerry on her own to face the world. She *did* love her. But she was torn between what she felt, and what she *should* feel – what magazines and TV and society in general insisted all women should feel.

And it just wasn't there.

Chapter 10

Nicola was discussing the following week's staffing arrangements with the leisure centre's assistant manager, when the *Mode* magazine team approached reception.

"Fidelma Corrigan looking for Nicola Peters, please," the woman announced bossily. Nicola looked up. Fidelma looked no older than twenty-two or three, not quite what she had been expecting.

"I'm Nicola – good to meet you." She moved out from behind the desk and extended a hand to Fidelma.

"Oh, I thought . . ." Fidelma was perplexed. "Sorry," she said, recovering herself, "I was expecting someone – someone older."

"That makes two of us then!" Nicola said, smiling brightly at her.

"Well, this is Sean Kenny, our photographer. Now, if we could just start with a photograph of you at reception . . ."

It soon became evident that the features writer was a bossy little madam, and Nicola didn't appreciate being ordered about. It had already been a long day and she just wasn't up to it, having had a night of broken sleep while wandering in and out of vivid, lucid, dreams – worryingly, Nicola thought, about Dan.

"Can you turn your head slightly to the left – no, to your other left, that's it – perfect. Now if your receptionist could again just move out of the way . . . great!"

Nicola knew that Sally had been desperately disappointed that she wouldn't be featuring in the article. She couldn't be consoled when Fidelma informed her that they wanted Nicola *only* for the photographs and could the receptionist stop 'popping up and grinning in the background'.

When the shoot was over, Nicola had a short interview with the journalist in her office.

"So how long has the centre been in business?" Fidelma asked.

"Well, after a very encouraging first year, we're now well into our second year in operation," Nicola said confidently. She wasn't going to let the woman know that their first accounting year had been a new lesson in mathematics. Ken had been expecting losses but none quite so heavy as they had experienced. Nicola knew that this year the pressure was on to ensure business improved beyond expectations, and hopefully this article would help do just that.

"You've been living outside of Ireland for some time, I understand?"

"Yes, in the UK – Fulham actually. I spent some time in a health and fitness centre there, and found that hydrotherapy was most beneficial to clients, and, of course, a huge selling point for any leisure club." Nicola was anxious to veer the interview more towards the business, rather than the personal side of things. "Ken and I decided that such a treatment would go down well here, and Motiv8 now offers the most diverse range of alternative therapies in the country."

Fidelma nodded. "You and Ken Harris, you two go back together quite a bit."

"Yes, years ago we worked together at another centre." Nicola was a little taken aback. The reporter had obviously done her homework, because not all that many people were aware of Nicola and Ken's previous association. She didn't want to be drawn on their present association either, and quietly resolved to deflect any questions of that nature, should they be asked.

After a while, Fidelma leaned forward in her seat. "I have to ask – isn't it unusual for someone like you to be involved in this type of industry?"

"What do you mean?"

"Well, you know . . ." Her voice trailed off, as she looked Nicola up and down. "You normally wouldn't expect someone – like yourself – to be involved in such an obviously 'active' business."

"Really?"

"Well, yes," Fidelma now looked uncomfortable. "Someone who isn't that, I suppose . . . well, you know . . . active herself."

Nicola bristled. She was sick to the teeth of people like Miss Fake-Tanned-Stick-Insect looking down their skinny little noses at her. Why did supposedly intelligent people think they could make instant deductions about others, based simply on appearance? It was so bloody frustrating! She crossed her arms and took a deep breath.

"Fidelma, if you're trying to point out that I hardly teach aerobics classes, and that I wouldn't be much good on a treadmill, let me assure you that my lifestyle doesn't stop me from doing my job, and doing it well."

The other woman at least had the good grace to look embarrassed. "I'm so sorry. I didn't mean any offence. I just thought . . ."

Nicola shook her head. There was no point in blowing what would be good publicity for Motiv8, by getting into a strop with someone who looked like she was barely out of nappies.

"It's not a problem. But I'd prefer if you concentrate on the Centre. You're not doing a feature on *me* after all."

"Sure." Fidelma duly backed off. She then at last began asking some useful questions about the Motiv8 facilities

"Well, thank you for your time," Fidelma said eventually. "The article will appear in our next issue and I'll get the office to send you on a copy."

"Thank you," Nicola said, pleased that Fidelma was finally leaving and she could get some real work done.

Not long after the journalist's departure, Ken popped his head around the door of her office. "Nicola, sorry to do this to you, but is there any chance you can cover for Sally at reception? There's a guy downstairs waiting to become a member, and Kelly's in the middle of another client's fitness programme. We don't really want to leave him waiting for an assessment so . . ."

"No problem," she said quickly. "Tell them I'll be down in a minute."

Ken studied her. "What's up?" he said, coming into the room and closing the door behind him. "Didn't the interview go well?"

Nicola shook her head, exasperated. "It was fine, but . . . oh, don't mind me. I'm just a little out of sorts today."

She still hadn't told him anything about Dan's new marriage and, the longer it went on, the harder it was to broach the subject. She didn't want Ken to think she was hiding things from him and she wasn't *really*. It was just . . .

"Will this help?" Ken had come round to her side of the desk and was now gently massaging her shoulders.

"Mmmm . . . that feels great," she said, closing her eyes. Ken bent down and planted a kiss on the top of her head. Immediately Nicola began to feel guilty. She should tell him about the Dan situation – it was only fair. She and Ken shared everything, and he knew better than most what Nicola had gone through to get to the stage she was at now. He understood how much things back then with Dan had affected her. So surely he would understand that things felt a little strange for her now.

"Ken –"

Just then, the intercom buzzed and Sally's voice blared over it. "Nicola, sorry to rush you, but Ken said he'd ask if you could cover –"

"Sorry, Sal, I'm just on my way down." She reached for Ken's hand and kissed it softly. "Duty calls, I'm afraid."

"Unfortunately. Sorry to do this to you, love. I know you have a lot on your plate at the moment . . ."

Nicola started. A lot on her plate? How did he know?

"But I'm already looking into taking on additional staff, and that will free you up a little. I know you hate being called on at the last minute to cover people." He smiled, obviously thinking Nicola was down and out because of pressure at work.

"Ken, it's fine. I don't mind doing what I have to, to keep this business going. You know that. Listen, why don't you come over to my place this evening – I'll cook."

He walked with her to the door. "Sounds great but I'm playing squash with Peter Kelly tonight," he said mournfully. Ken adored her cooking.

"Oh, I'd forgotten about that."

"I'll hold you to it, though – see you later!" He grinned and headed back towards his office, leaving Nicola unsure whether to feel relieved or upset that the opportunity to talk had gone amiss.

On her way down in the elevator to free Sally up for her fitness assessment, Nicola tried to remember the last time *she* had carried out one of those. Most leisure staff hated doing it and Nicola was no exception. She smiled There was one particular time though, when she hadn't minded at all.

* * *

Her appointment had been delayed and Nicola remembered clearly her impatience at having to stay late as a result. She had planned to go out on her mountain bike after work, maybe take a spin up as far as Johnny Fox's pub – anything that might clear her hangover.

She was working in Metamorph at the time, and if she remembered correctly, it wasn't long after that 'incident' in town with Laura.

Apparently, some overly enthusiastic new member –

enthusiastic for the first week, if the rest of these business types were anything to go by – had phoned reception first thing that morning and demanded an instant fitness assessment for the same afternoon.

Nicola couldn't understand the urgency. After all, if he was unfit today, he'd still be unfit tomorrow, wouldn't he?

Having visited most of Dublin's city centre hotspots with Helen the previous evening, Nicola certainly wasn't in the mood for another stuffy forty-something hoping to do something about his love handles, while still insisting that he had the fitness level of a twenty-year-old. She had once recommended a mild programme for the head of a well-known Dublin stockbroking firm, and he had been highly insulted when Nicola suggested that he might try some light weights to begin with.

"Light weights?" he had said scornfully. "Nothing about Jim Courtney is lightweight."

Nicola had to bite her tongue when days later the same man put his back out after a particularly disastrous session with a pair of heavy dumbbells. But it was the always the same, and the men were the worst. They joined the gym simply for the status that Metamorph membership would bring them, but when it came to their wellbeing, instantly disregarded the advice of trained professionals.

This guy would probably be just the same.

Just before six, the regular after-office crowd began to appear, and there was such a flurry of activity that Nicola failed to notice a tall man standing patiently alongside the counter, waiting for her to finish the signing-in.

"Hello again," Dan Hunt said in a friendly tone. "Sorry

I'm late. I had an appointment for a fitness assessment at five thirty but I rang earlier to say I'd be delayed."

To say that Nicola was taken aback at the sight of him would be a gross understatement.

"You!" she accused. "But the appointment book says . . ." She studied the name again, wondering why it hadn't hit her earlier.

"It should say me," Dan grinned.

So it does, Nicola thought, mind racing. The name had stirred a slight recognition earlier, and now she knew why. The cute guy from the traffic jam. But what was he doing here?

"How did you know I worked here?" she asked, thinking that he must have sought her out to make a further complaint.

"I didn't know, actually," he answered innocently. "I'm just here for a fitness assessment."

Nicola was thrown off balance. This was way too much of a coincidence for her liking.

"So will you be my fitness assessor then?" he asked, a smile playing about his lips.

"I suppose." She gathered her things and motioned him towards the gym.

"Just in here, please," she said, trying to sound professional, but as he passed her the faint scent of his aftershave set off an army of butterflies in her stomach. This wasn't like her. She was normally the epitome of cool, calm, and collected where men were concerned. What the hell was this guy doing to her?

She shook her head and tried to think of him as a client, nothing more.

However, it was soon obvious to both of them that Dan Hunt wasn't here just as a client.

"Right, where do we start?" he said eagerly, that megawatt smile lighting up her insides.

Nicola put a hand on her hip. Try and gain some control here, she told herself, try not to let him affect you. "Well, first of all I'll need to measure your height and your weight."

She glanced at his lean, well-defined torso as he removed his fleece top. He was well-built, but in a natural, effortless-looking way. Of course, Nicola was well used to seeing well-defined torsos and the like, but this was different.

This was very different.

She saw a faint smile cross Dan's features, and realised that she was staring. She managed to alter her features into what she hoped was a concerned-looking frown. "Have you used weights before?" she asked.

Dan nodded. "Not at a gym, mostly at home – whenever I get a chance. Why, does it look as though they are having some kind of effect?" he added innocently.

"Not really," Nicola said, intently studying the chart she held, his double entendre plainly evident. "You need to work a lot harder than you do at the moment to have any *real* effect."

"Oh." Dan feigned a disappointed tone. "I had hoped I might be getting somewhere."

"Sorry, still a lot of work to do." Nicola bit back a smile. "Now, first I'll measure your height and then if you could just hop up on the scales there, so I can take a weight measurement."

Dan obliged, and neither spoke for a while as Nicola entered his details onto the chart.

"Age?"

"Thirty, heterosexual, single."

Nicola raised an eyebrow and tried to keep a straight face. "The latter information has absolutely no bearing on your fitness, Mr Hunt."

He shrugged nonchalantly, those cool blue eyes fixed on her face. "Just thought it might be helpful."

"Right, flexibility test next," she said. "Sit down on that mat, and try to touch your toes."

"I can assure you that I'm very flexible." He winked as he sat down, then leaned forward and touched his toes with little effort.

She smiled. "I'm impressed."

"Good."

"Now let's try your peak flow." She opened a nearby cabinet, and produced a strange-looking piece of plastic apparatus.

"My what?" All of a sudden he looked nervous.

"Your peak flow." Nicola was enjoying his petrified look. "Just blow into this so that I can measure your lung capacity."

"Oh."

"Not bad." Nicola entered another set of figures onto her chart. "Now grip."

"Grip?"

"Grip strength. I need you to grip this piece of equipment as tightly as you can and then I'll measure how long you can sustain it." She couldn't resist adding, "I trust that you have some staying-power?"

Dan met her gaze full on. "That depends on what I'm doing."

"Right." This time there was no mistaking the flirtation, and despite herself Nicola felt her stomach do a little flip. *Stop it,* she warned herself. *Stay in control.*

"OK, now do twenty minutes on the exercise bike over there," she said sternly.

"Twenty? Bit of a slave-driver, aren't you?"

"I thought you were here for a fitness assessment, Mr Hunt?"

"I am."

"Well, your body's reaction to intense aerobic exercise is essential to an evaluation of your overall fitness."

Dan grinned. "You make it sound very serious indeed, Ms Peters."

"I'm very serious about my work."

"As serious as you are about your driving?"

Nicola smiled. "I wondered when you'd bring that up."

"Sorry." He didn't look the slightest bit sorry.

"What happened that day wasn't my fault," she said.

"No?"

"No."

"And did the Gardai see it that way?" he grinned.

"Not quite."

She had been about to drive away when a member of the Garda Siochana had pulled up beside her on his motorbike, and promptly issued three consecutive tickets: illegal parking, obstructing traffic, and threatening conduct towards fellow motorists. Nicola had objected profusely to the latter, and it was only when the guard suggested that he might just charge her with aggressive behaviour towards a member of the Gardai that she shut up and drove off fuming.

"It was all right for him whizzing around on his motorbike," she said, her irritation returning at the thought of it all. "He didn't have to sit in traffic for the best part of two hours."

Dan didn't answer, because he was trying his very best to maintain a consistent rate of pedalling. Minutes later, Nicola noticed that he was really struggling. She smiled.

"You're doing well there, Mr Hunt – hardly breaking a sweat." She checked her watch. "But, in order to accurately measure your aerobic fitness level, I think I'll have to order another twenty minutes on this."

Dan gasped and slowed his pedalling considerably. "What? Are you some kind of sadist or something? I'll die!"

The expression on his face made Nicola want to laugh out loud. "Not at all. You're here for a fitness assessment, aren't you?" She tried to be flippant. "And obviously I can't assess your fitness until I have all the necessary information. Now another twenty minutes on this, and then we'll put you on some weights to get an idea of your upper-body strength."

He finally stopped pedalling. "OK, OK, I give up!" he gasped. "I don't care about the bloody fitness assessment. That was a bloody cover. I only came here because I wanted to see you again."

Nicola's expression betrayed nothing. "Oh? How did you know where to find me?"

"I was stuck behind your car for almost an hour that

day, remember? I couldn't fail to notice the Metamorph sticker on the rear window, so I reckoned you were either a member, or you were staff. There was nothing else to look at, not until you did your disappearing act at any rate. So," he added, his voice still breathless after his exertions, "are you going to let me take you out to dinner, or what?"

Chapter 11

A frown sullied Chloe's usually attractive features as she studied Dan in the mirror. He was acting very strangely these days. There he was, sitting on the bed, his mind obviously a thousand miles away.

And he hadn't yet said a thing about her outfit.

"Well? What do you think?" she asked finally.

"What?" Dan was miles away. "What do I think of what?"

"My dress. You haven't even mentioned it." She turned sulkily back to the mirror and continued to apply her make-up.

"Nice." Dan was noncommittal.

She spun around. "Dan, what is *wrong* with you lately? For the past few weeks you've been going around in some kind of daze! This dress is John Rocha and it cost me an absolute fortune. What do you mean by just 'nice'?"

Dan stood up and ran a hand through his hair. "Jesus, Chloe, just because I don't fall to worship at your feet every time you ask me how you look, doesn't mean you look bad! You look fine. What more do you want?"

"'Fine'," Chloe repeated, putting a hand on her hip. "I look 'fine', do I?"

"Yes," Dan said through gritted teeth.

"Well, *I* don't think I look 'fine', Dan. As it happens, *I* think I look a lot better than just 'fine'. But you wouldn't give a damn if I went out tonight wearing a pair of your pyjamas, would you? You wouldn't even notice!" Stung by his attitude, she turned her back to him. Dan *always* commented on her appearance whenever they were getting ready to go out somewhere. He loved it when she dressed up and she loved the way his compliments made her feel so sexy and, nine times out of ten, they both ended up horny and indulged in some pretty good sex before going out at all. But lately, Dan seemed to have lost interest – in sex and more worryingly, in *her*.

"Chloe, please don't start." Dan slumped back down on the bed and began to knead his forehead.

"Don't start what?" Chloe approached the bed. "Seriously, Dan, what the hell is wrong with you? You're away with the fairies these days. I can hardly get a word out of you." When he didn't answer she continued, "Can't you tell me what's bothering you? Is it work?" It had better be something like that, she thought. It had better not be something else.

Like an affair.

But where would Dan get the time to have an affair? And why? Chloe turned back to study her expression in the mirror. She was still looking good as ever, wasn't she? She hadn't put on any weight, and her breasts were small, but full and definitely still in their rightful place – unlike some others she could mention.

At the last dress fitting, she had been shocked, but more than a teeny bit gratified to discover that Lynne's boobs had very definitely headed south with little hope of returning. And that spare tyre – oh dear! Lynne had better shift it by the time the wedding came around, otherwise she could end up *ruining* Chloe's wedding photographs.

Her skin was fresh and clear, and she had even upped her sunbed sessions lately in order to ensure she had a radiant glow for the photographs. She was always up for sex, admittedly a lot more than Dan was these days, so it couldn't be that. Dan's sex drive had dwindled a bit, but maybe that was because he was that much older than her.

Chloe grimaced. Nah, he wouldn't cheat on her, would he?

"So?" she turned her attention back to her fiancé. "Is it work?"

Dan gave a low groan. "Chloe, please, I'm just in bad form. You know well that I don't particularly want to go to this bloody party, and yet you expect me to be jumping up and down like a child on a promise of a trip to McDonald's!"

She shrugged. "I don't know why you're so against it. I thought you got on well with Mick. I know Louise can be a bit of a pain but –"

"It's not that – I'm just really not in the mood. Work is manic and . . ."

Good, it was definitely work then. Relieved that it was something simple, Chloe turned her attention back to the mirror, and began to tease her straight blonde hair into face-framing flicks. She had seen that very look on Cameron Diaz in a magazine the other day, and was certain that it would look great on her. Cameron always looked so stylish. In fact, Chloe thought, standing back to take another look at her profile, she didn't look too unlike the actress herself in this get-up. She wondered if anyone else would notice the resemblance.

Oh, stuff Dan, she thought, dismissing her worries. Just because *he* was in one of his moods didn't mean that *she* couldn't enjoy herself tonight. So work was mental but wasn't it mental for everyone these days? Not to worry, he'd soon get over it.

Studying her reflection once more and exhilarated by what she saw, Chloe relaxed and began looking forward to the dinner party.

* * *

Dan looked in the direction of Chloe's preening, but stared right through her. He'd have to ring Laura.

It was his own fault, anyway. He should have at least tried to contact Nicola. But what would he say? Maybe Nicola wouldn't give a stuff about his new fiancée and his new life. And who could blame her? Hadn't she told him in no uncertain terms a long time ago that she wanted him out of her life – completely? So why would it matter now whether or not he told her himself?

Then a thought occurred to him. Maybe Laura didn't even read the invites? Maybe she just glanced at them, realised that they weren't hers and brought them straight back to the shop. That Debbie one told him that they had been returned that same day. So, maybe he was worrying for nothing. And if Laura had read the invites, maybe she didn't recognise his name? Maybe the name meant nothing to her. But Dan knew that if Laura read the name, Daniel *Ignatius* Hunt, that, of course, she would recognise it. Hadn't Nicola made great fun of it during their wedding vows that time, making sure that the minister pronounced if fully and clearly, knowing that it would mortify Dan? Everyone at that wedding had known how much he hated that name, especially when he refused to repeat it back to the minister, saying simply 'I, Daniel Hunt, take thee Nicola Peters.' They had all laughed at that.

Dan exhaled deeply. That had been a good day. Definitely one of the very best of his life. So relaxed, so easy-going, exactly the way it should be. There was no great pomp, no great ceremony, just Nicola and him, pledging their vows in front of a few close friends.

Not like this up-and-coming charade, whereby at Chloe's insistence he would have to wear that ridiculous top and tails get-up, all trussed up like a circus performer. Why did some women go all mental over those kinds of things? It was all a load of bollocks as far as Dan was concerned. All about performance, and exhibition, and 'look at me'. He loved Chloe, but there were times when her obsession with impressing people got to him big-time.

These days he couldn't really give a shit about what anyone thought of him, because worrying about such things had before been his undoing.

But still, Dan thought, studying the pattern on the duvet cover, now he couldn't help but worry about what Nicola might think of his marrying someone else – after everything.

Chapter 12

Tangerine Praline, Cerise au Kirsh, Gianduji or Irish Mist Truffle – which to choose? The luscious selection of handmade chocolates, the scent of which wafted heavily throughout the air, was almost sinful.

Laura eventually made her choice, and along with cup of steaming hot chocolate, she nabbed an empty table in Butler's Chocolate Café. She took a sip of her beverage, and shivered deliciously as the decadent, mouth-watering aroma filled her nostrils.

Pure indulgence.

Laura sat back comfortably in her seat. Nicola, who was on a diet, would murder Helen for choosing this café as a meeting-place. The three had arranged to meet up for pre-wedding shopping in Grafton St, but the girls were so far running late. As Laura's bridesmaid, Nicola didn't need anything other than shoes, but Helen needed a hat, dress, bag, shoes – the works. Laura had also asked Helen to be her bridesmaid, but Helen had immediately refused, offering Kerry instead as flowergirl. She obviously had her own reasons for the refusal, and Laura didn't mind all that much, but it would have been nice to have her two best friends with her on the day. Laura also had her younger sister, but she and Cathy had little in common, and had never been particularly close.

So today they were shopping for Helen, and if she needed something there was no stopping her until she got it – and inevitably, a whole lot more. Boy, could Helen Jackson shop! Laura had always enjoyed shopping with her; she always made it seem so exciting, and was able to hunt out these fantastic little boutiques that only a select few knew existed. And of course, she had such great taste.

Laura stared out of the window at the busy street.

"Hey, what are you dreaming about?"

She looked up to see Helen, Kerry and a smiling Nicola approach their table. Nicola had a bundle of magazines under her left arm.

"Page 22," she said with a grin, tossing a copy of *Mode* magazine on the table, "and *now* I know what they mean about the camera adding ten pounds. I look like a whale in that one." She gave Helen a sideways glance. "And arranging to meet in a place like this *isn't* going to help. Oh, is that a Tangerine Praline – thanks." Nicola winked and popped one of Laura's chocolates into her mouth.

"Hi, Auntie Law-law!" Kerry grinned up at Laura, her wide brown eyes twinkling with fun. Her blonde curls were tied back in a high ponytail, and she looked the epitome of cute, dressed as she was in pink dungarees and a tiny denim jacket. Laura grinned back. Kerry was becoming so like Helen it was unbelievable.

Laura studied her friend enviously. How did Helen manage to look so amazing all the time? Today, she had tied her blonde hair in a casual knot, and wore a caramel belted leather jacket, knee-length denim skirt and highly fashionable, but, Laura thought, dangerously high-heeled tan and caramel suede boots. Laura wouldn't be able to walk ten yards in those boots, and she definitely wouldn't get very far before people started pointing and laughing at her short legs, and tree-trunk thighs. But on Helen's slender frame and long legs, the outfit was stunning. Laura felt as she always did in Helen's presence: dowdy and inconsequential.

Kerry held her arms out, and Laura lifted her up onto her lap. "Hi, darling! Were you and Mummy shopping today?"

Kerry nodded, looking happily at her mother.

"And what did you buy?"

The child paused and took a deep breath. "B-b-b-b . . ." Kerry screwed up her face, and Laura's heart went out to her. "Baawbeee!" she finished delightedly.

"A new Barbie," Helen clarified, sardonically, "to go with the other two hundred she has at home."

Laura looked at her and wondered, not for the first time, why Helen was so impatient with the child. When Kerry eventually got her words out right, she looked immediately to her mother for approval – approval that was never very forthcoming.

Helen removed her jacket and went to order coffee, while Laura and Nicola pored over the long-awaited Motiv8 feature.

"Well, what do you think?" Nicola asked with a broad

grin, leaving no one in any doubts about her own opinion on the article.

"I think it's fantastic," Laura said. "You look wonderful in the photograph and this will be terrific publicity for the centre."

Nicola gleefully rubbed both hands together. "I know. It worked out a lot better than I expected and luckily they didn't use any full-length photos of me. I told you what that Fidelma one said to me, didn't I?"

Laura nodded. She knew that some people could just be thoughtless but others could be downright ignorant. Nicola was fantastic at her job and no one had any right to make her feel bad about herself.

"I hate that photograph of me in the office, but the one of reception looks great, doesn't it?"

Laura smiled. For all her talk about the feature being more hassle than it was worth, she could see that Nicola was really pleased with the way the article had turned out, and rightly so. Things were going very well for her now – so much so that despite the initial shock of finding out about Dan's new marriage, Nicola had apparently taken the news in her stride. She was obviously long past letting Dan's actions get to her, Laura thought, and rightly so.

"I'm just so glad it's over and done with," Nicola said, referring to the article. "I have to admit, I was a bit apprehensive about the whole thing, but I think it's worked out quite well. At least now, I can concentrate on getting the client numbers up, and that should certainly help."

"Absolutely!" Helen appeared, laden down with a tray, and looking tired and harassed-looking. "As soon as they read this, people will be clambering for membership. You and Ken will be fighting them off. Speaking of which, how *is* the gorgeous Mr Harris these days?"

Nicola beamed. "Great, he was asking about the two of you, actually – and Neil of course. We'll have to organise a night out together soon."

Laura smiled. Ken was such a dote and so perfect for Nicola. It was funny, she thought, remembering – for ages before he and Nicola got together, *Helen* had had her eye on him. But apparently Ken had no interest, despite Nicola's attempts to set them up. Laura thought it was a terrible thing to be thinking, but she felt mildly gratified that not *every* man fell under Helen's spell.

"So where will we go first today?" she asked.

"Stephen's Green Shopping Centre?" Helen suggested, looking at Nicola.

She made a face. "Nah, too many escalators."

"True," Helen agreed. "OK then, I suppose we'll just hop in and out of the shops on Grafton St. Laura, tell us, what do you have to get?"

"Nothing really," she answered. "I just thought I'd tag along with you two, and maybe check out some of the competition in the accessories stores."

"Good idea." Helen took the milk jug out of Kerry's reach. "While you're at it, maybe you could pitch your stuff to some of the craft shops, or the gift stores."

Laura's heart raced. She didn't think she was ready for that just yet.

"Are you feeling nervous about the wedding?" Nicola asked, obviously sensing Laura's reticence. "It's only two months now till D-Day."

"Stop it! It's still ages away yet! And no, I'm not feeling

the tiniest bit nervous. I love Neil and I can't wait to marry him."

Nicola smiled. "Good for you."

"I've always thought that whole 'Big Day' palaver was a bit silly," Helen said airily. "If you don't know by now, you never will. Kerry, will you *please* stop messing with that!" She snatched the milk jug out of Kerry's grasp.

"I thought *I* knew," Nicola said softly, "but I was wrong, wasn't I?"

Helen exchanged nervous looks with Laura. "I'm so sorry," she said quickly, wiping Kerry's wet hands with a tissue. "I didn't mean that . . . I just didn't think."

"You made the right decision in the end, Nicola – don't forget that," Laura added, seeing Nicola's troubled expression, and wondering if she might have been wrong in her earlier assessment of her friend's reaction to the news of Dan's new marriage.

"Did I?" she replied, with a watery smile. "I can't help wondering that maybe we should have paid more attention to our wedding vows. I seem to remember promising 'for better or for worse'."

"Nicola . . ."

"I know, I know. It was a long time ago." She smiled but her eyes told a different story. "Sorry, Laura, I hope I'm not putting you off marriage altogether."

"Of course, not." Laura patted her hand. "We know how hard it was for you and Dan back then."

"For Dan!" Helen exclaimed, outraged. "How bloody hard was it for that bastard?" It was common knowledge that Helen had always thought there was nothing wrong with Dan Hunt that couldn't be fixed with a large brick to the head.

"Forget it," Nicola said, lightly. "It's all over and done with now."

She smiled, but Laura noticed her face tighten. She had definitely been wrong – the situation with Dan had affected Nicola a lot more than she had let on. There was no point in trying to discuss this when Helen was around, so Laura sat back in her chair and made a mental note to get her friend on her own, sooner rather than later.

"So how are the plans for LCD going?" Helen asked brightly, using her acronym for Laura's business. "Did that computer guy work out?"

Laura nodded. Despite her initial misgivings about Laura's plans, Helen had been terrific in helping her source a reliable CAD software developer. While pencil drawings would suffice for the moment, Laura eventually hoped to use 3D computer technology for her more ambitious designs.

"So, all systems go for the big launch, then?"

"Well, there's no launch as such. I'll be open for business next week, and everything is pretty much in place." She beamed. "My parents are coming over tonight to see my workshop."

"That's great. I must come over and have a look myself. Jesus, Kerry! Can you not sit still for one second?" Helen snapped, as Kerry got out of her seat, and went towards Nicola.

"Helen, relax. She's fine," Nicola soothed, stroking Kerry's silky blonde curls.

"She's *not* fine! She's far from bloody fine! Kerry, I'm warning you – sit *down*!" Helen's last sentence was uttered with such emphasis that people at the surrounding tables turned to see what the ruckus was about.

Helen stood up, and wrenched Kerry away from Nicola. "Look, I'm not dragging her around with us today. We'll have no pleasure. You two do what you have to do, and I'll organise to come out on my own some other time."

"Helen, don't be silly. She's no trouble." Laura was astonished. "She's just excited to see us, that's all."

"There's no point, Laura." Helen's mouth was set in a firm line. "She'll cause us nothing but grief for the day."

"I'm s-s-s-solly, Mummy." Kerry's bottom lip began to stick out, and she looked genuinely contrite. "I w-w-w-wanna go w-w-w-with you and –"

"Forget it, missy! After the way you've been carrying on you're going nowhere but home. I told you to be good, I told you that we had a lot to do today for Auntie Laura's wedding, and that you had to be a good girl, but did you listen? No!"

Laura gave Nicola a look of mild shock. Helen was often strict with Kerry, but this was going overboard. And the child hadn't done anything to deserve the rollicking she was getting.

"Helen, please calm down," Nicola urged. "She's only a child."

But Helen couldn't be persuaded. "I'm sorry," she said to Laura. "I'll ring you sometime during the week to see how you're getting on. Maybe then we can talk in peace." She roughly fixed a by-then tearful Kerry into her buggy, and lobbing her bag over her shoulder, walked resolutely out of the café, leaving Nicola and Laura looking at one another in shock.

"I don't know what's got into her lately," said Nicola at last, "but whatever it is, she shouldn't take it out on Kerry."

Laura nodded. "I wouldn't mind, but compared to some children, Kerry isn't at all bold. In fact, for her age, she's very well behaved. My sister's two lads – now they're another story altogether, constantly hanging out of her, moaning for this and that. And most of the time you can't hear yourself for their chattering and questions. Kerry isn't a bit like that."

Nicola looked thoughtful. "Cathy's two are about – what? Three, three and a half?"

"Three last February, why?"

"Well, when did you ever hear Kerry chattering about anything?"

"But that's because the poor thing can't get the words out properly."

"And why do you suppose that is?"

Laura shrugged. "It's just one of those things."

"I'm not so sure about that. Look, I love Helen to bits and I'm not suggesting that she's a bad mother or anything but . . ."

"She doesn't exactly encourage Kerry by the way she talks to her," Laura finished. "I know. I've often thought that too."

"But she doesn't talk to her. She talks *at* her. It's all 'Kerry don't do this, don't do that'. She seems to be constantly chastising the child. I don't think I've ever actually heard her talk *with* Kerry."

"Yes, but you don't know what she's like at home. I'm sure they have lots of time together." Although she partly agreed with Nicola, Laura didn't want to criticise Helen too severely.

Nicola made a face. "From what I can gather, Kerry's

in bed an hour after Helen gets home from work. Helen makes dinner, and then it's off to bed for Kerry while Helen does some more work on the PC. Now, I could be wrong, but, from what I can make out, they don't exactly spend any quality time together."

"You don't know that for sure, though – for all we know she could be trying very hard with Kerry. And I'm sure it must be frustrating for both of them . . ." Laura trailed off, becoming uncomfortable with the conversation, and Nicola read the vibe. "Look, I'm not suggesting it's Helen's fault or anything, and she did take her to that speech therapist, it's just . . . well, I think that a child like Kerry needs more attention and encouragement than she's getting."

"You wouldn't say anything?" Helen would undoubtedly react angrily to any suggestion concerning her parenting, as would any mother.

Nicola shook her head. "Of course, not – what Helen does with Kerry is her own business."

"In fairness, I'm sure it's pretty difficult bringing her up on her own. There's no one to consult with, and no one else to share the work."

"Laura, as single mothers go, Helen has it easier than most. She has her own apartment, an excellent salary, a reliable childminder and no shortage of friends who are only too willing to help out if needed. Not your typical single mother."

"Yes, but it's very easy for us to talk. I know I wouldn't like to be in Helen's position," she said, thinking how lonely it must be. "You said a while ago she was seeing someone – is that still on?"

Nicola shook her head. "She told me that he was good

fun, but in the end they weren't suited. Ah, she's just too damned fussy."

Laura looked up, surprised. "Do you think that's it?"

"Of course! Think about it, Laura – of all the guys she's been out with since Jamie left, every single one of them had some kind of fault. Either he was too young, too old, too short, too tall, too bald, too hairy . . !"

Laura laughed. "Maybe you're right. It'll take something special to satisfy our Helen."

"Jimmy Choo possibly?" Nicola grinned and drained her coffee cup.

"Maybe," Laura sat forward, her mind on something else. "Listen, Nic, you haven't really said anything since, so I don't know if you want to talk about it but . . ."

"The Dan thing?"

"Yes. Are you OK about it? I mean, it must have been strange finding out the way you did, and I just wondered if –"

Nicola shrugged and looked down into her coffee cup. "Maybe I'm stupid, but I think he could have told me he was getting married, Laura. Oh, I know I'm probably expecting too much of him. We both know what Dan is like – and we *are* divorced, after all. But still, I know that if *I* was the one getting married again, I'd make it my business to tell *him* about it."

Laura agreed with her, but then again, as Nicola said herself, they were now divorced. Dan didn't have to say anything but perhaps, just out of courtesy, he should have let her know. "I understand," she said, "but besides that – is the fact that he's getting *married* again bothering you?"

Nicola looked at her. "Difficult question. To be honest,

Laura, since Ken and I got together, I haven't given Dan a second thought. I mean, why would I? Ken's wonderful and everything's great between us but . . ." She trailed off and shook her head. "I don't know, I think all of this has just thrown me off balance a bit, and I'm not exactly sure why."

"What does Ken think?"

Nicola grimaced. "I haven't told him yet."

"Nic . . ."

"I know, I should have said something, but then again, is it such a big deal? If I tell Ken that I've known about this for a while and didn't tell him, then of course he'll wonder why I'm making an issue out of it."

Laura nodded in agreement. She was sure Ken would understand why Nicola was a little thrown by Dan's marriage, but still, there was no point in rocking the boat.

Nicola brightened. "Anyway, what's done is done. Dan's getting married again and he didn't have the decency to bother telling me – fair enough. Yes, it surprised me a little at first, but now it's not that big a deal. I'm getting on with my life, Dan's getting on with his – and good luck to him."

"You're sure?"

"Yes!" Nicola laughed, ending the discussion. "Now come on. We're getting nothing done nattering away like this!"

Laura reached for her coat. "Let's head down to Brown Thomas first, and take a look at some of the accessories they're stocking. It might give me some idea of what I'm up against."

"Sure," Nicola followed her towards the door, but moved so quickly she bumped hard against another table on the way out. She looked in dismay at the two women seated there, one of whom was mopping up what looked like spilt cappuccino. "Oh, I'm so sorry!" she said, horrified. "Please let me get you another one."

"It's no problem," the woman said, with a smile. "It had gone cold anyway."

Nicola looked apologetically from the woman to her companion, and suddenly her features broke into a wide smile.

"Carolyn?" she said, pleasantly surprised. "It is you – isn't it? How are you?"

"Hello," said the woman called Carolyn. "I didn't realise it was you . . . I hardly recognised you."

"Well, I certainly have changed since the last time you saw me!" Nicola said laughing. "But listen, how are you? How are things?"

"Fine, fine. This is Alma McGuinness. Alma – Nicola Hunt."

"Well, it's Nicola Peters, now." Nicola smiled and shook hands with the other woman.

"Hi." Alma warmly returned the handshake.

"Oh, I'm sorry, Nicola, I'd almost forgotten you and Dan were . . . well, it's so long since I've seen you."

"Not at all, it's no problem. So tell me, how's John?"

"He's fine." Carolyn didn't elaborate.

"Oh – well, tell him I said hello."

"I will."

There was a short pause, an *awkward* pause, Laura felt, but Nicola didn't seem to notice.

"Carolyn, I must go, my friend is waiting, but we should meet for coffee soon."

"Yes, that would be nice."

"I'll give you a ring at home sometime? You're still at the same number?"

"Yes. Good seeing you again, Nicola."

"Are you sure I can't get you another drink?" Nicola turned again to Alma, who smiled and waved her away. "Well, I suppose I'd better be more careful on my way out!" She gave a self-deprecating grin. "Lovely to meet you, Alma. Carolyn, we'll talk soon."

The others said goodbye, and the two girls made their way back out onto the street. "Carolyn O'Leary," Nicola said, shaking her head from side to side. "I haven't seen her in ages. She's John's wife, remember?"

"That's who she is – I couldn't place her." Laura knew that Nicola and Carolyn, the wife of Dan's business partner, had been very close before the split.

Nicola sighed. "She looks fantastic, as usual – and she's lost loads of weight since I last saw her. She must have got some shock when she saw me!"

Laura smiled but said nothing.

"I really must arrange to meet up with her, soon." Nicola continued. "I could do with a good night out, and Carolyn was always good for a giggle. Anyway, let's get moving, only three more shopping hours in the day left!"

The two girls waded through the crowds, and headed in the direction of Grafton St.

* * *

Later that evening, Maureen Fanning was shuffling around Laura's workshop, her mouth set in a firm, thin line.

It had been a few weeks since Laura announced her intention of going into business, and she still hadn't managed to get over her parents' reaction. She had asked her mam and dad to visit, in the hope that they would notice the professional set-up, and perhaps realise that she was serious about this business – that it wasn't just some silly idea. She had spent most of the previous weekend making a selection of pendants, necklaces and earrings, and had laid them out in full view, hoping her parents would be impressed by them.

If it wasn't for Neil, Laura wasn't sure if she would have the strength to continue with her plans. He and Nicola had been so supportive and enthusiastic about the idea that maybe they had instilled a confidence in Laura that she didn't really possess. Maybe her mother was right. Maybe her designs weren't really that good. Maybe she was mad to take a chance.

Yet, something else inside Laura was telling her that she should go for it. Neil's cousin had done a fantastic job with the website, and had used 'every trick in the book' to ensure the site would be well placed on the best-known search engines. Laura never tired of logging on and putting test orders through. It always thrilled her to see the orders appear as the subject line in her inbox. She just hoped that there would be plenty of those in the near future.

But while sometimes her excitement soared, there were times when her confidence dived sharper than a kite without a breeze. This she knew was mostly down to her mother's reaction.

"Looks like you've spent more money on this nonsense than you have on your own wedding," Maureen said, her caustic tone cutting her daughter to the quick. "Honestly, Laura, you'd think that making sure your own flesh and blood had a decent day out would be more in your line than all this."

She was still going on about the fact that Laura and Neil were only having a small wedding, and had neglected to invite Maureen's brothers and sisters, the majority of whom Laura considered embarrassing troublemakers.

"Mam, I know you'd like them all to be there, but we just want a quiet family wedding," she said patiently, hoping that Maureen would notice some of her newer designs. As her enthusiasm and her confidence grew, she had become more and more elaborate in her creations.

"But do you not realise that I'll get the brunt of it?" Maureen continued her complaint, and much to Laura's disappointment ignored her displays and returned to the kitchen. "It's all right for you, away up here in Dublin, but I have to live in the village. You *know* how Frances treated me down in the butcher's that time when I forgot her youngest's twenty-first. I've never been so mortified in my entire life!"

Apparently, Maureen's sister Frances had announced loudly to the rest of the queue, that 'some people were so up in themselves these days, that they couldn't be bothered even sending a card or a few euro to her poor Farrah'. 'Poor Farrah' was seven months pregnant at the time, so apparently she needed all the euro she could get. But Maureen had never got over what she saw as 'the humiliation of it'.

Laura couldn't understand how her mother failed to see that her siblings were a bunch of freeloading users. If any of them needed a loan (or more often a handout never to be repaid), Maureen was the first one they turned to. If they needed a lift to or from the town, she would hop in the car without complaint and take them where they wanted to go. She never got anything in return, but for some reason was afraid of her life to risk upsetting her family.

Laura filled the kettle with a heavy heart. Maureen obviously wasn't going to let this one lie. "Look, Mam," she said, opening a packet of chocolate malted milk, her mother's favourite biscuits, "if you like, I'll contact the Kellys and explain the situation with Neil's mother being so ill – let them know that it won't be your typical day out."

"They'll never forgive me for snubbing them," Maureen said, as if she hadn't heard a word. "I'm afraid to show my face down the village now."

"It's not you that's snubbing them, Mam – it's *our* wedding." Laura couldn't hide her frustration.

"Oh, for goodness sake, Laura, it's the same thing. If one of their crowd left us off the guest list . . . well!" A look of horror crossed her features. "I'd wonder what I had done to cause offence!"

Laura sighed. It was always the same with her mother's relations – one would somehow offend the other, and the result could be a family feud that lasted for years. Then having forgotten what the quarrel was about in the first place, they'd all be friends again, at least until the next family member rubbed another up the wrong way. Now Maureen was petrified she would be that member.

"Listen, love," Joe Fanning spoke in a conciliatory

tone, "why don't we give you a few quid to put towards your day? Maybe then you might be able to stretch to a few extra relations."

Laura was resolute. "I'm sorry, Dad, but Neil and I have made our decision. We're having no more than sixty guests on the day, and the others can come to the afters. I'm sorry but that's the way it has to be."

There was silence in the small kitchen for a few moments, and Laura soon began to feel Maureen's disapproval eat into her conscience. She wished Neil was here – he'd think of something to say that would bring the discussion to a close. As it was, Laura didn't even want to talk about the wedding. She wanted her parents to say something, at least make some comment about the business.

"So what did you think of the workshop, Dad?" she asked eventually. "Neil did a good job of the spare room, didn't he?"

Joe shook his head. "I don't know, Laura. It's a shame to waste a good room like that. I mean what'll happen when ye decide to have a few young ones. There'll be nowhere to put them."

Laura's heart sank. "Dad, that won't happen for a long time, at least not until the business is up and running. Oh, I forgot to show you the website – it's really professional –"

"Laura, would you . . . ah . . . would you not forget about this notion of yours, and just go back to work?"

"What?" She spun around in surprise. What had her father just said? "Is that what you think this is – a notion?" she said, her heart constricting with disappointment. Whatever about her mother, Laura had always thought that her father – her father who knew how much she loved to sit and draw quietly when all her friends were out playing on the streets, who loved arts and crafts and used to jump at the chance at making home-made cards and decorations every Christmas – would be supportive.

"Your father's right, Laura." Maureen smiled across at her husband. "I don't know what kind of ideas Neil Connolly's been putting in your head, but I think it's about time somebody put you straight."

"Put me straight?" Laura repeated. "Put me straight about what?"

"About the fact that you're never going to make a living for yourself with this jewellery nonsense." Joe's tone softened when he saw his daughter's pained expression. "Look, pet, would you not try it part-time first and see how it goes? It might not go well at all for you and you mightn't make much money out of it. You don't want to be putting yourself and Neil under pressure."

"You don't understand, Dad," Laura's voice was barely a whisper. "This is something I've wanted to do for most of my life. You know I'm good at it; I've always been good at it. And surely it's not all about the money; it's about being *happy*."

"It is all about money when you buy a house in a uppity place like this." Maureen wrinkled her nose. "Honestly, I saluted one of your neighbours on the way in here today, and she looked at me as if I was a bit of dirt! Well, I'll tell you, Laura, that wouldn't happen down our way – down home we all know where we come from, and none of us think we're something we're not."

Laura ignored the jibe. "Mam, it's Dublin – people don't live in one another's pockets here. The neighbour wasn't snubbing you – she just didn't know you. She doesn't even know *me*, for Chrissake!"

Maureen pursed her lips. "There's no need to speak to me like that," she said looking away piously, then added, "You've obviously settled in well to this kind of life."

Laura resisted the urge to roll her eyes to heaven. How could she win?

"Joe, we'd want to be making a move," Maureen said then, and Laura knew she had already lost the battle. Her parents weren't here to see her, or the work she had done for the business; they were here to try and talk her out of it. And, of course, to talk her into inviting the Kellys to the wedding.

Laura felt disappointed, manipulated, and very alone.

Joe helped his wife on with her jacket.

"So, there's no convincing you to give up this whole thing then, is there?" Maureen asked, her disapproving eyes boring strongly into her daughter's.

"No, Mam." Laura felt, as probably Maureen intended, that by deigning to do something a little bit different, she was stepping out of line. Laura was 'lifting her chin above the windowsill' as the villagers would say about anyone who thought they were that little bit better than they were, who *tried* to be that little bit better than they were.

"Right. Well, we'd better go." They went out into the hallway. "You're finished work now for good?"

Laura nodded. "The business will be officially open next week."

For a while nobody said anything, but eventually Joe cleared his throat. "Best of luck then," he said kindly but to Laura's ears, completely insincerely.

Her mother uttered something unintelligible and, at that moment, Laura didn't think she had ever felt so desolate and alone in her entire life.

As if on cue, they heard Neil's car pull up outside and shortly afterwards her fiancé bounded energetically into the hallway.

"Hello, folks!" he said happily, not noticing the chill in the atmosphere. "Hey, you're not leaving yet, are you?"

"We have to get back before the traffic, Neil," Joe said, looking at Maureen.

"Oh come on, there'll be no traffic on a Saturday. Sure you've loads of time!" Neil somehow managed to shuttle Laura's parents back into the kitchen. "So, did Laura show you all the work she's been doing with the business? Fantastic, isn't it?"

"Great, great," Joe answered.

One look at Laura's face told Neil all he wanted to know. He gave a nearly imperceptible shake of his head.

"So tell us, Maureen, are you looking forward to the wedding? I suppose you have a right snazzy number that'll put everyone else to shame on the day?"

Maureen beamed up at him, and not for the first time Laura marvelled at how easily Neil could handle her mother.

"I got a gorgeous coral two-piece and a hat. I didn't want to show it to you yet, Laura, so you'll get a surprise on the day. Expensive, mind, but it'll be worth it."

Laura smiled. "That's fantastic, Mam. That colour will really suit you."

"Do you really think so?" Maureen was mollified. "Sure, I'll soon find out when I see myself back on the video."

"The what?" Laura repeated, and she and Neil looked at one another in surprise.

"The video."

"We're not having a video, Mam. I already told you that."

Maureen waved her away. "Ah, I know you said that, but hasn't your sister already ordered it for you as a wedding present? You have to have a memento of your wedding, Laura. It'll be no good otherwise." Maureen wasn't about to have her visions dashed of watching herself over and over again in all her finery.

Laura knew that Neil would be livid. He didn't want to have the day recorded, as his mother was by now well into her chemotherapy, and to her distress had already lost most of her hair. Neither he nor Laura wanted Pamela Connolly feeling uncomfortable on her son's wedding day.

"Maureen, we've already decided." Neil was firm. "My mother is feeling bad enough about her appearance as it is, let alone having the entire thing recorded for posterity."

But Maureen wouldn't hear of it. "Sure, there are great wigs around these days?" she said artlessly. "Don't you see them all the time on these popstars, and no one can tell the difference."

"Mam!" Laura said, mortified. She knew Neil was struggling desperately to hold his tongue. "Wigs for cancer patients are completely different. Neil's mother is almost bald, and she finds wearing those wigs difficult – they're itchy and warm and they just don't look natural."

"Hmmph!" Maureen gave a dismissive shrug. "You'd

think that vanity would be the last thing on their minds."

Laura's mouth dropped open.

"We should go now, Maureen." Joe Fanning sensed – correctly – that they had outstayed their welcome, and he shepherded his wife towards the door. "Just think about it, love," he said softly to Laura, while Maureen settled herself queen-like in the passenger seat, "and good luck with the other thing."

"Thanks, Dad."

Laura felt cheated. She closed the door behind her parents and went back into the living-room, where Neil sat red-faced on the sofa.

"I'm so sorry," she said, sitting down alongside him. "She has no idea. She just doesn't realise."

"I know, Laura," Neil took one of her hands in his and held it tightly, "but the hair loss is a big thing to my mother. It's nothing to do with bloody vanity! How dare she?"

"I know that, love," Laura planted a kiss on his temple. He didn't often show his feelings on the subject of his mother's illness, but she knew he was like the proverbial swan, appearing to sail peacefully on the water, while kicking furiously underneath. "It'll be OK," she whispered softly, putting her arms around him, but uncertain whether or not she believed her own words. Neil's mother had another five months of chemotherapy left, and even then the doctors couldn't be sure it would have any effect.

The wedding was only two months away, and the business would be open next week.

Would everything be OK?

At that moment, Laura wasn't so sure.

Chapter 13

"Oh, it was just amazing, Lynne. Like paradise in your mouth. And I could feel the pounds creeping on as I swallowed it down! Oh, I *know* I'm not heavy, but I still *have* to be careful . . . I don't want to look like a giant snowball on the day!"

Hearing Dan come in, Chloe sat up. "Lynne, I have to go. Dan's here and he'll be dying to know how I got on with it. Talk soon!"

Chloe hung up and turned to face her fiancé. "Dan, I picked out the most amazing cake for us today – it was just unbelievable . . ."

She stopped short when she saw his face. "What is it?" she asked, taken aback by his bloodshot eyes and shaken demeanour. "Dan, you look awful!"

"I feel awful," he said, laying his briefcase on the floor and flopping down on the sofa. "I've just spend two hours in town in bloody bumper-to-bumper traffic, and my head feels as though a kanga hammer has been doing overtime in my brain."

Chloe bristled. "I take it that dinner is off, then."

"What dinner?"

"Dan, we agreed!" Try as she might, Chloe couldn't keep the whinge out of her tone. Dan was *always* tired these days. "You promised that we'd have dinner in the Four Seasons tonight – just to make sure that the food is up to standard before the wedding, remember?"

"Ah, Chloe, we can do it another night, can't we? I'm just not able for it right now. I'm sorry." Dan loosened his tie, and ran a hand through his hair.

"Right." Her tone did nothing to conceal her annoyance.

"Jesus Christ, Chloe – I come home after a bollocks of a day, I've got a splitting headache, and now you expect me to get all trussed up, and go gallivanting with you!"

"Gallivanting? Dan, this is our wedding – doesn't that mean anything to you?"

She had been looking forward to this for ages. Being fussed over in the Four Seasons, discussing the wedding preparations so far . . . it would be better than sex! Well, almost. But now Dan had to go and ruin it.

"Chloe, of course it means something! But if I had known how much hassle it was all going to be, I don't know if I –" He broke off.

"You don't know what, Dan?"

Dan relented. "Look, love, I said I'm sorry. What more can I do?"

"Well, now that you ask, there's a hell of a lot more you can do, actually. First of all, you could try showing just a modicum of interest in what is supposed to be the most important day of our lives."

"Chloe –"

"But of course, I forgot," she continued, putting a hand on her hip, "I forgot that this is all old hat to you – this is all just one big nuisance to you, isn't it?"

"For God's sake, Chloe, calm down."

"Calm down? Calm down?" Chloe blinked as she desperately tried to stop the tears from appearing. "Do you think I don't notice? Do you think that I don't see how uninterested you are in all of this? Well, remember something, Dan, *you* were the one who proposed to me. You were the one that wanted to get married, to make it official. And up until a few weeks ago, everything was fine." She stepped back, shaking her head from side to side, as Dan stood up to comfort her. "I don't know what the hell is going on with you lately. Have you met someone else, is that it? Well, if that's the case, Dan, you can go jump –"

"Chloe, stop it, please. It's nothing like that."

"Nothing like that . . . then there *is* something!"

Dan nodded, and with a sigh, slumped back down on the sofa. "You're right. There *has* been something on my mind lately, but it's not what you think. I mean, I haven't met anyone else."

"What, then?"

"It's Nicola, my ex."

Chloe felt her stomach constrict as she sat down beside him. She didn't know much about Dan's first marriage, other than the fact that he and his ex-wife had parted on unpleasant terms. Dan was loath to talk about it, and she wasn't sure who had initiated the divorce, but reading between the lines Chloe knew that something major must have happened back then. She had always privately suspected that the ex-wife had been a bit of a bitch. But she had never been completely sure of Dan's feelings towards this Nicola. Had she tried to contact him? Was she still in love with Dan, or maybe trying to get even more money out of him? There were no children, so what the hell was her problem?

"What about her?" she asked, realising that she was holding her breath while waiting for his answer.

"Remember the mix-up with our wedding invitations that time?"

Chloe nodded, frowning.

"Well, the ones we got by mistake, amazingly, were Nicola's best friend's invitations."

"What?" So much for Amazing Day Designs being original. Now the whole world and his mother were using them. She tried to recall the name. "The ones for that other girl?"

"Laura, yes."

"And?"

"And, because they mistakenly got *our* invites, there is a very good chance that Nicola – or at least Laura – knows about our wedding"

Chloe shrugged. "And why is that a problem?"

Dan began to knead his temples with one hand. "I haven't told Nicola that I'm getting married again. I didn't want her to find out like that, or to think that I was trying to keep it a secret."

Chloe was confused. "So what if you didn't tell her? What does it matter now?"

"I'm not sure it does," he answered softly. "I just didn't want her to be hurt by it, that's all."

"And why would it hurt her? You two are divorced, for goodness sake! For all you know, she could be married herself. Jesus, Dan, sometimes you can be way too considerate."

"She's not married," Dan said quietly.

"How do you know that?" Chloe asked, unsure as to whether she wanted to know the answer. Had Dan been keeping tabs on this woman? And if so, why?

"Because, believe it or not, I came across an article only yesterday about her in one of your magazines. She's back in Dublin, and she's running a leisure centre." Chloe saw him smile then, as though he was silently adding 'fair play to her'.

"What? What magazine?"

Dan shuffled through some newspapers on the coffee table. He found a copy of *Mode*, opened the page, and pointed at a small head and shoulders photograph.

"That's Nicola."

"*This* is Nicola?" Chloe repeated, staring at the photograph. The famous Nicola was a fair-haired, pasty individual, who to Chloe looked as though she could do with a few sessions in the gym herself. Somehow, she had always imagined Dan's ex as that bit more glamorous. The fact that Nicola was a bit of a plain-Jane was rather gratifying. "So why the big deal, Dan?"

"What?"

"Why is all of this bothering you?"

Dan looked strained. "Look, I know it's hard for you to understand, Chloe, but you don't know how things ended with us."

"You're right," Chloe said, seizing the opportunity to find out what this was all about. "I *don't* know how it ended with you. So maybe you'd like to tell me."

Dan's expression clouded. "Look, like I told you before, we just grew apart – I don't really like to talk about it."

"But why not? You're divorced now. What difference is it going to make?"

He wouldn't meet her eyes. "Nicola and I . . . we . . . we just couldn't make it work. I've never liked to talk about it because . . . well, I suppose I blame myself that we couldn't make it work."

"But it couldn't have been all your fault!" Chloe interrupted. "Surely she has to shoulder some of the blame too."

"Not really," Dan said quietly.

"Why not?"

He was silent for a moment. "It was me – I was weak," he said. "I should have fought harder. I should have been stronger, but I wasn't . . . I was a bloody coward."

"It was a long time ago, Dan." Chloe wasn't sure she liked where this was going. Of course she was curious about the break-up, but she didn't want Dan thinking that he should have 'fought harder' for his first marriage.

She tried to move the subject along. "So if you're so bothered about Nicola finding out about our wedding, why don't you just set the record straight?"

"What do you mean?"

"Well, the number of the leisure centre is plastered all over that article – they must be desperate for business – why don't you give her a ring at work?" Chloe didn't particularly want Dan being all pally with his ex, but if his conscience was giving him that much trouble, it would surely be better to get it over and done with.

"You wouldn't mind?" Dan looked unsure.

Chloe was flippant. "Nope, go right ahead."

"OK, then – I think I will," Dan looked relieved but, Chloe thought, a little nervous.

While he showered and changed, Chloe studied the photograph in more detail. Judging by the state of her in that picture, Nicola was nothing to worry about. Unglamorous, pale and ordinary-looking – Chloe thought she was the *last* person you would expect to be promoting a fitness centre.

Let Dan contact her and have it out with her. She didn't like it, but what could she do? Better that he got it out of his system and stopped worrying about it, and then maybe *she* could stop worrying about it.

Trust Dan and his principles. Sometimes her fiancé was too bloody considerate for his own good.

Chloe picked up the phone, and redialled her friend's number. "Lynne, hi, it's me again – listen, I'm coming over."

* * *

"I don't understand it," she said, sitting back on her friend's luxurious Italian leather sofa. "Why the obsession with what *she* thinks – after all this time?"

Chloe had gone straight to Lynne's, all thoughts of wedding cake abandoned, leaving Dan snoozing happily on the sofa in front of the television.

Lynne poured milk into her coffee. "Well, maybe it's just good manners on Dan's part," she said. "After all, it's only right that he should let her know about you two. They were married for what – a couple of years before they separated?"

"Yes, but if he's that worried, why didn't he let her know about me sooner?"

"You said she was out of the country – maybe he didn't have an opportunity."

Chloe sat forward. "Look, I wouldn't mind, but you should have seen Dan these last few weeks. He hasn't been himself at all. He has absolutely no interest in the wedding. I asked him the other day what he thought of the seating plan and he just blanked – as if he didn't have a clue what I was talking about. He seems –" she paused, "I don't know, obsessive or something."

Lynne raised an eyebrow. "I don't like the sound of that."

"Me neither."

"Well, why did Dan and what's-her-name split in the first place?" Lynne asked, echoing the thought that had been going around in Chloe's brain, since she first learnt of this Nicola business.

"I'm not entirely sure," she replied, feeling silly as she said it. Dan had always been so dismissive about his first marriage. Chloe hadn't asked, because up to now, she didn't really care. As far as she was concerned, the former Mrs Hunt was well out of the picture and out of the country to boot. Why *should* she care? As long as it didn't affect her, Chloe wasn't all that interested. But now, Nicola's return and Dan's reaction to it was beginning to fill Chloe with a very strong sense of unease.

"Well, I'm sure you could find out," Lynne continued. "The official reason, at any rate."

Chloe sat forward. "What? How?"

"Chloe, you work in a solicitor's practice," Lynne laughed, as if it was the most obvious thing in the world. "If anyone is ideally placed to get their hands on legal documents, then you are. Find out from Dan, casually mind, who handled his divorce, and then phone around and see what you can find out."

"Lynne, you're a genius!" Chloe would never have thought of that. In spite of her friend's apparent dimness, there was a sharp mind at work in there somewhere.

Lynne smiled beatifically. "I've always thought so. The separation agreement may or may not tell you anything, but there will have to be a cause stated in the divorce papers."

Chloe's mind raced. Dan wouldn't appreciate her going behind his back like that, but what did he expect? He wouldn't tell her anything!

No, she needed to find out what it all meant and, more importantly, if this Nicola was going to pose a threat to her wedding. And there was no way Chloe was going to let that happen. She had waited long enough for Dan to propose, long enough trying on all those wedding dresses (although that had been great fun), choosing the flowers, the wedding cake, the invitations – everything. She was determined not to let anything or *anyone*, disrupt this wedding.

"I wouldn't stop there, either," Lynne continued. "What about Dan's friends? Surely that's the most obvious place to start."

Chloe made a face. "Dan doesn't really have all that many friends, Lynne, not many that I know of anyway. I think he and Nicola were all part of the same circle, so when they split up . . ." She shrugged and trailed off. "You know we only socialise with you and Nick and the others now."

It was true. When she thought about it, it was kind of odd that Dan didn't have that many close friends. She hadn't really noticed before and, in a way, was glad that she had him all to herself, but this fact didn't help her when she needed someone who had known Dan and Nicola together.

Then it hit her. "I could always try John," she said. John O'Leary, Dan's creepy partner, would have been around at the time. She was sure that he would have no problem at all filling her in on the gory details of Dan's first marriage. Dan had said before that John was always great for gossip. While he was a lecherous creep whom Chloe didn't like, she would put up with it if it meant she might learn something to put her mind at ease.

Chloe sat back and smiled at Lynne, relieved that she had a plan of action.

She'd phone Dan's partner first thing in the morning.

* * *

John answered his private line on the second ring. "O'Leary Hunt, Accountants – John speaking."

"John? Hi, it's Chloe – Dan's Chloe," she clarified.

"Chloe, babe! How are you?" John spoke as if they were old friends. They weren't that close – in fact Chloe could count on one hand the number of times she had met the man. According to Dan, John O'Leary was not an ideal business partner, something he had discovered shortly after going into practice with him, and as a result they rarely socialised. "Listen, Dan's in a meeting at the moment. I'll get him to phone you later, will I?"

Chloe cleared her throat. God, she was actually nervous. She had spent all night thinking about what she was going to say, and how she was going to phrase it but now she didn't know if she could go through with it.

"Um, I'd like to talk to you, actually, if you have a minute."

"Oh! Fire away."

She could almost picture his bemused expression.

Chloe decided to get right to the point. "You knew Dan's ex-wife, didn't you?"

"Nicola? Of course. I hear she's back in Ireland now. Why're you asking me?"

Chloe's stomach tightened. Dan must have told John that Nicola had come home. But why would he do that? Why would he say anything about it at all unless . . . All of sudden, Chloe began to feel very threatened.

"No real reason, I just wondered what she was like, that's all." She tried to sound offhand, but despite herself Chloe's hands shook. "I mean, of course Dan told me a watered-down version of it, but I just wondered about the real reason they split up."

"Chloe, if you ask me that was doomed from the very beginning," John said in a tone that suggested he wasn't all that enamoured of Nicola. "They were having problems since day one, as I'm sure Dan told you."

"Um, yes." Chloe couldn't admit that she hadn't a clue. Dan was right about John enjoying a bit of gossip. She said nothing, suspecting that it was better to let him warm to his subject.

"Yeah, that whole thing with his parents and everything, a nasty business."

Chloe's ears pricked up at this. *Dan's parents?*

"They didn't approve of her?" she volunteered, imagining the most likely scenario.

"That's putting it mildly. The mother was hard work, as I'm sure you know yourself," John added with a laugh. "And as for the father – don't ask!"

Chloe's eyes widened. She knew that Dan didn't get on with his parents, but now she could understand why. Dan was obviously afraid that the same thing might happen with them as it had with Nicola. She sniffed. Dan was a fool if he thought that Chloe would let his mother, or indeed any woman, get in the way of their relationship. Nicola must have been a right sap.

John continued. "Being honest, Chloe, I don't know a great deal about how it went in the end. Of course, I felt sorry for Nicola and everything, but . . . well, she and I, we didn't exactly gel."

"Oh?" She was surprised by the admission. John O'Leary loved to give the impression that he was everyone's best friend, that he was a 'sound man'.

"Yeah. She and Carolyn got on well, but when me and Dan set up the partnership, she got this notion that Dan was the one doing all the work, and I wasn't doing enough. But Dan's like that. You know, he likes being the one in control. I was happy enough to let him." Chloe sensed him shrug. "It wasn't my fault that Dan stayed late at the office five nights a week in the early days. Maybe if he had someone a bit more relaxing to go home to, he wouldn't need to," he added bitterly.

"Nicola was uptight, then?" Chloe probed, pleased at this image of her predecessor. "Uptight? Compared to Nicola back then, the bloody taxman is relaxed, and believe me I should know!" John laughed at his own feeble joke.

Chloe clarified what she had just learned. "So Nicola and Dan were under pressure from the beginning, what with Dan working hard at the partnership, and the thing with his parents?"

"Yeah, with all the stuff that was going on, it was always going to be difficult. It's a pity, I suppose, and they were a great couple, but you need a very strong marriage to survive these things."

These things? *What* things?

"John –"

"Anyway, why the sudden interest in Nicola, Chlo? Want to see how you measure up, is it? Well, I can tell you that Nicola was nice-looking in her day, but now . . . well, I don't think there's any comparison."

"Thanks, John." Chloe was hugely gratified by this. She already knew how Nicola looked these days – obviously the break-up had taken its toll on the woman. Still, that was no excuse for letting herself go. Chloe idly wondered whether or not Dan would have any old photographs of himself and Nicola hidden away anywhere – a wedding photo, perhaps? "It's just Dan doesn't talk about her all that much, and I wondered what she was like."

"Ah, you've nothing to worry about, babe," John said condescendingly. "Dan's well over her now."

Over her? Chloe didn't like that. It could only mean one thing, that *Nicola* must have been the one who ended the relationship. She had always hoped somehow, that

Dan had dumped *her*, and she certainly didn't like the image of her fiancé pining over his ex-wife.

Was Dan over her? Or had Nicola's return sparked something in her fiancé other than guilt? She thought about how distracted and impatient he had been over the last few weeks, until he had finally told Chloe what was bothering him. How had he felt when he discovered Nicola was back in Ireland again? And worse, how would he feel when he made contact with her? God, was Chloe a fool to suggest that Dan contact her?

"Listen, Chlo, I really should go. I have a ten o'clock I need to prepare for and –"

"Sure." Chloe was about to say goodbye, but instead found herself asking, "John, can you remember who initiated the divorce? Dan told me, but I just can't recall at the moment. I think it was her, wasn't it?"

"Well, of course, it was her!" John said as if it was the most obvious thing in the world. "She claimed domicile in England, and got the papers drawn up from there. You know they didn't get married here in Ireland?"

"Yes, they did it abroad somewhere?" Dan had mentioned that.

"Yeah, so it was a quick divorce, no long separation period, or anything like that." Chloe made a face. If it had been an English divorce, it would be almost impossible to get her hands on the divorce papers. She'd have to strike that one off of her plan of action!

"Listen, Chloe, again, I'd love to stay and chat, but I really have to go."

"OK, thanks John – listen, you won't say anything to Dan, will you?"

John laughed. "Are you mad? That fella is still so touchy about Nicola that I wouldn't dare risk it!"

Chloe hung up, her unease multiplying with each passing minute. John's information hadn't exactly assuaged her curiosity; if anything, it had made it worse. She had learnt a little about Dan and Nicola's problems, but nothing to suggest a valid reason for their marriage break-up. Why would Dan be feeling guilty? If it was just that the relationship had disintegrated along with their feelings for one another, Chloe could accept that.

But something deep down inside was telling her that there was more to it than that. She couldn't explain why, she just knew it.

And what had John meant when he said: 'You need a very strong marriage to survive these things?'

She wasn't sure. The wedding was only a few months away, and Chloe was damned if she was going to let Dan's ex-wife get in the way of her Big Day.

She might not know the reason for Dan and Nicola's break-up but Chloe was determined to find out

Chapter 14

Laura could barely contain her excitement. As of today, Laura Connolly Design was open for business, and now she was officially proprietor of her own company! She looked around her small garage workshop with immense satisfaction. The presentation boxes had arrived a few days earlier, and Laura had been unprepared for the absolute joy she felt upon her first glimpse of them. For the Laura Connolly Design logo, she had decided upon a simple lilac, silver-tinged wording on a white background, and inside the box the jewellery would be presented upon white satin.

At Neil's suggestion, she had put together small samples of her work – earrings and brooches etc – and had boxed and sent them out to selected gift and jewellery stores, hoping to ignite some interest.

Laura wasn't fooling herself; she knew it would be some time before things began to move, but hopefully by Christmas she would have some idea as to whether or not the pricing structure had been correct, and her margins sufficient. If it hadn't been for Neil, she would be selling her jewellery for half nothing, but he had insisted that she maintain a decent mark-up.

"I know you don't want to price yourself out of the market, but remember that they're handcrafted products, not the mass-market stuff already out there," he had said. "If they cost too little, then people will think that they're not worth much."

If it weren't for Neil, Laura would probably be giving them away.

Helen had suggested that she have an official Laura Connolly Design opening, invite all and sundry and perhaps gain a little publicity, but Laura wanted to leave such an outward proclamation until closer to Christmas, when buying jewellery would be foremost in people's minds. For the moment, she was quite happy to start slowly, build up a decent catalogue, and hope that her profile might be raised by the Crafts Council and a few satisfied customers spreading the word.

Her family hadn't been much help, though. As far as she knew, her mother hadn't said a thing to anyone about the business.

So much for being proud of her.

Neil was becoming increasingly frustrated by Maureen's attitude towards both the business and the wedding, and Laura was feeling the strain of trying to defuse the growing tension between the two of them.

Joe hadn't said much, so she had no idea how he felt about the whole thing. For all Laura knew her dad could be secretly pleased for her but, because he always backed her mother, she had no way of knowing how he felt about it. Joe rarely let anyone know his personal feelings about anything – preferring instead to let his wife do the talking. It was a pity. Laura thought, because she could really do with someone in her corner. As for the wedding, Joe tended not to take any notice of Maureen's rants about it, having already experienced a similar scenario with Cathy's wedding.

Still, her mother's blatant lack of belief was difficult to handle. She had been so sure that Maureen would be thrilled, had been positive that her mother would be one of her greatest advocates, yet she was acting as though Laura's plans were something to be ashamed of. It was hard to take. And she had heard nothing from her parents, not even a quick phone call to say good luck, when they knew well that – as of today – their eldest daughter was officially an entrepreneur.

Deep in thought, Laura sat down at her bench, and began working on the design for a necklace that she hoped would become a popular seller, particularly at Christmas. As she worked, she tried to come up with an interesting-sounding description for the website:

"Fine silver vermeil mesh with an overlay of filigree squiggles and curls, cloisonné enamel flowers and a centre row of coral and turquoise glass cabochons . . . this necklace will have everyone talking . . ."

Everyone talking? Laura made a face. Should she say things like that? She didn't want people to think that she was blowing her own trumpet. But maybe that was what she was supposed to be doing. She was trying to sell not just the jewellery but the *image*.

She picked up her own personal favourite, one of the very first pieces she had designed since going out on her own. Going out on her own! Laura still couldn't believe it. This bracelet was pretty spectacular though, and it had taken her ages to make – the fine silver metal chain being almost impossible to thread. She had strung shimmering crystal aurora beads on the chain and covered the metal clasp with blindingly bright aurora rhinestones.

Laura ordered from a UK distributor who had sourced the stones in Italy, and while she was pleased with the results, she needed more materials to really achieve the designs she wanted. While she was concentrating on four, maybe five strong lines, using metals, beads and stone, she wanted to try a rather unusual ethnic range, using leather, and perhaps shell, or wood. She didn't know how well this might go commercially and this, Laura thought, was her biggest problem. The designs might look fantastic, but would people wear them? No, for the moment she should concentrate on the more conventional styles, and give them her own contemporary twist.

She was definitely going to experiment with her wedding jewellery, though. Laura had a clear idea of what she wanted in that regard. She was going to come up with something fabulous for Nicola and Cathy, something that her bridesmaids would hopefully treasure for years to come.

Laura was so engrossed in the work that she almost didn't hear the doorbell ring.

A deliveryman stood at the door, holding the most amazing and unusual arrangement of flowers Laura had ever seen. That morning Helen had a gift basket of handmade chocolates delivered, Nicola had sent her a Good Luck helium balloon, and Neil's mother, despite the fact that she was in hospital, had sent a magnum of champagne.

But these were from Neil.

> 'Congratulations, LC,
> Guess who has designs on your heart?'

As she read the card attached, Laura tried to hold back the tears. He was being so wonderful – *people* were being so wonderful. Blast her family! What did it matter what they thought? As long as she had Neil behind her, surely everything would be all right?

* * *

Helen checked her watch. She was sitting in the bar of the Stillorgan Park Hotel and Miriam Casey was late. Forty minutes late. If there was one thing Helen hated, it was professional discourtesy. If the woman was going to be late, why the hell didn't she ring ahead and say so?

As if on cue Helen's mobile rang.

"Helen?" The woman sounded rushed and harassed. "Miriam Casey here – listen I know this is awful, but could we possibly postpone this meeting until some other time?"

Helen bristled. She had been up all night working on a presentation for *Mizz* Casey and now the cow was cancelling! Blast her!

"Miriam, I have to admit I'm disappointed. I have a table booked and –"

"I know, I know and I'm very sorry, it's just that one of

the kids has taken ill, and I really can't leave him. Tell you what, why don't you stay for lunch and bill it to the company? Please," she insisted, when Helen hesitated, "it's the very least I can do."

It certainly is, Helen thought, after dragging me all the way out here for nothing.

So it looked as though Helen wasn't the only woman struggling to hold a career and motherhood together. Although she certainly wouldn't let something like a sick child get in the way of business. Couldn't the childminder deal with it?

She shook her head. "Call me when you want to reschedule," she said shortly, putting her phone back on the countertop.

Great! So much for rushing around like a madwoman earlier, trying to get a full day's work into one morning. Despite Miriam's offer she didn't fancy having dinner on her own. She debated going back to the office but it was such a gorgeous day . . .

Helen paused. It was just after two. She *could* just collect Kerry from pre-school and go home early, but there was hardly much point in doing that, when Jo was probably already on the way. And, Helen thought, Kerry didn't need collecting from Jo's until after five, so for the first time in as long as she could remember, she had an afternoon to herself! She mentally hugged herself. This was brilliant!

Maybe she should head out to Laura's and see how she was getting on in her first day in business or – even better – visit Nicola at the leisure centre, maybe stay for a massage or a long soak in the spa. She sighed. That would be absolute bliss.

Then, of course, there was the other option – an option that Helen could rarely resist. Grafton St was there to be conquered, so how better to spend an idle afternoon than shopping? She needed to get an outfit for Laura's wedding, Kerry's tantrums having ruined her last opportunity, so why not? She already had something in mind, maybe a racy little Julien McDonald or Jenny Packham number, something to get them all talking in Glengarrah.

Helen checked her watch. She could be in town by three, and still have plenty of time before she needed to pick up Kerry. And even if she was a tiny bit late, Jo wouldn't mind.

She finished her soda water, and glanced idly up at the television before leaving. Then Helen stopped dead in her tracks and her eyes widened as she watched the sports bulletin. On screen, one of her favourite footballers was pictured smiling at the camera, and holding a rival team jersey against his chest.

"I don't believe it!" she said to the barman. "Can you turn up the volume, please?"

The barman looked amused, and reached for the remote. "Bit of a shock, wasn't it?" he said indicating the news story. "He'll get some reception when he goes back to his home ground."

"But he's been with them since he was fourteen years of age!" Helen stood rooted to the spot, amazed. "I can't *believe* he's signed for a rival team."

"Well, that's what forty-five million quid will do for you." The barman shrugged and went to serve another customer.

Helen sat back down to watch to the remainder of the bulletin, her head still shaking in amazement.

"Someone you know?" a male voice piped up from her left.

"Sorry?" she asked, looking at him through dark eyelashes. It was almost second nature to Helen to flirt with *any* male who spoke to her, let alone one who looked like this. He was tall, lean and almost painfully good-looking, his tanned high cheekbones and slate grey eyes staring directly into Helen's dark ones.

"That guy," he indicated the television. "Is he a friend of yours or something?"

Helen laughed. "Oh no," she said, feeling little ripples of anticipation flood through her at the sight of his solid physique. "He's a footballer."

"Oh right." Mr Perfect looked confused. "It's just –"

"It's OK," she interjected, waving him away with a grin. "I get a little excited sometimes, that's all."

"I'd like to be around when you get *really* excited, then."

He gave her a meaningful glance and Helen almost blushed. *Almost.*

"Paul Conroy," he said, extending a hand, and flashing a set of perfect teeth.

"Helen Jackson." She gave him her most flirtatious smile.

"So, are you waiting for someone, Helen, or is this just my lucky day?"

It was a line if ever there was one, but Helen didn't care. Right then he could have asked her if she came here often and it would be the sexiest thing Helen had ever heard. And those *eyes* – it was as if he could see right through her. Just then Helen wouldn't have minded if he did.

"Well, I was waiting for someone but he appears to have let me down." She sighed.

It was lame to be fishing for compliments, but Helen didn't care. Anyway, it worked.

"Silly, silly guy." Paul shook his head and put a hand under his chin.

The way he was looking at her sent an involuntary shiver of excitement down her spine. The dark, downy hairs sneaking over his sleeve sent her imagination sprinting, and she began to imagine running her fingers along his undoubtedly hairy chest. She let the sensations work their way from her mind down along the rest of her body. God, if she touched him now, she wouldn't trust the light bulbs to stay in one piece, such was the electrical charge between them.

God, it had been ages . . .

"So what are you going to do?" Paul asked.

"Sorry?"

"Well, are you going to join me for a drink, or do you have somewhere else to go?"

Helen smiled and sexily crossed her legs. Jenny and Julien would have to wait.

* * *

Less than an hour later, Helen was writhing uncontrollably beneath Paul on the bed, his lean sculptured body fulfilling every one of her earlier expectations.

It had probably been the most intense flirtation she had ever experienced. Every word they said to one another had been heavy with meaning, and Helen had enjoyed every second of it.

It wasn't just the alcohol either, she decided – it was as if her mind had been taken over by some weird sensual drug. The man absolutely emanated sex, and Helen had felt unbelievably horny just sitting beside him.

Paul must have seen something in her eyes because at one stage he gave her an intense searching look and signalled almost imperceptibly towards reception.

Understanding immediately, Helen nodded instantly, before she changed her mind.

"Hold that thought," he said, before walking purposefully toward reception. Again she forced herself to ignore the cliché. Who cared?

It didn't matter that she didn't know him, or anything about him – all that mattered was that she was more turned on than she had ever been in her entire life. She clung to his damp body like her life depended on it. She was an experienced and confident lover, but soon discovered that she was no match for Paul. He had her in ways she never thought possible, ways that had her cry out with ecstasy and pain in equal measures. It was as though she was in some kind of sexual dream, one that she didn't want to end.

After what seemed like hours, Paul collapsed heavily on the pillow beside Helen, the hair around his forehead damp with sweat, and his tanned skin glistening in the afternoon light. She slung an arm across his chest.

Paul turned to look at her, his pupils still dilated with lust. "So, what was your name again?" he teased.

Helen kicked him in the leg. "Names were about as far as we *did* get before . . . this," she smiled slyly.

"Well, *this*, as you call it, this was fucking fantastic."

She shrugged. "If you say so."

179

"What?" Paul's eyes widened. "You're kidding me, right?"

There was a slight twang in his voice that Helen hadn't noticed before. She laughed. "Of course, it was fantastic."

"Well, now we should at least get to know one another, don't you think?" Paul began running a finger along Helen's ribcage, and she felt herself respond almost instantly to his touch.

"Yes."

"So, tell me all about yourself, Helen Jackson," He traced his tongue around one of her nipples.

Helen breathing began to quicken once more. "I'm thirty, I work in sales, I'm not married . . ."

"No," he whispered, putting a finger to her lips. "*Tell* me about yourself – for instance . . . tell me how you're feeling now, how this feels." He moved his hands lower along her body and Helen struggled to speak.

"Is this a getting-to-know-you exercise?" she asked him huskily, wrapping herself around him again.

Afterwards, they lay together in, Helen thought, a very comfortable silence. "So, what about you?" she asked eventually.

Paul sat up. "What about me?"

"Well, I know you're a businessman –"

"Pensions," he interjected.

"Pensions?"

"And investments," he finished. "Not what you imagined, huh?"

Helen smiled. "No, not exactly." She had thought him a partner in some high-powered corporation, not quite a pensions salesman.

"Does it matter?" he asked, kissing the nape of her neck.

"Of course not," Helen moved his head upwards, and kissed him sensually on the lips.

"So what do you think?" he asked with a daring smile.

"About what?" Helen felt a tingle of anticipation. She knew where this was going. He wanted to see her again.

"About dinner on Saturday night?" Paul confirmed her expectations.

"I'd love to," she said coyly, pulling him close to her, "but I think I need to know that little bit more about you first."

Paul willingly complied.

Chapter 15

Nicola closed the Accounts program on her PC, unable to concentrate on the figures. She heard a soft knock on the door of her office, and seconds later Jack's head appeared around the door.

"Nicola, one of Murphy-Ryan kids has had an accident in the swimming-pool again. I've had a word with the mother, but she's getting antsy."

She made a face. Oh, no – not *again*! "Have you taken care of it yet, Jack?"

"Not yet, remember you said before that the next time it happened – with the Murphy-Ryans in particular – that we should leave it as 'evidence'." He gave a slight grin.

Nicola groaned. "Where is it?"

"Near the exit on the left-hand side."

"OK, Jack, can you call the lift? I'll be down in a minute. And thanks for letting me know."

Nicola ran a hand through her hair and buttoned the top button of her shirt. Mrs Bloody Murphy-Ryan again!

Who did she think she was? Double-barrelled surname or not, this time Nicola was going to give this particular client a piece of her mind.

Jack reappeared at reception, having located a pair of rubber gloves. He grabbed the 'fishing net' (which, in this case, doubled as a pooper-scooper) and Nicola followed him out towards the swimming-pool. The offending item was indeed floating near the surface of the water, not far from Mrs Murphy-Ryan and her toddler twins. Ugh!

Nicola affected her most menacing expression and approached the woman.

"Mrs Murphy-Ryan, I've told you before that your children *must* wear the appropriate swimming pants when you take them into the pool," she said curtly.

"Pardon?" the woman's eyes widened as she trod water. "What on earth are you suggesting?"

"I'm not *suggesting* anything. The *fact* is that one of your boys has soiled himself *and* our pool." Nicola's voice rose an octave. She couldn't believe the cheek of this woman. "You need to follow the rules, Mrs Murphy-Ryan. It's very unfair not only to the rest of our clients, but also to the staff. We're the ones that have to clean it up."

"How *dare* you!" the other woman exclaimed. "How dare you suggest that one of my children would do such a thing?"

Nicola gave her a solid stare. "Mrs Murphy-Ryan, as you can see for yourself, there are no other children here this morning."

"But that doesn't mean . . ." Realising she was beaten, the other woman trailed off and muttered something under her breath, while Jack scooped the floating object out of the swimming-pool.

Nicola grimaced. Poor old Jack.

As she left the room, she noticed that some of the other swimmers had already made their way back to the changing-rooms, the idea of a morning swim no longer appealing. Oh, dear. But then, who could blame them?

Blast the woman! This was the third and – if Nicola had her way – the *last* time Mrs Murphy-Ryan would do such a thing. She'd have to ask Ken to speak to her, because so far the woman hadn't taken the blindest bit of notice of her, and if anything had treated her with downright contempt. Nicola knew some people felt uncomfortable to see someone like herself running a leisure centre. Some people felt uncomfortable with her, full stop. And she hated getting Ken involved because it looked as though she couldn't manage the situation on her own.

Nicola went to increase the pool chlorine level and, through the window of the control room, she saw Mrs Murphy-Ryan still brazenly lazing around in the water with her boys, obviously unperturbed by the incident. Still, she supposed she couldn't blame the kids. It wasn't the boys' fault that they had incompetent parents.

She heard Sally call her from reception. "Nicola, telephone – line three!"

"I'll take it from upstairs, Sally, thanks!" Nicola dried her hands and called the lift. Back in her office, she pressed the blinking extension light.

"Nicola Peters speaking."

A slight throat-clear at the other end. "Hello, Nicola, Dan here."

It was as though she could feel every cell in her body constrict with tension but amazingly, her voice when she spoke sounded casual, almost ordinary.

"Dan, how are you – it's been a while."

He cleared his throat again. "Um, welcome back . . . um . . . I mean, I didn't realise you were back in Ireland and . . ."

Welcome back? Was that it?

"What do you want, Dan?" she asked, sitting forward in her seat.

He hesitated. "I just wondered if we could meet up – for coffee, or something."

Silence.

"Please, Nicola. I'd really like to talk to you."

Nicola bit her lip. She wanted to see him too but she didn't know if she could stand it. How could she look into those eyes again, those ice-blue eyes that would undoubtedly remind her of what they had lost? She had battled too long and too hard for that. Anyway, she was fine now, she had Ken, and she loved him and . . .

"I'm not sure, Dan. We're very busy here at the moment."

"The leisure centre, yes. I'm pleased for you." She knew by the sound of his voice that he was smiling.

"Yes."

Then he sighed. "Nicola, I don't know if Laura told you . . ."

"About the wedding? Yes, she did." She wasn't going to tell him that she had actually *seen* the wedding invitations.

"Well, I'm sorry you had to find out like that. I would have told you, but I had no way of contacting you, and I didn't know you were back. I'm sorry. I hope that –"

"Dan – forget it. It's not a problem," she interjected breezily. "If it's the reason you're phoning, or if you're worrying about it, then don't. You didn't have to tell me anything. We're divorced now, remember?"

She heard him breathe deeply – with relief, she thought. Good old Dan and his guilt. Not that his guilt had stopped him before. Back then guilt was the last thing on Dan's mind . . .

"I know, but I just thought –"

"Dan, I'm sorry, but I really have to go. It's very busy," she interjected quickly. "I wish you well with the wedding, and I hope you'll be very happy."

"Do you really mean that, Nic?" he asked, his voice soft and hopeful.

Nicola felt her heart sink to her stomach. *Did* she mean it – after everything? But surely she *should* be happy for Dan – happy that he had found someone else to love, as she had with Ken.

But had she moved on, really? Lately, Nicola wasn't sure. Sure, everything was going fantastically for her now, and she had absolutely no regrets about coming home to Ireland, and no regrets about the divorce. And, of course, falling in love with Ken was the best thing that could possibly have happened to her.

But yet, news of Dan seemed to have stirred up old feelings – feelings Nicola thought she had successfully buried a long time ago. Why couldn't Dan have just got on with his life, and she with hers, without any interference? Why, out of all people, did Laura's wedding invites have to get mixed up with her ex-husband's? Why drag it all up again?

But then again, Nicola thought, maybe this was it. She hadn't seen Dan in almost four years since . . .well, since everything. Maybe, if she met with him now, and didn't feel anything, then she would be free to move on for good.

So maybe that's what she should do.

Nicola took a deep breath. "You're right, Dan. We should meet up for coffee, sometime. I'd love to hear all about the new Mrs Hunt." She injected some warmth into her voice.

"That would be really great, Nic. I'd love to see you." He sounded pleased, but Nicola thought, also a little surprised.

"Well, I'll give you a call then."

"Where are you living at the moment?" Dan asked, and she sensed that he didn't want the conversation to end just yet.

"Stepaside, at the moment," she said, not giving him too much information.

"Oh – nice area. What's the house like?"

"I'd prefer that we didn't meet at my place, Dan."

"Of course." Dan sounded as though he had temporarily forgotten himself.

"Well, as I said, I'll give you a call."

"You have the number?"

"I think so." The number of O'Leary Hunt Chartered Accountants was etched somewhere in her brain, even after all this time.

"OK, well, nice to talk to you again, Nic. Oh, by the way, I saw the magazine article. You looked great."

"Oh!" Nicola was surprised by this. "Thank you."

"I'd better go – talk to you soon then."

"Yes."

187

She replaced the receiver, and stared unseeingly at the phone for what seemed like ages, trying to decide whether or not she had made the right decision.

* * *

Nicola drove home afterwards, her thoughts going a mile a minute. It was so strange, speaking to Dan again after all this time. And the conversation had been almost . . . well, almost *casual*, considering.

And he had seen the article in *Mode*, too. She wondered if Dan realised that Motiv8 was Ken's enterprise, as he hadn't actually been mentioned by name in the article. What would Ken think of all this, she wondered. She'd certainly tell him about Dan's phone call anyway, and that they had arranged a meeting. He wouldn't be too pleased, but she was certain he would understand that she had to see Dan and more importantly, *why* she had to see him. He had always known there was a possibility that Dan would re-emerge in Nicola's life at some stage, so why not now?

She wished she could tell him immediately, but he was over at his dad's tonight. Nicola smiled. The Harrises were a close family, and Ken was an extremely dutiful son. She had met Pat and Clodagh Harris many times over the last few months. They were fantastic people who had taken to her immediately, and thankfully, Nicola thought, had absolutely no reservations about her relationship with their son. She had been a little concerned at the beginning that they might have a problem with her being a divorcee and all that, but she needn't have worried.

Still, she thought, turning into her driveway, she couldn't

be blamed for worrying – after all she had to put up with from the Hunts.

Nicola recalled how, at the beginning of her and Dan's relationship, she had been so looking forward to meeting his parents. She had no idea what kind of reception awaited her when, one Sunday, he suggested that they pop up to Longford to see them. By then, Nicola was sure that Dan was The One. There was no question about it. She loved this man with all her heart, and she wanted to spend the rest of her life with him. And as far as Nicola knew, Dan felt exactly the same.

So it was with great excitement, and not an ounce of trepidation, that she jumped at the chance to meet Mr and Mrs Hunt for the very first time.

Actually thinking back on it now, Nicola remembered that the first time hadn't been all that bad.

The Hunt residence was situated just outside Longford town, and Nicola's immediate impression upon approach was that someone in the family – probably Mrs Hunt – must be an adept gardener. The grounds were magnificent. A host of rhododendron bushes in full spring bloom, some of which must have been about fifteen feet tall, bordered the cobbled driveway – and the house itself, an impressive mock-Swiss design, was swathed with mature clematis intertwined with a heavy vine creeper. Towering cordylines, eucalyptus and monkey-puzzles surrounded the perimeter, and various species of ornamental grass flourished dramatically from underneath the windowsills. To Nicola, who was idealistic about gardening but in reality couldn't keep potted geraniums alive, the place was an absolute paradise.

Judging by the silver Mercedes S-class and the Cherokee Jeep parked in front of the house, the Hunts weren't short of a bob or two. Dan had told her that, although now close to retirement, his father was managing director of a building firm and that his mother had never worked.

"I know it's unfashionable these days," he had said, "but Mum never wanted to be anything other than a housewife. Both her parents were doctors and rarely at home and Mum decided that she didn't want that for me – she wanted to be there and have a home-cooked meal waiting for me after school each day."

Nicola nodded. Her mother had always been there for her and her brother, Jack, too.

"Well, here we are," Dan announced, as they pulled up outside the house. Nicola stepped out of the car and looked around. She had brought some handmade chocolates and a small bunch of lilies as a gift for Dan's mum, but the arrangement looked pathetic against the lush blooms surrounding the house.

Dan took her hand and gave an excited smile as they entered the hallway.

"Mum, Dad – it's me, where are you?" he shouted.

"Well, hello there." An older, more distinguished, but equally attractive version of Dan appeared in the doorway. "You must be the famous Nicola," he said, extending a hand.

As they shook hands she sensed that Jarlath Hunt must have been one hell of a charmer in his younger days. And although his hairline had receded to nothing and his face was lined and weathered, she thought that Dan's father was, even now, a very attractive man. It must be the eyes, she thought. It had been Dan's ice-blue gaze that had melted Nicola's heart in the first place, and now an older, but altogether colder version of that gaze was concentrating on her at that very moment.

"Welcome to our home," he said formally. "My wife is in the kitchen, just through there."

Upon first impression, Nicola thought that Annabel Hunt looked considerably older than her husband, although she wasn't sure if it was the poorly applied make-up or the shapeless clothes that gave her that idea. She was tall and wiry, and her white-blonde hair had obviously been freshly styled, but did nothing to disguise her drawn features. When shaking hands, Mrs Hunt looked distinctly unfriendly, and Nicola wondered if perhaps this visit had been forced upon, rather than been invited by her.

"You have a very beautiful home, Mrs Hunt," she said, hoping to break the ice, which seemed thicker than the iceberg that sank the *Titanic*, "and your garden is truly amazing – it must have taken years of great care to have it looking like that."

"You'll have to ask Jarlath about that," she replied dismissively. "It's always been his baby and I don't have much time for gardens myself." The edge to her tone was unmistakable, and Nicola knew instantly that Mrs Hunt didn't like her. She wondered then if it was just her, or was Dan's mother distrustful of all her son's girlfriends?

"Well, it's very beautiful, anyway," she said with a polite smile as Mrs Hunt turned away and went back to chopping vegetables.

"Nic, will you have a glass of wine, or something?" Dan asked her.

She smiled with relief. "I'd love a small one, thanks."

"Dad?"

"Drinking in the middle of the day, Dan? I don't think so."

Nicola looked at him. Oh, well, *excuuuse* me, she thought. You'd swear that one glass of wine would result in her and Dan getting fluthered and starting an all-out rendition of 'The Green Fields of France'! What was Jarlath's problem, she wondered, taking a large gulp from her own glass and praying that the wine would help settle her unease.

Mrs Hunt said little throughout dinner. Nicola complimented her on her genuinely delicious cooking, but when Dan's mother declined to comment other than with a quick nod, she gave up. What was the point? Nicola knew enough about human nature to know that it was hopeless ingratiating herself with the woman in the hope that she would soften her attitude. For reasons unknown, she was plainly determined not to like Nicola.

Jarlath's curiosity more than made up for his wife's reticence, however. He was full of questions and wanted to know everything about her – where she worked, she lived, her family, her ambitions – everything. He was so businesslike about it that Nicola was expecting him to come out with the 'where do you see yourself in five years time?' question.

"Leisure management? What does that involve – organising golf-trips, or something?" He laughed as he said this but to Nicola, there was no mistaking the scorn behind it.

"Not exactly," she said with a tight smile. "Leisure management involves the day-to-day running of a leisure centre – swimming-pool, gym, fitness programmes, spa, aerobics, that type of thing."

"Oh? And how did an intelligent-looking girl like yourself get into something like *that*?" The way he said it, it was as though Nicola was down in Benburb Street every night touting for business.

"I studied for three years in college to get into something like that," she answered, wishing that she could tell him where to go. This felt like some kind of test. The way Dan went on about them, you'd swear that his parents were contenders for a remake of the Waltons. But his mother had been rude from the very beginning, and now his father was being downright condescending.

After dinner, when the plates had been cleared, the foursome went into the Hunts' spacious and comfortable lounge. Nicola tried to relax and assumed a casual posture on the comfy leather suite.

"How are plans for the practice going, Dan?" his father asked.

"Very well, actually." Dan's eyes lit up. "We're drawing up the final draft of the partnership agreement at the moment, and hopefully we'll secure the lease on the office by the end of the month."

Jarlath nodded. "Let me have a look at the agreement before signature, will you?"

"Dad, I've worked with John O'Leary for years. I know what I'm doing." Dan sounded annoyed.

"No matter. With any legal document you should always have a professional look it over."

"You hardly think I'd get into this without at least consulting a solicitor, Dad. I'm not totally stupid."

Nicola listened to the exchange with interest. Jarlath was speaking to his son as though he was an immature sixteen-year-old.

"Nevertheless . . ." Jarlath insisted.

Dan gave up. "OK, I'll fax you a copy of it when it's finished."

The two men chatted some more about the practice, leaving Nicola and Mrs Hunt sitting in uncomfortable silence together on the couch. Eventually Mrs Hunt brought herself to say something.

"So, Nicola, you're from Dublin?" she asked as though she was trying to coax a spider out of the bath by talking to it.

Nicola nodded. "Through and through. I was born in the Coombe and raised not far from it – Crumlin, to be precise."

"Oh – the inner city, then?" Her patronising tone was unmistakable.

"Well, not exactly, but close enough." Nicola was half tempted to tell Mrs Hunt that she had been raised in a block of drug-dealing flats, rather than a perfectly respectable corporation three-bedroom semi. That would give the silly bitch a shock. And so what if she had been? Nicola's parents had done a great job and she and her brother had never wanted for anything. They had a full education, had both gone to college – Nicola to study Leisure Management in Finglas and Jack Computer Science in DIT – and went on to have successful careers as a result. Carmel Peters, in particular, had instilled a fierce sense of independence into both of her children. How she had been raised had a lot to do with the person Nicola was now and, if anything, it had ensured she was more than able for the likes of these two snobs. How the hell had the Hunts raised someone as mild-mannered and down-to-earth as Dan?

"Yes. I live in Rathfarnham now, but ideally I'd love to move back. Impossible though," she shook her head sadly. "Unfortunately property prices there have gone through the roof!"

"In Dublin certainly, but hardly in the *inner city*?" That expression again, Nicola thought. She might as well have been talking about downtown Kabul.

"Absolutely. It's *the* place to live at the moment. Rather like Manhattan, I suppose – you know – the closer you are to everything the more expensive the property prices? Anyway my parents are still there, lucky things – sitting on a goldmine they are, but, of course, they wouldn't sell up for anything."

She wasn't about to add that the Peters were still trying to pay off their corporation mortgage but Mrs Hunt's look of bewilderment was worth the fib.

"I see," Annabel poured herself a glass of mineral water and didn't ask any more questions. After a while, Nicola found the silence and tension unbearable and she was desperate to leave. She was relieved when finally Dan looked at this watch and suggested they head back to Dublin.

"I think they were crazy about you – what do you think?" he asked happily as they drove towards town.

Nicola looked at him. "Um, I'm not really sure about that, Dan."

"Oh, come on! My dad was drooling over you!"

"Do you think so?" Nicola thought that she might have misread the signals.

"Definitely. And Mum . . ." his face clouded a little, "Mum can be a bit shy sometimes."

Shy? Stuck-up dragon, more like!

"I guessed that," she said diplomatically. She suspected the Hunts detested her, but if Dan thought they got on OK, then that was the main thing. "Although I'm sure that once your mother gets to know me better," she added, knowing it was probably wishful thinking, "we'll all get on absolutely fine."

* * *

The next time she and the Hunts met, it was to announce the engagement. It wasn't long after he and John had officially opened O'Leary Hunt Chartered Accountants and Dan had invited them for dinner at the apartment he was renting temporarily in Bray.

"Dad, Mum – we have an announcement to make," he said, looking boyishly from his parents to Nicola. "We're getting married."

"*Married*?" Mrs Hunt pealed. "What do you mean married? You've only been going out a wet week."

Nicola remembered her heart dropping like a stone at the time. God only knows what Dan felt.

"Dan," Jarlath began nervously, "surely you should wait a little longer before you start making decisions like this, at least until the business is up and running."

"What are you talking about, Dad? The business has got nothing to do with this. I've asked Nicola to be my wife, and she's accepted. We want to get married as soon as we can."

"But what's the rush?" his mother cried, giving Nicola

a look of such blatant disdain that she recoiled. "Oh, you've gone and got yourself into trouble, haven't you?"

That was enough for Nicola. She kept her voice even, but her tone was pure ice.

"Mrs Hunt, with all due respect, this isn't the Dark Ages. I suspect that 'getting into trouble' refers to the possibility that I would deliberately set out to get pregnant in order to trap your son. Please give Dan and me *some* credit. We're hardly a pair of immature teenagers." She could tell that her calm and eloquent speech had completely disconcerted Mrs Hunt, who stood there with pursed lips as Nicola continued. "We're in love, and we want to get married. What could possibly be wrong with that?"

"Well, it's all a little bit convenient, isn't it?" she spat. "A few months ago we didn't know you from Adam, and then no sooner than Dan sets up on his own, you're crawling all over him."

"Mum!" Dan was aghast.

"Mrs Hunt, if you're implying that I am some kind of money-grabber, can I remind you again that we're living in the new millennium, and that very few women these days are in need of a man to support them." *Except yourself*, she wanted to add.

"Rubbish! The likes of you will always be looking for a man to support them. You think you've really landed on your feet, don't you? Well, we know all about you and your corporation upbringing."

"What?" Nicola didn't think she had heard right. She knew that Dan's parents were snobs but surely . . . at that moment she had been too gobsmacked to come up with anything in reply, but Dan had no such problems.

"Get out, both of you," he shouted at them. "How dare you! How dare you speak to my fiancée like that? I've met her family and their pet *cat* has more integrity in his right paw than either of you two put together – now *get out!*"

"Dan, you could be making a big mistake here," Nicola heard Jarlath say as they were unceremoniously escorted to the hallway. "We know what we're talking about and that girl is all wrong for you."

"Dad, you haven't a fucking clue!"

"Well, it's easy to see where you picked up language like that," Annabel said nastily, before Dan closed the door in her face.

He looked shocked when he came back into the room. "Jesus, I'm so sorry, Nicola. I don't know what to say. Mum has always been a little stuck up but, Christ, you'd think Dad would have a little more cop-on!"

"It's OK, Dan," Nicola said quietly.

"It's not bloody OK! What I said about your family there was true! Your parents are both terrific people, which is more than I can say for mine!"

"Dan, stop," Nicola had never seen him so upset. "Look, I don't mind. It's just the way they are." She was upset too, but she didn't want to risk an all-out war with the Hunts. She loved Dan too much.

"Well, *I* mind! I'm so embarrassed, Nicola. I don't know what to say."

Nicola smiled, put her arms around her fiancé and told him to forget it – they shouldn't let it cloud their happiness. Still, she knew then that any notions she might have had of easing her way into the Hunts' affections had that day gone completely by the wayside.

The Peters family's response to the news of their engagement however, had almost made up for the Hunts' unpleasant reaction. Tears of happiness and copious amounts of sparkling wine flowed for hours in Crumlin that night.

"Oh my God!" her mother whooped for joy when Nicola displayed her stunning solitaire. "My baby is getting married!" With that, she had hugged Dan so hard that he laboured for breath. "Welcome to the family, love!" she said, struggling to speak through happy tears.

Nicola grinned as her father shook Dan's hand and clapped him on the back. "Congratulations, lad!"

"Well, when's the big day and oh! When do we get to the meet the in-laws?" her mother said excitedly. "Oh, I've *always* wanted to say that!"

Nicola tensed. How could she tell her wonderful trusting mother that the in-laws were ignorant snobs who had already formed a derisory opinion about her?

"Well, I'm sure we'll all meet up before the wedding." Dan interjected quickly, seeing Nicola's torn expression. "Mum and Dad don't get down to Dublin very often, what with Dad being so busy."

"Of course – what with him being a big businessman and everything." Carmel nodded in agreement. "God, Nicola, wait 'til I tell Betty Corcoran! She'll be green!" Carmel clapped her hands together.

Later that night, Nicola informed her brother of her news and Jack was equally thrilled for them, assuring that he would be home soon and then they could have a real family celebration. She couldn't remember the last time there was such a jubilant atmosphere in the Peters household. Nicola wished with all her heart that the

Hunts had reacted the same way – it was the one blight on her happiness.

Later that evening, when she and Dan returned to her apartment, Nicola confessed her worries about the two sets of parents meeting at the wedding.

"With all due respect, I'm not really concerned about your parents. They've made their feelings about me more than clear, but I don't want them upsetting my mother. She's doesn't deserve that."

Dan nodded. "I've thought about that myself. Nicola. You don't know how sorry I am about all of this. I cringe when I think about the things they said to you."

"I can handle myself. I'm just not so sure about Mam. You know what she's like, Dan – she'd be all over your mother, hoping to get friendly with her. I know that it would break her heart if your mother snubbed her, not to mention that it would break mine too."

"I know that, love. I want our wedding day to be the happiest day of our lives, and believe me, I'm not about to let my parents ruin it by causing aggro."

"So what can we do? It's not as though we can keep them apart on the day."

"I think there's only one way out of it, then," Dan said seriously, but there was a twinkle in his eye.

"What?"

"Well, you said yourself that you weren't into the big white wedding thing, and all the hullabaloo surrounding it . . ."

Nicola smiled. Those were her words exactly. "So?"

"So why not just go away and get married, then – in the Caribbean, or Las Vegas, or something like that."

"Are you serious?" Nicola grinned, realising that he had come up with a perfect solution. If they went away somewhere and got married by themselves, then both sets of parents could be kept apart, and there would be little or nothing to organise.

"And maybe Jamie and Helen, and Laura and Neil might be tempted to come with us," said Dan.

She was sure the gang would jump at the chance. Jamie and Helen took foreign holidays on a regular basis, and although Laura and Neil Connolly hadn't been together all that long, Nicola was sure they would be thrilled to travel over for her wedding.

Maybe her mother might be a little taken aback, and disappointed that there would be no Big Day, but Carmel had raised her children to be completely independent, and Nicola knew that her mother would support her in whatever she wanted to do.

She laughed as Dan engulfed her in a huge hug, and swept her off the ground.

"That's settled then!" Dan said, and Nicola laughed as he whooped for joy. "The Caribbean, here we come!"

Chapter 16

Helen stood almost transfixed outside Brown Thomas.

That dress! Well, if you could call it a dress, Helen thought. It was Issey Miyake, daringly short – black and silver-embroidered at the bust. It was demure, but very sexy and would look just amazing with her newly bought, silver strappy heels. Not quite right for a wedding, but Paul would absolutely love her in it, and probably, Helen thought with a grin, love her even more *out* of it.

Lately, she couldn't keep the smile from her face and Helen felt better than she had in years. She and Paul had met a number of times since that first wonderful afternoon in the hotel and, each time, the sex was becoming more intense. It was crazy, they hardly knew one another, and yet it was as though they were in perfect sexual synch. Twice they had planned to meet for lunch, and twice they had ended up in bed at Paul's place in Ranelagh, unable to even *think* about food. And today, Paul had rung Helen at work and asked her to meet him for 'lunch' tomorrow.

Helen didn't know why he even bothered pretending that it would be lunch.

"Afterwards, we could try your place for a change of scenery," he had said, in a tone that had Helen already shifting in her seat.

But Helen wasn't prepared to have him stay at her apartment, not yet anyway. She needed to see how things went first, and whether or not she and Paul were as well matched personally, as they were physically.

Not to mention the tricky subject of Kerry.

Paul knew as little about Helen as she did about him, and they had barely got round to discussing their jobs, let alone their family situations.

No, Helen thought, imagining Paul's reaction to her in that dress, there was no point in saying anything about Kerry until the time was right.

She gave a quick glance at her watch. Six twenty. It was late-night shopping, and Jo had agreed to keep Kerry until seven o'clock, to give Helen a chance to pick up something for Laura's wedding.

Right. She'd go in, try on the dress, and maybe have a quick run-around. She'd be a little late collecting her daughter, but Helen *had* to have that dress. Yes, it was expensive, but sometimes a girl just had to treat herself, didn't she? And what was the point of having these feel-good endorphins gushing around your insides if you couldn't enjoy them? It wasn't all that long ago that she was miserable, so she might as make the most of her current mood. Helen raced into the store, conveniently forgetting about her shoe blitz in Office only a week before.

But Brown Thomas was no place for a 'quick run-around'. Once inside, Helen was dazzled by the fantastic array of clothes, handbags, and as for the shoe basement – God – it was almost indecent! By the time she left the store almost an hour and a half later, Helen had picked up a cute Marni handbag, another pair of Jimmy Choos (but these would go with just *everything*), and probably the entire Agent Provocateur Spring/Summer Collection. And because she would now almost certainly be late collecting Kerry, Helen had raced downstairs to the perfume and make-up department, and chosen a 30ml bottle of Gucci Eau de Parfum for Jo. There was something terribly indulgent about buying anything Gucci, she thought, handing over her credit card and idly wondering if maybe she should get a bottle for herself while she was at it. No, she decided firmly. Enough was enough. Although she could do with some new make-up and Ruby & Millie did some amazing lipsticks . . .

By the time Helen reached Jo's house near Cornelscourt, it was well after eight.

"I'm so sorry, Jo," Helen started with the explanations as soon as she got out of the car. The front door was open, and as she approached, Helen knew by her expression that Jo was *very* annoyed. Shit! "The traffic was crazy and –"

"Helen!" Jo interjected angrily. "I told you that Pete and I were going out for an anniversary dinner tonight. The only reason I agreed to keep Kerry late was because you promised me you'd be back by seven, and you told me you were desperate!"

Helen stopped short. She had never even heard Jo raise her voice, let alone bite her head off. Still the perfume would pacify her, wouldn't it?

"Hold on a second, Jo," she began. "It's not as though I was late on purpose. I told you that the traffic was mental and there was no way I could have got here by seven." She looked behind Jo in the hallway. Where the hell was Kerry? After a day like Helen had at work today, she just wasn't able for this tirade. At this stage, she just wanted to just grab her daughter and run. "Oh, and I got you a present," she added, quickly holding out the tiny Brown Thomas bag.

"Really?" Jo drawled, completely ignoring Helen's peace offering. "The traffic was mental, was it? So how come my husband, who works on the Northside, left the office at *six*, and was well home by seven?"

Helen cringed inwardly. Shit – she'd forgotten all about Pete.

"Jo, look, I promise I'll make it up to you, OK?" she began quietly. Maybe honesty was the best policy here. "I was in the *centre* of town and it was very busy, and I just didn't notice the time going and –"

Jo's eyes narrowed. *"You didn't notice the time going! In other words, you just didn't bother your backside leaving town until you were good and ready."*

"No, no, that's not it at all."

"It *is* it, Helen Jackson. It's *always* it with you. Honestly, only for the fact I adore that daughter of yours, I would have told you exactly where to go a long time ago!"

Helen stepped back. Where was all this coming from?

"Jo, I was only a half an hour late –"

"Try an *hour* and a half, but that's not the point, is it? You're *always* late, Helen! You're *never* here at five, and then you flounce in all excuses for being late, but no apology for putting us out. Then in the mornings you call too early! Jesus, Helen, if you're not interrupting our dinner, then you're interrupting our breakfast by dropping her off at all hours of the morning! But then again, we're lucky if you remember to collect her at all!"

Helen reddened. Jo was referring to that first afternoon Helen had met Paul.

She had been so dazed and so euphoric after their afternoon together, she had driven straight home in another world, almost forgetting to pick up Kerry. And of course at the time, Helen had to open her big mouth and jokingly admit to an unimpressed Jo that she *had* almost forgotten.

"Now, hold on just a minute, Jo. That was only one time and –"

"But it shouldn't happen, Helen!" Jo lowered her voice, and glanced behind her in the hallway. "Look, I asked Pete to keep Kerry occupied, because I didn't want her to hear any of this when, and *if*, you called. She's upset enough as it is."

"Jo, that's not fair."

"Helen, of *course* it's not fair. It's not fair to that poor little sweetheart in there who absolutely adores you, but doesn't get anything in return! Do you realise Kerry spends most of the day telling us, in her own sweet way, what Mummy does and what Mummy says! But we can see the worry in her eyes when five o'clock comes around and Mummy's not here yet. Your daughter is as good as gold, and she genuinely worships you, but you don't realise it. You don't realise what a blessing that child is and how any mother, any *norm*al mother would be so proud to have her as their own."

There were tears in Jo's eyes, and Helen knew that she was no doubt getting maudlin over the child she herself had miscarried last year. Still, there was no need for her cheek and downright rudeness towards Helen, who, after all, paid her handsomely for the privilege (or so it seemed) of looking after Kerry!

Helen's expression was hard. "I'm very sorry that you feel that way, Jo. However, you seem to have conveniently forgotten that I *pay* you for looking after my daughter – you're not doing me any favours. And I'm not stingy with Christmas presents or any other kind of presents for you. That is Gucci perfume, Jo! And how many times have I asked you if I can get you anything when I'm going into town?" Helen crossed her arms across her chest. "Funnily enough, I thought you and I were friends. How was I supposed to know you were pissed off at me for turning up late to collect Kerry? You never said so." What did Jo think Helen was, some kind of mind-reader?

"For God's sake, Helen –"

Helen put up a hand to silence her. "No, no, we might as well have it out here and now. As Kerry seems such a trial to put up with, then you won't mind me taking her off your hands for good." That'd change her tune, Helen thought, knowing that Jo and her husband Pete weren't exactly rolling in it. They relied on Jo's childminding to keep them going.

"That's fine, Helen." Jo said shortly. "Because that's exactly what I came out here to tell you. I don't want to take Kerry any more, and God knows it has nothing to do with the child. It's you, Helen! You and your blasted selfishness, and the way you treat her! It breaks my heart to see her struggling with her speech like she does, and I know damn well that your attitude isn't helping."

"How dare you? What the hell do you know about bringing up a child?" she said nastily. Jo winced, but Helen didn't back down. "Yes, you think you know it all, don't you, sitting on your backside every day watching Marty Whelan on the telly while your husband goes out to earn a crust. Well, you know nothing about it, Jo. You know nothing about having to work long hours, and your fingers to the bone to keep that child in the luxury she's used to!"

Jo gave her a sceptical look. "Your fingers to the bone? Helen. You have a professional manicure twice a month, so fearful are you of messing up your nails. So don't play the martyr with me!" She turned back inside. "I'm going to say goodbye to Kerry now, and goodness knows I don't want to. If it were up to me, I'd probably put up with all your carry-on just for the pleasure of spending time with that wonderful little girl. But Pete has put his foot down."

"Well, Pete can bloody well lift his foot back up again, before I stamp on it!" Helen said shakily to Jo's retreating back. "And I'd never have left any of you *near* my daughter in the first place, had I known you felt that way about me!"

Just then a grim-looking Pete appeared in the doorway. "I'd appreciate it if you didn't carry on like a fishwife on my doorstep, Helen."

"Oh, well, *excuse* me!" Helen stormed. "I'll wait in the car, and when you and Mrs Sanctimonious are finished 'saying your goodbyes' you can send my daughter out to me."

Pete shook his head. "You know, I feel sorry for people like you," he called after her.

"Excuse me?"

"I feel sorry for people who don't appreciate what a wonderful gift it is to have a child, especially a child like Kerry."

Helen rolled her eyes. "Spare me the sentimental rubbish, Pete," she said, getting into the front seat and slamming the driver door.

A few minutes later, a tearful Kerry joined her in the car. "J-J-J-Jo don't w-w-want to m-m-mind me any more, Mommy," she said, her bottom lip curling.

Helen started the engine. "No, *Mommy* doesn't want Jo to mind you any more, pet."

"Then w-w-who –" Kerry tried to take a breath, but was so upset she couldn't get the remainder of the sentence out.

But Helen knew exactly what she meant.

"I don't know who'll mind you from now on, Kerry," she answered grimly, thinking of her upcoming lunch with Paul, "but we'll have to find someone."

* * *

The following afternoon, Laura soldered the last freshwater pearl onto a thin strand of silver wire. Then, holding it carefully with a tweezers, she lifted one of the silver coated leaves she had painstakingly fashioned the week before, and positioned it at the base of what now was beginning to look like a tiara. It was so delicate though; Laura knew it wouldn't tolerate any abuse. She'd have to make sure the hairdresser at home was gentle with it on the day of the wedding.

Next, she would begin work on her own and the

bridesmaid's neckpieces, as well as a smaller replica of her own tiara for Kerry. It was just as well that she had all that to do, she thought with a sigh, because there was precious little else.

Laura Connolly Jewellery Design hadn't taken off with quite the fanfare Laura had expected. Not that she *really* imagined everything would just fall into place, and that people would be climbing over themselves for her designs. It was just that after a few weeks in business, she thought there might have been *some* interest. She had invested a lot of time and money in the sample packs she sent to the jewellers and gift stores, and had followed some of them up with timid phone calls, enquiring as to whether or not they were interested in stocking her. But the response so far had been dismal.

Laura didn't really mind initially, because she was so excited and enthusiastic at the prospect of actually having time to get stuck into her designs. In the beginning, she often lost herself in her work, and the days would be gone before she knew it. Days whereby the phone might only ring once or twice, with either Neil or the girls wondering how she was getting on. And Laura was getting on fine, she was getting on wonderfully, she was coming up with all sorts of ideas, and was trying lots of different designs and lots of different materials.

"But have you sold anything yet?" Helen asked, in her typically direct manner.

And Laura had to admit that no, she hadn't sold a thing. She hadn't even had a single enquiry. Apart from that big order on the internet.

Laura cringed when she thought about it now. How

could she have been so stupid? She had logged into her email one morning, and was thrilled (and relieved) to find a huge order for a selection of items from one of her key ranges – namely the silver ethnic-style chokers and matching bracelets. Laura had put the (considerable) amount through the credit-card terminal, and had spent all day and most of the night crafting the additional items she needed to fulfil the order.

Neil was delighted for her. "What a boost!" he had said. "And imagine someone all the way from Indonesia ordering from you!"

The customer had sent Laura a follow-up email, asking that she 'overnight' the order, and that she should charge the additional expense to his credit card. Thinking that he must really be keen, Laura had done so, and had sent the entire order off to Indonesia with an astonishing sense of achievement. Things were finally starting to happen.

Her sense of achievement was very short-lived. One day soon after, she received a letter from Amex Credit Card Services, explaining that the transaction was invalid, and that the full amount would be charged back to her business account.

Laura had phoned the credit-card centre, almost in tears. "But how could it be invalid?" she asked. "The terminal authorised it – twice!" With dismay, she thought not only of the cost of the order, but the expensive courier charges.

"Well, it appears that your customer was using a stolen card, dear." The bank's representative was terribly sympathetic. "Unfortunately, if the transaction is through email, you have no way of knowing if the person ordering is the authorised user."

"But the payment system on my website is completely safe. It's encrypted – there's no way anyone could –"

"Unfortunately this has nothing to do with website safety. The person involved gained possession of a stolen card. How, we don't know. But in the absence of a signature . . ."

And that was it. Laura had lost not only some of her most expensive stock, as well as the staggeringly expensive overnight courier cost, but she had also lost a great deal of confidence.

In fairness, Neil was great at keeping her spirits up. "Well, you should just chalk it up to experience, and be that little bit more cautious the next time," he had said.

"Maybe now is the time to concentrate on fine-tuning your product range, and getting your stock built up, to sell directly to suppliers. Who knows, when you *are* busy, you mightn't have any time to spend on actually making the things!"

But Helen had suggested a different approach. "Get out on the streets! Talk to the store managers face to face. Don't hide behind a telephone call," she urged Laura. "I'm betting they haven't even seen your designs – the staff probably took one look at them and thought 'great, a freebie' and took your gorgeous handcrafted earrings home with them. To have any hope of selling any product, but especially *your* products, you have to get them in front of the right people."

But Laura couldn't bring herself to start doing that, not just yet anyway. It was all right for Helen; she was a natural saleswoman, good-looking, flirty and unashamedly confident. Laura wouldn't know what to say; she'd more than likely end up causing more harm than good, her potential customers wondering what on earth was that eejit mumbling about? Anyway, they could always visit the website if they wanted to see what her designs were like.

In fairness, if Laura got a big order now she might not even be able to fulfil it, what with the wedding coming up and everything. Maybe it was just as well that things were slack, at least for the time being.

And the Golden Pages wasn't out yet, so she couldn't really expect the phone to be ringing off the hook, when nobody knew where to find her. Once the directory was in circulation, and the half-page ad on which she had spent a fortune appeared, she was sure to have some enquiries. Weren't they always saying in those radio ads that people's business doubled and tripled as a result of having their number in the Golden Pages?

Still though, double and triple of nothing wasn't much good.

Laura tried to clear her mind. She really had to stop thinking negatively. Things were bound to improve.

In fairness, it wasn't all doom and gloom. The Crafts Council had promised to circulate her name throughout the trade, and of course there was always the Crafts Exhibition, which incidentally was coming up soon. Yes, it was coming up soon after the wedding! Laura had almost forgotten about that.

That's what she'd do then, she thought, feeling a burst of energy that she hadn't felt in a while. She'd concentrate on coming up with the best possible designs, and showcase the very best of her skills at the exhibition.

Surely something would come out of that?

With renewed vigour, Laura set about finishing her wedding tiara and making a start on the jewellery for her bridesmaids.

Half an hour later, she was so engrossed in her work that she almost didn't hear the phone ringing.

Heart pounding in expectation (as always), Laura picked up.

"Laura, where were you? I almost hung up!" Helen sounded frantic.

"In the workshop – why, what's wrong?"

Helen took a deep breath. "I need to ask you a really *huge* favour."

"Sure, what?"

"Is there any chance you can collect Kerry from playschool today? She finishes at two."

"Out in Loughlinstown?"

"Yes, look, I'm really sorry to ring you like this, but Jo has let me down and I have meetings all afternoon. Please, Laura? You'd be doing me a massive favour."

Laura thought about it. She'd hardly get the wedding jewellery finished today if she had to traipse all the way out to Loughlinstown and back on a Friday afternoon. Still, what else could she do? She wouldn't dream of leaving Kerry stranded out there. She wondered idly why Jo wasn't doing it. Helen's childminder was normally so reliable. Maybe she was ill or something.

"Laura?" Helen was waiting for her reply.

"Sorry, yes, yes, I'll do it – no problem."

Helen breathed an obvious sigh of relief. "I owe you one, Laura, I really do. I'd go myself only – only we're hoping to nail down a big account here, and I really need the commission."

"It's fine, Helen. Just make sure that her teacher knows *I'm* collecting her. If they're expecting her childminder – well, these days, they have to be sure."

"Oh, I've already told them – I mean, they already know that someone other than Jo will be collecting her," Helen said quickly. "I'll give them a ring now and tell them to look out for you."

"Right. And do you want me to drop her down to the office to you or . . .?"

There was a sharp intake of breath. "Is there any chance you could hold onto her for me? I'll call and collect her from your place after work."

Laura shrugged. "Sure. I'll see you later then. Good luck with the meeting."

"Yeah, thanks."

Laura hung up and went back into her workshop. It was just after twelve thirty so she might as well have a bite to eat now, before heading off to collect Kerry. She'd need to leave here by quarter past one at least. She sighed. Not a chance of getting any more work done before lunch, then. Still, it wasn't as if she was bogged down, and Helen needed the favour.

Wasn't it really lucky though that she was able to get away when she felt like it? Otherwise poor Helen would be really stuck.

* * *

At two o'clock that afternoon, exactly the time Laura reached Kerry's playschool, her phone began to ring.

After six rings the answering machine came on, and Laura's pleasant tones filled the empty workshop.

"Hello, thank you for calling Laura Connolly Jewellery Design. We are unavailable to take your call just at the moment, but please leave your name and number, and we will call you back as soon as possible."

A short throat-clear after the beep. "Hello? Sorry, I'm on a mobile and it's a bad line. I saw your stuff on the internet and I . . . ink it's great! My name is Ge . . . lden and I wanted to speak to someone . . . out the possibility of having an engagement ring commissioned. I was hoping for something really unusual, and I have a few ideas myself. Something . . . pecial and money's . . . object. I'm planning to propose soon – during a holiday, actually – so I'd really like to . . . someone as soon as possible. My number is 086-2 . . . 26 . . . 68 . . . Thank you."

Chapter 17

That same evening, as she sat in a quiet pub on Bray seafront, Nicola was staring out the window at a young couple pushing a buggy along the pier. She was sipping frothy cappuccino and taking in the view around her.

It was a spectacular August afternoon. Seagulls soared above the sea, occasionally dipping down towards the waves, and further out a flotilla of yachts passed slowly along the coast, obviously making the most of the settled weather. It had been a long time since she'd been here.

"Are you OK there?" the young barman enquired, emptying the ashtray. "Is that table a bit high for you – or do you want me to move it?"

"Not at all, I'm fine thanks." Nicola smiled up at him. The pub was busy and it was a rare pleasure to find someone so helpful, not to mention considerate, in today's hustle and bustle.

When they lived in their rented apartment in Bray, she and Dan had spent many a Sunday afternoon walking lazily along the pier with the day-trippers, skateboarders and dog-walkers. She smiled. Dan could never resist stopping off at a kiosk to buy one of those whipped ice-cream cones he was so fond of. And according to him, it was no good at all unless it was totally slathered in raspberry sauce.

"Hi."

He appeared suddenly at her table as if from nowhere. Nicola felt her stomach spasm as she looked up into his face for the first time in over four years. He had aged, she thought. His hair was cut in a short crop, which emphasised his lined forehead, and he looked as though he could do with losing a few pounds. But he was still a very attractive man.

"Hello, Dan."

He was smiling, but she noticed that he too, looked slightly unsure. "I was almost afraid to disturb you. You looked as though you were miles away just then."

"Sit down." She gestured to the seat across from her. "Can I get you a coffee or something?" It was strange, but it was as if she didn't recognise her own voice.

"I've got one on the way – thanks." He pulled his chair forward, and rested an arm on the table. "Thanks for agreeing to meet me, Nic – I really wanted to see you. You look . . . terrific. How have you been?"

She wished he wouldn't call her 'Nic' like that. It was way too familiar.

"I'm very well thanks – you?"

"Not too bad."

He cleared his throat, and she sensed that he was struggling to say more, to move the conversation forward, yet he didn't quite know how. Nicola wasn't about to make it too easy for him.

There was a long tension-filled pause.

"So how did things go for you in London?" he asked eventually.

Nicola studied the bubbles on her cappuccino. "Not too bad. I'm still the same old me." She forced a smile. "I'm sorry, I suppose I should have told you I was back."

"No, you shouldn't. It would have been more than I deserved." He gave her a sad look. "It was a hell of a shock getting those papers like that."

"I know. But there was nothing else I could have done." Her mouth tightened. "I didn't want to see, or even speak to you back then."

"I know. I'm sorry."

Another pause.

"Did you get . . . I mean did your aunt pass on my letter?"

Of course, Ellen had passed it on. At one stage back then, Nicola could recite every word, every sentence. "Yes, she did, thank you." Then she smiled. "Look, let's not talk about old times, Dan." Nicola now felt unsure as to why she had come here, but she was certain she didn't want to rake up the past. What was the point? Anyway, seeing Dan in the flesh hadn't affected her as much as she had expected. All that time in London, she had thought about him, wondered how it would feel, how she would feel when she saw him again. But in truth, Nicola felt nothing other than . . . nostalgia. It was rather liberating.

Dan gave a rueful smile. "If you prefer. So tell me, how long have you been back?"

"Well over a year now. Ken Harris asked me to manage his new leisure centre. It's in Rathfarnham."

"Oh, really – and how *is* good old Ken these days?" His voice was hard.

Instantly Nicola put down her cup, and reached for her handbag. "This was a mistake."

Dan's face fell. "Oh look, I'm sorry. I couldn't help it. I have no right to say anything –"

"Dan, I didn't agree to meet with you so that we could take up where we left off. If we're trying here to be someway civil towards one another it would be best if we didn't drag up the past – *any* of it."

He nodded. "I'm sorry," he repeated. "It just popped out. I don't want to bring up the past either."

She nodded and tried to relax a little. She didn't want this meeting to blow up into a big waste of time. It had taken a lot to come here, and she had felt guilty enough about it as it was.

As planned, she had told Ken about Dan's phone call, and he hadn't been as understanding about their forthcoming meeting as she had expected.

"What the fuck does *he* want?" Ken had said, in a tone she had never heard him use before.

"He wants to talk, I suppose."

"But why now?"

"What do you mean?"

"Well, why didn't he want to *talk* when you came back home in the first place? Why didn't he want to *talk* long before you two divorced? But no, Dan couldn't do that, could he? He had to wait until you were back on your feet and living your life properly again, before he could burst his way back on the scene and cause maximum damage."

"That isn't it, love." Nicola was taken aback. Ken didn't think much of Dan and in fairness she couldn't blame him, but she hadn't expected him to be so bitter. "He's not 'back on the scene' as you put it. He's getting married again."

"Oh?" Ken was silent for a moment. "And who's the poor misfortunate he's marrying?"

"Ken!"

"What? What do you expect me to say – that I hope the two of them will be very happy, or something?"

Nicola looked at him. "What's really going on here, Ken? Why are you so annoyed about this?"

"I'm annoyed because it took you long enough to get over it all, and now you seem quite happy to invite Dan back into your life without a second thought!"

"Without a second thought? Of course I've thought about it, Ken! I've done nothing but think about it since . . ." she trailed off, realising she had revealed more than she intended.

Ken immediately picked up on this. "Since what? Have you been hiding something from me, Nikki?"

She sighed. "No, not as such. But I knew Dan was getting married again before he told me himself." She explained about the mix-up with the wedding invitations.

"Jesus! So, he probably had no intention of telling you himself and yet he snaps his fingers and you come running!"

"Hey, I'm not running anywhere, remember?" Nicola said, eyes flashing.

Ken hung his head. "I'm sorry. I just don't understand

why you feel such a need to meet with him. Surely a telephone call is enough."

"It's not that I need to – I *want* to."

Ken looked at her sadly. "Why? Do you still have feelings for Dan Hunt? Because if you do, then you really need to think hard about what you're doing with *me*. I love you, Nicola, and I know how things were for you back then. I don't want you to have to go through it all again."

"I know that, love. But meeting Dan again isn't going to affect what you and I have now. He's moved on, and I've moved on. That's all there is to it, believe me."

Ken gave her a watery smile, but Nicola knew he was still unsure – and definitely unhappy – about it all.

Now she looked across at Dan. "I suppose I might as well tell you – Ken Harris and I are together now."

"Together – as in *together*?" Dan's eyes widened.

"You look surprised." No, Nicola thought, he looked totally *shocked*.

"No, no – not surprised as such. I mean, I just didn't expect that you –"

"That I would find someone else? Whyever not, Dan?" Nicola chuckled inwardly at his panicked expression.

"No, it's not that. I mean . . . of course I knew you'd find someone else," he said, flustered. "I just didn't expect it to be Harris, that's all."

She smiled. That had certainly pulled the rug out from under him!

"So what about you?" Nicola asked, changing the subject. "How are the wedding plans coming along?"

Dan shot her a wary look, as if he hadn't expected her

to be so casual about it. "Ah, it's all busy, busy, busy. A bit too much fuss for my liking, to be honest."

"I can imagine. Is she younger than you – your fiancée?"

"Chloe? Not too much younger – she'll be twenty-eight soon."

"Chloe – nice name."

"Yes."

"So how long have you two been . . .?"

"Together? Not that long, just over a year," Dan said quickly.

"Oh, a short engagement then."

"Yes, Chloe was anxious to get married." He shrugged and trailed off as the barman approached with his coffee and they were both silent until he had retreated.

Dan sighed. "Nic, I just want to say how sorry I am that you found out second-hand about the wedding. I would have told you myself, but I had no idea you were back."

"Well, I hadn't planned on staying away for that long, but things seemed easier when I was away."

"I know."

Do you? She wanted to ask. Do you really?

Instead she asked, "What about you?"

"Me?"

"Yes. How are things going for you now? The practice going well?"

He nodded and took a mouthful of coffee. "Almost too well. We're constantly up to our eyes, and we can well afford someone permanent, but instead John keeps insisting that we take on these part-timers. Most of them are fresh out of college, and haven't the foggiest." He rolled his eyes as he set his cup down.

Despite herself, Nicola grinned. Even if these poor misfortunates had been in the business for years, Dan would still maintain that they hadn't 'the foggiest'. But trust John O'Leary to be watching the pennies.

"How is John these days – and Carolyn?"

"John's fine, but he and Carolyn are separated now."

"Oh!" Nicola was surprised. She had sensed that Carolyn was a little distant with her that day in town with Laura. Now she knew why.

"I know. I thought they'd make it but you just never know, do you?" She could feel the weight of his gaze on her face.

"No, you never know." Nicola looked out towards the pier.

There was a short strained silence.

"And what about Laura and Neil?" Dan said eventually. "They finally decided to tie the knot."

"Yes." Nicola smiled.

"I'm so pleased for them."

"Well, she deserves it, and Neil is a good man."

"Unlike some we could mention?"

Nicola giggled, knowing exactly what he meant. Before she and Dan were married, and long before her friend had even met Neil, Laura had been going out with a pompous know-it-all called James Gallagher, whom they all hated. Dan had managed to get on with him for appearances' sake, but Nicola, and indeed Helen, had disliked him passionately.

"You and Helen gave him such a hard time," Dan said with a groan. "Remember the time we went to that restaurant, that Thai one in town –"

"Do I what!" Nicola groaned. "And there he was, going on and on about the menu, pretending to be some kind of Thai connoisseur, just because he had a flight stopover in Bangkok once."

"And Helen told him that the Nurr Pud Piroth was the mildest dish on the menu, knowing full well that he couldn't even handle a Tikka Masala!" Dan guffawed at the memory. "For as long as I live, I'll never forget the expression on his face when he tasted that. It's not called Angry Beef for nothing."

Nicola grinned. "Well, it served him bloody right. And then, of course, he got in a big sulk with Jamie for laughing at him."

"How is Jamie? God, he was a gas man altogether. I haven't seen him in years."

"Neither has Helen," she said drily.

"What? What happened? I thought those two were together for life."

"A lot's changed since then, Dan. Helen has a daughter now. Kerry – she's a beautiful little thing, the spit of her mother."

"She met someone else?"

Nicola made a face. Trust Dan to assume that Helen was the one who caused the problem.

"No, Kerry is Jamie's daughter. But the pregnancy was unplanned and they went through a tough time after they found out about it." She shrugged. "Jamie took off to South Africa after deciding he wasn't able to face up to his responsibilities. He left her on her own, apparently not caring whether she sank or swam."

"Well," Dan said pausing carefully, "maybe he was

just frightened by the situation, and wasn't quite sure what to do."

"And what about her? She didn't have much of a choice, did she? What was *she* supposed to do?"

"Give him some time to get to grips with it all maybe?"

Dan looked her straight in the eye, and he and Nicola both knew that they were no longer talking about Jamie.

She looked away, and again there was a slight pause.

"Bloody Angry Beef!" Dan laughed again at the memory. "God! He really looked like he wanted to thump Jamie there and then. I've never seen a man look so upset!"

Despite herself, she smiled. "Well, as far as I know old Gallagher hasn't changed a bit."

"Well, more power to him, although I'd say it was a very long time before he ate Thai food again – if ever!"

The two talked some more about mutual friends, carefully skirting around their own circumstances, before eventually they ran out of inconsequential subject matter.

"Tell me more about Chloe." Nicola was satisfied she could speak about it so easily.

Dan looked unsure. "Chloe? Well, she works as a legal secretary at her dad's firm."

"Her dad's a solicitor?"

"Yes."

"Oh, your mother must be pleased." Nicola couldn't keep the bitterness out of her voice.

"Actually, she doesn't know Chloe all that well."

"I see." She waited for Dan to elaborate on this but he didn't. Instead he reached into his pocket and from his wallet produced a photograph of a stunning blonde.

Nicola studied the picture for a long moment. Wow.

"She's gorgeous," was all she said.

Dan laughed. "And doesn't she just know it!"

Nicola's chest tightened. Was she mad? Here she was sitting with Dan after all this time, and she was joking with him about his new wife-to-be! Was that progress, or just downright stupidity?

Just then, Dan's mobile shrilled loudly.

"Hello?" He looked at Nicola, and when he heard the voice on the other end his expression became guarded and his eyes lowered. "Hi."

By his tone, Nicola discerned it was Chloe. She looked away.

"No, I wasn't at the office. I'm – meeting a client."

Nicola marvelled at easily he could lie – still.

"No, hold on, Chlo . . . just slow down a minute . . . I don't understand . . . what kind of problem?" From what Nicola could make out, the other woman seemed frantic.

"What?" Now Dan was agitated. "You've got to be kidding me! OK, OK . . . just give me a half an hour or so and I'll meet you there." He hung up and then looked at Nicola, his expression weary and apologetic. "I'm so sorry about this, Nic, but I really have to go."

"Problems?"

"Yes." He rolled his eyes.

"Oh dear."

"Well, look – I really shouldn't –"

"Of course you should." Nicola put her empty mug on the table. "Dan, it was nice seeing you again."

Dan hesitated for a second and looked directly at her. "Nic, I really am so sorry."

The way he said it, she knew he wasn't just talking about having to rush off.

"It's OK, Dan, really." She gave him a small smile. "We'll talk again sometime."

"It was really good seeing you again."

"You too," Nicola said quietly, and let the man who had once been the love of her life rush away to meet another woman.

Chapter 18

Nicola had suspected from the very beginning that Shannon Fogarty was after her husband. She and Dan had worked at the same accountancy practice long before Nicola came on the scene, and before Dan and John went into partnership. The trio were close friends, and Shannon made no secret of her dislike of Dan's new girlfriend.

Dan had invited Nicola to a company dinner, and John's wife had tipped her off about Shannon beforehand. Dan and John were leaving directly from the office, and Nicola had arranged to drive to Bray for Carolyn and give her a lift to the restaurant. Nicola had always liked John's wife, and the two women clicked immediately upon their first meeting. Carolyn was chatty, bubbly and well able to handle John.

Carolyn had described Shannon in her typical succinct fashion.

"She's a fucking cow," she said, while retouching her lipstick in the car. "Very possessive of her 'boys', and she'll talk to you only if she feels like it. The first time I met her – a year or two ago now – I didn't know what I had done to offend. She looked at me like I was Myra Hindley!" Carolyn smacked her lips together. "So, I doubt she'll make *you* feel very welcome."

Nicola grimaced. "Great. We've only being going out a few weeks, I don't know half the people there and already one of them hates me."

Carolyn gave a little smile. "Oh, something tells me you'll be more than a match for our Ms Fogarty. And I for one can't wait for the sparks to fly!"

By the time they reached the restaurant in Terenure, Nicola and Carolyn were a little on the late side. John was seated at the table, but the chair beside him was empty and Nicola deduced that Dan must be either at the bar, or in the gents'. Carolyn giddily approached the table, having already had a few glasses of wine while waiting for Nicola to collect her.

"Hi, everyone!" she beamed. "Nice to see you all again. This is Nicola – the main reason Dan's been going around with a big fat grin on his face lately."

Nicola knew instantly that the tall, but surprisingly young redhead looking daggers at them was the famous Shannon. She could have killed Carolyn. Talk about winding the woman up. John's wife obviously took a sadistic pleasure in unsettling Shannon and while the people Nicola didn't already know shook hands with her and introduced themselves, Shannon sat button-lipped and completely ignored her.

"Hey, girls!" Dan appeared at the table, and put a protective hand on Nicola's back. "Sorry . . . I was talking to a guy in the gents'." Then he stood back and looked her up and down. "Wow, you look amazing!"

Nicola was wearing a white, knee-length silk dress with tiny gold butterflies running diagonally across the bias-cut skirt. The neckline plunged to a sharp 'v' emphasising her deep cleavage, and the white looked stunning against her dark colouring, helped of course by the copious amounts of fake tan she had been applying for most of that week.

"I know – she looks so stylish. I'd kill for a figure like that!" Carolyn, who was considered the epitome of glamour, and was also dressed to the nines, gave Nicola an almost imperceptible wink. "And I've never met *anyone* with such curves."

Nicola smiled self-consciously, and took a seat beside Dan.

Shannon peered across the table at her. "I must be mixing you up with someone else. You're not the aerobics girl, are you?"

Nicola pasted a smile onto her face, having already decided that she was not going to like this girl. "Not exactly. I'm a fitness instructor but we do a lot more at the centre than just aerobics."

"Oh?" Shannon took a sip from her wine. "You'd never know to look at her, would you, Maurice?" She nudged the quiet, grey-haired man beside her who in truth seemed slightly embarrassed by her comments. "And you seem *very* different from Dan's usual type," she added.

"You're right," Dan laughed, the implied insults going way over his head. "To be honest, I can't believe my luck. Nicola's *way* too good for the likes of me."

The others laughed as did Nicola, but daggers were

drawn as far as she was concerned. She'd let Shannon get away with her last comment, but only just.

All throughout dinner the other woman ignored her to the point of extreme rudeness. Twice Nicola asked her to pass the Parmesan, and twice Shannon paid no attention. The younger girl tried a number of times to engage Dan in conversation about past experiences, mutual friends, work – anything, it seemed, that would prevent Nicola from participating. At one stage, when Nicola vacated her seat alongside Dan to visit the ladies', she returned to find Shannon happily ensconced in her place, her arm linked possessively through her boyfriend's.

Nicola had known instantly that Shannon was little competition. She was coarse, loud and bitchy, and whatever looks she might have had were grossly overstated by her garish make-up, and shapeless clothing. Anyway, if Dan *was* interested in her, Nicola was sure he would have done something about it long before now.

No, it was the girl's ill-mannered behaviour that galled her.

Nicola walked purposefully back to her seat. As he saw her approach, Dan looked up and smiled. True to form, Shannon ignored her and tried to continue her poor attempts at flirtation. Out of the corner of her eye, Nicola could see Carolyn watching them with interest.

"Shannon, isn't it?" Nicola said sweetly, as if she hadn't really noticed her since their earlier conversation. "Hi, I'm Dan's girlfriend. We haven't really had a chance to chat properly. Why don't you pull up a chair and have coffee with us?"

In one fell swoop, Nicola had marked her territory,

made Shannon feel like the outsider and reclaimed her seat – while all the time coming across as being nothing other than friendly. In any other circumstances she would have told the girl exactly what she thought of her, but this was Dan's night, and these were Dan's friends. She wasn't about to make a show of him.

Shannon, it seemed, held no qualms in that regard.

"You're being a bit possessive, aren't you?" she said, still firmly rooted beside Dan. "He and I are just old friends."

"Really? You don't look *that* old," Nicola's tone was ultra-sweet. "I'd say thirty-four, thirty-five at the most." Truthfully, Shannon didn't look a day over twenty.

The younger girl obviously wasn't used to being on the other end of a bitchy comment, and couldn't think of anything in return. Nicola heard a muffled guffaw from behind, and knew that Carolyn was silently applauding her.

That was only the beginning. Dan gradually became aware of the fact that his girlfriend and close workmate didn't get on, but most of the time it wasn't a problem. They rarely met other than at company gatherings, and there hadn't been too many of those.

Soon, she and Dan were married and by the time they moved into their apartment in Bray, Nicola had almost forgotten about the dreaded Shannon. Dan and John had been making plans to set up a partnership and go out on their own. John, who already lived in Bray, had already amassed some potential new clients as well as poached others willing to move business to their new practice. It was unethical, but a silver-tongued John had convinced them by promising lower fees and a little 'tax avoision'.

He and Dan were working around the clock to get things moving.

Then, a few months after their wedding, Shannon began phoning Dan at the apartment at all hours of the morning, whining and crying over this guy and that, expecting him to comfort her.

"She's getting desperate," Carolyn had said, when Nicola complained to her about it. "She knows that Dan's leaving the company, and she's pulling out all the stops."

"He's married! Dan's no longer a free agent. Shouldn't that scupper her plans a little?"

Carolyn shrugged. "That one's imbalanced. There's no other word for it. Who knows what goes on in her head?"

"But still Dan can't see it, Carolyn. He thinks he's being such a good friend to her and has no idea what a scheming bitch she really is!"

"Well, whatever you do, don't let her rattle you. It's exactly what she wants."

For the time being, Nicola had held her counsel and said nothing to Dan. It was true for Carolyn. There was nothing to be gained from arguing about it. Dan was blind to Shannon's true colours, and Nicola would be the loser if she complained about their closeness. Anyway, Dan didn't need the hassle what with all the pressure he was under trying to get the new business up and running, while still working in his present job.

She kept up her good intentions for as long as she could – until one evening Shannon appeared at her front door looking for Dan.

"He's still at work, Shannon," she said shortly from the doorway.

The younger woman looked pointedly at her watch. "You mean he's not here?" she looked surprised. "He left the office early this afternoon. I wonder what he's up to?"

It took all of Nicola's strength not to deck the smirking bitch there and then. Who did she think she was, trying to place doubts in her mind about her husband?

But she refused to rise to the bait. "Shannon, is there anything else you wanted?" she asked in a bored voice.

"No, not at the moment. But look," she added with, Nicola thought, a scheming smirk, "tell Dan I was looking for him and I'll be at home later if he *wants* me." She put particular emphasis on the word 'want', apparently for Nicola's benefit.

Nicola and Dan had the mother of all arguments when he arrived home not long after. Nicola was sick of holding back. This time she told Dan exactly what she thought of his so-called 'friend'.

"I'm warning you, Dan, I won't be walked over in my home. That woman is poison! And I'll tell you something else, if I ever find out that you have been up to anything with that one, you won't get the chance again. 'If he *wants* me', my arse! What Lorena Bobbit did will be mild compared to what I'd do to you!"

Dan was almost afraid to speak. This was their first argument as man and wife, but he was already aware that an angry Nicola could be a very scary prospect. Her face had flushed crimson and she had a dangerous-looking glint in her eye.

"Nic, there's no way on earth I would *ever* be unfaithful or lie to you. Why would I? You're my wife – my *life*, for Christ's sake! Why would I do something like that?"

"You'd better not!"

"But I wouldn't! I don't know why Shannon would say something like that – really I don't! We're friends and she knows full well that I'm totally in love with you. OK, I may have played around a little bit in the past, but that was *way* before I met you!"

"It'd bloody better be!"

Still, Nicola knew almost instinctively that he was telling the truth. Dan was a very good-looking man who attracted female attention wherever he went but, in fairness, he didn't court it. Not to mention the fact that she loved and trusted him. And who *didn't* play around in their younger days?

Dan spoke softly. "Nic, there will never be anyone else but you. OK, you think Shannon might have a bit of a thing for me –"

"*Might?*"

"Seriously, Nic, you've got the wrong end of the stick completely. Shannon and I have known one another for a long time, and we've never been anything other than friends. Anyway, she has her own problems now, believe me."

She said nothing, letting him stew for a while.

"Nicola, I would never dream of it, not when I have you."

"And is it only because you have me that you wouldn't dream of it, Dan, or does it mean that you *would* go for Shannon if I wasn't around?" Nicola knew she sounded juvenile, but she couldn't help it.

"No, no, that's not what I meant." Dan shook his head from side to side, unsure what to say, afraid he might get himself into even more trouble.

He looked so forlorn, so serious then, that Nicola couldn't stay angry with him any longer.

And fighting with Dan always made her horny.

She reached across, put a finger on his lips and without another word led him slowly towards their bedroom.

It was good to get it all out in the open, she thought, kissing him hungrily. Now that Dan knew exactly how Nicola felt about his 'friend', and the damage she was trying to inflict on their relationship, surely they wouldn't see that much more of Shannon Fogarty?

* * *

It was that very night, Nicola deduced, that she and Dan had conceived.

They had been trying for ages, admittedly long before the wedding, neither caring about the mathematics, both hoping to have a baby sooner rather than later.

Nicola had come off the Pill, and they had been at it at every spare opportunity. She remembered one time, Dan called in to her at work on the spur of the moment, and she managed to sneak him into one of the changing-rooms for a quickie.

At that stage, they couldn't get enough of one another. But it had taken longer than expected, and Nicola now clearly recalled the excitement she felt when she realised that her period was late. At that stage she had been so conscious of her cycle, the period was conspicuous by its absence. When she went nearly two weeks over, and there was still no sign, Nicola didn't need the predictor test to tell her that their wish had finally come true.

It was late summer, not long after their wedding, and

she remembered Dan's nervousness while waiting for the little blue line to change colour.

"I feel like Homer Simpson," he had said. "Purple means 'doh!', red means 'wohoo!'."

Nicola was so fraught with anticipation that she was unable to answer. When finally the line began to change colour, and continued to darken until it was clearly red, Dan picked her up and spun her around the room.

"Wohoo! Woohoo!" he shouted.

"Stop it, you idiot!" Nicola was laughing through her tears, as then Dan laid her on the bed and the two of them made love, both exhilarated by the fact that an extra link was soon to be added to their almost unreal bond.

Nicola couldn't remember ever feeling so elated. You'd think that it would be enough that a most wonderful man had out of nowhere walked into her life and swept her off her feet. And now, just when she thought things couldn't get any better, she was about to become a mother.

Nicola tried to get her head around it, tried to abandon herself to the pure unadulterated elation she felt; yet deep down inside she couldn't help feeling afraid. She was afraid that all of this could come crashing down on top of her. What had she done to deserve this bliss? She was nothing special, had done nothing extraordinary in life – in fairness she could be a downright cow from time to time. She was always moaning about her job, was impatient with people, and yet somebody somewhere had seen fit to bestow all this happiness upon her.

Dan had by now fallen asleep at her side and, as she studied his peaceful expression, Nicola felt a tiny sliver of fear. What would she do if anything ever happened to him? Dan was her life.

She had always laughed at those silly stories and films about that 'special person' out there for everyone, had always scoffed at Laura's notion of a 'better half'. But Dan was without doubt her better half – and a considerably better one at that. It sounded corny, and she wouldn't dare say it loud, but her husband was a 'good' person by its absolute definition. Nicola had never come across a man like him and, if he had any bad traits, she didn't know about them. He was an honest, gentle and loving person, always open about his feelings, and never afraid to express them – unlike some of her past boyfriends who were Neanderthals by comparison.

Nicola couldn't help feeling afraid that maybe his parents were right. Perhaps Dan was way too good for her and one day, eventually, he might realise it.

She gave a mental shrug as she tried to suppress her unease. They had a wonderful relationship and their happiness had just been completed.

She really shouldn't worry so much. Perhaps it was perfectly natural for a new mother to be having feelings like this.

Or maybe, Nicola thought, a slight grin on her face, just maybe she had done something wonderful in a past life, and was getting her rewards in this one.

* * *

Ken, who had a key to Nicola's house, was waiting for her when she returned home that evening. As she pulled into the driveway, she saw Barney and him standing together in the doorway – the Labrador's tail wagging so hard she thought there was a danger it might fall off.

"Well, how did it go?" Ken asked when they were inside, his expression completely unreadable.

Nicola grimaced and rubbed Barney's glossy coat. "The only word I can think of at the moment to describe it is – strange."

"Strange?"

"Yes. I don't know what I had expected exactly, but he's still the same old Dan."

"But how did it go?" Ken repeated, an anxious edge to his tone. "I mean, what did you two talk about?"

Nicola sat back in her chair. "Well, seeing him face to face after all this time felt very odd – it was quite tense at the beginning. Still, after a while, I think we both began to relax. I'd imagine it was weird for Dan too."

Ken's facial muscles twitched slightly, but he said nothing.

"But somehow, it wasn't the big deal I thought it would be. I mean, what could we say to one another? So much time had passed and –"

"Surely he must have at least asked how you were, and how you've coped these last few years?" Ken interjected. "Didn't he say *anything*?"

She grimaced. "Well, we didn't get much of a chance to talk, actually. The ice had been broken, we were laughing over something stupid and then, the fiancée rang."

"Oh! And did she know he was meeting you?"

Nicola shook her head. "I don't think so – he went shortly afterwards. But he showed me a photograph of her."

"He *what*?"

She grinned at his reaction. "Yep, she's blonde, petite, and obviously well off – a typical trade-in model, really."

"Jeez, he showed you a picture of his new fiancée!" Ken was amazed at the cheek of him. He gave her a sideways glance. "And did it . . . did that bother you?"

"No, it didn't." There was a slight pause, and then she smiled. "I'm really glad you're here."

Ken finally sat down beside her. "I wasn't sure whether or not you wanted me here, considering. I mean, I haven't been exactly supportive about your seeing him again and I didn't know if you wanted some time alone after –"

"Look, I wouldn't blame you for worrying, and, of course, I want you here." Nicola looked at him. "Ken, as I told you before, my meeting Dan today wasn't going to change anything between us. I love you – there's never been any doubt about that." She sat forward. "Actually, I think today really brought it all home to me."

"What do you mean?"

"Well – and you might think this is silly – but when I pulled up in the car just now, and saw you and Barney at the doorway, I felt like . . . I don't know . . . like I had come home, or something."

Ken was smiling. "Are you *sure* you're all right, Nicola? Nothing happened to you on the way back – like a blow to the head, or anything?"

"Stop laughing. You know what I mean," she said lightly, pleased that he had relaxed a little. "Here I am, trying to be nice to you, and you start taking the piss!"

"You're being nice to me now?" Ken said, eyes twinkling. "When did that change of heart come about?"

She fixed him with a hard glare.

"OK, OK, I'm sorry!" he said. "Go on with what you were saying – about 'coming home' and all that."

"Ken . . ."

"No, seriously, go on."

"Right. Well, on my way home, I got to thinking about everything that had gone wrong between Dan and me, especially in the later stages, and I came to the conclusion . . ." she paused, and blushed a little, "I suppose I've always known that if it had been *you* I married – if you had been my husband at the time, then things would have turned out differently." She felt him lightly squeeze her hand. "And then, turning into the driveway tonight and seeing you and Barney standing together like that, I felt a kind of –" she searched for the right word, "clarity, I suppose. Like I said before, I felt like I'd really come home and that this was exactly where I belonged – with you."

Ken's relief was palpable. "So, that's it then?" he asked softly. "You and Dan – there's nothing left between you now – no unfinished business, or anything?"

Nicola reached across and kissed him. "That's it," she said decisively.

Chapter 19

Was there anything more mortifying than having to postpone a wedding? Chloe didn't think so.

It had been so *embarrassing* having to ring each and every guest on the wedding list, explaining that their wedding would have to be postponed until early next year. She could almost sense the sniggers behind the masked sympathy. She'd *never* get over this.

Last week, and with only a month to go until the big day, Chloe had called the hotel to confirm the arrangements for their wedding on September 25th. She should have guessed that something was wrong when the receptionist first sounded confused, and then nervous, quickly promising that she would 'check the arrangements and have someone phone back'.

Minutes later, the hotel manager phoned, and in smooth tones informed Chloe that yes, there *was* a wedding booked for September 25th – in the name of Collins/Moran. "I've examined our records, and it appears that a Fallon/Hunt wedding is scheduled at this hotel for September 25th *next year*." He spoke slowly, as if Chloe was some kind of simpleton.

"No, no, that must be a mistake," Chloe spoke quickly, her heart racing madly. "Our wedding was booked months ago. I signed the booking form myself."

There was a slight shuffle at the other end of the phone. "Yes, I have the booking here in front of me," the manager said. "Ms Fallon, next year's date has indeed been entered here."

"*What*?" Chloe tried to keep the shriek out of her voice. "What do you mean 'next year's date'? Surely I, of all people, should know when my own bloody wedding is happening! Why would I fill in next year's date?"

"I'm sorry, Ms Fallon, but this is the information I have here. As I said, we already have another wedding for Friday 25th this year."

"Well, we'll see about that," she said resolutely, before hanging up on the annoyingly placating manager.

That evening, after finally managing to trace Dan, who had been away at a meeting with some client or other, the two of them called to the hotel to personally examine the booking form. To Chloe's absolute horror, she discovered that next year's date had indeed been entered – and she had signed for it.

"I don't believe it," she said tearfully, putting a hand to her mouth. "How could I have done something so stupid? Why would I have done that? At the end of last year, I phoned specifically enquiring about 25th September, and the receptionist told me it was free."

Then she recalled a recent conversation with the hotel

about the flowers. There had been some confusion as to whether the 25th was a Thursday, or a Friday. She also remembered that the receptionist sounded a little bit strange on the phone. Probably wondering why anyone would be making arrangements for flowers a whole year in advance, Chloe thought glumly.

Damn! She should have realised then that something was up. Now some other couple would be celebrating their wedding here on *her* wedding day. How could this have happened?

"Isn't there anything you can do?" Dan asked, frowning. "Maybe accommodate us in a conference room, or something?"

"*What*?" Chloe cut in before the hotel manager could answer. "I'm not holding my wedding reception – the most important day of my life – in some dingy conference room! No way, Dan! We'll have the banquet hall, or nothing. That's part of the bloody reason I chose this hotel in the first place!"

The hotel manager intervened. "Ms Fallon, Mr Hunt, unfortunately all our facilities are fully booked on the 25th. Obviously, you have additional arrangements made, and I'm sure you don't want to wait another year –"

"We *can't* wait another year!" Chloe said, gritting her teeth. "Everything's arranged, the flowers, the cake, the invitations . . ." At this, she broke off, remembering the day she went to choose those bloody invitations – the same day she broke that car wing-mirror on Wicklow main street.

That was it! Chloe realised suddenly. All of this had to be her punishment – her seven years' bad luck. First the mix-up with the invitations, then Dan's ex coming back into his life – and now *this*!

"Well, maybe we could try and get a booking somewhere else –" Dan began.

"But where?" Chloe felt as though someone was twisting a knife in her heart. She *couldn't* give up on this hotel, not when it was to be the *pièce de résistance* of the entire wedding. She wasn't going to end up in some kip on her wedding day. No bloody way. It was the one thing that she wouldn't – she *couldn't* – compromise on at the beginning, when she and Dan were planning it. God knows she had fought long and hard enough to convince him.

"Everybody else just picks these ordinary run-of-the-mill hotels," she had said at the time. "I want something different, something elegant, something –"

"Expensive," Dan had finished with a groan, but eventually he agreed.

And now after all that, it seemed that Chloe wouldn't be dancing her first dance as Mrs Hunt in these sumptuous surroundings. What had she done to deserve this?

"Dan, it's only a few weeks to the wedding," she said mournfully. "What chance do we have of getting anywhere at such short notice?"

He shrugged. "We hardly have much of a choice."

No way. No *way* was Chloe going somewhere else. There had to be other possibilities. She turned to the hotel manager. "Don't you have any other days free around that time – a Thursday or even a Monday?"

He shook his head. "I'm sorry, Ms Fallon, but we're completely booked for weddings almost up to the end of January."

"January?" Chloe's mind began to race overtime. A winter wedding! OK, she might have to rethink the dress, and instead of a veil possibly go for one of those Snow Queen cape-type thingys, but that wouldn't be a problem. The flower arrangements would have to change, of course; orchids would die a quick death in January, but just imagine a winter bouquet with berries, and ivy and frosted apples and things!

"January would be perfect!" she announced happily.

"Chloe, hold on a second." Dan pulled her to one side, out of the manager's earshot.

"We should discuss this – what about all the arrangements?"

"What's to discuss?" Chloe spoke quickly. "We can wait a little longer to get married, can't we? I mean, we're practically married as it is, and I'm sure everything else can be put off until a later date, the flowers, the photographer and all that."

She was having visions of a snow-decked church as background to her wedding photos. And if there was no snow, Chloe was sure they could organise some fake stuff for the photographs – the church was only down the road from RTE, after all.

God, it would be gorgeous. And much more unique than any old run-of-the-mill, summer wedding. She didn't know why she didn't think of it before. OK, it was disappointing to have to wait that bit longer, but at least she wouldn't have to spend her wedding night in some grotty hotel!

Dan nodded thoughtfully. "Well, I have no problem waiting, but are you absolutely sure you don't want to try somewhere else?"

"I want our reception in this hotel, Dan. If I have to wait a little longer, so be it, and it's certainly better than having to wait a *year*."

They'd have to check with the priest, but it was unlikely to be a problem, especially in January. The honeymoon would need to be rethought – they didn't want to be in Thailand for the rainy season. Still, there was always the Caribbean. The only problem was . . .

"We'll have to get the wedding invitations reprinted," she said wearily, although she'd be damned if she'd give that Debbie one the satisfaction of knowing that something had to be changed. She remembered how condescending the designer had been on her visit to the Amazing Days store. "You just never know." Now her words were coming back to haunt Chloe.

"Well, if you're sure." Dan turned to the manager. "If you could accommodate us in January, we'd be very grateful."

The hotel manager smiled and spread the diary out in front of him. "Let me see . . . we have Friday 13th ?"

Chloe looked horrified. "I really don't think so."

Turning the page, the manager tried to hide a grin. "Perhaps the following Friday?"

"That would be great." Chloe's heart soared as she watched him enter their names in a space beside Friday 20th January, *next* year.

A winter wedding. It would be just perfect.

In the meantime, though, they had to withdraw the blasted invitations to this year's wedding.

Now Chloe looked over at Dan, who was busily engrossed in his newspaper. Even though he was as disappointed as she had been with their wedding being delayed, she still got the feeling that his mind was continually elsewhere. She wondered if he had ever got round to contacting that Nicola. With this latest uproar over the wedding, she herself had forgotten all about his troublesome ex.

"Dan?"

"Hmm?" he answered idly.

"Remember you said you were going to contact your ex – about your getting married again, and all that?"

He stiffened, and Chloe instantly knew that he had already been in contact with her. Why hadn't he said anything?

"I spoke to her last week," he said. "She's fine about it."

Chloe was instantly annoyed by this. Why *shouldn't* she be fine about it? And so what if she wasn't? They didn't need her permission, did they?

"Did her friend – you know, the one with our invites, did she tell her about us?"

He nodded. "It didn't seem to bother her, though – in fact she wished us well. I showed her a photograph of you. She thought you looked gorg –"

"*What?*" Chloe interjected, before he could finish the sentence. "You met with her – face to face?"

Dan reddened, and Chloe knew then that he had let that last comment slip out inadvertently. He hadn't planned on telling her about his little rendezvous with Nicola at all. Why the hell not? Instantly, Chloe felt her hackles rise.

"Yes, I was going to tell you but –"

"Well, why didn't you then?"

"Because I knew you'd react like this – that's bloody

why!" Dan's eyes flashed with annoyance. "I knew you'd try and make something of it."

"Well, would you blame me?" Chloe stood up. "When you're sneaking around behind my back, having secret meetings with your ex-wife!"

"I wasn't sneaking around. It wasn't like that. It was tense on the phone, and to break the ice I asked her to meet me sometime for coffee. Then she rang me one day last week and –"

"*And* of course you had to up and meet her, just like that, and without a second thought about *my* feelings! What is it, Dan? She says jump and you say 'hold on 'til I get my trampoline'?"

"Of course not. Look, Chloe, I told you that I felt bad about not telling her personally about us and –"

"Yes, but you said you'd *phone* her. You certainly didn't tell me you'd be having cosy dates with her!"

"Oh, please!" Dan put a hand to his head. "I'm not able for this any more, Chloe, really I'm not."

"Oh, well, s-o-r-r-y! But don't you think that as your future wife, I deserve to know about these secret meetings with your bloody *ex*-wife! What's going on, Dan? Why do I feel that you're not telling me everything here?"

"Chloe, can you please just give it a rest – *for once!*" Dan stood up, infuriated.

"For once? What the hell is that supposed to mean? Anyway, what do you expect me to think?"

"There's nothing *to* think, Chloe! All I was trying to do was treat my wife – my ex-wife – with a little bit of respect. After all Nicola's been through, it's the very least she deserves!"

"What's that supposed to . . . where are you going?" Her tone dropped a level, seeing him head for the door.

"Out!" he said. "Where I don't have to listen to this!" With that, Dan grabbed his jacket, walked out the door and slammed it loudly behind him.

Chloe stared after him, her thoughts running a race alongside her heartbeat. She sank down in her seat, and with more than a little trepidation, recalled Dan's words.

After all Nicola had been through? What did the hell that mean?

Right, that was it, Chloe thought, angrily throwing aside the guest list. Seeing as Dan seemed to have no problems with sneaking around behind her back, why shouldn't she do the same? John O'Leary had given her something to go on, and with a little persuasion, she might just be able to find someone who would go that bit further, and know that much more about Dan and Nicola's relationship.

Now that she had more time on her hands, Chloe was going to do a little digging around, and she wouldn't stop until she got to the bottom of this Nicola thing – once and for all.

* * *

Dan drove furiously down the Stillorgan dual carriageway.

Shit! Why did he let that slip? Chloe would never shut up about it now, and God knows she was a nightmare once she had something to complain about. She would be on and on at him forever.

Chloe was so unlike Nicola really, he thought, turning onto the coast road. In fact, the two of them couldn't have been more different. Nicola had always been most pragmatic and level-headed about things, whereas Chloe would fly off the handle at nothing. Not that Nicola would hide from a confrontation, he thought with a wry smile. Indeed, quite the opposite. But Nicola didn't get her knickers in a twist over things like . . . well, like the *colour* of her knickers, and whether or not you could see it through her trousers, or if it went with this dress, or these boots or . . .

Dan found himself tuning out during Chloe rants about her clothes, her shoes, and lately, about this bloody wedding. He was sorry in a way that it had had to be put off, because now he'd have to put up with another five months odd of planning – not just the Perfect Wedding – but the Perfect *Winter* Wedding. She was already talking about dressing the men up in some kind of Russian-themed get-up, complete with furry hats and high leather boots. His father would certainly love that!

What was it with Chloe and weddings? Why did she feel that she had to impress people? He knew that most women went a little bit batty over their Big Day, but was only realising now how lucky he had been the first time round. Wedding trivia had never bothered Nicola, and she was quite happy with their cosy, intimate wedding in the Caribbean that time.

In fact, Dan thought, there was very little that could bother his first wife.

He stopped in the carpark overlooking Sandymount Strand. Despite himself, Dan was thinking about Nicola more and more these days, and a lot more than he should be. He was getting married in a few months, for goodness sake! But yet, since meeting her last week in Bray, he just couldn't stop thinking about her.

She had been so calm and so *together*. He had expected the worst – anger, admonishment, bitterness – *something* after all that time. But Nicola seemed fine; she seemed strong, calm and amazingly, she seemed . . . happy. Dan wasn't sure what he had expected, but he certainly hadn't expected that.

She looked beautiful too, he thought wistfully – despite her weight gain. No amount of physical change could dampen that spirited, determined glint in her eye, the very thing that had attracted him to her in the first place. Nicola had always been strong-willed; whatever had made him think that she would fall to pieces? Dan smiled wistfully, remembering their very first encounter in O'Connell St that time.

Yes, Nicola had always been the strong, forceful one in their marriage, always able to handle anything that was thrown at her, never letting anything faze her. Dan looked out to sea.

Except for that one time, of course.

* * *

They were almost a year married at the time. Nicola was losing it, and Dan didn't know how to help her. It was like as if he didn't know who she was any more. What had happened to his wonderful, sunny, carefree wife?

Well, of course, Dan knew what had happened. It had been a tragedy, and a devastating disappointment to both of them. But however much they wanted that baby, and however much it hurt, there was absolutely nothing they could do to bring it back. The miscarriage had happened. There was no reason, no explanation; it just happened.

Dan could see it, could partly understand it, so why couldn't he help Nicola see it?

How could he help? How could he bring her out of the fog that had now surrounded and completely consumed her – the most important person in his life?

He couldn't get into her head, couldn't even begin to understand how she was feeling. "Time will heal," they all said, doctors, nurses, Laura, her mother.

So each day Dan would come home from work, hoping for some improvement, some tiny glimpse of the old Nicola but no, she'd still be sitting listlessly in front of the TV, not having bothered to get dressed, barely having bothered to get out of bed.

She'd just about look up when he came in, would only seem to come out of her trance when she heard the door close behind him. And when he went to kiss her, instead of throwing her arms around him and hugging him tightly like she used to do, Nicola would barely respond – she would barely even move.

Dan knew she was grieving but he also thought she blamed him. He should have looked after her better, or should have at least realised that something was wrong. But could he be – *had* he been at fault? Dan didn't think so. These things *did* happen. Maybe he shouldn't have suggested they go out as much as they had at the weekends? God knows sitting in dank and smoky pubs wouldn't exactly have improved the baby's chances.

They had been having a lot of sex too, especially in the early days, but the doctors had told Nicola that it was safe, hadn't they? And it wasn't as though he was pushing her or anything; it was just he and Nicola the way they always were, reaching for each other, reaffirming their love as often as possible. But perhaps even more so once her pregnancy was confirmed. They had been so happy.

Maybe they were wrong.

Eventually as the days went by, Nicola seemed to at least come out from under her blanket of fog, and start becoming human again. After almost two weeks she got up, got dressed, went back to work, and went about her day-to-day business just as before.

Except she wasn't the same Nicola. She was this faraway, preoccupied Nicola, and Dan didn't recognise her any more. He couldn't remember the last time they had had a conversation that lasted longer than two sentences, and it was never about anything other than trivialities. She got on with her life as though he didn't exist.

It hurt. It hurt desperately. He was losing her, and he didn't know how to prevent it. After a while, it became almost impossible to stay in the same room with her evening after evening, and be unable to share, to talk, to laugh like they once did.

So Dan found that he began to avoid spending time with her. It started out subconsciously; he would stay late working on a set of accounts that needed to be ready for sign-off before Friday. And he told John that yes, of course they could take on more clients, even though the practice had already been more successful than either had anticipated, and their respective offices were already overburdened.

And eventually it was easier that way. Dan could live with himself. He could live with himself because he didn't have to see the pain and disappointment in his wife's eyes every time he looked at her, and he thought that maybe if he stayed away long enough, then one day the old Nicola would return.

One evening, Dan was sitting in his office staring at the computer screen, and thinking about all that he was about to lose, or worse, about what had already been lost.

"Dan?"

He jumped.

Someone popped a head around the door of his office. "What are you still doing here?"

Dan caught his breath. "Shannon, you scared the living daylights out of me! I didn't think there was anybody else here. I'm working on – on the P35 for Manning Packaging." He picked up the first company file that came to hand. John had recently taken on Shannon to act as PA, hoping that an extra person would help them deal with the workload. The decision had been resented by Nicola, and indeed by Carolyn. But Dan couldn't do anything about it at the time, as it had been John's decision. Anyway, he wasn't sure if he wanted to do anything – he liked Shannon.

"At eight o'clock?" she frowned. "Dan, don't you think you should be heading home soon?"

"I just have a few small things to finish up, then I'll go. What about you? It's not like you to be working late."

"I wasn't, actually. I left earlier but I forgot my mobile, so I came all the way back to get it." She gave him a mischievous look. "I'm expecting an important call tonight."

Dan grinned back. "Oh? Do I know about this one?"

Shannon always had some man on the go – be it past, present or future.

"No. He's new on the scene," she said coquettishly. "I met him at the weekend. He's nice, seems like my type."

"Nice? That definitely doesn't sound like your type." Dan laughed for what seemed like the first time in ages.

"Oh, well. I'll see how it goes, anyway." Shannon went back towards the doorway. Then she paused. "Dan, is everything OK?"

He stiffened. "Sure. Why wouldn't it be?"

"Look, I hope you don't mind me saying so, but you look awful."

"Thanks a bunch."

"No, I don't mean . . ." She floundered. "Look, I just wondered how things were going – at home, I mean. You haven't said much and, well, we haven't really had a chance to talk about it."

Dan looked at her. Shannon knew about the miscarriage, everyone here did. Should he confide in her his fears about Nicola? God knows he needed to confide in someone, but it almost felt like a betrayal. Especially as Nicola and Shannon had never seemed to get on all that well, and as a result Dan had consciously cooled his friendship with her. Yet they were still friends and before Nicola they had been very close. He threw down his pen. Fuck it, he needed to talk to someone, otherwise he'd crack up soon.

"Things are a little . . . delicate," he offered eventually.

Shannon gave him a compassionate look. "It's understandable, you know. I'm sure losing a much-wanted baby wasn't easy for her."

"It wasn't easy for me either, but nobody seems to understand, or even consider that."

"I can imagine." Shannon nodded, then looked at her watch. "Look, Dan, you need to get out of here. Let's go next door for a pint, and we can have a good long chat." She gave him a winning smile.

Dan thought that sounded great. "Are you sure? Don't you have somewhere else to be?"

She shook her head. "Not really. If lover-boy rings, I can talk to him from there. Go on, get your things."

"Great." Dan looked relieved.

As he shut down his computer and collected his briefcase, he discovered he was feeling better already. This was exactly what he needed. A cosy pub, a decent pint of plain and a good listener.

As Dan followed her out to the hallway and locked the office door behind them, Shannon looked across, and flashed him a beaming grin.

Chapter 20

"Good afternoon, Laura Connolly Design?" Laura closed her eyes in silent prayer. Please, please, let it be that man calling back – the one who was looking for the engagement ring that time.

Three weeks later it was highly unlikely. That day, having returned from collecting Kerry, she had waited and waited for him to phone back, but no call had been forthcoming. The disappointment had been almost unbearable, as was the fact that there was no chance of piecing together his name, or his mobile number.

Still, Helen had been so grateful for the favour, and when she came to collect her daughter that same evening she had presented Laura with the most gorgeous bottle of designer perfume for her trouble. But the favour turned out to be longer-lived than Laura had expected. Since then, she had collected Kerry from playschool nearly three nights out of five in the last few weeks and again this afternoon.

"Hello?" she repeated, when there was no reply.

A short pause at the other end. "Um, hello? Is that Laura?"

"Yes, it is. Who's speaking please?"

"Laura, how are you, pet? Kathleen Brennan here."

"Oh, hello, Kathleen, how are you?"

Kathleen Brennan, Laura thought. Kathleen Brennan from Glengarrah. What the hell did *she* want? Then Laura collected herself. Was it possible – could it be that Kathleen was looking to buy something from her? Perhaps her mother had been telling people about the business, after all. Why else would the village busybody be phoning her?

"Well, it's like this, Laura," Kathleen began, as if reading her thoughts, "your mother told me all about how you're working for yourself these days."

Brilliant! Laura thought. Maureen had come through for her, after all. Now what would Kathleen be looking for, a brooch to wear at Mass on Sunday, or maybe a present for her husband? She could do a gorgeous set of cufflinks that would suit Cornelius Brennan, something simple but very elegant, something he'd love . . .

Kathleen's voice broke into her thoughts. "And she told me that you know all about the dubbleya-dubbleya and wouldn't mind doing me a turn."

"Sorry?" Laura's eyes widened. *Dubbleya* what? The woman was babbling. She remembered Kathleen had a mild stroke a few years ago but, as far as Laura knew, it hadn't affected her speech.

"It's just myself and the other women on the bingo bus would love to see Daniel O'Donnell playing at the Opera House down in Cork, but we wouldn't know how to go about it, and then Maureen said you could get it on the dubbleya-dubbleya."

Now Laura was really lost. What was she on about?

"Kathleen, I'm not really sure –"

"I have it written here on the back of my hand," Kathleen said, and then took a deep breath as if reciting something. "Dubbleya, dubbleya, dubbleya, ticketshop, dot –"

"Oh!" Laura interjected, realisation finally dawning. "You mean the internet!"

"Well, yes of course," Kathleen sounded put out. "The dubbleya-dubbleya. You're supposed to be able to get tickets from that. So if you wouldn't mind booking twelve of us for Thursday 14th . . ."

Laura bristled. This was the *second* time she had played booking agent to someone from Glegarrah. Only the other day, one of Cathy's friends had phoned to ask if Laura could go online and help book flights to London *and* a cheap hotel for her and her husband. "It's supposed to be the cheapest way to do it," she had said cheerily. After spending nearly an hour and a half trawling through various tourism and hotel-reservation websites, Laura had eventually found something that would suit. To top it all off, she had to use her own credit card to make the booking, as Cathy's friend had none.

"I'd be dangerous with one of those things," she laughed, as Laura stonily input the details. "Anyway, I'll get Cathy to set you right next time you're home."

Laura wouldn't mind doing anyone a favour, but she was getting a little sick of being used as the Glengarrah internet café. Her last phone bill had been huge as a result and if Kathleen Brennan and her bingo buddies had got wind of the internet, then Laura could end up doing this full-time.

Yet she hadn't the heart to say no to the woman.

"I'll have a look for you, Kathleen," Laura told her, logging onto the ticketshop website. "How many tickets did you say you'd like me to book?"

"Twelve, please," Kathleen said in the manner of someone who was ordering mushrooms from the vegetable man, "and try and get us as close to the man himself as you can."

Laura tried to think of something to talk about as she waited for the website to appear on screen. She didn't know Kathleen Brennan all that well. "So, Kathleen, how are things at home?"

"Fine, pet. You haven't been home yourself in a while, have you? Although why would you? There's nothing here for young ones these days. Yourself and Helen Jackson had the right idea emigrating to Dublin and getting good jobs for yourselves."

Emigrating! Good God, Laura thought. Glengarrah was, and always had been, one of those villages in which the inhabitants were suspicious and dismissive of the 'Big City'. Carlow was fine, small enough to get around, and no fear of anyone trying to stab you or run away with your purse or anything. God help any of them if they ever had to go to New York, Laura thought giddily.

"And how *is* Helen these days?" Kathleen asked, and Laura sensed a tone of faint disapproval behind the supposedly off-hand question. Helen could never be considered as a candidate for Glengarrah Person of the

Year. In fact, she abhorred the place and only returned a few times a year to visit her widowed father. Most of the older women found this almost as scandalous as the fact that Helen, in no uncertain terms, had told Maisie Davis where to go, when one time Maisie had the cheek to ask after 'the poor child's father'.

"And Maisie only trying to be friendly!" Laura's mother had relayed the story to her word for word about an hour after it happened. Laura wasn't surprised that Helen had reacted the way she did. When they got together, the women of Glengarrah were like a pack of vultures, pouncing gleefully on any piece of gossip or information about one of their own.

"Helen is fine, Kathleen," Laura answered, vaguely satisfied to discover that the Daniel O'Donnell concert was booked out.

"I'm very sorry, Kathleen," she said, after explaining the situation to the older woman. "Maybe if you had given me a bit more notice –"

"Are you sure now?" Kathleen sounded sceptical. "They couldn't be all gone, could they? Even the ones down the back?"

"Well, I can't actually see the theatre on screen here. It just tells me that the show is sold out."

There was a sniff at the other end. "I was so looking forward to it too. Are you absolutely certain, Laura?"

The woman was almost in tears. Laura knew that Kathleen and her bingo cronies would be devastated. And, of course, it would be all Laura's fault for not being able to get the tickets on the 'dubbleya, dubbleya'.

"Definitely. Maybe some other time." Shit, why had she

said that? Now half the village would be ringing her up looking for things.

"OK, Laura. I'll tell your mother you tried, but I'd say she'll be very disappointed altogether."

Laura sighed. Her mother would probably be on the phone within seconds, wondering why Laura couldn't oblige Kathleen Brennan, and didn't Laura know how embarrassing it was?

Perhaps this was part of the reason her mother was loath to boast about her business to the neighbours, Laura thought suddenly. If the business failed, which at this stage was looking like a true prospect, Maureen would never be able to live it down. Never mind that her own daughter would be shattered and disappointed, never mind that Laura was following her dream, and doing something that a lot of people would call courageous. As long as the neighbours weren't able to say that Maureen Fanning's daughter was a failure, that was the main thing. She shook her head sadly. Such a shame that her mother couldn't see beyond what the neighbours thought, but then again Maureen had always been the same, and at sixty years of age was unlikely to change.

Still, this thought didn't make Laura feel any better. Failure? The way things were going, it was a very distinct possibility.

* * *

Later that evening, Helen breezed into Laura's sitting-room, looking like someone who had just stepped off the fashion pages of *Cosmo*, rather than the supposedly harassed mother she was supposed to be.

Laura thought she saw Neil throw her friend an admiring glance, and felt immediately self-conscious in her Dunnes-Stores-bought trousers and T-shirt. Laura spied her friend's stylish Karen Millen top, worn over black woollen trousers that fitted so well it looked as though they had been custom-made for her.

OK, so working from home didn't require dressing up, and Laura wasn't exactly inspired to go through the entire make-up rigmarole, when the only living thing with which she came into contact from nine to five was Eamonn the cat, who couldn't care less whether she wore SuperCurl or Superglue on her eyelashes.

Still, Laura decided she should start making more of an effort to look the part of the professional career woman, even if it was just for Neil.

"Hi, Mommy!" Kerry brightened instantly on seeing Helen. "Look what I d-d-did today." She handed Helen a drawing she had done earlier that day at preschool. "This is me, this is you and this is B-B-Baawney."

Helen took the drawing and smiled. "That's lovely, darling. Aren't you a clever girl?"

Pleased, Kerry took her mother's hand. "Mommy, when can we get a doggy like Baawney?"

Helen sighed, and made eyes at Laura. "Now, pet, I know how much you love Barney, but I told you before that we're not getting a puppy. Barney looks after Auntie Nicola because she lives on her own, but you don't live on your own, do you?"

Kerry shook her head from side to side, her eyes filled with disappointment. "But Auntie Law-law has Eamonn, and s-s-she lives with Uncle Neil," she countered.

Helen paused, unsure how to answer, and Neil decided to help her out. "Yes, but that's because Auntie Laura is at home on her own all day, while I'm out at work."

Kerry pondered this. "Can I stay at home all d-d-day while you work, Mommy? Then I could have a d-d-doggy to look after me."

"But wouldn't you miss pre-school?" Laura asked.

Kerry shook her head. "No, I h-h-hate pwe-school."

"This is the latest thing." Helen rolled her eyes.

"But why don't you like pre-school? Aren't there lots of nice boys and girls there for you to play with?" Neil probed.

Kerry shook her head from side to side, her eyes wide.

"No nice boys and girls – at all?" Laura asked

"No – don't like them."

Helen made a face. "Don't mind her. She's been like this ever since she stopped going to Jo's."

Laura wasn't so sure. She'd collected Kerry from playschool a lot in the last couple of weeks, and not once did she mention another child or playmate, which Laura thought was quite strange for someone her age. Kerry was a naturally shy child as a result of her stutter, and Laura wondered if maybe she was having problems making friends. She resolved to speak to Helen about it. And speaking of Jo . . .?

"So have you found another childminder, yet?" she asked Helen, surprised at her own forthrightness.

Helen reddened. "I know. I know. I'm sorry. But it's been so busy at work, I just haven't had a chance to put a decent effort into it."

Laura instantly felt like a heel. Kerry was a dream to look after, and it wasn't as though she was rushed off her feet here – she just hated being away from the office in the afternoons, especially since she missed that call. Still, what else were friends for? And Laura was sure that Helen would do the same for her, if the situations were reversed.

"Listen, why don't you two stay for dinner?" she said, anxious to make amends. She didn't want Helen to think she was being unhelpful, or Kerry to think she was unwanted.

"Oh, can we, Mommy?" Kerry looked delighted. "Auntie Law-law made sheep's pie!"

"Would you mind?" Helen looked from Laura to Neil, unsure.

"No, not at all. Come through to the kitchen. It's nearly ready."

"Great. Thanks, guys – at least this will save me having to order out. I tell you, there's only so much Chinese food a girl can eat in one week."

Once again, Laura felt sorry for Kerry. Helen's diet of constant takeaways at irregular hours couldn't be that good for the child. Then she immediately berated herself. It was all right for her, being able to start the dinner two hours before Neil got home from work, whereas some nights poor Helen didn't get home until well after seven. At that stage, Laura too wouldn't feel like cooking.

"So how's the business going?" Helen asked, taking tiny morsels from her overloaded plate.

Laura's insides tightened. She hated speaking to Helen about this, because her friend was always on at her to be more proactive about her selling.

"Getting there," she answered, trying to sound more enthusiastic than she felt. "The website is working out well and I've had enquiries from the States, Germany, even Saudi Arabia."

"She'll be going international before we know it!" Neil added proudly, shovelling a forkful of potato into his mouth.

Helen gave her a genuine smile, and once again Laura felt mean for thinking badly of her. Of course, Helen would want things to work out for her. They were friends – why wouldn't she?

"Any stockists yet?" Helen speared a carrot onto her fork.

Laura looked uncomfortable. There had been a few, but they weren't ordering enough to make any kind of impact on her accounts. The internet orders were picking up, but Laura was slightly wary of it after what had happened the first time. "The Crafts Council have my name on file, and I'm sure it's only a matter of time . . ."

"The trade fair should help too," Neil said. "That's when? A few weeks after the wedding?"

Laura nodded, and Helen must have felt her reticence on the matter because she changed the subject soon after.

"Did you see Henry's free kick on Saturday?" she asked Neil, who like Helen was a big fan of Premiership football.

Neil nodded, and his eyes widened with interest. "Unbelievable stuff. I couldn't believe the speed of the ball, thought it would blast through the net."

"103 miles per hour, apparently," Helen stated knowledgeably.

"If not more. But I'm not sure the ref should have even given the foul in the first place. It was a nothing tackle and the defender definitely got the ball."

"What?" Helen put down her fork. "Are you blind? He went straight through his man – the ball was long gone!"

"He would never have gone on through goal from there – it was never a scoring chance."

Watching her husband and her oldest friend keenly discuss their favourite subject, Laura suddenly felt left out.

"I don't know what you two find so interesting about a load of supposedly intelligent men following a white ball around the place each week," she said winking at Kerry, who was happily wolfing down her dinner. "It's so boring; nothing ever changes."

Helen and Neil looked at her.

"Put it this way," Neil said. "It's a hell of a lot more exciting than watching *Coronation Street* or *EastEnders*, like you do."

Helen nodded. "A lot more exciting."

"I don't see how," Laura wrinkled her nose. "At least there's a bit of drama in the soaps. In football, it's just the same thing week-in week-out. They might lose or they might win. Big deal."

"No drama? Helen, tell her."

Helen sat up in her seat, only too happy to have a point to argue. "OK, what about relegation battles, teams struggling to stay alive against the millionaire big teams? Every game is massive. Or the derbies – you won't get better drama anywhere, Laura. These guys aren't just playing football, they're out there fighting passionately for their team and their fans, and all of that is real!"

Neil took up the baton. "And what about the last World Cup and all the drama in Saipan? The whole country talked about nothing else for weeks!"

Laura still wasn't impressed, but she envied the way Helen could enter a room and just kick-start a conversation about something interesting. It was something she had always been good at, irrespective of subject, be it football, business or even politics. She was just so knowledgeable, so intelligent and so *interested* in all of these things, whereas Laura couldn't care less.

Did that make her boring and uninteresting then, she wondered, letting the other two finish trading Football's Finest Moments. Did Neil look at her these days and have second thoughts about marrying someone dowdy and unintelligent, when he could have someone like Helen?

Laura's confidence was rapidly eroding with each passing day. It was as though her self-esteem, her entire self-worth were tied up in this business venture, and what had started out as a great business idea and a rush of excitement had now turned into something Laura was almost ashamed of.

What if she couldn't make this work? What if she had to admit defeat, and throw in the towel? How would she face them all? Nicola would support her, but probably feel for her at the same time. Helen would undoubtedly think 'I told you so' and Laura didn't have to even wonder about her family – *they* would probably start celebrating on the streets. But what about Neil? What about loving, supportive, hard-working Neil? Would he be disappointed in her? Would he begin to pity her, or even resent her if she packed this in?

Because the way she was feeling at the moment, Laura thought, watching Helen engage her fiancé in what must have been riveting conversation, she wasn't sure if she could carry on much longer.

Chapter 21

"Nice place." Paul sat up, zipped up his jeans and glanced fleetingly around Helen's ground-floor apartment in Monkstown. "You're obviously very good at what you do."

From where she lay half-undressed on the ground, Helen gave him once of her most provocative smiles. "I thought you of all people should already know that?"

He laughed and kissed her again. "Well, if you work half as well as you shag, then I can only imagine." Then he ran a hand though his hair and checked his watch. "Come on. It'll be closing time soon."

Helen got up, straightened her clothes and went to the bathroom to retouch her make-up and brush her hair.

"Come on, come on. You don't need that shit. You look gorgeous as you are," he called after her impatiently.

"I am not going out with bed-head," she retorted. "Even if it is only as far as the local."

"You look best with bed-head," he said, pulling her close and kissing her again.

She followed Paul out the door, and took one last look around the apartment to ensure that none of Kerry's toys – which had been deliberately hidden earlier – had managed to evade her. All she needed now was some Tweenie doll sticking its head out from one of the sofas. *That* would certainly make an impression.

Helen smiled as Paul took her hand and they walked towards the pub. Thank goodness Nicola had agreed to look after Kerry again this evening. Helen had pleaded a work do, but Nicola was having none of it.

"Wow, you lot at XL have a great social life," her friend had said. "Any chance of a job there for me?"

Because she was desperate, Helen didn't even bother with a pretence. She sighed. "OK, OK, I might as well tell you. I've met someone – someone new."

"Oh?"

"Don't 'oh' me – that's all you're getting, for the time being anyway."

There must have been something in her tone because Nicola knew straight away that this guy wasn't quite 'new'.

"You dark horse, Helen Jackson," she said. "Why didn't you tell us?"

Helen giggled. "There's nothing much to tell," she said, unwilling to elaborate. "Anyway, Nicola, can you baby-sit, or not? If not, I'll have to ask Laura, and I feel bad enough as it is, asking her to collect Kerry from school during the week."

And Helen did feel bad about it. But she just hadn't had the chance to find another childminder at such short notice. Anyway, Laura loved having her and Kerry loved being there – in fact, Helen thought, she couldn't think of a better person to take Kerry. And Laura wouldn't have to mind her for that much longer, what with Kerry starting school in a couple of weeks' time.

"I'll take Kerry on Friday night," Nicola said. "I won't be going anywhere anyway and Ken is away this weekend."

"Oh," Helen said, remembering, "Laura told me you met up with Dan again recently. How did it go?"

"Not bad," Nicola said guardedly, and Helen knew instantly that her friend didn't want to discuss it with her. In a way, she could understand why. Helen hadn't been all that supportive of Nicola throughout her marriage break-up – what with everything that was going on with Jamie at the time.

To this day, Helen still felt guilty about that – after all, Nicola had always made time for her. She must pop over and have a proper chat with her about it all soon, but then again, she was just so busy these days with work and Kerry, and everything . . . Anyway, Nicola didn't really need her friends around her all that much any more – not since Ken. It was great really that Nicola had found someone else, although Helen had been a bit taken aback all those months ago, when she discovered her friend's new man was none other than Ken Harris. She'd really never have put the two of them together but . . .

"So are you going to tell me anything about lover-boy, or what?" Nicola asked her and Helen grinned, pleased to be back on more familiar, guilt-free, territory. "Well, his name is Paul, he's a little younger than I am – about twenty-eight, twenty-nine, I'd say."

"*About* twenty-eight – you mean you haven't asked him?"

Helen chuckled. "I haven't really had the chance," she said, her voice heavy with meaning.

"Well, how long have you been seeing . . . oh!" Nicola exclaimed, understanding immediately. "It's one of *those*."

Helen laughed. It wasn't *all* just sex, although there had been plenty of that. Things had begun to get serious between them lately, at least as serious as they could be with Paul away from Dublin so often. His work as an investment adviser meant that he was constantly on the road for days on end. Then apparently his mother wasn't very well, so most weekends he travelled to Cork to spend time with her – which is why he would have to leave Helen's early tomorrow morning.

Aside from Paul's obvious magnetism, it was this fact that particularly endeared him to her. Who would have thought that this sexy, macho man was nothing but a big softie inside? Travelling hundreds of miles each weekend just to be with his mother. It wouldn't have been Helen, that was for sure, but then again her own mother was long gone, and she didn't have to worry about visiting her father, who tended to be much happier left to his own devices on the farm in Glengarrah.

But because of this side to Paul, Helen was almost certain he would eventually take to Kerry. But when to tell him? She had thought about that a lot lately, but then as the weeks went by, it was getting harder and harder to broach the subject. What was she supposed to say? 'Oh, by the way, Paul, I nearly forgot – I have a three-and-a-half-year-old'?

No, she had to think a little more about it. After her experience with Richard Moore, Helen wasn't going to just rush into telling him. She had to bide her time, and wait for the right opportunity. In the meantime, she was just going to enjoy being with a man who obviously adored her. It had been a long time.

"So what are you up to tomorrow?" Paul asked her.

Helen grinned at him. "Well, because I have the day to myself *for once*, I'm going shopping . . ." She trailed off, realising what she had said. "I mean, I normally have a lot of work to do at home, and this week I got it all finished early and –"

"You're really dedicated to your job, aren't you?" Paul didn't notice anything amiss, nor did he hear the fearful pounding of Helen's heartbeat.

"I suppose so, but as I said, I'm going shopping tomorrow. I need to get an outfit for a friend's wedding next month. I don't have much time so –"

"A wedding?" Paul interjected. "I love weddings."

The way he said it, Helen knew he was angling for an invitation. But how could she invite him, when Kerry would be there as flowergirl!

"Well, I'd invite you, only – only one of my friends is single too, and we said we'd stick together, and –"

"Single? Just remember that *you're* not single any more, Helen Jackson," he said, pushing the pub door open and gesturing her in ahead of him. "Your friend can do what she likes but I don't want you running off with the best man or anything!"

Helen was so excited by this she was afraid she might giggle out loud. Tingles of excitement travelled up and down her spine. They were a couple – she and Paul were really a couple!

Oh God, how she'd love to bring him to Laura's wedding! It had been so long since she'd had a partner at a social event. For once, she wouldn't be on her own – and she'd have someone other than Ken to sit with on the day. Helen didn't really connect with Ken. He was a nice enough guy, of course, but could be a little on the boring side. Helen had conveniently forgotten that not all that long ago she had viewed the same Ken Harris as a promising romantic prospect. "Super-sex on legs" were her exact words to Nicola, until she discovered that the object of her attention wasn't interested.

She bit her lip, and grabbed a stool at the bar while Paul stood waiting to order drinks. Maybe she should just bite the bullet and tell him about Kerry. Now that they were a couple, a real couple, well – she was almost obliged to, wasn't she? It might only do damage to keep him in the dark any longer. That was probably where she went wrong with Richard – she should have told him long before she did. Anyway, Paul was different – he was softer, more approachable, not a hard-nosed corporate freak like Richard. Helen wasn't sure what, but there was something telling her that Paul wouldn't mind at all – in fact, he might be pleased. Yes, Helen thought, feeling better about it already. She would tell Paul about Kerry tonight. Well, maybe after a few drinks, but definitely tonight.

Helen chuckled inwardly, imagining herself arriving at Laura's wedding in Paul's sleek, black Audi. She'd emerge outside the church in a show-stopping outfit, something expensive, tight and probably indecently short (definitely something to scandalise the Holy Marys in Glengarrah). Then, as the rest of the congregation stood back and stared, Helen would enter the church on the arm of the sexiest man this side of Carlow. That might finally stop the old biddies going on and on about 'the poor child's father' every time Helen met any of them in the village.

She smiled. Yes, she would definitely tell him. Helen just wished her heart would stop pounding and her palms would stop sweating. Still, a drink would soon soften her nerves.

Helen glanced idly round the darkened pub, trying to remember the last time she had been in here. Generally, she and Paul met for dinner or drinks in town. This was the first time they had gone out near her place and, after their little bonking session on the floor earlier, it was likely that he would stay with her tonight. She was probably pushing her luck in asking Nicola to have Kerry stay over, but Nicola adored Kerry and luckily seemed to love having her. It couldn't have worked out better really, Helen thought, smiling to herself. For once, she wouldn't have to trudge all the way in and out of town, just to spend a few hours with him.

The pub was very busy, and judging by the banners and balloons hanging from the ceiling, a 50th birthday party was being held there. As if on cue, sixties music began blaring out of the speakers on Helen's left. She looked across at the revellers who, surprisingly for that hour of night, included a few young children – probably grandchildren, she reasoned. The kids looked tired and sleepy.

The barman put a quarter bottle of white wine in front of her and let Paul's Guinness settle on the bar.

"I think we should stay up here," Helen said to Paul. "It could get dangerous down there." She indicated the busy seating area where the birthday girl and her companions were now dancing around the tables to 'Brown Girl in The Ring'.

Paul shook his head. "That's why I can't stand these local-type pubs," he said, with, Helen thought, a real edge to his tone. "They're always filled with bloody kids."

Helen looked at him. She knew what he meant; sometimes children could overrun pubs like swarming locusts, causing maximum destruction with crushed crisps and red lemonade, but these particular kids weren't doing any harm. Actually Helen felt a bit sorry for them as the grown-ups showed no sign of leaving anytime soon – in fact, they looked as if they were just getting going.

"Well, at least they're not running around," she said as if in agreement, although his tone had unnerved her.

"Doesn't matter, I think they should all be bloody banned, anyway." Paul took a sip of his drink. "Pubs are no place for kids."

Helen wondered whether he meant this out of concern for the kids, or concern for the drinkers. She couldn't be sure.

"So you're not a big fan of children, then?" she asked, trying to sound casual.

Paul nearly spat out his Guinness. "Jesus, no way!" he said. "I can't stand being within two feet of the little whingers. My sister has three and they're right little bastards, with all their moaning and groaning and 'I want this' and 'I want that'. I ask, you what's the bloody attraction? You're expected to feed, clean and clothe the little feckers day in, day out for the best part of twenty years, and what do you get in return? Grief, that's what!"

Helen's throat felt dry. She took a huge gulp from her glass. Shit!

"Well, I'm sure most parents feel differently," she said, rubbing her hand provocatively across his thigh. "Anyway, we won't stay here too long."

His earlier annoyance forgotten, Paul grabbed her hand and squeezed it. "Helen Jackson," he said, "you're my kind of woman."

* * *

Laura was sorry she had ever made a phone call to Maureen, enquiring as to whether her sister had remembered the wedding-dress fitting this coming weekend. .

"Honestly, Laura," Maureen sniffed, "I can't understand why you had to go and get your dress made in Dublin. There's plenty of dressmakers down this way too, you know. And poor old Cathy having to traipse all the way up there on the bus for a fitting, every time you snap your fingers."

Laura heart quickened with annoyance. Traipse *all the way* up there! The way her mother carried on, you'd think that Dublin was on the other side of the world! And Cathy, being a modest size twelve, didn't have to come for fittings all that often. In fact, Laura remembered, she had only come twice. Anyway, wasn't the shoe on the other foot when Cathy was getting married, and Laura had to 'traipse' all the way down to Carlow for *her* dress fittings? And poor old Cathy didn't mind coming to Dublin unexpectedly, and landing herself in on top of Laura when she felt like a bit of shopping, did she?

"Anyway, Laura, you know that poor old Cathy is having a tough time of it at the moment."

Laura frowned. "How's that?"

Maureen lowered her voice conspiratorially. "Apparently, all isn't well with herself and Packie."

"Really?" Laura hadn't heard anything. Then again nothing ever seemed to be 'well' with Cathy. Her sister was a perpetual moan. Laura couldn't remember if Cathy had ever acknowledged Laura's business, let alone wished her well with it.

"Yes. So I really think you should forget all about this fitting nonsense, and not be putting your sister to any trouble."

Putting her to any trouble! Jesus, Laura wasn't asking her to *make* the bloody dress!

She took a deep breath, trying to calm herself. Lately everything her mother said – everything *anyone* said – was getting on her nerves. She wasn't usually so touchy or irritable, but of late she found she was becoming oversensitive and irrational. And it was something she was finding more and more difficult to control.

"Mam, it's the final fitting before the wedding," she said as calmly as she could muster. "Cathy knows that."

Maureen harrumphed. "Well, that's all very well, but I'm the one that's stuck looking after the twins while the two of you are living it up in Dublin."

Stuck looking after the twins! And the same one wouldn't hear of anyone else minding them, Laura thought uncharitably. For all her mother's whingeing about being landed with baby-sitting, Laura knew that Maureen would die before she'd let Cathy's mother-in-law look after them.

"That woman breastfed Packie as a baby," she'd told Laura one day, in shocked tones. "It's small wonder he turned out to be such a Mammy's boy. Seriously, did you ever hear such rubbish in all your life? But then again, the likes of Milupa wouldn't have been good enough for those Kennys and all their fancy notions."

Laura did wonder about the research that claimed breastfed children tended to be more intelligent than those who were formula-fed, because her brother-in-law seemed to fly in the very face of that research. Packie was one of the dimmest people she had ever come across. "A nice oul divil," as her father had described him, Packie tended to take everything and everyone at face value, but somehow always ended up being involved in every moneymaking scheme that was going. He always had a couple of quid riding on a 'sure thing' and the only thing sure about it was that Packie would be minus his couple of quid after the race. He was one of the first to get duped by the illegal Pyramid schemes, having handed the majority of his and Cathy's savings to some chancer in the hope of making it big. Her younger sister too could be a little naïve at times, and the combination of herself and Packie was a recipe for financial disaster and possibly the reason 'all was not well' now.

"Tell her to bring the twins with her if she wants," Laura said, feeling magnanimous, although she was sure Cathy could do with the break. The twins weren't exactly placid. Monkeys jumping on hot coals would be a more apt description for Laura's wayward nephews. "They can all stay here for the night."

There was a sharp intake of breath. "And I after cancelling my bingo night in order to mind them?" her mother shrieked. "She will *not* bring them with her. She'll go up on the bus on Saturday morning, get the fitting over and done with, and then come back home straightaway. There'll be no gallivanting round Dublin with you, either."

Not for the first time, Laura wondered how Cathy managed to stay living in the vicinity of her mother, let alone two doors down. Maureen still treated her grown-up daughters as if they were children who didn't know how to behave, and were likely to embarrass her at any given moment. Didn't Cathy feel like Laura did sometimes, and want to strangle her? Yes, she loved her mother, but a lot of the time Maureen wasn't easy to love. She was just so – so bloody contrary!

She recalled the way her mother had nearly eaten her that time she couldn't get the concert tickets for Kathleen Brennnan.

"I can't believe you were too busy to do the poor woman a good turn, Laura," her mother had admonished soon after. "Do you know I couldn't show my face at the bingo for two whole weeks after it?"

I couldn't give a shit about your bingo, *or* bloody Kathleen Brennan, she wanted to say, but in true Laura fashion she asked Maureen to again pass her apologies on to Kathleen, and to tell her that she would be happy to try and book something for her again in the future.

"Well, that's not much good to her now, is it? Just because you were too busy to –"

"It wasn't that I was too busy, Mam," Laura reiterated, knowing that her words were falling on dear ears. "That show was completely sold out."

"Well, I think the very least you could do to make it up

to her is invite herself and Cornelius to the afters of the wedding," Maureen had said – no, Laura thought – *ordered* and of course, she had complied. Despite the fact that she hadn't seen Kathleen Brennan in years, and had never known the woman all that well in the first place. But as usual, her mother's guilt trip had done the trick.

"Listen, Mam, I have to go," Laura said now. "There's another call coming in and it could be important."

Laura hoped it would be. She *needed* it to be.

"It's like that now is it, Laura?" Maureen was put out. "Too high-flying these days to have a decent conversation with your own mother?"

Laura gritted her teeth, and tried to dispel the feelings of resentment rising up within her. She shouldn't be feeling this way, but lately her family were driving her mad. Lots of things were driving Laura mad.

"I really have to go," she said, refusing to rise to her mother's bait. "Tell Cathy I'll meet her outside Easons on Saturday morning."

"Well, make sure you don't leave her waiting too long . . . with the way things are going in Dublin these days, you wouldn't know what could happen – she could get shot or anything –"

"Goodbye, Mam." Laura disconnected and briskly picked up the other line. "Good afternoon, Laura Connolly Design?"

"Hello, I'd like to speak to the owner or manager please?" a chirpy female voice asked.

"Speaking. How may I help you?" Laura said, a slight smile crossing her features. Owner or manager. That she most certainly was. This sounded promising.

"Oh, hi, how are you today? My name is Jenna McCauley, and I'm calling from Business Network Marketing Management. We're a marketing consultation company, and I wondered if you might be interested in our services?"

Laura's heart sank. *Another* sales call. It seemed that every time the phone rang these days it was some telemarketer or advertising rep, trying to sell services that the business just couldn't afford. Neil told her not to entertain it, that maybe someday she could afford them, but it always irked Laura to have to explain that this was a small company, and the advertising budget 'just couldn't stretch to additional advertising'.

Still, some of these reps seemed to have been genetically engineered to sell, and were incredibly persistent. Laura always found it difficult to get rid of them, and wondered how on earth her business name managed to circulate so quickly amongst sellers, and so slowly amongst what she really needed – buyers.

Unfortunately for Laura, chirpy Jenna was an über-seller and couldn't be fobbed off by non-existent marketing budgets, or Laura's feeble attempts at being firm.

"If I could just have a few minutes of your time, it won't take that long, and if you could give me some information about the company I could design a sample business strategy and –"

"Look, I'm sorry. We're really very busy here," Laura began.

"Well, maybe we can arrange a more convenient time. I could perhaps call to the premises, and explain exactly what we could do for Laura Connolly Design. You wouldn't believe what a constructive marketing solution could do for your company. Say ten am, Monday?"

"No, I really don't think –"

"Ten it is then. Looking forward to it, I really feel that Business Network Marketing can grow –"

"I said *no!*" Laura bellowed, her hands shaking with adrenaline. "I don't *want* you calling here for a meeting. I don't *need* a constructive marketing solution – whatever that might be. I *told* you I wasn't interested. Now stop annoying me!"

Her face hot and her heartbeat going a mile a minute, Laura hung up. For a long moment, she stared at nothing in particular, trying to get a grip on herself. Why was it that everyone thought they could roll her over like a trained dog, thinking that they could take advantage of her? She was so sick of them, so sick of *all* of them, her mother, her family – Helen.

The other day, Helen had asked Laura to drop off a disc to a client in Dun Laoghaire.

"There's no rush with it or anything. But seeing as it's on your way to the preschool . . ."

It was nowhere *near* the preschool – in fact it was an extra forty minutes in Dublin traffic *out of the way* of the preschool, and Laura had been livid, absolutely livid.

And what had she done – what had she said? She hadn't said what she wanted to say which was: 'No, Helen. Shag off, Helen. I'm sick and tired of doing your messages and taking in your deliveries, and being your childminder and your general dogsbody – so you can go and stuff it!'

No, Laura hadn't said that. Instead she had simply said: "Fine, just give me the address and I'll drop it off on my way."

"Thanks, Laura, you're a star," Helen said airily.

Laura sighed. At the beginning she had been happy to do Helen a turn, and get her out of a spot, but why couldn't Helen do the same? Why couldn't she see that Laura was working, that she was trying to get her business off the ground, and that being away from the phone every afternoon while she was off collecting Kerry wasn't going to help? She took a deep breath. Well, at least Kerry would be starting school soon, so hopefully Helen wouldn't need her any more. Then again, as far as she knew Helen hadn't found another childminder – as far as she knew she hadn't even looked! So it would be the same old story – Laura would now be collecting Kerry from school, and trying to keep her entertained until her mother decided she would turn up to collect her.

Just then, the phone rang again and Laura snatched up the receiver, deciding that if this was Ms Telemarketer bothering her again, she was really going to give her a piece of her mind. But she was wrong.

"Hello, is that the jewellery design place?" the caller tentatively asked.

"Yes, this is Laura Connolly – how can I help you?"

"Well," the caller began, "I know this might be a bit short notice, but my boyfriend and I are getting married at the end of October and we were thinking of . . . well, I was thinking of, getting our wedding rings specially designed. I have a few ideas in my head . . ."

Laura was so excited she barely heard the rest of the

sentence. A customer, a real live customer – and someone looking for a one-off design! Oh, this was good, this was really good!

"So, I wondered if I could maybe call into your studio and show you what I have in mind?" the caller went on. "I'm really anxious to get this organised. You're in Ballinteer, aren't you? I could call on my lunch break – around two o'clock if that would suit? I'm so sorry for calling at such short notice but –"

"Of course, yes! That would be fine, absolutely fine!" Laura replied and then her heart sank. Kerry! She had to collect Kerry from playschool at two. Oh, blast it, this wasn't on. She had to be here for this. It was her first personal consultation for goodness sake! No, Laura thought, her thoughts tripping over themselves as she tried to find a solution. She would ring Helen, explain the situation and hopefully her friend could make some alternative arrangements for today. She knew Helen's work was important, but damn it, Laura's was too.

"Oh, that's terrific! I sooo appreciate it," the caller said, and Laura couldn't resist a smile.

This was a sale. It was definitely a sale. She could feel it in her bones. Maybe things were finally looking up.

"See you at two then," Laura said, after taking the girl's details and giving her directions to her studio. "My studio," she repeated out loud to herself. Yes, that sounded good, and much better than a simple old workshop. "This afternoon *I* am having my first consultation in my *studio*," she told a bored-looking Eamonn, who was sitting on the floor across from her, his long tail swinging from side to side.

Then she grimaced. Now, she had to tackle the rather unpleasant task of telling Helen she couldn't collect Kerry this afternoon. For all her giving out about Helen earlier, Laura did feel as though she was letting her down. After all, Helen was depending on her. First she dialled Helen's mobile, and not getting any answer from that, tried her direct line at XL.

"Hi," Helen's sultry tones came through the mouthpiece and Laura idly wondered if sounding like an advertisement for one of these phone-sex lines was good for business. Maybe she should try it herself. It certainly seemed to work for Helen anyway! The woman could buy and sell anyone. She was about to answer, when Helen went on, "You have reached Helen Jackson's voicemail. Please leave a message and I will call you back as soon as I can."

Shit! Not at her desk, what should she do? She couldn't just leave a message. What if Helen was in a meeting and didn't get out 'til well after two? Poor Kerry would be in an awful state. No, she couldn't do that – she'd have to find some way of letting Helen know. Laura bit her lip and mulled over it for a while. Then it hit her. Reception! She could ring reception, find out where Helen was and if she was contactable or, alternatively, leave the message with reception to pass on.

"Good morning, XL, Paula speaking."

"Hello, I was looking to speak to Helen Jackson please," Laura said pleasantly.

"I'm sorry, Helen isn't in today," Paula said, and Laura sat up in her chair.

"Isn't in? Isn't in the *office* today, you mean?"

"No, she isn't in at all."

"So, she's out sick?" Laura said, more to herself than to

the receptionist. But how did Helen get Kerry into the preschool this morning if she wasn't well . . . wait, she thought, mind racing, *that* was even better because there was a chance that Kerry wasn't in preschool at all today, so she wouldn't need to collect her – but then why hadn't Helen let her know?

"No, she took an annual leave day. I spoke to her yesterday and promised to hold all her calls 'til tomorrow, so if you'd like to leave your name and number –"

"*What*?" Laura said. "She knew she'd be off today?"

"Well, yes, as far as I know she has a personal matter to attend to today, but I'm sure that someone else here can help you and –"

"It's fine, thank you," Laura said shortly and hung up.

What the hell was going on? When Helen had called to collect Kerry yesterday there was no mention of a day off or a 'personal matter'. If Helen had the day off, why the hell didn't she tell her? Here she was, feeling bad about letting Helen down and all the time Helen didn't need her because she could collect Kerry herself! And the worst part was, she didn't even let her know!

Laura stood up and, trying to clear her mind, began tidying her office space, hoping to make it look a little bit more presentable for her potential client's visit. Then she stopped dead, remembering something Helen had said yesterday when picking Kerry up. "I might be a bit late collecting her tomorrow, if that's all right," she had said, on her way out the door. "The boss has scheduled something last-minute and, knowing him, it could go on for a while. I hope you don't mind," she added, with her trademark angelic smile.

Laura didn't think she had ever felt so annoyed in her entire life. What the hell was Helen Jackson up to?

Two hours and umpteen phone-calls later to Helen's apartment, her mobile, Kerry's playschool and back again to the XL office, and still Laura was none the wiser. The only thing she knew for sure was that yes, Kerry *was* in playschool and she had no choice but to go and collect her. She had been lucky in a sense that the school – by now well familiar with Laura – agreed to let her pick up Kerry an hour earlier than normal, so at least she could be back in time for her consultation. But she didn't feel right about doing that and it was bloody embarrassing having to ask. And after all, she shouldn't even have to – Helen was the child's mother after all.

But she was nervous enough about this meeting without having to worry about whether or not Kerry would be okay by herself in the next room watching TV, or whether she might come in and interrupt them, giving the client a terribly unprofessional first impression.

As it turned out, the client was lovely and was so impressed by Laura's designs that she there and then signed up to commission her wedding rings. Laura was more relieved by this than anything else, her annoyance with Helen so great that she just didn't have the mindset to enjoy her small triumph. By the time the client left late that afternoon, Laura was hassled, weary and very very angry.

In fact, she was livid. Livid that Helen could lie so easily to her, livid that she would take advantage of her, livid that she was such a bloody soft touch. She was just so sick of it. It was all Laura, do this, Laura, do that, and not one – not *one* of them offered a word of thanks or anything in return. Making sure once more that Kerry was okay watching TV, Laura went back into her office, slumped down on her chair and put her head in her hands. What was happening to her? Why was she feeling like this? It wasn't as though this was anything new. She had always been this much of a pushover, hadn't she? She was always the one people turned to – the one that never said no to anyone.

Most of the time it didn't bother her, but these days Laura felt wound up like a tight spring. And lately the spring was being stretched beyond belief. Maybe it was all finally getting to her – the stress of the wedding, the worry of the business, the self-doubt.

Maybe this was all wrong.

Well, no more, Laura thought, her mouth set in a firm line. When Helen Jackson deigned to turn up here this evening, boy, was she going to get it!

"Hey Laura!" Later that evening, Helen sailed into the hallway in a cloud of *J'Adore*.

"Where the hell were you today, Helen?" Laura snapped, giving it to her straightaway with both barrels, Kerry safely out of earshot in the kitchen with Neil.

"What? What do you mean where was I?" Helen stopped short and, Laura noticed, looked a little wary.

"Well, you weren't at work," Laura said, her tone faintly sarcastic, "because I tried to phone you earlier to tell you that something had come up, and I wasn't available to be your gofer today."

"My gofer? I'm sorry, Laura, but I don't understand. Is

this about collecting Kerry from playschool? I spoke to you yesterday and you said –"

"No, *you* said, Helen, *you* said that you would be late collecting Kerry today because you had some meeting or another, yet they knew at work that you were taking a day off!" Laura's voice shook with anger and her heart pounded. "Isn't it well for you to be able to take a day off and leave the worry of looking after your child to someone else – someone who actually *was* working today?"

"Laura, I'm sorry, really I am but Paul and I had organised this trip and . . ." Helen, stopped short, and her complexion reddened.

"Paul? Who the hell is Paul?" Laura said frowning, although one look at Helen's face told her all she needed to know. Paul was obviously some new Romeo she'd hooked up with. She didn't *believe* this!

"Look, he lives in Cork and we haven't seen one another in a while. I just didn't think you'd mind. I wasn't that much later so –"

"That's not the point though, is it, Helen? The point is that weeks ago you asked me to do you a favour, and because you're my friend and you were stuck, I obliged. But it's not an open-ended favour, Helen. *I'm* working too, although you don't seem too concerned about that. If I was working in an office, would you expect me to take time off every day to collect Kerry – would you?"

"Well no, but –"

"But nothing. It's the same thing, Helen. But just because you don't take me – and this business – seriously, don't think you can walk all over me. Even worse, now you're using me to spend time with some guy!"

"Oh, Laura, that's not true," Helen said, putting a hand on her arm. "I promise you. I have been looking for another childminder, really I have. But it's really difficult to get someone at this time of year . . ." She trailed off, her shoulders slumped. "Look, I'm really, really, sorry, Laura," she continued, her voice barely a whisper. "I know I've been taking advantage of you, and I would have told you about Paul. It's just . . ." she blushed slightly, "well, it's early days with us, and I didn't feel comfortable saying anything before now."

"Helen, you did a very dangerous thing today. Forget the fact that I couldn't contact you because it wasn't convenient for me to collect her – what if something had happened? What if she got sick or there was an accident or something?"

"I know, I know, shit . . . I just didn't . . . I should have thought to leave my mobile on." Helen bit her lip and looked away, her eyes troubled and upset.

"I just don't know, Helen." Laura gave a deep sigh and all of a sudden felt unbelievably jaded.

The entire afternoon she had been going over what she was going to say, and how she was going to put Helen in her place, but now that Helen was here, looking truly apologetic and pouring her heart out, she just didn't have the same resolve. Was it worth it? Was it worth arguing with her friend just because she had had a tough day and Helen had been a little bit late? Kerry was no trouble and, admittedly, everything had worked out fine in the end, what with her getting the commission and everything.

Being in business was bound to bring some challenges,

wasn't it? And if she couldn't manage something simple like re-organising her day to suit unusual circumstances, then she wasn't going to be much of a businesswoman, was she? Oh, sod it, it just wasn't worth it. She'd give Helen the benefit of the doubt this time . . .

Sensing that Laura had calmed down somewhat, Helen looked up at her, her beautiful eyes deep and sorrowful. "Laura, I promise I will make it up to you, and I'll get moving on another childminder first thing in the morning. You know I really appreciate what you're doing, and I promise you won't have to mind Kerry for much longer."

Silence.

"Laura?" Helen urged. "I swear."

Eventually, Laura sighed again and nodded wearily.

* * *

The following Saturday morning, Laura and Nicola drove into town for the dress fitting, accompanied by an unusually sullen Kerry. Apparently, Helen had gone out again with the famous Paul the night before, and had left Kerry at Nicola's for the night, proclaiming that there was no point in Nicola having to drive all the way to Monkstown to collect her for the fitting the next morning. Better to have Kerry stay there all night.

"Better for Helen maybe," Nicola had said grouchily, while collecting Laura at the house. Kerry had gone looking for the cat and was out of earshot. "Ever since she's met this Paul, the poor child has been shunted from pillar to post. I've had her the last two Friday and Saturday nights and I'd say poor Kerry is sick of it."

"But she loves staying with you," Laura said, while at

the same time feeling sorry for Kerry. Obviously, Helen was making this new guy her utmost priority.

"Maybe, but I'm sure she'd like to spend *some* time with Mummy at the weekends too – she hardly sees her during the week."

Nicola sounded put out, Laura thought. She wouldn't blame her. Even though Kerry was a very well-behaved child, she was still a child and Nicola couldn't watch her twenty-four hours a day. Since her own argument the other day, she found Helen had been much more appreciative of her help and was actively trying to find a new childminder. But, in the meantime, she was still asking favours of people.

"I'm going to have to confront her about it soon," Nicola said grimly. "It's not good for the poor kid."

Laura grimaced. Nicola or Helen disagreeing with *anyone* was not a pretty sight, let alone with one another. Arguments had occurred between the two a couple of times over the last few years, but thankfully not for a long time now. Unlike Laura, Nicola would go straight for the kill and wouldn't back down as easily as she had. If they locked horns over Kerry's welfare, Laura wouldn't want to be within throwing distance.

"I still can't understand why she gave up going to Jo," Laura mused. Helen had told them little or nothing about that.

Nicola sniffed. "*I'd* say Jo copped on to herself and told Helen where to go. It's a shame because Kerry was mad about her. She went on about Jo nearly as much as about Helen. I think Jo helped her a lot with her speech too."

Laura looked at her. "You're in very bad form today," she said. Nicola looked tired, as though she hadn't been sleeping well. Despite her friend's insistence that meeting Dan last month had had a positive effect on her, Laura worried that she might have been deluding herself. She certainly didn't look the better for it.

Nicola exhaled deeply. "It's Dan," she said, confirming Laura's suspicions. "He rang me at work yesterday, wanting to meet up again."

Oh dear, Laura thought. What was Dan up to now? "Meet again – why?"

"He reckons we didn't get all that much of a chance to talk properly last time, what with his having to leave unexpectedly."

"And what do you think?" she asked carefully.

"To be honest, I don't see the point. It's over and done with, Laura. We've both got very different lives now, we're moving on with other people, and we're both happy with that – well, I am, anyway."

Laura paused. "And Dan?"

"Honestly? I think he just wants us to remain friends. The thing is, I don't want this causing trouble between Ken and me. He was wary enough about my seeing Dan again in the first place, and I know he wouldn't be too happy about my meeting him for chats on a regular basis."

"You couldn't blame him though." Typical Dan, Laura thought, as she settled Kerry in the back seat of Nicola's Focus. Couldn't he leave well enough alone?

Nicola got in front. "I know that, which is why I told Dan no – there's no point in our meeting up again. But

I'm not sure if he'll leave it at that." She sighed. "I haven't told Ken about it, because as far as he's concerned it's all over and done with. I hate keeping anything from him, especially this."

Laura frowned. "I feel guilty. If it wasn't for me and my invites –"

"But it wasn't your fault they got mixed up," Nicola said, looking sideways at her. "Anyway, I doubt the invites had anything to do with it. Dan rang me as a result of the Motiv8 magazine feature. He would have contacted me in any case."

"I suppose so but, Nic, do you think the fiancée knows about you?" Laura had been wondering about that.

"About me? Of course! Why wouldn't she?"

"Well, did she know that he was meeting with you that day?"

Nicola shook her head. "Not sure about that, although it might explain why he had to run off so quickly." She shrugged. "I suppose I wouldn't blame her though – *I* wouldn't be too pleased if it was the other way round."

Laura nodded. She wondered idly what Dan's fiancée made of it all.

Nicola checked her rear-view mirror. "We'd better get a move on – poor Cathy will have been kidnapped or something by the time we get there." She gave a broad grin, Laura having earlier relayed the conversation she had with her mother about 'poor Cathy' being left waiting all alone in the Big Bad City. "Now, do you have the neckpieces with you, and the earrings?" she asked, starting the engine.

"Shit, I almost forgot!" Eyes wide, Laura put a hand to her mouth, having momentarily forgotten that Kerry was in the back seat. "Don't tell your mommy I said that," she said, and for the first time that morning Kerry giggled.

Laura raced back to the workshop. She'd spent long enough working on the wedding jewellery to have it all ready for the final fitting – she'd have gone mad if she'd left everything behind.

"Can I have a peek?" Nicola asked, when she returned.

"Nope. Not until the dresses are on." Laura grinned. She had worked especially long and hard on these pieces so that they would be like nothing any of them had ever seen before. Hopefully, the girls would treasure them.

An hour later, Laura, Nicola, Kerry and a dishevelled Cathy lined up for the final dress fitting at Brid Cassidy Bridal Design.

"I've been here almost an hour!" Cathy had whined, as Laura greeted her outside Easons with a hug. "Where were you?"

"It's not easy for me to find a decent parking-space in here," Nicola said shortly. Cathy reddened and was silent all the way to the bridal boutique.

Finally, Laura stood before the mirror in full wedding regalia. The dress was ice-white with a fitted bodice, and a slightly flowing chiffon-layered skirt – the hem on the rear dropping low to a short train. It fitted perfectly. Well, perfectly, Laura thought, apart from her spare tyre, but shrink-wrap knickers would soon put paid to that.

She looked at the others. Kerry, in her violet-coloured flowergirl dress was leaping around in delight, proclaiming that she was a fairy princess. Cathy was studying her reflection and making a determined attempt to suck in her (worryingly, Laura thought) rounding stomach. The boned bodice sat awkwardly on her midriff and the crushed silk skirt strained across her hips. Laura shook her head. Cathy's supposed marital problems obviously weren't as bad as Maureen had made out. Cathy either didn't know, or hadn't bothered telling Laura, that she was pregnant again. Laura gave her a look that conveyed her dismay, and Cathy had the good grace to look ashamed. Indeed, she didn't look at all happy about it.

Neither for that matter, did Brid Cassidy. The bridal designer was today joined by an assistant named Amanda that Laura hadn't met before, and the other woman, noticing Cathy's expanding waistline, gave Laura a conspiratorial look. Laura returned the look. She knew that Brid could be temperamental at times, and this new development was not going to go down well – at all.

"Well, we need to put an extra panel in there, anyway," Brid concluded briskly to Cathy before turning to examine Laura. "What do you think, Laura? Are you happy with your dress?" She tugged gently at the straps. "I think maybe we could tighten these a tiny bit, just to lift you slightly at the bust and . . ."

"It's perfect." Laura glanced across at Nicola who was studying her earnestly, a proud look on her face. "You look beautiful, Laura," Nicola said. "Just perfect."

"Thanks," Laura was pleased.

"Still, the rest of ye won't hold a candle to *me* on the day," Nicola added with a wicked grin. "I'll be the talk of Glengarrah!"

Laura laughed. She understood her friend well enough to know that, despite her self-deprecation and offhand jokes, Nicola was a little self-conscious about going up the aisle. But Brid had done a fine job with the two-piece, and Nicola would look just as good as everyone else on the day.

Laura opened the box and took out the jewellery she had designed for her bridesmaids. She smiled shyly. "See how this looks with it."

The neckpiece was fashioned with silver so fine it looked like hand-spun thread. Each concentric circle was intertwined with amethysts, the stones accentuating the colour of the bridesmaid's dresses. There were earrings to match, and the designs had a vague tribal-princess look – an effect that Laura had been trying to perfect for quite some time. Nicola and Cathy were wearing strapless and relatively undecorated bodices, and would be wearing their hair up, so with the neckpieces the overall effect would be stunning.

Brid and Amanda moved over to take a closer look. "Wow," Brid gasped. "Laura, where did you get these – they're fantastic!"

Cathy looked across with interest, but her face fell when she realised what she would be wearing. "I thought you'd buy us something," she said mournfully. "Something decent, or at least something we could keep."

"But it *is* something you can keep!" Nicola gave Cathy a look of mild surprise. "This is astonishing, totally originally – Laura, this is just – incredible!" Nicola couldn't think of enough superlatives to describe it.

Cathy was unmoved. "When I was Sharon Costigan's bridesmaid, she gave us a gold T-bar chain each. I have enough of your plastic at home already. Honestly, every Christmas or birthday or –"

"You made these, Laura?" Brid interrupted, goggle-eyed in amazement. "But how?"

"Laura's a jewellery designer." Nicola said proudly. "Didn't she tell you?"

"No, she did not." Brid gave Laura a reproving look. "You never said a word, Laura."

Laura reddened, unused to all this lavish praise. "I haven't been doing it for very long," she said, almost apologetically.

"Give us a look at the one you made for yourself," Nicola urged, suspecting that Laura's own piece would undoubtedly be something special. She wasn't wrong.

The bridal neckpiece was again the same circle design, but using gold and mother-of-pearl, instead of amethyst. And then there was the corresponding tiara and Kerry was thrilled to see that Laura had fashioned a smaller tiara for her too.

"Now who's a real princess!" Laura said, placing the replica tiara on Kerry's little blonde head.

"This is just amazing," Brid said, fastening the neckpiece on Laura, and standing back to admire the effect. "All this time, I couldn't understand why you wanted such a plain dress, but now I do. This puts my work to shame!"

Laura laughed. "Don't be silly, Brid. It's just something simple."

"Something simple! I wish the rubbish I get to go with my dresses was more like this. Instead I get beads and bits of wire that fall to pieces in minutes. 'Exclusive Tiaras', my foot!"

Laura's heart began to pound. This was the part where she should offer to show Brid more of her designs. Maybe

Brid might become a customer. No, she couldn't ask her, not now in front of everyone. It would be too embarrassing and she didn't want Brid to feel as though she had to say yes. Laura was still Brid's customer and she couldn't put her on the spot like that. No, she'd wait until after the wedding – then she might say something.

Cathy had taken her neckpiece off, and Amanda was carefully examining the detail. "Do you specialise in bridal jewellery only, Laura?" she asked.

"No, not at all," Laura said, suddenly embarrassed by all the interest in her work. "But I've never done anything quite so elaborate before."

"Really gorgeous," Amanda said, putting down the neckpiece and picking up the earrings, which were basically miniature versions of the neck design. "Where are you stocked, Laura? You must be run off your feet with these."

Laura reddened. "I am – sometimes I can't keep up with the demand." The words were out before she could stop them, and she gave a short nervous laugh to cover her discomfort. Luckily Nicola was now being helped out of her bodice, and didn't overhear. She'd murder her for not seizing what could be a real opportunity.

But she couldn't admit the truth to this woman who was so admiring of her designs. Laura's pride wouldn't *let* her admit that, most of the time, she sat twiddling her thumbs at home.

Chapter 22

When she was absolutely positive that Dan and John had left for their late afternoon meeting in town, Chloe entered the offices of O'Leary & Hunt, Chartered Accountants.

"Hello," she said to the young receptionist at the front desk, who had absolutely no idea that the blonde woman standing before her was her boss's fiancée. "I'm looking for . . ." she made a great show of studying the folder she carried, "for a Mr Hunt, please."

"I'm sorry, Mr Hunt is out of the office for the afternoon." The girl spoke as though she had rattled off that line many times before.

"Would Mr O'Leary be available, then?" Chloe asked, knowing full well what the answer would be.

"I'm afraid Mr O'Leary is meeting with clients at the moment. He's also out for the afternoon."

"Oh, dear." Chloe feigned an unimpressed frown.

"Did you have an appointment?"

"No, it's is a spur-of-the-moment visit, actually. I'm

here on behalf of a previous client of Mr Hunt's. I'm her legal representative, and I was really hoping to speak to one of the partners about my client's affairs." She flashed a business card.

"Oh. Well, if you'd like to leave your name and number, I can get Mr Hunt to phone you," the receptionist offered.

"No, I'm on my way down the country this afternoon, and just popped in on the off-chance. I was really hoping to speak to someone, though." Chloe sighed dramatically, but then her eyes widened, as if she had just thought of something. "Tell you what, maybe *you* could help me. You're Mr Hunt's personal secretary, yes?"

The girl blushed, flattered. "No, I'm only a student on work-experience here for the summer. Mr Hunt's PA is upstairs. Would you like to speak to her?"

Chloe pretended to study her folder again. That was exactly what she'd like. Chloe had spoken to his PA on the phone a few times but luckily they had never met. The woman wouldn't know Chloe from Adam, so hopefully by using the solicitor's ruse she would be able to glean some information from her on events from a few years ago ie, Dan's marriage break-up.

She looked up and smiled beatifically at the young receptionist. "If you wouldn't mind checking that she's free. It's Miss Fogarty, isn't it?"

The receptionist nodded, and dialled the extension. She spoke pleasantly into the mouthpiece. "Are you free for a moment, Shannon?" she asked. "There's someone at reception hoping to speak with you."

* * *

"So, you knew Nicola well then?" Chloe asked, offering a cigarette.

The other woman shrugged. "Not that well, but you could say that I knew a lot *about* her. Dan and I were close and he confided in me, particularly when things weren't going well."

"I see."

"Nicola wasn't right for him. I could see that from the very beginning. When they got married John and I gave it three years max." She gave a short laugh. "Still, I didn't think we'd be that close to the mark!"

"So what went wrong for them?" There was no point in beating about the bush, and Chloe sensed that the other woman seemed only too happy to dish the dirt.

"A number of things," she said, echoing exactly what John O'Leary had told Chloe. "His parents hated her. She wasn't good enough for him in their eyes, quite rightly too I think."

"Not good enough? How?"

She exhaled a cloud of cigarette smoke. "Come on! She had nothing going for her. Dan has his own business, he comes from a very well-off family and his father was a self-made man for Chrissake! But *her* parents – well, let's just say they weren't exactly the Rockefellers."

Chloe looked at her. "That sounds a bit harsh," she said and, despite herself, felt a bit sorry for Nicola. Would Dan really let that kind of snobbery affect him? And who the hell these days worried about backgrounds when choosing a partner?

"You asked, I'm just telling you how it happened."

"So was that it then? Did Dan's parents succeed in breaking them up?"

A derisive snort. "You could say that. But there were other things too."

"Like what?"

"Well, Nicola was mad for a baby from the very beginning. Dan wasn't so sure though. I think – no – I *know* that he wanted to wait for a few years, didn't want the pressure of a young family along with the pressure of running a new business. But he said that Nicola kept pushing him and pushing him and eventually she got her wish."

"Her wish? You don't mean that she got pregnant?"

"Yep – eventually."

"What?" Chloe nearly fell off her chair. Her heart pounded with panic. Dan had never told her. He had a child with Nicola and he never told her. But why not? And where was the child now? Was that why he had been so anxious about her coming back to Ireland? Was it because he was hiding a secret child? "You can't be serious!" she exclaimed. "Dan and Nicola had a child together?"

"I never said that they had a child – I said that she got pregnant. She lost it."

"Oh." Chloe felt something akin to relief. That explained a lot, a hell of a lot, actually. She breathed deeply. Things were finally beginning to make sense now. Dan doesn't want a child, Nicola does, she gets pregnant, loses the baby and blames Dan for not wanting it in the first place.

End of story and – more importantly – end of marriage.

She didn't have to try too hard to imagine how it all went after that. Nicola devastated by her loss and Dan's rejection of their baby initiates the divorce, Dan sick to the teeth of it all agrees, they separate, Nicola moves away and all concerned (including Dan's parents) are happy.

"But of course the affair didn't help either."

"*What*?" Chloe couldn't hide her surprise. An affair? This was incredible! Dan had an affair! She didn't think he had it in him.

"Yep. Not long after the miscarriage."

Wow! Now Chloe was really shocked. Dan just didn't seem the cheating type. He just wasn't that *interested* in other women. OK, he had a few female friends but that was it. He never noticed things other men noticed, like long legs and big boobs – the normal things! Whenever they were out together she might point out a good-looking woman across the room, just to see if she had caught his eye, but nine times out of ten he wouldn't even have seen her. Chloe supposed she should be flattered, but then again Dan was so used to women making eyes and practically throwing themselves at him, that he didn't really give a shit. And although she hated admitting it, even to herself, it had taken Chloe weeks to get him to notice *her*.

The very first time she saw Dan, he had been a guest at one of her friend Alison's Sunday barbecues. He and John had been invited by Alison's fiancé, who used Dan and John's accountancy firm. Chloe remembered thinking he looked exactly like Mel Gibson did in that film *Forever Young*, all sweet-faced and blue-eyed. For most of that day she had followed his every move out of the corner of her eye, laughing and joking loudly, trying to get him to notice her. It had been impossible, and he seemed the only man in the room that wasn't drooling over her in that short red Ben de Lisi she had been wearing.

Eventually, she had no choice but to walk right up to him and introduce herself.

"Haven't we met before somewhere?" Chloe cringed when she thought about it now, but at the time it was as good a line as any.

"I don't think so," he said, a slight smile playing about his lips, leaving Chloe in no doubt that he was used to this kind of thing.

"Oh, I'm sorry. I thought you might be a client of my father's."

"And your father is . . .?"

"Jeff Fallon. As in Fallon & Co? Solicitors?"

Dan shook his head.

"Are you sure? I'm almost positive I saw you in the office last week, with one of the partners?" She was getting desperate now and she was sure he could see it in her eyes.

"Afraid not."

"Oh – OK." Chloe feigned nonchalance. She might as well give up. "Well, nice meeting you then – Dan, isn't it?"

He nodded. "See you later."

"Yes, enjoy the party."

Chloe remembered walking off in a right mood. Who the hell did he think he was? Then a thought struck her. Maybe he was gay! Of course – that had to be it. Why else would Dan have kept his gaze on her face throughout the entire conversation, when the neckline on her dress plunged deeper than Angel Falls? He was almost definitely gay.

"Isn't he gorgeous?" she heard Alison say beside her. "Only for I'm an engaged woman," she flashed her white gold solitaire, never missing an opportunity to show it off, "I'd probably be running after him too!"

Running after him? Chloe didn't need to *run after* anyone!

"I think you'd be wasting your time." Chloe growled sulkily. "I don't think he's that way inclined."

"What? Don't be silly. According to Scott, he's not long separated from his wife. Upped and left to England apparently." She leaned forward conspiratorially. "I mean, who in their right mind would leave someone like that? He's an absolute angel!"

Chloe stopped her mind wandering and brought her attention back to the present. Well, apparently Nicola had left someone like that.

Because her beloved husband hadn't turned out to be such an angel, after all.

Chapter 23

Nicola's extension buzzed. "Nicola, can you come down to my office for a moment, please?"

"Um, just two minutes, Ken. I'm in the middle of something here."

Nicola made a face, and speed-read the remainder of the *Cosmo* article she'd been engrossed in. Ken sounded pissed off. That only meant one thing. The end-of-quarter figures were in and obviously weren't up to scratch.

Shit! She had thought that *Mode* article would do wonders for the membership figures. It wouldn't have been worth posing for all those embarrassing photographs otherwise.

She wondered how she and Ken could explain away her lack of success to the partners. Hell, she couldn't even explain that to herself. Her heart just didn't seem to be in it these days. There was just way too much going on in her head.

Nicola fiddled with a strand of her hair. She hadn't

heard from Dan since his call the other day, which was good. At least it meant she wouldn't have to keep secrets from Ken. She wondered now, as Laura had, if Dan had ever mentioned meeting her to his fiancée, and if not, why not?

She wondered too, and not for the first time, about the quality of the relationship between them. Dan wasn't devious – at least, he *hadn't* been, not for most of their relationship, and even for most of their marriage except towards the end really.

She recalled their conversation in Bray that day. It was strange how he reacted when she told him about Ken. It had obviously bothered him to find that the two of them were together, but what did it matter now? It was no longer any of his business.

But yet, Nicola thought, remembering, Dan had never really got over her and Ken, had he?

* * *

At the time, Nicola didn't think she could cope. Dan had been quiet – distant even. But how could she be expected to help him through it, when she couldn't even help herself? It was as though a dark cloud had descended on their marriage since . . . since she lost the baby.

It had been too difficult to even think about it, let alone talk about it. Even as the weeks went by, the pain was still physical, vivid and all too real. It was just so *there*.

She remembered what the doctor had told her afterwards.

"You're young, Mrs Hunt. Leave it a few months and then you can start trying for another one," he had said after performing a D&C. Nicola had wanted to kill him then. She had wanted to catch him and strangle him and make him feel some of what she was feeling.

Try for another one? How could he even suggest that? Did he not realise how she felt? How she felt as though a part of her insides had died? Because in theory that's exactly what had happened. Her baby, her and Dan's baby had died. OK, so she had only been five and a half months gone, but that baby had meant everything to her and Dan.

They had been so happy, so thrilled about it all. She should have known, though. She should have known that it was bad luck going into Mothercare every time she happened to be in town, picking out bits and pieces 'for the baby'.

What baby? Now those purchases were locked away up in the dark attic, never to see the light of day. Much like Nicola's feelings.

Would she and Dan ever see the light of day? Would she ever be able to look into his eyes again without seeing blame and sorrow reflected in them?

Because she knew he blamed her. She knew that he thought she should have gone straight to hospital when the pains started, instead of ignoring them and hoping they would go away. But she was at work at the time, the pains weren't that bad, and to be honest, she didn't really think that anything was wrong. How could she possibly have known?

Yet Dan blamed her. He blamed her for everything. She couldn't remember the last time they talked about it, if ever; the last time he had taken her in his arms and told her he loved her. It was as if the old Dan had been abducted by aliens, and a new more morose Dan had been left in his place. He never laughed any more.

He never even cried. Not once.

Nicola had cried and cried for days afterwards. She still cried sometimes.

If it weren't for those pills the doctor had given her who knows what she might have done, how she would have coped? The medication helped her get through it, helped her sleep at night and admittedly, sometimes during the day, thank goodness. And because of those pills, Nicola had been able to let it go, to come to terms with it all – eventually.

But Dan wouldn't let it go. He couldn't come to terms with it. Instead, he worked all hours of the day and often long into the evening.

"The practice is still in its infancy," he had said. "I need to put the hours in."

Yet the practice had been going well long before any of it had happened. Work had been important, sure, but never as important as their relationship had been. Dan didn't need to work late – at least not for the sake of the practice. Dan needed to work late because he couldn't face her. He couldn't bear to see, hear, or speak to her – that Nicola knew well.

But what could she do? How could she help? Then again, maybe she couldn't do anything. Maybe Dan couldn't be helped, didn't want to be helped.

She knew he was spending a lot more time with Shannon Fogarty these days. Nicola could smell the woman's Camel cigarettes on Dan's clothes every time he walked into a room.

313

Maybe Shannon was helping him.

Work was her only refuge, and Nicola spent as much time at the leisure centre as possible, albeit in a world of her own, until one day her manager had taken her up on her bad humour and unhappy disposition.

"Nikki, what's wrong?" Ken asked, his face full of concern. Nicola wouldn't meet his eyes. Ken was the only one who ever called her Nikki and normally she hated it. This time though, it sounded reassuringly familiar.

She wiped her nose with a tissue. "It's nothing, Ken. I have a bit of a cold and I'm just feeling under the weather, that's all."

"Don't give me that." He looked sceptical. "I know you, and you haven't been the same since . . . well you haven't been your usual bubbly self for a while."

"Sorry." She looked away.

"Hey, I didn't mean it like that!" Ken put an arm around her and led her away from reception towards his office. It felt good – strong and comforting. When he let her go in order to close the door behind them, Nicola was sorry the contact was broken.

"Look, I'm not having a go at you," he said, motioning her towards a seat. "We're friends. And friends look out for each other, don't they?"

She bit her lip and nodded.

"So are you going tell me what the matter is, then?"

"It's Dan," she said flatly. "Our marriage is over."

"What? You can't be serious!"

She nodded again and blew into a tissue. "He's having an affair." There – it was out. She had finally said it, finally admitted it out loud.

"What?" Ken exclaimed again. "Dan is having an affair! With whom, for goodness sake?" Without waiting for an answer he went on. "How do you know? Did you catch him? Did he confess?"

She shook her head.

"Well, what then?"

"I just know," Nicola wailed.

"Oh, for Chrissake." Ken gave her a look conveying that he would simply never, as long as he lived, be able to understand women.

Nicola sniffed and looked up. "He doesn't have to confess, Ken. All the signs are there."

"What kind of signs?"

"You know, avoiding me, supposedly working late, all those things."

"Nikki," Ken walked around his desk and knelt beside her chair, "you and Dan have been through a lot lately, what with the baby and everything."

Nicola looked at his kind face and noticed for the very first time how attractive Ken was. His eyes were like pools of melted chocolate. And his eyelashes were so long, feminine almost.

"Maybe you're just jumping to conclusions. Dan adores you. He wouldn't cheat on you."

Nicola sniffed again. "Don't be so sure."

"Well, tell me what happened to make you so sure."

"He's been out – drinking late into the night with a woman colleague, his so-called friend." Nicola wanted to slap the silly bitch's face. How dare she? How dare Shannon throw herself at her husband, trying to take advantage of their misery!

"She's been after him for years," she told Ken bitterly.

"So, why hasn't anything happened before now, then?"

"Because . . . because things were going well between us. We loved one another. He didn't blame me."

"Blame you for what – the miscarriage?" Ken put a hand on hers. "OK, I don't know Dan that well, but I do know that he loves you. Everyone knows that. And he knows as well as I do that nobody is to blame for what happened. It's just one of those things."

Nicola said nothing.

"Has he ever actually told you that he blames you?" Ken asked.

"He doesn't need to. He keeps avoiding me. He doesn't touch me. Ken, he can't even look at me. Jesus, my husband hates me so much that he can't even look at me!" The tears were flowing freely now, and Ken put an arm around Nicola and held her close.

"I hate to see you like this," he said. "Look, go home early, get some rest and then talk to him – tonight. You two need to get some things out in the open."

"I can't."

"Of course, you can. Nicola, you and Dan are the happiest couple I have ever come across – and you guys are married!" he added. "It's almost weird!"

She smiled a half-smile.

"OK, so you're going through a rough patch at the moment, but the only way to get through that is to talk about it. Chances are he doesn't have any clue that you're feeling this way, so tell him. Tell Dan how isolated, worried and lonely you feel."

"Is it that obvious?"

"It's obvious that you've been very unhappy lately,

and with good reason. But you need to sort it out before it gets too late."

Nicola nestled comfortably in the crook of his arm. It felt good. Good to be comforted, to be cherished. She and the rest of the staff at Metamorph had always joked that their hard-nosed manager was like the Tin-Man in *The Wizard of Oz* – no heart. But today Nicola had discovered that beneath that tough, businesslike exterior, Ken Harris's heart was not made of tin, but of solid gold.

"Thanks, Ken," she said, wiping her eyes again. "I feel a little embarrassed now, to be honest."

Ken smiled. "There's no need. I can't say I know what you're going through, but I can imagine how tough it must be . . ." He trailed off, his dark eyes full of concern and compassion.

Nicola looked at him. "I had no idea you were the sensitive, in-touch-with-your-feelings type," she said jokingly, beginning to feel better.

Ken looked at her meaningfully. "You'd be surprised."

Nicola couldn't pinpoint why, but at that exact moment the atmosphere in the room transformed. All of a sudden, her nerve-endings were sharp as knives and her stomach began to tremble. Ken was still holding her and, when she looked up at him, she saw his expression had changed too. She watched the attractive curve of his mouth, the faint beginnings of dark stubble on his chin.

He had a very sexy mouth, dangerously sexy, even. At that very moment and for some strange reason, Nicola very badly wanted to feel that mouth on hers. She imagined him planting tiny kisses on her neck, then moving down towards her collarbone, then her breasts, then . . .

Suddenly, she didn't have to imagine any more. Suddenly, Ken's mouth *was* on hers, kissing her, his tongue probing and teasing and then they were both standing, clinging to one another, desperate for one another.

Nicola pressed herself tightly against him and with a single swift movement, Ken lifted her up onto the desk and Nicola wrapped her legs around him, not wanting to break the contact, not even for a second. They gasped. He kissed her again, pulling her body even closer.

Neither of them heard the slight rap on the glass, nor the sound of the office door opening.

"Ken? Do you know where Nicola Hunt is supposed to be today? Oh! Oh, shit!"

The voice brought Nicola back to reality, and the two of them looked towards the doorway, to see Lisa, the gym attendant, staring wide-eyed and embarrassed at them.

Followed by a white-faced, stunned, and utterly horrified-looking Dan.

* * *

Nicola shook her head at the memory. She recalled Dan's face, the look of sheer dismay, the horror and disappointment in his eyes.

It was only when Lisa burst in on top of them that Nicola had realised what she had been doing. And Ken, poor old Ken, he had realised it too. It was as if someone had cast some weird lustful spell on the two of them, because before then there had never been an attraction. Dan had looked from Ken to Nicola, and then had – wordlessly – spun on his heel and walked out.

Ken, full of remorse, had rushed out after him. What

had happened, or what had been said between the two men then, Nicola had never known. All she had known for sure at that very moment was that she truly wanted to die.

She remembered sitting there on the desk, stunned, immobile, unable to think straight while the gym attendant stood there watching her, mortified. Lisa was new at the centre and Nicola barely knew the girl.

"I'm so, so sorry," Lisa said. "I had no idea. Believe me if I had any idea there was no way I would have come in here. I knocked but," she looked away, embarrassed, "but obviously Ken didn't hear me."

Nicola had been unable to do anything other than nod.

"Your husband –" Lisa swallowed nervously, "came in looking for you at reception and I told him I hadn't seen you around for a while. I thought you'd gone home early, what with your cold and everything, so I said I'd just pop in here and ask Ken and he followed me and . . . well, you know the rest."

Nicola put her head in her hands. "What in God's name was I doing? Lisa, you must believe me. There has never been anything going on between Ken and me. It was just a spur of the moment thing, I – I don't even know how it happened – one minute we were talking, I was upset and Ken was being tender and . . . oh *God*!"

Mortification burned through her all over again as Nicola heard herself speak. Why would Lisa believe that, why would anyone believe it? It had been nothing like a tender moment. She remember the ferocity of their kissing, the animalistic lust they had displayed.

"What are you going to do?" Lisa asked, her voice so full of sympathy that Nicola wanted to cry.

"I have no idea," she answered with a slow shake of her head. "I have absolutely no idea."

How could she go home and face him now? Dan wouldn't want anything to do with her. Unless, and the thought hit her like a speeding car, unless he had something to confess too, unless he decided to come clean about Shannon.

Nicola then experienced a moment of sudden clarity, and realised the damage she had caused to her marriage these past few weeks. She had been totally selfish and self-indulgent after the miscarriage. Instead of sitting down and talking to Dan about how she was feeling, about how they were *both* feeling about it, she had instead pushed him away and distanced him from her, trying to put the blame on him, to punish him. It made the pain easier to control if she had something to hate. And she *had* hated Dan. Yes, she had tried to turn it around, and make herself feel as though he was the one doing the blaming, but inevitably she had been the one at fault. *She* had been the one to drive him to despair, and possibly into someone else's arms. But even if it hadn't, even if Dan hadn't gone that far, then she, through her own self-absorption and childishness had. She had gone *too* far. So, she resolved to sort things out.

* * *

The extension buzzed again, startling Nicola out of her reverie.

"Nicola, what's going on. I phoned you about ten minutes ago!" Ken's exasperated tones drifted through the air.

"Shit – Ken!" She had completely forgotten about him.

She hurried to the elevator and was in his office within minutes.

"Sorry," Nicola said with a mischievous smile, "I got waylaid by a client."

Ken grinned. That was normally the excuse they used on the other Motiv8 staff when they wanted to steal a moment together. They were either 'seeing a client' or 'phoning a client'. "Oh, was he worth it?"

"Not as good as some." Nicola was surprised to see him smile.

Ken shuffled through a number of print-outs on his desk, picked one up and without a word, handed it across the table to her.

Nicola's heart thumped as she began to read it. She was silent for a moment. Then her eyes widened and she looked up, delighted. "I don't believe it!" she exclaimed. "The figures for July/August are sky high!"

It was simply incredible. Membership uptake was always at its slowest throughout the mid-summer months. People out and about in the fine weather saw little need for pounding on a treadmill when they could enjoy the exercise much more in the park or on the beach. But the report Nicola held for the summer read as well as the one for January! She couldn't believe it.

"That article was an absolute godsend, Nikki," Ken smiled. "Those figures should carry us through for the rest of the year. The accountant will be happy, as will the partners so I'm confident of getting a capital top-up for next year. Should free us up to spend a bit more on this place. Well done!" He winked at her. "I always knew you were the right person for this job, you know."

Nicola smiled at this. Initially, she had her reservations about coming back to Ireland and taking up Ken's job offer, unsure as to whether she would be able for it – unsure if coming back home was a good thing. She had also been quite touchy about it, suspecting that Ken had suggested her for the job simply because of her situation and because he was feeling sorry for her. But Ken had been insistent that she would be perfect for Motiv8 and, as it turned out, he was right. She loved this job and within months had dispelled any of her own qualms about Ken's ulterior motives for offering her the manager's post. She was good at this, and she knew it.

Soon she realised that Ken had offered her the job because he understood her need for independence and a chance to regain some normality – and also because he cared deeply about her.

Nicola hadn't known it at the time, hadn't known it that day in his office when Dan walked in, hadn't known it for a long time after they began working together at Motiv8. But when she eventually did find out, she didn't care about Ken's original intentions, because by then she had fallen in love with him too.

She had been very lucky, she thought, studying Ken who looked as pleased as Punch with himself as he reread the figures. She had been very lucky in finding a man like him; maybe she should put more of an effort into making sure he knew it.

And, she thought cheerfully, recalling her recent

musings about Dan and the problems in her first marriage, she really had been worrying for nothing. Dan could continue phoning her all he liked, but she and Ken were happier than ever. Whatever Dan Hunt's intentions might be, there was little he could do to change that.

Chapter 24

Nicola had had the affair. Oh, God no. Chloe hadn't expected that. Why hadn't John O'Leary said anything about it? Shit! Shit! Shit!

Chloe started up the Jeep and headed towards Lynne's house. She needed to talk to someone about this, get someone else's opinion on it.

What a bitch! And a silly cow. What woman in her right mind would cheat on someone like Dan Hunt?

Then a thought struck Chloe. Nicola hadn't been in her right mind though, had she? She had been full sure that Dan was carrying on with Shannon. Chloe had thought so too, with the way the way the story was going. After all, Nicola had rejected him and kept pushing him away, refusing to let him share her grief.

But Shannon hadn't a hope, because obviously Dan was too much in love with Nicola, too much in love with their marriage.

Still, that gave Nicola no excuse to start having it off with her boss!

And Dan had actually *caught* them at it too! No wonder he didn't want to talk about it! Now Chloe understood. No man likes to admit they've been cheated on, least of all a man like Dan.

But if Dan and Nicola's marriage ended because of her fling, then goodness only knows how he felt about her now. Maybe he was still in love with her. Chloe remembered what John had said before about Dan having to 'get over her'. Maybe Dan had got over Nicola, but meeting her again had brought all the old feelings back.

Nicola had broken Dan's heart, and their marriage had ended because of her affair. But now she was back. Chloe's heart sank.

What in God's name was she going to do?

Chapter 25

Laura carefully eased the dress over her shoulders, and pulled the skirt down over her hips. She hoped that the false tan she'd applied earlier had fully dried; otherwise she would have some orange go-fast stripes down each side of her wedding dress. Lovely.

She turned sideways and struggled to view her rear in the mirror, hoping that it wouldn't be obvious to all and sundry that she had had to wear industrial-strength knickers under the dress.

She giggled as she put on her garter. The lace garter combined with those knickers didn't exactly make for sexy viewing. But she didn't think Neil would mind. In fairness, by the time they got to bed tonight she might as well be wearing knickers made of steel for all the interest he would have in them. A few pints and Neil could barely stand up, let alone anything else. Laura smiled. She and Neil wouldn't be the first or last couple that didn't consummate their marriage on their wedding night.

She hoped that today would be a good day. She was a little bit nervous about the reception, thinking that perhaps she had been mistaken in omitting her mother's family from the guest list.

Maureen was barely talking to her over it. For some reason, she had been convinced that Laura could eventually be talked round into inviting them, and had been apoplectic when Neil had finally put the kybosh on it by admitting that the invitations had been sent out two months earlier, and not one had been addressed to the Kellys in Glengarrah.

"It's nothing but bad manners," Laura had overheard her mother say to him, and had nearly died with embarrassment.

But Neil was well able for her. "Isn't it bad manners that not one of them have ever congratulated Laura on her engagement, Maureen? Isn't it bad manners that they didn't bother turning up at the church for the twins' christening, but were the first into the hotel for the dinner?"

It was true. There had been so many Kellys ensconced at the hotel beforehand, that upon the christening party's arrival, the hotel had actually had to set a second table, while all the while Maureen's sister-in-law Francis had moaned about the delay in being fed. Laura couldn't understand why Cathy had never said anything, but her sister was too like her mother, always eager to please, always afraid to risk insult.

Still, neither Cathy nor Maureen seemed all that afraid of insulting Laura. Only that morning, she had overheard Cathy complaining about the 'cheap tat' she had to wear with her dress.

But Laura wasn't going to let any of them get to her. Not today.

She finished dressing and for a long moment studied her reflection in the mirror. She was so looking forward to this, so looking forward to starting married life with Neil. She had been feeling strange about things lately, strange about the business, about her mother, about Helen. But today was about Laura and Neil. The rest could wait for the moment.

There was a low knock and a slight throat clearing outside.

"Can I come in?" Joe Fanning asked.

"Of course, Dad. I think I'm ready to go now." Laura smiled, her dad being the first one to see her in full wedding regalia. She waited expectantly for him to comment. After all, it wasn't every day that your daughter got married.

"You're looking very – em – nice," he said in such a way that Laura knew he had been warned to say it. Her heart sank. "But your mother was wondering if you might hurry things up a little bit. The photographer is downstairs, and she doesn't want to hold him up."

Hold him up – where else would Kieran be going? He was her bloody photographer, for goodness sake – and an old schoolfriend at that!

"Fine, tell them I'll be down in a minute," she said, annoyed that her mother couldn't even let her savour a few moments alone before her own wedding. *Hurry things up!*

"Right," Joe turned towards the door, paused slightly, and then turned back to Laura. "Whatever happens, love, with your business, with everything . . . just try to be happy. You deserve it," he said quietly and almost embarrassedly, before heading back downstairs.

Laura looked after him, tears in her eyes. That from her father meant more than any pride-filled speech or words of encouragement. A man of very few words, Laura knew that those few came right from Joe's heart. She also knew that it was his way of telling Laura not to let Maureen's antics get to her. Her father was one of the kindest, most patient and easy-going people she knew, and he had a lot to put up with in Maureen. Yet he never complained and merely went about defusing arguments and smoothing over problems without ever losing his cool.

Laura wondered how he managed it all these years. How had he let himself be henpecked and browbeaten by his wife, a selfish woman who didn't know the meaning of the word compromise? Had Maureen always been that way? Did her mother begrudge and belittle people and their intentions when she was Laura's age, or had getting older blighted her vision and closed her mind? Laura didn't know, but she knew that she was determined never to be that way. If Laura had a daughter, she would give her every encouragement possible, she would let her make her own mistakes and be there for her to pick up the pieces. Had her mother ever done that for Laura? The simple answer was no. From an early age, she had tried to stifle her artistic abilities and discouraged her from following her dream to such an extent that Laura had lost faith in herself. It wasn't because she *wanted* to go to design college that she ended up there – no – it was because her Career Guidance teacher had *recommended* Laura should go. A professional person, a person who knew what she was talking about, not an 'ordinary person' like Maureen. As far as Laura's mother was concerned, if a professional person thought her daughter should go to design college, then that was fine. What did it matter what Laura wanted? What did Laura know about things like that?

But then, when it didn't work out afterwards, when Laura didn't easily find a job in that field, Maureen had stepped in and insisted she find a 'proper' job. She was only too happy to let her daughter's talents go to waste in an uninspiring and unchallenging office career, her hopes and dreams drifting further and further away with each passing day.

It really wasn't until she met Neil, wonderful, kind and patient Neil, that Laura had given her ambitions a second thought.

And look where that had led.

Laura shook her head. Today was not the day to be thinking about the business and whether it would or wouldn't succeed. She wasn't going to allow her mother's doubts in her abilities creep into her conscience and ruin her chances.

Today she was getting married, and Laura was going to enjoy every minute of it.

* * *

Nicola and the others waited for Laura's arrival outside the church. Helen, who Nicola noticed was looking very sexy – possibly a little *too* sexy for a wedding – had just arrived and was doing her best to calm down a hyper Kerry. Her friend was wearing figure-hugging Lainey

Keogh – the hem of the bright, multicoloured dress just long enough to be decent. There was no denying that Helen had a fantastic figure and amazing legs, and judging by the gawks she was getting from some of the male guests, Nicola wasn't the only one to notice.

"Where's Paul?" Nicola asked immediately, hoping to finally get a glimpse of this supposed sex-god.

"Oh, he's not coming," she said airily. "Something cropped up at work. Last minute, you know yourself." She indicated Nicola's neckpiece. "Wow, look at that. It's gorgeous."

Nicola caught Ken's eye. Last minute . . . on a Saturday?

Hopefully this Paul wasn't just another of Helen's come-a-day, go-a-day boyfriends, and if he was, she hoped that at least her friend would have the sense not to let him get too involved with Kerry. Although Helen was great like that. She rarely introduced her boyfriends to her daughter, ostensibly because she was unsure of how the relationship would go and, of course, didn't want Kerry getting attached to someone who could eventually disappear from her life.

For all the giving out she did about Helen's maternal shortcomings, Nicola had to admire her for that. Kerry had never known Jamie, so it wasn't as though she needed a father figure in her life. Yet, Nicola thought, it would be good for Kerry and indeed for Helen, to maybe eventually have someone she could call 'Daddy'. She wondered briefly if this Paul might be that someone.

"You know, we should try and arrange something after the wedding," she said to Helen. "Get all of us round to the house for something to eat, and you could bring Paul."

"Yeah," Ken added, "it would be much easier than meeting everyone at something like this."

"He really is working, you know – he didn't just bottle out, if that's what you're thinking," Helen said testily.

"That's not what we meant." Nicola decided she had better shut up. If Helen was going to be touchy about it, there was no point in pursuing it. And she didn't want Helen in bad form on Laura's wedding day.

Laura arrived shortly afterwards, helped out of the car by her father. She was the picture of radiance and, as she smiled down at Kerry, who had raced across to hug her, Nicola thought she had never seen her friend look so beautiful.

The ceremony was wonderful. Nicola felt silly for worrying about how she herself would look going up the aisle in front of Laura – although there had been a few curious sideways glances, nobody took much notice of her. And why would they? They were all watching the bride.

There were tears in Neil's eyes when he caught sight of his wife-to-be and Nicola knew that those tears weren't just for Laura. His mother had taken a bit of a turn the week before the ceremony and both he and Laura were concerned that she might not make the wedding. But there Pamela was, sitting behind him and looking as well as she could be in a lilac two-piece and a Philip Treacy hat.

Throughout the day Nicola thought she looked very tired and very drained. She sensed that Pamela was struggling to enjoy her son's wedding reception and, to her credit, a proud smile never left her face.

Today was also the first time that Nicola had met Laura's family, and her friend certainly hadn't been exaggerating about her mother, she thought wryly, thinking that perhaps Laura had been *too* kind in her assessment of Maureen Fanning. For most of Laura's wedding day, and particularly throughout the dinner, Maureen Fanning looked petrified. Petrified that something would go wrong, petrified that the food wouldn't be good enough and petrified that the uppity Connollys might not approve of the arrangements. Nicola could see all of this written in the older woman's anxious face. Maureen was petrified, it seemed, of everything but whether or not her daughter was having a good time and making the most of her big day. At one stage, when Neil had finished his speech and invited his new wife to say a few words, Maureen had looked as though she might go into cardiac arrest. As it turned out, Laura shyly refused, but Nicola thought she knew exactly why Maureen had been so alarmed by this. A bride making speeches, expressing happiness, thanking everyone who shared in her special day? It just wasn't 'the done thing'!

Being as close to her own mother as she was, Nicola found it all very strange. Why was Maureen Fanning so self-conscious? Surely she should just settle down, enjoy the day and be proud of the fact that she had raised a daughter like Laura, be proud of the fact that her daughter was today the happiest woman alive? But no, Maureen looked as though she was waiting for the bomb to drop any minute. It was all very sad.

A little after the meal, when the wedding guests were reseating themselves for the evening, a crowd of – well, they looked to all intents and purposes like a horde of

Neanderthals – barged into the hall and colonised at least three tables at the top of the room. She had *never* seen so many young children at a wedding before. It turned out that this crowd were relations of Laura's that hadn't been invited to the wedding, presumably because they were loud, unruly and could drink for Ireland. And that was only the women! One of them had nearly toppled Nicola over in her rush to the bar.

Seeing Laura's wide-eyed alarm upon their arrival, Nicola was sure that one of her parents would have a word asking them to calm down, but lo and behold, there was Laura's mother smiling and handing out balloons to the kids, who with obvious glee immediately set about bursting them and frightening the heart out of poor Pamela Connolly.

Helen returned to the table then with an orange juice for Kerry, a pint for Ken, and more wine for herself and Nicola. She looked around and made a face.

"Where did that crowd come from all of a sudden?" she asked, then recognition dawned. "Oh no, not the bloody Kellys!"

"Laura's relations, apparently." Nicola raised an eyebrow as one of the said Kellys approached their table.

"Jaysus, Helen Jackson, I nearly didn't recognise ya!"

Nicola was nearly knocked out from the stench of drink on his breath, so goodness knows how Helen felt with him in her face like that.

"Nicola, meet Charlie Kelly," Helen said drily.

"And you must have had one of them boob-jobs since I seen you last 'cos you've a fine pair of knockers on ya today!"

Helen gave him a look that would definitely hurt tomorrow. "Charlie, if you don't take your stinking mitts off me *this minute*, you'll be living out the rest of your days as a eunuch."

Nicola caught Kerry's eye and winked. Kerry put her hand to her mouth and gave a little giggle. She knew *that* tone of her mother's only too well.

Charlie Kelly wasn't a bit put out. "Ah, Helen, you're gone awfully up in yourself. God be with the days when you were happy to ride anything that looked at you sideways."

Nicola's mouth dropped open and Ken moved to challenge him, but Helen shook her head as if to say 'don't mind him'. She was obviously well used to his blather.

Charlie guffawed. "Ah, relax, sure I'm only having you on," he said, nudging Ken. "I wouldn't mind but the likes of any of us couldn't get next nor near her. So is this the young one?" He sat down next to Kerry. "Jaysus, she's the spittin image of ya, Helen. Howya, young one, I'm Charlie – what's your name?"

He extended a huge sweaty hand and Kerry, far from being afraid of Charlie Kelly, as Nicola most definitely would have been at that age (she was even now!) seemed delighted with him.

"My name is K-K-Kerry," she said taking his hand shyly, and Nicola offered a silent prayer that Charlie wouldn't make fun of her stutter.

"Well, aren't you a gorgeous little thing," he said. "I'd say you'd get on grand with my Shelley. Shelley!" he roared, and a tiny dark-eyed child of about Kerry's age came running over. "This is Mary – I bet she'd love to see your new Barbie doll, wouldn't ya, Mary?"

"No, it's *Kerry*,"she corrected with a giggle, and Nicola knew instantly that Charlie had mispronounced her name on purpose in order to put her at ease. It worked. Within seconds Kerry and young Shelley Kelly were playing happily under the table with Shelley's Barbie dolls.

Charlie too seemed determined to grace them with his company for a while longer.

"So you must be one of the bridesmaids?" he said, giving Nicola the once-over, when Ken had gone to the gents'. "Jaysus, you're a fine lump of a woman! Will you give us a dance later, when the wife isn't looking?" He gave her a lecherous wink. Helen looked horrified.

"Maybe later," Nicola answered, with a slight smile, remembering that Charlie hadn't been at the wedding ceremony.

"Ah, I know a blow-off when I hear one, not to worry." Charlie was unconcerned. Then he leaned closer to Helen and his voice dropped conspiratorially. "Tell us, whose yer woman over there with the toupee?"

"Charlie!" Helen was shocked. "That's Neil's mother. She's very ill."

"Oh God," to his credit, Charlie looked shamefaced, "oh feck it, I'm sorry. I didn't know . . . I didn't mean anything by it . . . I didn't know."

"That's all right," Helen said. "Just make sure that the rest of your crowd don't start making fun of her – you know what they can be like with a few jars on them."

Glancing across at the table next to them, Nicola thought she wouldn't like to see what the Kellys were like 'with a few jars on them', when they looked totally smashed as it was.

"Do you mind if I ask you something?" Charlie said after a short while, a thoughtful look on his face.

"Go on." Nicola wondered what was coming this time.

"Well, is it my imagination – or do you have a rake of sparkly chicken wire wrapped around your neck?"

Chapter 26

A week later Nicola and Ken were relaxing in front of the television, Barney sleeping peacefully at their feet, when she got a call.

"Hello, Nicola?"

She smiled. "Hello, yourself. How are you? I'm so glad you rang. I was just talking to Laura about you a while ago, actually. When are we meeting for coffee?"

"Soon, I hope. But look, this isn't actually a social call."

"Oh? What's wrong?"

"Well, someone came to see me a few days ago, someone who was asking a lot of questions about you."

Nicola took the cordless handset into the kitchen and closed the door behind her. "What do you mean? Who? What kind of questions?"

"It was Dan's fiancée. She was pumping for information about when you two were married. I couldn't get you at home before now, and I didn't want to disturb you at work."

"You can't be serious! What did she want?"

"Well, she's a cute one. She let on that she was some kind of solicitor or something. Only for I've seen her before, and I knew damn well who she really was, I might have been taken in by it. John pointed her out to me one night."

"What? She didn't even tell you who she was?"

"No. She obviously doesn't want anyone, including Dan, to know that she's digging around. Obviously, I didn't say much to her and I told her that the two of us were friends, but only through Dan and John."

"And?"

"And she said she was under the impression that I had been a close friend of yours, so I told her that if I was such a close friend, why didn't I even know you were back in Ireland until recently?" She paused. "She was very persistent. I didn't really take to her, to be honest."

Nicola couldn't believe it. If Dan's fiancée was looking for information about her, then she must know that she and Dan had met up again lately. Maybe she was the jealous type, Nicola thought, recalling how unnerved Ken had been by it all. But surely if Dan had told her everything, then she'd know there was absolutely no reason for her to be jealous.

"Do you think I should tell Dan about this?" she said, thinking out loud.

"Well, if it was me, I'd *have* to tell him. I wouldn't want her poking around in my business like that. I mean, she could be talking to anyone."

Nicola sighed. "I wonder if she *has* spoken to anyone else?"

"To be honest, I kind of got the impression that she had, because she seemed to know an awful lot about your marriage. But she didn't get much from me."

What would Chloe want to know about their marriage? Her first guess was that Chloe was basically insecure, but she couldn't imagine how any woman could be so bad that they'd resort to sneaking around like that. "Look, thanks for putting her off."

"No problem. I just thought you should know, though. I wouldn't like someone asking questions about me behind *my* back like that."

"Thanks. And listen, you should come over soon, for dinner or something."

"I will, we'll arrange it soon."

"Who was that?" Ken asked easily, when she returned to the living-room.

"What? Oh, it was Helen, wondering if I could baby-sit Kerry this weekend," Nicola lied. She couldn't tell him about this. Ken would go mad. *And* she couldn't risk the possibility that he might confront Dan about it. Shit! She had thought this thing was over and done with.

"Oh." Unperturbed, Ken changed the television channel.

"I'm going to make a cuppa," Nicola said, needing a little time to think about this. "Do you want anything from the kitchen?"

Ken looked up, pondering. "Mmm, I think I'd like the table, please," he teased, "and maybe a couple of chairs while you're at it?"

"Ha! Somebody's in fine form tonight." Nicola smiled absently and left the room, her mind fully focused on what she had just heard.

Dan's fiancée asking around about her? Why? She'd have to tell Dan and let him deal with it. It was up to him to sort it out.

Luckily, her old friends were supportive, and of course they wouldn't tell Chloe anything. Laura certainly wouldn't, neither would Helen, and no better woman than Carolyn O'Leary to tell her where to go! But Chloe wouldn't be bold enough to approach her closest friends, would she?

* * *

The following day, still annoyed, Nicola dialled Dan's number

"O'Leary, Hunt Accountancy. Can I help you?" It was a voice Nicola didn't recognise.

She cleared her throat. "Is Mr Hunt free, please?"

"He's in a meeting at the moment," the telephonist told her in a song-song voice. "Would you like to leave a message?"

Nicola paused. Should she leave her number? Dan would surely wonder why she was calling him. It was probably better to phone back later and speak to him directly.

"Or possibly his PA could help you? Shall I put you through?" the girl continued, unnerved by the lack of a response.

"No, no, that's fine. I'll just leave my number, thanks." Nicola recited her office number and hung up.

Nearly an hour later, she was in the gym conversing with one of the newer instructors when Sally roared across at her.

"Nicola, phone!"

It was Dan.

"Nic?" he sounded pleased, but a little surprised. "Did you phone me earlier?"

She nodded, forgetting he couldn't see her.

"Nic – you still there?"

"Yes, sorry. Dan, can you hold for just a minute? I want to use the phone in my office."

"Sounds ominous," he joked.

When she was safely ensconced in the privacy of her own office, Nicola told him what she had learned about Chloe.

"Are you serious?"

"I wouldn't make something like this up, Dan."

"I know – that's not what I meant . . . Jesus! What the hell is she playing at?" he asked, voice raised in anger.

"Look, I'm not telling you this to cause any trouble between you two, but I have to tell you that I don't like it."

"Shit! I just can't believe that she would do something like that. And pretending to be a solicitor? Did it ever cross her silly little mind what would happen if she were found out? I just don't believe this!"

"Well, why *is* she doing it?" Nicola asked shortly.

"I don't know . . . I . . . well, I know she's been very anxious about you and –"

"But why?"

Dan was silent for a moment. "I didn't . . . Nicola, she doesn't know."

"What?"

"I just couldn't . . . I wasn't able to . . ." he trailed off.

"Oh, Dan . . ." Almost immediately, Nicola felt sorry for Chloe. The girl obviously felt threatened by her, and was trying to allay her fears by finding out as much as she could. Nicola tried to put herself in Chloe's position, and knew that she herself would probably have done the same, albeit a little less underhandedly. Dan was a fool to keep things from her.

"Dan, you need to sit her down and tell her everything," she said. "It's only right."

"It's got nothing to do with her, Nic. It's to do with you and me."

"That's exactly why she's sneaking around – you're shutting her out."

"For God's sake, why should it matter to her?"

"Well, it does, obviously."

"It's none of her business," he said again, then sighed deeply. "Look, what has she found out so far?"

"I'm not too sure – she was asking questions about our marriage, about any problems we were having."

"But she was told where to go?"

"Apparently."

"Right." His voice was hard. "Well, look, let me sort it out from here and don't you worry about it a second longer."

She nodded. "Dan . . . it's important that you know I'm not trying to cause any trouble between you. It's just –"

"I know that, Nic," he interjected, "but I'm glad you told me this. It gives me some idea of the type of person I was supposed to marry."

Was *supposed to marry*?

"Oh – I thought you two were married by now," Nicola said, surprised. Their wedding was to take place the day before Laura and Neil's. Was Dan saying that it hadn't?

"No, it's a long story but the hotel messed up on the booking. We had to postpone, and the way things are going, it's a bloody good job we did."

Oh! At least it had nothing to do with her anyway, Nicola thought, unsure if she was pleased or worse, *relieved*. She had worried a little when he kept phoning, asking to meet up again, hoping that they could maintain some kind of friendship. But what Dan was doing wasn't fair to Chloe. The girl deserved better.

"Dan, if Chloe thinks you're hiding something, then you can't blame her for wanting to find out what it is. She's just trying to protect herself and your relationship."

"I know that." He sounded contrite.

The conversation was suspended in silence for a moment, as both Dan and Nicola were lost in their own thoughts.

"Look, Nic, I promise I'll sort this out but . . . please, can we meet again soon?" Dan's voice was soft. "We didn't really get a chance to –"

"Dan, no. As I said before, I've moved on – we've *both* moved on. I've got Ken to think of and there's no point in our going over what went on before. It's history now."

He exhaled deeply. "OK, I understand. But look, I know you don't want to hear this now, least of all from me but maybe . . . maybe sometime soon you might feel like talking about it. If you do, let me know."

"Thanks." Why couldn't he just leave things well enough alone?

"All right then. Take care." Dan hung up.

* * *

"What the hell did you think you were playing at, Chloe?" Dan raged. "Sneaking around like that – pretending to be someone you weren't?"

"Dan, I'm sorry, really I am. I didn't know what else to do!"

"*What else to do!*" he repeated savagely. "Chloe, I told you before that what happened between me and Nicola is none of your business. We're divorced now and it's over."

"But you were always so cagey about it . . . and I was just afraid that it was something terrible."

"Well, did what you find out put your mind at ease then?" he snapped. He had no idea what Chloe had found out, if anything, so he was particularly interested in how she answered now.

She looked away, ashamed. "I know that you and Nicola lost a baby, and that . . . that she cheated on you." When she saw his eyes widen, Chloe floundered. "I'm sorry, Dan. I had no idea, I thought it might be something else . . . oh, I don't know what I thought." She shook her head.

Dan's mind raced. What she had said surprised him, because there were only a few people who would have known about Nicola's 'fling' with Ken Harris back then.

Unless Harris had been shooting his mouth off. But no, as much as he hated the bastard, Dan knew that Ken Harris had nothing but the utmost respect for Nicola. In fairness, Harris had been the one to convince Dan that there was nothing between them – that they hadn't been carrying on some torrid affair behind his back, that Ken couldn't help the feelings he had always had for Nicola, despite the fact that she was a married woman. The man had been distraught with guilt, and although he'd wanted to tear the fucker limb from limb, Dan respected him for his honesty. Harris had even tried his best to get them back together and for a while it had worked. Anyway, weren't he and Nicola an item now – much as the idea galled Dan and made him sick to his stomach. So Ken would hardly go shooting his mouth off about it, would he? No, it wouldn't have been Harris.

So who then? Dan thought back to that time, one of the most difficult periods of their short marriage. Who had he and Nicola been confiding in back then? He never told John anything. So who else? Then the thought struck him. Shit, shit, shit!

Dan clapped a hand to his forehead. There was one person who would be more than happy to blab all about it. Dan raced from the room, leaving Chloe white-faced with remorse.

* * *

"You stupid cow!" he shouted down the telephone. "Don't you have a single shred of compassion or *decency*? You know how hard things have been for Nicola – why drag it all up again?"

"Dan, calm down."

"What? You're telling *me* to calm down! Why did you talk to her in the first place?"

"Look, I didn't know who she was, OK? She showed me her business card and she said she was on official business, so what was I to do?"

"You could have kept your mouth shut! I thought you were supposed to be a friend."

"I said I didn't know, OK? Jesus, it's not a fucking state secret that you and Nicola were having problems back then – you two are divorced, for God's sake! What's the big deal?"

"You're a spiteful bitch, and I think you knew damn well what you were doing and what you were saying."

She sniffed. "You think I did this for revenge, Dan? You think I did it because I wanted you all for myself? That one night wasn't good enough for me?"

Dan's heart sank. He didn't want to discuss this with her. He didn't want to have to feel guilty about it all over again.

"I think you did it because you were pissed off that it *was* only one night," he said. "You knew I wasn't myself. You knew I was going through a terrible time yet –"

"Yet I dragged you into bed," she said mockingly, "and made you go through with it – not once, but twice! Give me a break, Dan. You wanted it as much as I did. Going through a terrible time, my arse! What about *my* problems. What about all *I* had to put up with? We needed each other at the time, and that was all there was to it."

"Look, we've had this out before. There's no point –"

"No, that's true. There is no point," she said. "In fairness, it wasn't all that good anyway. I could have done a better job on myself."

"God, you're a cold-hearted cow! You pretend to be my friend, and then at the first opportunity you turn around and shoot me in the back."

"Shoot you in the back? I only told your *fiancée* what she wanted to know, and if you had any decency you'd tell her the rest. No wonder the poor girl has to sneak around behind your back. *You* obviously don't trust her."

"It's not fair to Nicola."

"Jesus, Dan, you and Nicola are finished! When are you going to accept that? She wasn't there for you when you needed her; she was too busy feeling sorry for herself, without a second thought as to what you might be going through. *I* was the one who was there for you, Dan. Yet you're still carrying a torch for *her*. "

He shook his head. "You have no idea, do you?"

"What?"

"You have absolutely no idea how hard it was for Nicola. Have you even *seen* her since she's come back?"

"Yes, and she seemed perfectly all right to me," she snapped dismissively.

"She's better than all right, luckily. And she's gotten over all of this, and put it behind her, so why are you doing this?"

"Doing what? Dan, I haven't done anything. Chloe's the one asking all the bloody questions!"

"God, to think that I defended you –" Dan broke off and shook his head from side to side. "I was there for you when you were down and out, when you were having problems of your own. And even when you threatened to tell her, trying to break up *my* marriage, I still forgave you – because I thought you were just upset over John, and I didn't want Nicola to think badly of you."

"Dan, you broke up your marriage all by yourself, and without help from me or anyone else. You were happy to come to me when you wanted it, so don't you dare try to transfer *your* guilt on to me."

"It was a stupid mistake . . . I . . ." Dan trailed off. And it *was* a mistake. He hadn't meant to do it, but he had been so lonely at the time, and he couldn't get through to Nicola – by then she was a different person and he couldn't do anything or say anything right, so what else was he supposed to do. . .?

"You said you'd tell her – that you couldn't live with the guilt. You never did though, did you?"

He paused, remembering. "I couldn't tell her," he said sadly. "I wanted to but I just couldn't – she'd have been devastated. Things were bad enough –"

She gave a short laugh. "It's hilarious, really. Poor old Nicola never had a clue and the funny thing is, she still thinks we're friends! I met her in town a while back and the dozy cow asked me to go for coffee with her. What a joke!"

Dan gritted his teeth in anger. She was one dangerous bitch – that was for sure. If only he had realised that at the time.

"I promise you," he warned, "if you do anything, or say anything else to Nicola *or* to Chloe, so help me God, I'll do damage to you. It's none of your business, so from now on you'd better keep out of it."

Carolyn O'Leary smiled.

"Don't worry," she said smugly, "your little secret is safe with me."

Chapter 27

The following weekend, Nicola was buzzing around the living-room tidying things away while a giddy Barney skipped around alongside her, tongue out and tail wagging.

She was so engrossed in her tidying that only for Barney she almost missed the pasta boiling over on the hob. Hearing his shrill bark, Nicola zoomed into the kitchen and reached the cooker only seconds before the starchy water boiled over. Thank God for that, she thought, reaching down to scratch her conscientious doggy behind one ear. She didn't have time for mopping and scrubbing, particularly when her visitor was due within minutes.

The doorbell rang, and Nicola looked up at the clock. It was almost eight. Just in time. She went out to the hallway and opened the door.

"Hello, stranger!" she said, giving the caller an effusive hug.

"It's great to see you." Shannon stood back, and gave Nicola the once-over. "How are you doing?"

"Great, great, come on in." Nicola led her through to the kitchen, Barney sniffing curiously at the new visitor's heels. "Don't mind him. He'll be all over you for a while but he's harmless." Nicola gave her dog a mock-stern look while she poured wine. "He looks after me though, don't you, Barn?"

Barney responded by enthusiastically wagging the entire bottom half of his body.

"He's amazing," Shannon said, caressing his silky ears as he nuzzled into her. "How long have you had him?"

"Well, it seems like forever, but he's only been around since I got this place."

Shannon looked around. "It's a great place – really well laid out, isn't it?"

"It needed a lot of work," Nicola said with a grin as she handed Shannon a glass of Chardonnay. "Luckily I had a very patient builder."

"I can't believe it's taken me this long to pay an actual visit!" Shannon grimaced. "I should have called round long before now." Then her expression grew serious. "Look, I hope I didn't upset you the other day with the Chloe thing. I just thought I should let you know."

Nicola waved her away. "Quite the opposite. I'm glad you told me."

It had been very decent of Shannon to tip her off about Chloe's digging. So far, the girl hadn't approached Laura or Helen, and Nicola had yet to find out whether or not she had spoken to Carolyn O'Leary. But Nicola knew that if Chloe did, there was nothing to worry about. Carolyn would be the first one to send the girl off with a flea in her ear.

It was such a pity that she and Carolyn had lost contact

after her move. Then again, she thought, their friendship had cooled somewhat as a result of her relationship with Shannon.

Nicola had been completely mistaken in assuming, as she had in the early days, that Shannon was chasing Dan. After a series of arguments about the girl, and Nicola's complaints that Dan spent too much time with her, Nicola soon discovered that Dan's insistence that he was just a shoulder to cry on was actually just that.

He eventually admitted that Shannon had been having an on/off relationship with John O'Leary for years before Carolyn came on the scene. Shannon was deeply in love with him and heartbroken when he married. Carolyn gradually became aware of Shannon's feelings, and as a result the two women detested one another. Employing Shannon at the accountancy practice had been a massive flash-point for John and Carolyn. Nicola now suspected that this might have eventually led to serious problems in their marriage, and their eventual separation, which incidentally, Nicola had known nothing about until Dan had told her that day in Bray.

Well, at least *she* and Shannon had got their initial distrust out of the way, and had eventually become firm friends, Nicola thought fondly. Once she discovered the truth, Nicola had felt terribly sorry for Shannon, not to mention guilty about her early treatment of her. To make it worse, John kept leading the poor girl on by using her for sex whenever he felt like it. Many was the night Nicola had sat up until all hours with the other woman pouring her heart out over John and how she would 'never love anyone else'.

As difficult as it had been, Nicola hadn't said anything to Carolyn about her husband's faithlessness, having been warned by Dan not to.

"There's no point in either of us getting involved," he had said. "I tried to speak to John about it before, and he told me exactly where to go."

"But surely Carolyn deserves to know what a rat he is!" Nicola had countered vehemently, after John had wooed and then promptly dumped Shannon for the umpteenth time, Carolyn having been away at her mother's in Mayo.

"Well, with the way John is going, she'll find out herself soon enough," Dan said. "In the meantime, we should just stay out of it."

"Dan, she's a friend. If the situations were reversed I'd expect her to tell me."

"Well, from what I can make out," Dan had said cryptically, "Carolyn is no angel herself."

At the time, Nicola resolved to keep her mouth shut, at least for the time being. Her loyalties were torn. On the one hand she hated not telling Carolyn that her husband was being unfaithful, and on the other she felt desperately sorry for Shannon. The girl had been totally powerless to break free of John O'Leary's hold over her.

Until recently that is. Nicola and Shannon had always kept in touch, Shannon being one of the first to visit her after the break-up, and Nicola smiled at what Shannon had told her recently.

"I've been seeing someone," she had said one day on the phone, "someone nice. He's a little older than me, but we get on really well and I think this could be it."

The girl really was a total romantic at heart. Nicola

hoped things worked out for her and her older man. God knows she deserved that this relationship be 'it'.

Shannon brushed a strand of auburn hair out of her face. "You obviously told Dan all about it anyway," she said. "He was straight on the phone to me the following night, wondering if Chloe had got anything out of me."

"He was?" Nicola was puzzled. "Surely he knows you wouldn't have discussed anything with her?"

"Well, apparently she knew about you and Ken – back then, I mean . . . you know before . . ." Shannon looked embarrassed.

"What? You're kidding! But how?" Nicola's mind raced. Where had Chloe got *that* from? Shannon didn't tell her, and obviously Dan didn't either so who else . . .?

Suddenly it hit her. "Carolyn!" she exclaimed breathlessly.

The other girl nodded. "That's what I thought, and exactly what I told Dan." She hesitated. "Look, I'm not exactly impartial here, and I know you two were friends but I've always thought Carolyn was a sneaky bitch."

Nicola recalled again Carolyn's unfriendliness towards her that day in Butler's Chocolate Café. At the time, she had put it down to her friend's surprise or even *shock* at bumping into her like that after so much time. And she knew that a lot of people just didn't know what to say to her since she'd come back. Nicola was used to it, and normally didn't let it bother her.

But now she knew it was something more. Carolyn had changed, and like so many others, had obviously decided to pretend that Nicola no longer existed. That hurt. Nicola had expected more from Carolyn. Alongside Laura and Helen, Carolyn was the only person she had confided in about the problems in her marriage. She had thought the woman loyal and trustworthy. Obviously, she had been wrong

Shannon looked thoughtful. "I've always thought that she resented you," she said.

"Me?"

"Yes." Shannon took another sip from her glass. "You and Dan were so happy together. You were so well suited." She laughed when she saw Nicola's expression. "Well, you were most of the time, anyway," she added wryly. "I think Carolyn held your marriage up to the one she had with John, and knew that hers was lacking. She was no fool, Nicola – she knew that she and John were far from perfect." Suddenly, Shannon stopped talking, and her eyes danced with amusement as something caught her attention.

Nicola followed her gaze, and her eyes widened. "Oh, Barney, don't do that!" The dog was busily pulling clothes out of Nicola's washing-machine. "You'll mortify me – those haven't even been washed yet!" The dog dutifully stepped back from the machine, and apologetically rolled over onto his back, looking for forgiveness. Nicola smiled. "Sorry, Shannon, go on with what you were saying. You think Carolyn knew about you?"

"Of course she knew about me! You saw for yourself how much she hated me, and how she always tried to turn everyone against me."

Nicola nodded in agreement. Carolyn had done exactly that on the very first night Nicola had met Shannon. The two women already had a history of mutual dislike, so when Carolyn intimated to Nicola that Shannon was after Dan, she had been immediately on the offensive. As a result, Nicola and Shannon had got off completely on the wrong foot, each wrongly perceiving the other as some kind of threat.

"Look, I can't say I blame her. John is her husband, after all." Shannon looked ashamed. "I'm not proud of the fact that I carried on with a married man but –"

"You were besotted," Nicola finished for her. She paused for a moment. "And I suspect you still are."

Shannon looked up. "Is it that obvious?"

Nicola went to check on the pasta. So much for Shannon's new romance. "Maybe now that he and Carolyn are finished . . ." she began.

"He'll hook up with me? I doubt it," Shannon said miserably. "From what I can gather he's quite enjoying his freedom."

"Maybe you should try letting him go, Shannon. It's been years now."

"I know," Shannon looked frustrated, "and it's the same old story. Just when I think that I'm getting over him and I can move on without him, he comes back, all smiles and flowers and . . . oh, sometimes I just don't know what to do."

Nicola couldn't for the life of her imagine what Shannon had ever seen in John O'Leary, and she certainly couldn't figure out why the lively redhead couldn't find someone else. But she knew too that there was a side of Shannon that didn't want to. She enjoyed the excitement and the danger arising from an affair with a feckless man. There were plenty of women who did.

"I still can't believe Carolyn would blab about the thing with Ken, though," Nicola said aloud. "What would she have to gain by doing that? She has no allegiance to Chloe, so why bother?"

"That one always enjoyed dishing the dirt –" Shannon stopped short and looked apologetically at Nicola. "Sorry, I'm probably not the best person to talk to about this."

"Don't worry," Nicola said. "It's all over and done with now. And Carolyn obviously wasn't the great friend I thought her to be."

* * *

Later that evening when Shannon had left in her taxi, the two having spent a pleasant evening discussing old times and making plans to meet again soon, Nicola thought some more about Dan and Chloe. She felt sorry for Chloe, trying to imagine how curious and worried the younger woman must be about her, not to mention insecure.

She could appreciate why he might not want to share the finer details, particularly the miscarriage and the thing with Ken, but why not the rest? She could also understand that maybe he didn't want to delve too deeply into the mistakes that had been made in the past, particularly not with the woman he was about to marry, but Dan should certainly have told her the circumstances surrounding his and Nicola's separation.

He obviously hadn't told Chloe much about her, assuming or hoping that the two would never meet.

And that was it, Nicola realised. He hadn't told her because he was still feeling ashamed and guilty, probably still wondering if he should have done things differently and wondering what Chloe, his bride-to-be, would think of him.

Well, Nicola thought, as she finished tidying the kitchen and prepared to go to bed, there was no point in beating about the bush any longer. She didn't appreciate anyone digging around in her affairs, and if Dan wouldn't do it, then maybe she herself should put poor Chloe out of her misery.

Maybe then, Dan and his problems would toddle off for good, and stop disrupting *her* life. Luckily Ken, being so preoccupied at the Centre these days, hadn't seemed to notice she had been a bit off form lately, or that she was a bit preoccupied herself. Good. Nicola didn't want this Dan thing affecting Ken any more. He had put up with enough already.

"Ready for bed, Barney?" she asked, ruffling her dog's silky ears.

Barney wagged his tail in agreement and, waiting until his mistress went through to the bedroom, he jumped up and hit the light switch. Then he pawed the door, closing it softly behind the two of them.

Chapter 28

"Laura, can you mind my two tomorrow afternoon? I'm going into Holles St for a scan."

On the other end of the phone, Laura bristled. Why did Cathy have to pick this weekend of all weekends to have her scan? Today was Thursday and the Crafts Exhibition would be running from Friday until the middle of the following week. Laura was going to be there every day from noon until six in the evening, and had been working overtime to get her collections ready for display. She and Neil weren't taking their honeymoon until after Christmas, when the travel business would be that bit quieter, and to give Laura a chance to prepare for what would hopefully be an encouraging Christmas for Laura Connolly Design.

Tonight she had invited the others over for dinner, where hopefully they would meet Helen's elusive boyfriend Paul.

"I'm very sorry, Cathy – and normally I wouldn't mind,

but at the moment I'm way too busy," she said, explaining the situation to her sister. Cathy didn't say anything for a long moment and Laura realised just then how like Maureen she could be when it came to getting her own way.

"Couldn't you ask Mam?" she offered meekly.

Cathy sighed loudly. "I was hoping you'd do me the favour and Josh and Dylan are always going on about staying with Auntie Laura in Dublin, seeing as Auntie Laura doesn't visit them very much at home."

There it was, right on cue. The Guilt Trip.

"Cathy, normally there wouldn't be problem and I'd love to have them but the Crafts Exhibition is being held this weekend and it's really important for the business."

Cathy laughed. "Laura, when are you going to get it into your thick skull that you're wasting your time with this jewellery thing?"

"What?" Laura was taken aback at her sister's bluntness. OK, so Cathy was cheesed off about her not baby-sitting but that hardly meant . . .

Cathy continued. "I know you like fiddling around with those things, but do you really expect people to buy them? I mean, I was never so mortified in my life, having to wear that yoke at your wedding. Honestly, Laura, everyone was laughing at us."

"What?" Laura repeated. Everyone laughing at them? Why?

"I think that maybe you should come back down to earth and remember who you are and where you're from, sis. In fairness, it's not really all your fault. I know that Neil probably puts strange ideas in your head but –"

Laura was so upset she dropped the phone. Sitting at her workstation, tears flowing freely down her cheeks, she tried to deflect the raw pain, the blow that her sister's words had inflicted. What was wrong with her family? Why couldn't they support her? Could they not see how difficult this was for her, and how hard she was finding it, without making it ten times worse? What about support – or encouragement?

And how dare Cathy accuse her of trying to be something she was not? How dare she try and make her feel guilty for trying to do something with her life? She and Maureen were cut from the same cloth – and Laura had had enough of their doubting and their taunts. She was going to make this business work. She was going to display at this Crafts Exhibition and she was going to talk the talk and walk the walk just as well as the rest of them – even better. Why shouldn't she? She was good at what she did. Why was she always apologising for it? By the time Laura was finished building her jewellery business, she'd have her family *begging* her to design stuff for them.

Even though Cathy was probably long gone, Laura banged down the receiver and immediately felt a rush of energy, a rush of exhilaration that she didn't think she'd ever felt in her entire life. Bring on the Crafts Exhibition – bring them *all* on.

Laura was going to make this business a success even if it was just to shove it down her family's begrudging little throats.

* * *

That night, Nicola and Ken arrived at Laura's at a quarter to eight, Ken clutching a bottle of wine and a multi-pack of Pringles.

"*Ken!*" Laura eyed him when they joined her in the kitchen. "You brought crisps?"

"What? I just thought we might be hungry later, that's all." He winked at Neil who was trying his best to stifle a grin.

"Thanks a million! And here's me slaving over a hot stove all day."

"I know," Nicola teased. "That's exactly why we brought the crisps."

"Seriously, Laura, don't mind us – the food smells great," Ken said, sniffing the air approvingly. "When do we eat?"

"Not until Helen and the Famous Paul get here, I'm afraid," Laura answered. "But I told Helen dinner was at eight, so I'm sure they won't be too much longer."

"Is Kerry coming too?" Nicola asked.

"No, one of Helen's neighbours is looking after her tonight." To Laura's relief, that same neighbour had also been obliging enough to collect Kerry from school the last few days, leaving her free to prepare for the exhibition. She couldn't help wondering whether or not this poor woman knew what she was getting herself into by being roped into doing one of Helen's 'favours'.

"Oh, so we're not the only misfortunates at her beck and call then," Nicola said, her tone disapproving, as she removed her jacket. " Still, I can't wait to get a look at this Paul. Things must be pretty serious there – when was the last time Helen introduced us to one of her playthings?"

"*Playthings?*" Ken repeated sardonically. "That's what we're reduced to these days, is it? God be with the days when ye women couldn't do a thing without us. Now we're practically redundant."

"Not quite," Laura said, face red as she struggled with a large pot of steaming vegetables. "Neil, is there any chance you could pour some wine for our guests, please? I have my hands full here," she added pointedly. Still wound up from her conversation with Cathy earlier, and unused to cooking for more than two people, Laura couldn't keep the frustration out of her tone.

"Oh, sorry, love, we'd better get out of your way," Neil said, having earlier picked up on his wife's unusually low spirits. "Guys, I'll open a bottle and we'll leave the missus alone to get on with the important stuff." He gave Laura an encouraging wink and, bottle in hand, led the others through to the dining-room.

Oh, stop it, Laura, berated herself, just because *you're* in bad form and can't handle the cooking, don't go taking it out on poor Neil. If she was perfectly honest with herself, she wasn't really in the mood for having guests tonight but all the plans had been made and it wouldn't have been fair on the others to cancel last minute.

"You OK?" Nicola asked.

Laura looked around and almost automatically felt guilty. She was sure Nicola had followed the others into the living-room.

"I'm fine," she answered shakily, "just a little hot and bothered with all this cooking."

Nicola looked at her. "Nervous about the exhibition, huh?"

Laura smiled. "You could say that." Nicola had a knack of hitting the nail on the head. Despite her fighting talk earlier, she *was* feeling nervous about the Crafts Exhibition. To Laura this was make or break for the business. If her designs didn't go down well or she didn't pick up some new customers, well . . . well, then it was all over. She hadn't had to think about it that much before the wedding but now, when there was nothing else to think about . . .

"Oh, I'll be fine," she said. "After all, I've had plenty of time to get ready for this."

Nicola smiled encouragingly. "It doesn't happen overnight, you know," she said. Laura's stomach gave a nervous flip. Sometimes Nicola was too damn perceptive for her own good. She had obviously seen through Laura's false bravado these last few months – she had known that all wasn't well. Yet, Nicola had never pushed it, had never said a thing because she knew that Laura wouldn't want to admit it out loud that the business might be a failure. She suddenly felt very grateful to her friend.

"I know that," she said, "and I always told myself that I'd give it a shot, and if it didn't take off, well . . . at least I tried." She gave a watery smile. "But nobody told me it would be this hard to admit defeat."

"Hey, what's all this 'admitting defeat' business?" Nicola said cheerfully. "It hasn't been all that long – you have to give it time."

Laura looked at her. "I think you and I both know that maybe I didn't think this through properly. Helen was right

364

– I'm just not the right type of person for this kind of thing."

"Laura," Nicola put a hand on her arm, "please don't tell me you're thinking of throwing in the towel – not after everything you've done."

"But that's exactly it. I haven't done *anything*. A few orders a week from the internet and the odd bit of interest from the shops – it's hardly setting the business world on fire, is it?"

"It's something," Nicola countered, "not to mention something to be proud of. Don't lose faith in your abilities, Laura, and don't write yourself off just yet."

"I suppose I'll just have to see how the exhibition goes." Suddenly, Laura didn't want to talk about it any more.

"It'll be fine. To be honest, I think part of the problem is publicity. Your product is great – you just haven't had enough exposure."

"Thanks, Nic," Laura smiled.

"Um, Laura?" Nicola sniffed the air, and gestured towards the oven. "I think your roasties might be ready."

"Oh, shit!" Laura opened the oven door and a thick blanket of smoke rushed out. She looked at Nicola in dismay, her cheeks reddening with annoyance. "Nicola, I think now would be a good time to join the others," she said through gritted teeth.

"Yes, Mammy." Nicola sped off, anxious to make a quick exit.

"And Nicola?" Laura called.

"Yes?"

"Do you think Sour Cream & Onion Pringles would make a decent substitute for roast potatoes?"

365

"With lamb?" Nicola grinned. "They'll be absolutely perfect!"

"Good, and I hope Helen and this Paul guy won't be too much longer," Laura said, taking a fistful of crisps and trying to calm herself. "I'm absolutely starving!"

* * *

An hour and a quarter later, they were still waiting, Ken and Neil having hungrily demolished the crisps between them.

"I've tried Helen's mobile and there's no signal," Laura said, trying to suppress her annoyance. The lamb would be like rubber at this stage.

"They're probably just running late," Neil said, his tone soothing.

"If they're running late, the least she could have done is to have phoned," Nicola said, her irritation palpable. "But of course that would mean Helen thinking about someone other than herself, wouldn't it?"

"She'll be here," Ken said, giving his girlfriend a warning look. "There's no point in our –"

A loud shrill of the doorbell cut short the remainder of his sentence.

"That's them," Laura said, getting to her feet. "Neil, can you get that, and I'll get the starters?"

"Sure." Neil hopped up to answer the door.

Seconds later, Helen joined Laura in the kitchen. Laura thought she looked amazing, with her blonde hair swinging freely around her shoulders, and dressed in a stunning black beaded dress, the material clinging faintly to her curves – what few there were, she thought, with uncharacteristic sourness.

"Hi," Helen said happily, moving forward to give her a hug. "Everything nearly ready here? I'm famished!"

Laura was taken aback at this casual greeting and barely returned it. She had expected an apology, or at the very least some kind of excuse as to why Helen was over an hour late. "What kept you?" she asked. "And where's Paul?"

Helen beamed. "Outside showing Neil his new Audi. The two of them seem to have hit it off already, thank God."

Laura bit her tongue. "Well, go on in and join the others. Dinner might not be great after being kept this long," she added pointedly, "but I know they're all so hungry they won't care –"

"What?" Helen interjected, her eyes wide with alarm. "What others?"

"Well, Ken and Nicola of course," Laura said, puzzled.

"*What*? You didn't tell me *they* were coming! I thought it was just the four of us – you, Neil, me and Paul!"

"What's the problem? Did you and Nicola have an argument or something?" Laura asked, puzzled. She suspected then that Nicola might have said something to Helen about all the extra baby-sitting. Great, aggro between those two was all she needed tonight.

"No, nothing like that – it's just . . ." Helen bit her lip and looked decidedly panicked.

"What is it, Helen?"

She took a deep breath. "It's just . . . I kinda haven't yet told Paul about Kerry, and I was hoping you and Neil might do me a favour by not mentioning her tonight."

"*What?*"

Helen grimaced. "I know, I know. It's stupid. It's just we haven't been going out very long and the subject never came up and –"

"The subject never came up! Helen, she's your daughter!" Laura was incredulous. "That's so unfair! To Kerry *and* to Paul! And he was bound to find out sooner or later. What did you think would happen then?"

"Laura, I thought I'd cross that bridge when I came to it –"

"That's crazy, Helen!"

"I know, I know. It's high time I told him but I'm just not ready yet. I really thought it would be just you and Neil tonight and I was so sure you would . . ."

"Help keep it a secret for you?" Laura finished, shaking her head in wonder at Helen's unbelievable silliness, not to mention downright cheek at expecting her to lie on her behalf. She shook her head. "Look, Helen, you'd better take him aside now and let him know, otherwise –"

"But I can't just drop it on him all of a sudden!" Helen cried, and then her voice dropped sharply to a whisper, as she remembered that the others were in the next room. "Not when we're in company – it wouldn't be fair!"

"But you must! What about Nicola and Ken? And Neil? They're bound to talk about Kerry tonight!"

"Oh, God, what will I do? Should I talk to Nicola . . . ask her not to . . . ?"

"Sooner you than me! You can imagine how Nicola would react to that! But go ahead –"

She stopped dead, as just then the door to the dining-room opened. Helen had her back to the doorway and appeared not to notice.

"Do you need help with anything here, Laura?" Nicola asked easily, and Helen nearly jumped ten feet off the ground.

"Nicola – hi!" she said, her tone high-pitched.

"I see you've finally decided to honour us with your presence then."

Helen smiled warily. "Um, yes, Paul was working late and . . ." she trailed off as they heard voices in the hallway and footsteps approach the kitchen.

"Laura's just in here," they heard Neil say, and Laura felt her breath catch as, just behind Neil, the most stunning man she had ever seen entered the room. Long hair, sculpted cheekbones, piercing slate-grey eyes – lucky old Helen.

"Hey!" Paul said in a distinct American twang. "Glad you guys didn't start the party without us!"

Nice, Laura thought. No apology, no excuse, just 'Hey!'

"This is my good friend Laura –" A clearly flustered Helen made the introductions, glancing meaningfully at Laura as she did so. "And this is Nicola."

"Hello, Paul. Nice to meet you," Laura said, smiling warmly at him.

"Good to be here, Laura." He grinned back at Laura, his smile faltering as he turned to Nicola who gave him a curt nod.

"Glad you could make it –" Laura said, and couldn't help adding, "eventually."

"Paul was working late," Helen offered quickly, by way of explanation. "So, by the time he got to my place, and then, of course, our little detour . . ."

"I got a bit lost on the way," Paul admitted bashfully.

"In the metropolis that is Ballinteer?" Neil asked, winking at Laura.

"Well, I tried to give him directions but you know what men are like!" Helen batted her eyelids playfully at the two men present.

"Hey!" Neil piped up, rising to her bait. "I'll have you know that men are proven to be much better orienteers . . . orientators . . . what's the right word again, Paul?"

"Exactly my point," Helen jibed. "You know what men are like." She ducked giddily as Neil aimed a tea towel at her.

"Can everyone go inside and sit down now?" Laura said testily, deliberately refusing to make eye contact with Helen though she could feel her anxious gaze fixed on her. At Laura's words, Nicola promptly headed back to the dining-room, thereby robbing Helen of any chance to have a private word with her. Out of the corner of her eye, Laura saw Neil put a friendly arm around Helen's shoulders and usher her out of the kitchen in Paul's wake.

Laura was now seriously annoyed. Not only had Helen landed her in another dreadful situation, but she was sick to the teeth of her friend's incessant flirting with her husband. It was the same every time Helen called to pick up Kerry – *if* they weren't talking football, that was. Laura knew that her friend just couldn't help herself – get her within two yards of a man and she was batting her eyelids as if she was in a sandstorm, and wiggling her backside like Kylie Minogue – even in her present state of tension.

After taking a minute to try and calm herself, Laura began carrying the first course into the dining-room.

"So, are you a farmer or a forester or something, Paul?" Nicola was asking.

Paul looked at Nicola as if she was on drugs or something. "No, why?"

"Well, seeing as you were working late, I suppose I just wondered why you couldn't get to a phone."

Ken nudged her chair beneath the table, and Helen shot her a venomous look.

"Paul misheard the time. He thought I said dinner was at *nine* o'clock."

Paul gave Helen a quick glance, which suggested he thought anything but.

"Well, look, we're all here now, anyway," Laura said, trying to relieve the obvious tension. "Now get stuck in before it all goes cold."

"Great!" Paul rubbed his hands together. "I'm starving, haven't eaten a thing all day and I'll tell you this, I have one hell of an appetite." He winked at Helen.

"Good thing we waited for you then, isn't it?" Nicola said sweetly enough but, to anyone who knew her, her voice was tinged with sarcasm.

Laura rolled her eyes. It was going to be a long night.

* * *

Nicola sat and watched the gorgeous Paul wolf down his

lamb as if he had never eaten before in his life. Asshole!
What did Helen see in him? OK, that was fairly obvious:
he was bloody fantastic-looking! But still! He was as
artificial as you could get. And where did he think he was
going with the American accent? All 'hey' and 'wow' and
'guys' this, 'guys' that.

"So, Paul, where are you from?" she asked innocently.

He wiped the side of his mouth with a napkin.
"Mitchelstown."

"Oh!"

Helen shot Nicola another look, knowing exactly what
she was getting at. "Paul spends a lot of time abroad on
business," she explained.

"What you do?" Ken asked him.

Paul looked pleased to be asked. "I'm an investment
advisor – pensions, stocks, bonds – things like that. We
advise our customers on how best to invest their extra cash."

"He's given me fantastic advice," Helen trilled. "Now
I know exactly what to do with my money."

"Oh, are shoes considered a valid form of investment
these days?" Neil teased, and Helen made a face at him.
Grinning, he got to his feet. "I'll get some more wine, will I?"

"I'll get dessert." Laura shuffled out to the kitchen
with him, leaving the others alone at the table.

Nicola thought it odd that, despite her earlier enthusiasm
about her new man, Helen seemed rather tense and
uncomfortable at the table tonight. Every time Paul
opened his mouth to say something, Nicola noticed that
her friend's eyes kept darting here and there as if she was
afraid he might not make a good impression on everyone.

And any time the others opened their mouths, Helen all but started, as if nervous of what they might say. She supposed she might have been a bit unfair to her, really – it had evidently taken a lot for Helen to work up the courage to introduce him to her friends and, looking at her now, it was obvious she was anxious they all get along. She hadn't been fair to her really, coming down on the two of them for being late like that. OK, the 'guy' (as Paul would probably describe himself) was a bit of a show-off and clearly had no manners but, as long as Helen was happy, that was the main thing. For her friend's sake, she should try and get on with him.

"So, you two have been seeing one another for a while now?" Nicola injected some enthusiasm into her voice.

"Yes, and she's one hell of a babe." Paul looked at Helen with real devotion, something Nicola hadn't seen anyone other than Kerry do in a long, long time. Yes, men loved Helen; men had *always* loved Helen but usually didn't have a hope once her friend decided they weren't up to standard.

Might Paul actually be the right one for Helen, the one to banish the ghost of Jamie for good? For her friend's sake, Nicola hoped so. It would be terrific if Helen could finally find someone for her and Kerry to love.

Speaking of which . . .

"So have you met Kerry?" she asked Paul, just as Laura and Neil returned from the kitchen. Laura's eyes widened, and she shot a look at Helen who, horrified, was sitting ramrod straight in her chair, her eyes fixed on Laura's for support, inspiration, anything.

Paul looked blankly at Nicola. "Kerry?"

She watched him curiously. "Well, of course, Helen's –"

"*Dog!*" Helen cried out.

Paul turned to her, his mouth full. "What?"

"My dog," she said again, and Nicola stared at her, shocked. "Kerry's my dog, a Kerry Blue, lovely little thing, I've had her for years." Helen gave an apparently carefree little laugh but her eyes told a different story.

"Oh right." Paul laughed too. "You never mentioned a dog before."

"Yes, well, I have to lock her up when I have visitors. She's very possessive of me, can be a bit funny sometimes, about me – and – and who I bring home – isn't she, Laura?"

Laura stood rooted to the spot, and Nicola glared at her. Surely *she* couldn't be in on this too?

"Yes, she can be very possessive." Laura spoke slowly, her expression stony as she stared right back at Helen.

Nicola looked from one girl to the other. What the hell were they trying to pull here? Well, she was going to bloody well find out. She turned resolutely towards the kitchen, her mouth set in a thin angry line "Helen!" she barked. "Let's get the coffees and give Laura a little break!"

She heard Ken and Neil engage Paul in mindless chatter, anything it seemed to relieve the tension. But apparently Paul had noticed nothing amiss.

Alone with Nicola in the kitchen, Helen was shamefaced. "Look, he doesn't know. I haven't got around to it yet." She studied a piece of carrot that had fallen on the ground. "I didn't expect you and Ken to be here this evening and –"

"You haven't got *round* to it yet?" Nicola repeated.

"Helen, excuse my language but what the *fuck* does that mean? You've been going out with this man what, nearly four months, and you've just told him that your daughter –" Helen winced, and looked back towards the dining-room, presumably hoping that Paul couldn't hear, "yes, your *daughter*, Helen, is a – a *dog*! What the hell were you thinking?"

"Nicola, please, I know, I'm sorry – it was the first thing I could thing of –"

"First thing you could think of? Helen, why should you *have* to think of anything? Why didn't you tell him the truth? That Kerry is a sweet, loving child, the most important thing in your life, the most precious thing in all of our lives!"

And it was true. Kerry was the child that Nicola had never had, that she might never have and she loved that little girl with all her heart. And as far as she knew, Laura felt the same. The two of them had been there for Helen and for Kerry through thick and thin, and Nicola knew that, if she had to, she would fight to the death for Kerry. If she felt this way, then how could the child's mother, her own *mother*, deny her like that?

"Nicola, please, I know it was awful! And I really didn't mean for this to happen but I wasn't prepared for . . . I just . . ." Helen shook her head sadly. "I know it was stupid and I feel so guilty about not telling him, really I do!" Her eyes brimmed with tears. "But you don't understand. You don't know how it is. You don't know what it's like trying to find someone, someone decent and nice and – and I'm just afraid that if I tell him about Kerry it'll all be ruined. Men run a mile when they hear about

Kerry. I don't want that to happen this time. You don't understand – I really *like* Paul."

At this Nicola felt a familiar rage rise within her, something she hadn't felt in a long, long time. She took a deep breath, and struggled to remember every piece of advice she had ever heard about anger management. She began to count to twenty but didn't even reach five. *'I really like Paul.'*

Her face hard, Nicola looked one of her oldest friends straight in the eye.

"Helen, you are a selfish bitch." She spoke slowly, pronouncing each word clearly and precisely.

"What?" Helen stared at her, dazed. "What did you call me?"

"I called you a selfish bitch!" Nicola's temper was well and truly lost now, and the way she felt at that moment, it would probably never be found again. She couldn't believe Helen's selfishness, her callousness, her blatant cruelty towards her own child. Kerry adored Helen, looked up to her, would do anything for her. What was it with people like Helen? They had everything going for them, had everything to look forward to and yet, yet it still wasn't enough. They had to have it all.

Helen's back straightened. "Nicola, you're my friend. I know you're angry but believe me that is the one reason – the *only* reason I am taking this from you."

"The *only* reason?" Nicola went on. "The only reason, huh?"

"Yes." Helen amazingly seemed to be keeping her calm.

The two woman glared at one another, barely noticing as Laura quietly entered the room.

"Are you sure it's the only reason, Helen?" Nicola

went on. "Because I'm such a good friend? Or is because I know what you're really like?"

"Girls, don't . . ." Laura was soothing.

Helen frowned. "What I'm really like? What the hell is that supposed to mean?"

"You know damn well what I'm talking about and don't pretend that you don't."

"Nicola, I don't know where all of this is coming from but –"

"No, of course you don't, Helen. You don't know where this is coming from because you're so consumed in your own little life, you're so immersed in what's happening with *you*, that you don't know or *care* what's going on around you, do you?"

"What? What the hell are you talking about?"

"I'm talking *not* just about denying your own child in front of your new boyfriend, but denying on her on a regular basis. You're never with her, Helen! If you're not dumping her on me, you're dumping her on Laura, who God knows has had enough to contend with these last few months between planning a wedding and setting up a new business without having to look after a four-year-old!"

"Helen, it's OK. I don't mind having Kerry –" Laura began.

"But you don't care about what Laura has to contend with, do you, Helen?" Nicola went on as though Laura hadn't spoken. "As long as she serves your purpose, you don't give a shit! And she's just too nice and too *loyal* a friend to tell you to stuff it. She's too good to you and you and I both know you don't deserve that."

"Anything else?" Helen said, her hand on her hip.

"Well, now that you say it, Helen, yes there is. Kerry needs her mother's attention, she needs you to help her with her speech, she needs you to listen to her. You know that – the speech therapist has advised what you need to do. But you don't give a shit about that, do you? You don't believe in helping people, you'd just prefer to bury your head in the sand and pretend it isn't happening!"

Helen's expression would have been same had Nicola slapped her across the face.

"That's not true . . . I try my best. You have no idea how hard I try but it just doesn't work –"

"It *is* bloody true!" Nicola spoke over her. "That's what you always do. You're not there for Kerry, for your friends – anyone. Jesus, Helen, we've all done our best for you over the years, and you've never been there for any of us! Quite the bloody opposite!"

"Oh! Oh, I get it now," Helen began, her eyes hardening. "Now I know *exactly* what you're getting at. It's all coming out now, isn't it?"

"Yes, it certainly is." Nicola felt like she was on a runaway train. She was on dangerous ground but couldn't stop herself – she just wanted to catch the silly bitch and shake her.

"Nicola, please calm down," Laura beseeched.

"No, Laura, let her speak. Let good old Nicola get it over and done with," Helen interjected, glaring at Nicola. "So come on then! While you're at it, why not get it *all* off your chest, why not have a good old dig at me – you haven't done it for ages so go on!"

"You stupid cow –"

"No, seriously, go on." Now Helen was in full flight, her voice high and artificial. "I know you're dying to bring it up, you've been dying to bring it up again for years so why the hell don't you?"

"Helen, *please!*" Laura implored.

"All right then, seeing as you asked me, seeing as you seem to take some kind of sick pleasure in hearing it, then I *will* tell you straight out. Do you think I'm bloody stupid? I *saw* your carry-on earlier and you just can't help yourself, can you? Old habits die hard and you're *still* nothing but a slapper, Helen Jackson – a sad, selfish, man-stealing slapper!"

"Good girl!" Helen clapped her hands in fake applause and the two women stared angrily at one another. "That must have felt really good, did it, Nicola? All the old resentment coming home to roost, yes? Just because *I* didn't drop everything and come running when you wanted me to. Just because I made a mistake – a *single*, stupid mistake – something that could happen to anyone! Just because I wasn't a candidate for best friend of the century! Then again," she added bitterly, "I couldn't possibly beat good old Laura for that particular prize, could I?"

"Don't be so bloody stupid, Helen."

"No, seriously, you've always held that against me, haven't you? You've always held it against me just because back then I wasn't there to hold your hand like everyone else did!"

"I didn't care about you holding my hand! I cared about Laura!"

"Nicola, you're no bloody angel yourself. You –"

"For goodness sake, *will you two stop it!*"

In shock, the two women spun around to see Laura standing there, tears in her eyes.

"This is my home," she pleaded, her hands held out in front of her. "This is my home."

For a long, long moment a tension-filled hush descended on the kitchen.

Then Helen looked at Laura and her hand flew to her mouth. "Oh, Laura, I'm so sorry," she whispered. "I'm so sorry, we didn't mean . . . you don't know what we were –"

"What you were talking about?" Laura finished for her, her expression hard. "Of course I know what you were talking about, Helen. I've always known."

It took Nicola a little longer to come to her senses. She tore her gaze away from Helen and looked at Laura as if seeing her for the very first time.

Oh no, she thought, looking again from one woman to the other. What in God's name have I done?

Chapter 29

"I've always known, Helen," Laura said, wearily slumping down on one of the kitchen chairs.

Helen stood rooted to the spot, unable to meet her friend's eyes.

"Did you think really that Neil – my *husband* – would have hidden something like that from me? What kind of a sap do you think I am – both of you?"

Nicola tried to make amends. "Laura, it was nothing, really. I saw the whole thing – it was a long time ago . . ."

"I know!" Laura said wearily, her head in her hands. "I know all about it. Only unlike you two, Neil thought enough of me to tell me. What kind of a relationship did you think we had? Neil loves me; there was no way he would have kept it a secret from me. Helen, I've known since the very beginning."

Just then, the door from the dining-room opened softly and Neil popped his head around it. "Is everything okay, love?" he asked.

Helen looked guardedly at him.

"Everything's fine," Laura answered stonily, not taking her eyes off Helen.

"Well look, the lads and myself might pop down to the local – get out of your hair for a while, okay?"

"Okay," Laura gave a tired nod as the door closed after him.

Helen looked at Laura, guilt written all over her face. "Oh, Laura . . ." she began, "why didn't you ever say anything? Why didn't you ever confront me about it?"

"Because I'm a bloody coward, that's why," Laura said bitterly. "I should have said something. In fairness I should have slapped you hard, but you're my friend and at that time I knew you were hurting."

Oh God, Nicola thought. She should have told Laura at the time. She wanted to but it wasn't her place and she had been torn . . .

* * *

Nicola remembered the whole thing as clearly as though it happened yesterday. It was Christmas – not long after Jamie had abandoned Helen and six-month-old Kerry. Nicola was living in England at the time. She had come home that Christmas to see her family, mostly to convince them she was doing OK, but also to attend a New Year's Eve party at what had been Laura and Neil's old rented house in Goatstown.

There was quite a crowd, and everyone had been drinking heavily with the exception of Nicola, who that night was feeling particularly sorry for herself. New Year's Eve was often a very lonely night for single people, especially newly separated single people. Laura was well out of it, she and Neil having consumed nearly a full bottle of Southern Comfort between them – eventually, she went to bed early while Neil stayed up mingling with the guests.

Despite her recent pregnancy, Helen looked absolutely stunning that night. She had a salon tan, and was wearing a jaw-droppingly sexy gold knitted dress, which clung to every curve and emphasised her newly flat stomach. Every inch the social butterfly, Helen flitted teasingly from one man to the other, flirting madly all night.

Nicola was being chatted up by a friend of Neil's, who seemed greatly intrigued by her. "Aren't you great altogether?" he was saying. "The way you get out and about – not a bother on you."

"I'm not an imbecile, you know," Nicola answered, trying to be annoyed, but despite herself, *amused* at the reaction she had been getting from people on her return home. It was as though everyone expected that she should have lost her mind, as well as everything else.

Feeling a bit of a headache and deciding she might just go to bed early, she made her way to Laura's spare bedroom, trying to remember if she had left her overnight bag there or in the living-room upon her arrival earlier. She hoped it was in the bedroom, otherwise she would have to make a big song and dance about saying goodnight to the others. Anyway, the party was already beginning to break up and she suspected Helen might have left already, as she hadn't seen her in a while. Idly thinking it was a bit rude of Helen not to say goodnight, Nicola opened the bedroom door and, switching on the light, stopped short.

There, on the bed, bodies moulded tightly together and kissing passionately, were Helen Jackson and Neil Connolly.

"What the fuck?" Nicola couldn't contain her anger. "What the hell do you two think you're doing?"

Eyes glazed, Neil sat up and, horrified, looked drunkenly at Nicola and then back to Helen. Immediately he pushed Helen off him. "Oh Jesus," he said, "oh God, Nicola, I . . . it's not what you think . . . I would never –"

"Not what I think? Then what is it, Neil? Because I sure as hell don't know what else it could be!"

Helen rolled onto the other side of the bed and said nothing, watching Neil flounder.

"Nicola, I swear to you – I just don't know what happened . . . I –"

"Get out of my sight, Neil," Nicola ordered, ignoring his pleas. "I want a word with Helen."

Neil stayed rooted to the spot.

"Out, Neil – now!"

"OK, OK, I'm going but . . ." He stood up and, quickly buttoning up his shirt, he looked directly at Helen. "There was nothing . . ."

Nicola flashed him another look and Neil bolted, swaying slightly as he went. Her hair and clothes greatly dishevelled, Helen swung her legs off one side of the bed and the two friends faced one another, daggers clearly drawn. Helen didn't look in the slightest bit guilty – in fact Nicola thought she looked almost triumphant.

"What the hell are you playing at?" she spat, when Helen didn't say anything. "Laura is your friend!"

Helen waved a hand in the air. "Laura, Laura, Laura,"

she slurred. "Seems poor old Laura is just as fucked up as the rest of us."

"What?"

"Well, look at how things turned out," she said, as if it all made perfect sense. "*You* get messed up by Dan, *I* get messed up by Jamie – now we're *all* quits."

Nicola was so angry at her she could hardly speak. She knew Helen was finding things hard in the last few months but to deliberately . . .

"You're telling me that you set out to seduce Neil tonight, just to get back at Jamie?"

"Nope." Helen slumped drunkenly back onto the bed. "To get back at Laura."

"What? But why? What has Laura ever done to you? She's your best friend, for goodness sake!"

"Oh, she's so bloody perfect!" Helen hissed, sitting up. "Everything always goes so well for our Laura. She has her nice little job, and her nice little boyfriend and she never loses her temper, everyone loves her and I'm just so bloody sick of it!"

Nicola resisted the urge to strangle her. "You stupid cow! Just because you're jealous of Laura, just because your life is a mess right now doesn't mean that you can go around messing things up for her! She loves Neil and, despite what I saw just now, I'm sure he loves her too! What kind of a person are you, Helen? If we all went around doing things like that, just because our own lives weren't going according to plan –"

Helen seemed bored by the conversation. "Yeah, I know, I know. It could be worse. I mean, I *could* have ended up like you!"

This time there was no restraint. This time Nicola moved forward and slapped her friend hard across the face. What had happened to Helen? Was she so full of bitterness towards Jamie that she was no longer able to feel compassion for anyone else?

Helen had given her a look that would cut diamonds before picking up her shoes and exiting the room.

Things changed the next day though. The next day, a clearly mortified Helen turned up at Nicola's parents' house in Crumlin.

"I'm sorry," she bawled, a sleeping Kerry in her arms. "I don't know what I was trying to prove. I didn't want to hurt Laura . . . I was just so lonely and fucked up and . . . I'm sorry for what I said about you."

Nicola wasn't having any of her self-pity. "Just promise me that you will never *ever* do anything like that again. Grow up and start taking responsibility for your actions. You're an adult, and now you have a child to look after. Cop on, Helen!"

"I'm sorry," she said again. "I'm just finding it hard. I miss him so much, and I'm terrified that I won't be a good mother."

Nicola had sat Helen down and told her that it was early days, that she had just been through a tough time, that she was still in mourning for Jamie and that everything would eventually fall into place.

And, Nicola thought, it had. Helen seemed genuinely contrite, had afterwards stayed away from Neil and Laura, and began to pick up the pieces after Jamie's departure. Neil had phoned her too, beside himself with remorse and begging her not to think badly of him.

"Nicola, you have to believe me. I've never done anything like that before in my life. I can't believe I could have been so stupid. I adore Laura, I'd do anything for her and I would never, ever do anything to hurt her."

"You didn't think a quick shag with her best friend while she was upstairs asleep would do anything to hurt her?" Nicola had said.

"Oh God, Nicola it wasn't like that. We were just talking in the kitchen and then Helen got upset and somehow we just ended up in the bedroom and . . . oh God, I want to die!"

Nicola had agonised for a while, but eventually decided not to tell Laura anything about that night, perceiving it to be a drunken lapse by Neil, who in fairness was pretty out of it and suffering badly now as a result. There was no point in upsetting Laura by telling her that her best friend and her boyfriend had had a drunken, meaningless fling on New Year's Eve. Not wanting to think about what might have happened had she *not* interrupted them, Nicola had thought it the right thing to do.

Apparently, Neil hadn't felt the same way, yet the thought had never crossed Nicola's mind that he would come clean with Laura. She had always thought he would be much too afraid of losing her. Yet now that she thought about it, it wasn't too surprising he had confessed all. Neil Connolly was a kind decent man, who was prepared to sacrifice his relationship, and possibly Laura's trust in him by being honest with her. Although, she had had her doubts, and it had taken her some time to trust him after that night, Nicola now had to admit that he had behaved admirably.

* * *

Now Laura looked at them both, her expression stony. "I know you two thought 'Oh poor Laura, we'd better not tell her, she couldn't handle it – no need to upset her.' Why does everyone think that? Why is Neil the *only* one who gives me any credit? You," she said, pointing at Helen, "my supposed best friend tried to undermine my relationship like that and, Nicola, you knew about it but never told me!"

"Laura, it wasn't like that," Nicola began. "We were only trying to protect you . . ." She trailed off when Laura held her hand up.

"I'm sick of it," she said. "I'm sick to the teeth of it all. Why does everyone think I need protecting? I'm nearly thirty years of age!"

"But at the time . . ."

At the time, Nicola had been placed in a horrible position, dealing with doubts in her mind about Neil, trying to cover up for Helen and feeling bad about keeping secrets from Laura. This wasn't friendship – this was a bloody nightmare!

What had happened to the three of them? What had happened to trust, loyalty, support – all the things that should be taken for granted in friendship, *real* friendship? How had they let one another down like this?

"Laura, it was all my fault," Helen began. "It was New Year's Eve and I was feeling lonely and I just wanted someone . . . a man, to hold me and to comfort me and –"

Laura's tone was hard. "It wasn't just any man, Helen – it was Neil. And he wasn't exactly fair game. Okay, he wasn't actually innocent either but at least he had the guts to come and tell me about it, at least he respected me enough to let me decide what to do about it. I know you two think I'm too soft, too emotional. Oh, believe me, I know you've always thought that. But I'm not as stupid as you seem to think. I said nothing to Helen, because I had heard Neil's side of the story, and I believed him when he said it was nothing but a stupid drunken fling that had got out of hand. After all, I know full well what Helen can be like."

At this Helen hung her head, clearly ashamed.

But then Laura's tone softened. "But I also knew that you were suffering, Hel, and I tried to be there for you. I've always tried to be there for you, but in the last few years you and I have grown apart. You're different, Helen. Ever since you had Kerry, you're different."

"Why wouldn't I be?" she said hoarsely. "Why wouldn't I be different after nearly four years of being on my own looking after her –"

"She's your daughter!"

"I know," Helen said softly. "I know that. I just . . . I just feel so lonely sometimes."

"Helen, from where I'm sitting, you have bloody everything! A wonderful job, designer clothes, a fantastic apartment and, more importantly, a daughter any mother would be proud to have. What more do you want?"

"I want someone," Helen said in a low voice. "You two are so lucky with what you have and you don't know what it's like to be on your own, without someone to love."

"And what about Kerry?" Laura asked impatiently. "Don't you love her?"

"Of course I do – but not – not the way I'm supposed to – not the way other mothers do."

"Other mothers?"

Helen looked uncomfortable. "I don't think I feel the way I should – I – I just don't know."

Nicola studied her friend's expression. She hadn't seen Helen let her guard down like this in a very long time. And she certainly had never seen Laura behave so coldly towards her, towards *anyone*.

"And how should a mother feel, Helen?" Laura asked.

"I don't know!" Helen cried. "That's part of the problem. I don't know how I should feel. I love her but I've never felt as though she was the most important thing in my life. I should feel that, shouldn't I? I should want to kill, to *die* for my child!" Helen put her head in her hands. "But I don't feel that way. I just feel . . . lonely."

Nicola looked at her. She had no idea Helen had been battling with her feelings like this. Yes, she was selfish, Helen had always been selfish – but lonely? Nicola would never have used that word to describe her. Not when there was an army of male admirers ready and waiting at every turn.

Laura's tone was firm. "Helen, I'm not trying to be cruel, but, with the way you've been behaving recently, it isn't surprising that you feel lonely."

"I know."

Helen looked lost, Nicola thought. She looked as though she had been landed in a strange, unfamiliar world, a world from which she desperately wanted an escape. She couldn't handle confrontations, *real* confrontations whereby she had to give a little and admit her true feelings. Helen was dying a slow death in front of Laura – her inadequacies and shortcomings laid bare for all to see.

What had she started by arguing tonight with Helen,

Nicola thought sadly. This had opened a right can of worms. Although, maybe it was a good thing that this was all finally out in the open. Laura and Helen's relationship was an unequal one, Laura's lack of confidence causing her to feel somehow subordinate to her oldest friend, and Helen had clearly taken advantage of this. As much as she loved her friend, there was no denying that Helen had a dangerous, selfish streak in her, something that she would need to check soon, otherwise she would be looking forward to a sad, and very lonely life.

Both Helen and Neil had let Laura down very badly, and Nicola didn't think that Helen had ever appreciated how much she had betrayed her friend. Then again, that was Helen. Although always great for a laugh, she had never been able to handle trouble. When Nicola was going through the darkest period of her life, a time when she needed her friends and as much support as she could get, Helen couldn't be seen for dust. She just wasn't comfortable around her and it showed. Granted, Helen had her own problems, with her relationship deteriorating, so Nicola couldn't be too critical. Yet, she knew her friend well enough to know that had life been an absolute bed of roses for Helen back then, she would still be unable to deal with Nicola's situation.

Still, despite Helen's faults, and seeing her standing there shamefaced in front of Laura, Nicola's heart went out to her.

"Look, I think I should go," Helen said quietly, her head bent low.

"Perhaps you should." Laura was stony.

She and Nicola watched in silence while Helen retrieved her coat and bag from the cloakroom.

"The others are down at the Bottle Tower," Laura said, her expression unreadable. "It's a bit of a walk from here. And," she added, coldly, "you can make your own arrangements to have Kerry collected in the future."

Helen nodded, and opened the front door. She turned back. "Laura . . . I'm very sorry and I really mean that," she said, unable to meet the other girl's eyes. "Not just for the thing with Neil but . . . but for everything."

"So you should be." Laura gave an almost imperceptible nod of the head, and closed the door firmly behind her oldest friend.

Chapter 30

The following Monday morning, Chloe was sitting at her office desk, depressed. She knew now that she had made a very big mistake.

She stared at her screensaver, a picture of Dan and her taken last Christmas at her mum and dad's. Chloe loved that picture. She knew she looked particularly gorgeous in it and, looking at it now, it struck her that she really should wear purple more often. It seemed to complement her skin tone and highlight her cheekbones. She sighed. Of course, Dan was always equally striking in photographs, his attractive features lit up by that amazing grin. Their wedding photos would be truly spectacular, better than anything seen in *Hello* magazine.

If the wedding took place, that is.

Chloe had spent what *should* have been her wedding day alone in front of the television, while Dan went in to the office. He didn't have to go in, but Chloe knew that he was trying to avoid her. He was hardly talking to her.

And to top it all off, this Nicola thing wasn't such a big deal after all.

Chloe sighed, and checked her in-tray to see what fascinating gems her father's partner had given her today. Stapleton looked after probate estates and transfers so no doubt everything would be mesmerising.

Why had she bothered? So what if Nicola had a miscarriage, so what if she had a little fling? Dan was right. What did it all have to do with anything now?

Her life was a mess, and she knew that most of her so-called friends were laughing behind her back. So much for the wedding of the century in The Four Seasons Hotel. So much for the Sharon Hoey wedding dress, the exotic honeymoon and the supposedly wonderful Amazing Days wedding invitations.

The bloody wedding invitations! If it wasn't for the stupidity of that crowd in Wicklow she wouldn't be having any of these problems now. Well, maybe the wedding would still be postponed, but at least her fiancé would be talking to her, and probably just as eager to marry her.

She was losing him and Chloe knew it. Dan was hardly at home any more and most of the time she didn't even know where he was. They rarely spent any time together these days – she couldn't remember the last time they had gone out for a meal, or to the cinema or any of the things he loved doing. She had apologised and explained and tried to make it better, to make him see why she felt the need to go behind his back, but Dan no longer trusted her, Chloe knew he didn't.

She had hurt him, had displayed a complete lack of faith in him.

And because of it all, things were no longer the way Chloe wanted them to be.

Maybe that was it, though. Maybe it had all been about the way Chloe wanted it to be. If she was being completely honest with herself, did she ever once think about Dan in all of this? Had she ever been able to see past her own suspicions, worries and distrust?

No, Chloe had never once, throughout this whole – this whole hunt, search, whatever – she had never once thought about the consequences. She had worried only about what she might find, not about how it would affect her relationship. In fairness, she hadn't expected Carolyn O'Leary to tell her as much as she had, considering the woman was supposed to be Nicola's friend. And considering what Carolyn had told her about Shannon chasing Dan, she certainly hadn't expected the PA to send her packing! She knew now that it was probably Shannon that had spilled the beans on her digging. At the time, it was a chance Chloe had been willing to take. She really needed to know what had happened back then to make Dan so covert about his previous marriage.

But now, she wished she hadn't bothered. Although, if Dan hadn't been so bloody secretive about it all in the first place, she *needn't* have bothered. The way he carried on, you'd swear the reason for his marriage break-up was the third secret of Fatima! No, Chloe decided, why the hell should she beat herself up about this? Dan was as much at fault she was. Actually, if she really thought about it, *none* of this was her fault. What could he expect? He wouldn't tell her anything, so what else could she have done?

Well, there was no point in thinking about it now, Dan was mad at her and she'd already done enough damage as it was.

Chloe tried to clear her mind and to read the note Stapleton had attached to a current file. It was so bloody unintelligible; it was like transcribing the book of Kells. Didn't the man learn how to write in school all those years ago? Obviously not.

After a while, Chloe gave up and rested a hand on her chin.

There was one thing that was still bothering her about the entire situation, and try as she might she couldn't stop thinking about it. It was in the back of her mind all the time and she couldn't leave it alone.

Why, she asked herself, if Nicola had done the dirt on Dan, had he fought so hard to keep her? As far as she knew Nicola and Ken Harris hadn't run off into the sunset immediately afterwards – at the time it had just been a stupid, one-off fling.

So what else had gone wrong?

In her heart of hearts, Chloe knew that there *was* something else. Why else had Dan so readily agreed to the terms of the separation and divorce – most of which were in Nicola's favour? Why had Nicola gone to London?

And, more importantly, why had Dan always said that *he* felt guilty?

After all, Chloe reasoned, if Nicola had been the one at fault and Dan had done nothing wrong, well, what on earth would he have to feel guilty about?

* * *

Later that afternoon, she was still daydreaming when the receptionist put a call through to her desk.

Chloe wondered if she had heard right.

"Are you sure?" she asked Carina.

The receptionist sounded hassled. "That's what she said – line three, okay?"

Chloe's heart pounded. What the hell did *she* want? If she was calling here to give Chloe a lecture, then she could go to hell . . .

"Chloe Fallon speaking."

"Hello, Chloe, Nicola Peters here. I'm pretty sure I don't have to introduce myself any further . . ."

Chloe was surprised. Nicola sounded . . . quite pleasant, actually. But what did she want?

"Um, hello." Chloe was hesitant.

"Look, I won't waste your time. I just wondered if you were free after work this evening?"

Chloe's eyes widened as Nicola continued.

"I just think that with all that's been happening lately, maybe we should meet and clear the air."

"If you're referring to my questioning your friends like that . . . I'm very sorry. I just didn't –"

"It's fine, Chloe. I probably would have done the same," Nicola interjected breezily. "Anyway, do you think you could pop over to my house for a coffee later – after work, maybe? I'm in Stepaside."

Now Chloe was really frightened. Was this some kind of ploy?

"I'm not sure . . . "

"I'd really like to meet you, Chloe."

Overwhelming curiosity eventually made the decision

for her. She was *dying* to find out what Nicola was like. Despite all the information she had gleaned about her over the last while, there was no substitute for meeting Dan's ex-wife face to face. Dan mightn't be too happy though, she thought worriedly. Then again what could he say? Nicola had invited her; it wasn't as though she was going behind anyone's back or anything.

Chloe swivelled around in her seat. To hell with the consequences, she'd go.

"OK," she said to Nicola. "Just give me directions and I'll call over after work, maybe six?"

"Great." Nicola sounded pleased. "I'm really looking forward to it."

So am I, Chloe thought, her thoughts going a mile a minute as she wrote down Nicola's address on a Post-it note.

So am I.

* * *

Dan drove slowly through Stepaside village, trying to spot the turnoff to Nicola's house.

He was looking forward to seeing her again – probably a lot more than he should be, he thought wryly, reminding himself yet again that he was about to marry somebody else. Still, he was glad they would have the chance to talk, and he was ashamed and more than a little embarrassed about the whole situation with Chloe. He also knew that Nicola would no doubt by now have figured out that Carolyn had blabbed about her. He would have to try and explain that to her too, although he certainly wasn't going to admit the whole truth – that one night he and John's wife had somehow ended up in bed together.

398

Dan shook his head. He had regretted that almost immediately, especially when Carolyn had begun to practically stalk him afterwards! Talk about timing! Dan didn't know what had come over him that night. At that stage he had been so upset about Nicola and everything and even thought he might have to sell out his share of the business. It had been a tough, dark period in his life and Dan needed solace. Carolyn had been only too happy to oblige.

The thing is, Dan *knew* that Carolyn was a twisted, jealous bitch. He knew that her own marriage was in tatters, that she couldn't bear the fact that John had been cheating with Shannon. God knows he had had enough of listening to the two of them, with all their moaning and whingeing about John. Carolyn was a warped woman and had tried her very best to drag Dan down with her. She had almost succeeded too but for once – just once in his life – Dan had managed to put somebody else before himself.

And that was why he had let Nicola go. He wasn't good enough for her, he knew that. There was no point in trying to pretend that everything would be OK, that they could pick up the pieces and go on as normal. They weren't strong enough for that – *he* wasn't strong enough for that. Once he had been tempted by Carolyn, Dan was made only too aware of his own limits. A marriage would need to be solid as a lump of titanium to get through the whole thing and at that stage the strength of Dan and Nicola's marriage had been tested way too often.

No, he had done the right thing by leaving Nicola when he did.

Yet, after all these years, Dan was convinced that he

and Nicola had unfinished business – business they hadn't even scratched the surface of at their last meeting. Again, he didn't know what he had been expecting, but it certainly wasn't the strong and confident Nicola he had met that day. OK, she had put on quite a lot of weight but she had still looked so well and so *content* that it was almost frightening.

Then again, Dan thought, he should have known that Nicola would survive. She had always been the stronger one, hadn't that been proved over and over throughout their short marriage? No, he was the one who had fallen to pieces, who had let her down in the worst way imaginable. But was it possible that Nicola now might be ready to forgive – even forget?

Dan really hoped so.

He had been thrilled at Nicola's invitation to her house tonight – especially for dinner – well, in retrospect he hadn't been quite sure she had actually mentioned dinner but obviously that was what she'd intended. He knew this was a breakthrough; she wouldn't have let him near the place a couple of months ago. Anyway, he'd decided to come a little bit earlier than they'd agreed on the phone, so he could maybe give her a hand with preparing dinner. That was something they used to really enjoy when they were together and perhaps might make things a bit more relaxing and less formal than just him turning up when everything was ready. Dan was really looking forward to sampling some of his ex-wife's fantastic cooking. Nic had always been a whiz in the kitchen and usually went all out with her culinary creations. Dan had really missed that – Chloe could barely make toast.

And this supposed 'thing' she had with Harris at the moment couldn't be up to much if Nicola was inviting her ex round for dinner now, could it? Dan wasn't too worried. If there was a chance that he and Nicola could make amends, then Harris could just go and feck off for himself.

Suddenly spying the turnoff, Dan indicated and quickly jammed on the brakes. The loud blast of a horn behind him suggested that he hadn't specified his intentions fast enough.

"Indicate this!" Dan grinned, giving the other driver the finger before turning off to his left. He continued on a little way down the road, recalling the instructions Nicola had given him. "About half a mile down, yellow bungalow, third house on the left."

Dan was surprised she had bought a bungalow; Nicola had always hated that type of house. "Unimaginative and functional," she had said, when she and Dan were making plans to buy a house of their own. "No character whatsoever."

Nicola had fallen in love with a chalet-style house she had seen for sale in the Wicklow Mountains once, a mammoth place with indigenous stonework, woodwork and 'tons of personality'. That had been some house, Dan thought, shaking his head in wonder. He had been partial to the place too; it was ideal for a dynamic, up-and-coming businessman like himself and had been without doubt their idea of the 'perfect house'. Not for the first time, Dan wondered how their life together would have turned out, had things not gone sour.

And after all that, Nicola had settled for a bungalow. Why? It couldn't have been the money; financially she was pretty well off at this stage. And it wasn't as though she was stuck for choice; there were lots of period-style houses in this area, particularly in Bray or Enniskerry. If Nicola loved character so much, why didn't she go for one of those? Dan considered this for a few moments and then, realising his stupidity, mentally slapped himself on the forehead. Gobshite!

Seeing a row of houses come into view on his left, Dan slowed his driving, deciding that he must be almost there.

One, two three . . . Dan mentally counted the houses, and then trailed off as he spied what must be Nicola's house

"What the . . .?" he said out loud, puzzled. Right in front of him, pulling into Nicola's driveway, was none other than *Chloe's* Rav4. But it couldn't be . . . why would she be . . . ?

Dan's heart raced with panic as he watched his fiancée stop the Jeep. Chloe got out, took a quick, uncomfortable look around and seemed unsure as she locked the car door.

Oh God! Dan had to reach her before she got to the house – he *had* to!

Dan hit the controls for the electronic passenger window. In his haste, he pressed the wrong button and wound down his own window instead.

"Fuck!" he shouted, fumbling with the controls.

Chloe was now running a hand through her hair, and walking unsurely towards the house. She had almost reached the door when Dan put his head out the window, hoping that Chloe would hear him from this distance.

He needed to talk to her first, to explain . . .

But when he saw Nicola smiling and welcoming his fiancée from the open doorway, Dan knew that it was already too late.

* * *

Ken lightly ran his index finger over the newly polished diamond. Would she like it? He certainly hoped so. He was taking a hell of a chance choosing the ring beforehand, he knew that, but he wanted this to be a real proposal, a *proper* proposal. Ken closed the box and put it in inside his coat pocket.

Nearly sick with nerves, he put the car in gear and drove towards Stepaside. He couldn't believe how terrifying all of this felt! Would she say yes immediately, thrilled with the thoughts of marrying him, or would she maybe ask for some time to think about it? Ken steeled himself for every possible scenario, even one where she might say no. She might not yet be ready and if she wasn't, then, of course, Ken would accept that. He would have no problem waiting for Nicola – he knew she loved him and she was most definitely the one for him. Sometimes, Ken couldn't quite comprehend the strength of his feelings for her.

He was glad the thing with that other moron was finally over and done with. He knew there was always a chance that Nicola might see Dan Hunt again – might *need* to see him again – especially after so long, and after what she had been through.

But Ken hated the fact that Dan had sauntered back into Nicola's life lately – almost casually – as if she was some kind of afterthought. Ken would never treat her like that, would never have let her go in the first place. Dan

Hunt was nothing but an idiot, a self-serving, spineless idiot, and if that same idiot was only realising now what he had lost, then that was his tough.

Ken knew that Hunt had been phoning her recently. He knew because the asshole had phoned her at the house a couple of times, and Ken had answered. He was sure that Hunt had recognised his voice too, but typically had been too much of a coward to speak, and had simply hung up. He knew it was Dan because lately Nicola had been preoccupied and when he asked her about the hang-ups, she'd been nonchalant, almost too nonchalant. Ken didn't blame her for wanting to keep it this from him – after all, he hadn't reacted too well when she *had* confided in him about Dan's desire to meet up again in the first place.

Still, the main thing was that Nicola wasn't reciprocating. And Ken knew she wasn't reciprocating because Nicola was over Dan. Hadn't she told Ken that she wished *he* had been the one she was married to back then? Hadn't she told him that he and Barney were her family now?

Well, Ken thought, taking the turn-off to Nicola's road, if things went as well tonight as he hoped they would, they were about to become a proper family.

He began rehearsing the words again in his head, how he would say it and how he would lead up to it. Ken grimaced, almost unable to *look* at the house. He shook his head. God, this was nerve-wracking! He had been practising the build-up these last few days and hopefully, things would all go according to plan. Such a pity though, that he had to go off to Galway tomorrow for an impromptu meeting with the Motiv8 partners. By rights, he really should put this off until he came back. But he had found the perfect ring at the weekend and he knew it would be burning a hole in his pocket if he didn't do it soon. Anyway, he didn't think he could wait much longer. Upon arrival at Nicola's, he would tell her that he had just popped over on the off-chance for a visit before he left for Galway, all the time being really casual, and *then* he would go out and get . . .

Suddenly, Ken slammed on the brakes, icy daggers shooting up his spine.

Hunt! What the hell was *he* doing here? Ken was still a little away from the house, but he could quite clearly make out the other man's fat, ignorant head. And Dan was eagerly running up Nicola's driveway, running towards something – or some*one* . . .

Ken sat back, stunned.

Had she been lying to him all along? Had she been covering up the fact that she and Hunt were in much greater contact than she was letting on? After all, she had been secretive about the phone calls – what else was she being secretive about?

Immediately, he wrenched the ring-box from his pocket and flung it furiously onto the floor of the car. Then, reversing into a nearby gateway, face red with anger and tyres screeching wildly, Ken sped off in the other direction.

Chapter 31

"Neil, it was fantastic!" Laura danced excitedly around the kitchen. She had just returned from another day of the Crafts Exhibition, and although Neil had come with her on the first day to set up her exhibition stand, she was on her own once the doors opened to the public.

"I couldn't believe the amount of people that were interested in my work. I must've given out at least two boxes of business cards!"

Neil crossed the room and gave her a massive hug. "That's fantastic, love – didn't I tell you it would be brilliant?"

Laura beamed at her husband. It *had* been brilliant. Finally her designs had been exposed to the right people – or to the right market as Helen would say – and the feedback had been enormously positive.

Helen. Laura's heart lurched again as she thought about her friend. She had heard nothing from her since the other night.

Maybe Helen didn't want to discuss it at all. Maybe she just didn't want to deal with it, preferring instead to just get on with it and cut Laura out of her life like she had the first time round. That was Helen's way, after all. When faced with unpleasantness or trouble, she generally preferred to pretend the problem didn't exist. That was what she had done with Nicola, and to a lesser degree with Laura, immediately after the thing with Neil.

Laura doubted that Helen was troubling herself about it, although she looked very shaken upon her departure the other night. Laura didn't think she had ever seen her look so ashamed.

But it was good to have it out in the open. She was pleased too that she had had the guts to stand up for herself, and not let Helen paper it over with excuses and pleas of drunkenness. She smiled to herself. Nicola had been amazed to discover that Laura had known all along and had never said a word. But what was the point? Neil had told her all she needed to know. And because he hadn't hidden it from her, because of the fact that he respected Laura enough to come clean and in effect risk losing her, Laura believed what Neil had told her.

Yet, in spite of everything, in spite of their ups and downs, Laura didn't want to lose Helen as a friend. They had been through a lot together and lately life hadn't exactly been all that rosy for Helen. Her friend was lonely – who would have thought it?

Laura collapsed onto a chair, unwilling to let thoughts of Helen get her down.

"Oh, and guess who I met there?" she said.

"Who?" Neil asked with a grin, pleased at her enthusiasm.

"Debbie – from Amazing Days in Wicklow."

Neil looked blank.

"The stationery designer?" she prompted.

"Oh, right."

"She's a dote – we had a great chat."

Laura had bumped into Debbie while rushing off to grab a coffee – trusting the girl displaying handmade fudge across the way to watch over her stand. She had felt a tap on the shoulder while standing in the queue, and saw a smiling Debbie standing behind her.

"I thought I recognised you, earlier," Debbie said cheerily. "Are you just browsing or . . ."

"No, I'm exhibiting," Laura said proudly. Now she was amongst like-minded people and was getting so much positive feedback, she wasn't at all apologetic about her work. "I'm a jewellery designer."

"Really? I had no idea. I must pop over and have a look at your work. You already know what mine looks like," she added grinning. "Oh, and cheers for the 'Thank you' card – do you know you're the first bride ever to send me one?"

Laura was amazed. "But you did such a fantastic job! We were delighted with the invitations; people were mad about them."

"Mmm, a fantastic job all right – apart from the fact that we gave them away to someone else!" Debbie bought two coffees and, Styrofoam cups in hand, she and Laura walked back towards the stands.

"That's right!" Laura pretended she had forgotten, not wanting Debbie to think that it had been a problem.

But Debbie had something else on her mind. "Actually,"

she said, "I don't mean to gossip or anything, but your one was such a stuck-up cow, and you were so nice about the whole thing . . ."

"What?" Laura was intrigued.

"Well, it turned out that . . ." Debbie paused at Laura's stand and stopped mid-sentence when she saw her display. "Are these yours? They're fabulous!"

Laura hardly heard her. "What? Tell me about that other girl."

"Oh right. Well," Debbie lowered her voice conspiratorially, as if Chloe might pop out from under the pile of Aran sweaters at the next stand down, "it turned out that her wedding had to be postponed."

"Postponed? Why?"

"She didn't say. I know it galled her to have to ring me and ask for a reprint and another date, but what else could she do? It would cost her a fortune to get them made up from scratch again somewhere else."

Dan's wedding postponed! Laura was amazed. But why? Did it have anything to do with Nicola? More importantly should she *tell* Nicola? No, there was nothing to be gained by doing that – it might only make things worse.

But wasn't it a bit of a coincidence that Dan's wedding had to be put off not too long after he met up with Nicola again? Not to mention the fact that he had been pestering Nicola ever since?

"Anyway," Laura said to Neil now, "we went for coffee together when the exhibition closed, and she told me all about how she got started in the business, and how it took her ages to get going. Neil, to hear her talking, it was like listening to my own story! Her family were always popping in unannounced for coffee when she was trying to get some work done, and she too got landed with baby-sitting her friend's children while they went off shopping, or whatever. People used to send her off collecting laundry, or get her to wait at their houses to accept furniture deliveries and things like that."

Debbie's experiences had practically mirrored her own.

"They acted as though I was just sitting at home, with my feet up and nothing else to do but watch Sally Jessy and Jerry Springer," Debbie had confided. "Eventually I had to put a stop to it. I was getting nothing done, and being out of the house as often as I was didn't help the business."

"So, what did you say to them?" Laura was particularly interested in how she handled that, although Debbie didn't seem the type of woman to take nonsense from anyone.

Debbie grimaced. "I ended up falling out with some of them for a while," she said. "Most of my friends understood, but only after I sat them down and explained that even though I was working from home, I was still *working* and they couldn't just call in when they felt like it and expect me to be free. After that they were very supportive. Of course, once I got the shop I was able to separate business time from personal time and that helped enormously. But I'll tell you," she said with a shake of her head, "it wasn't easy."

Laura nodded sympathetically, thinking about her own family situation.

"But in order to keep going, you have to keep believing

not just in your product, but in *yourself*. And you have to condition your mind into believing that failure is not an option. It's not easy and no matter what the papers tell you, there are very few overnight successes and instant millionaires out there." She took a mouthful of coffee. "You just stay determined and keep working away and eventually you'll get the break you need." She gave Laura's hand an encouraging squeeze. "You know, sometimes that's all it takes – just one break. And by exhibiting here today, Laura, you're definitely on the right track."

Sitting now in her kitchen, Laura wondered about that.

Just one break? If that was all it took, would she recognise the all-important opportunity when it came?

Or, she thought nervously – recalling Brid Cassidy's interest in her wedding jewellery – had the opportunity already passed her by?

* * *

That same afternoon, a weary and despondent Helen called to Kerry's primary school.

She was still reeling from events at Laura's. How could her friend have known all those years and never said a thing? Helen didn't know how Laura could even have forced herself to stay friends with her, never mind being such a good one at that.

She knew she had taken Laura's friendship for granted, asking her to pick up Kerry from school and look after her daughter while she slipped off for sex sessions with Paul. She had taken advantage of Laura's kind heart and gentle nature in the same way she had mistreated Jo, who had always been helpful and accommodating where Kerry was concerned, even when Helen treated her like muck.

She had finished with Paul that night. What was the point? Nicola was right. She had gone too far in her lies, so far that she had even denied her own daughter's existence. No matter how much she wanted someone, there was no excuse for that. She hadn't even told Paul about Kerry in the end, better letting him think that she had just gone off him. In fairness, he hadn't seemed all that bothered. Then again, Helen thought, it wasn't as though it had been a deep and meaningful relationship; they had spent most of their time together in bed. And Helen was pretty certain that the so-called 'sick mother' he kept visiting was a lot more likely be a 'long-term girlfriend'. She knew enough about men to read the signs. All Helen had to do was admit to herself that she had been nothing more than a weekday fling for Paul.

That time with Neil – *of course* she had felt guilty about it afterwards, realising how nasty she had been in coming on to him. Poor thing, he was so drunk and so innocent he hadn't a hope, really. But the guilt hadn't lasted that long, and certainly wasn't severe enough for Helen to really comprehend the damage she might have done.

At the time, Helen hadn't been too worried. Nicola had interrupted them and they hadn't ended up sleeping together, so really, it was no big deal, just a bit of a fumble. Why feel guilty, when there was nothing to feel guilty about?

But the fact that Laura knew all along – had been her friend and had still managed to help and support her without question – now made Helen felt very guilty indeed. Laura's decency towards her, even immediately afterwards, served to truly highlight Helen's own inadequacies as a person.

She felt sick when she thought about it. Would she have done the same as Laura had? Would she have examined the situation and thought about Laura's state of mind at the time, and her motives for trying to steal Jamie away? Helen didn't think so. In fact, Helen would have probably have punched her in the nose. She certainly wouldn't have kept her as a friend, and she most definitely wouldn't have understood!

How could Laura be so understanding and so forgiving of people all the time?

Helen had always thought it a huge weakness in her oldest friend, but now she knew she had been very wrong. It was an unbelievable strength, a strength of character that no one, not even Nicola, had given Laura credit for.

And when Nicola too was struggling on her own after Dan, when her life was in tatters, it had been Laura helping her pick up the pieces, Laura the one who had sat with her day in day out, listening to her fears about how she might never be the same again.

Again, Helen felt ashamed that she hadn't been able to do that. It was another blight on her character that she had all but abandoned Nicola when her friend was at her lowest. She kept telling herself at the time that she had her own problems, that Jamie was about to leave her, but of course that wasn't it.

The truth was that she was afraid – afraid of what might happen to Nicola, afraid of how she as Nicola's friend might then be expected to cope.

Guiding the car into a free parking space, Helen realised that she was not only a terrible friend and a terrible mother but, all in all, a terrible person.

* * *

The headmistress, Mrs Clancy, looked at her gravely from across the table. Helen knew that the older woman was annoyed with her for not having met with her sooner. Kerry had started here in early September, and Helen knew her daughter hadn't really taken to it.

Mrs Clancy had been trying to arrange an appointment with Helen for quite some time, and after a lot of procrastinating (and particularly following recent events) Helen had finally decided to bite the bullet and meet the woman. She knew what this would be about; obviously Kerry's speech problems were impeding her learning and Helen suspected that the headmistress would want Helen to consider taking her out and starting her again next year, when she was a little more advanced.

"Ms Jackson, as I'm sure you're aware, Kerry has quite a severe speech problem," the headmistress began.

Helen nodded. "I am – I mean I *do*. She's seen a therapist but she doesn't seem to be getting any better. I had hoped," she continued, seeing the principal was about to interrupt, "I had hoped that going to school and being around other children would help her, although I realise now that she may have problems keeping up."

Mrs Clancy's eyes widened. "Far from it, Ms Jackson," she said. "In fact, Kerry is one of the brightest children in her class."

"Oh?"

"Yes, although Mrs Cosgrove – that's Kerry's teacher, by the way," she added, in a poorly disguised jibe at Helen's lack of interest to date, "rarely asks her to read out loud in front of the others because of her stutter. But she has a keen ear for grammar and, from what I am aware, tries her utmost to keep up in class."

"I'm confused," Helen said frowning. "I thought you were going to tell me her stutter is causing problems for her here." She certainly hadn't expected Mrs Clancy to be complimenting Kerry's progress.

The other woman looked at her. "Ms Jackson, how does Kerry seem at home to you?"

"At home? Well, she's fine, usually. What exactly do you mean?"

"Does she seem quiet, distant – upset, even?"

"Well, Kerry is always quiet, Mrs Clancy. She spends a lot of time in her room and – now that you mention it – she spends a lot of time alone perfecting her reading."

"Perfecting her reading – or her speech?"

Helen briefly considered this. "Both, I'm sure."

"Ms Jackson – may I call you Helen?" she asked, in what Helen perceived as a kindly tone. She wondered what was coming. "Because of her stutter Kerry has been the subject of some teasing in class." This was said apologetically, as if Mrs Clancy believed herself personally responsible for it.

Helen shifted in her seat. "Mrs Clancy," she said evenly, "this doesn't come as any great surprise to me. Children like Kerry are bound to be taunted, particularly at that age. I'm sure you know as well as anyone how cruel kids can be, but they're young, they don't know any different.

I always knew that there might be a possibility that she'd be called names."

The headmistress fixed her with a hard glare. "This isn't just verbal, Helen, and it's a very serious matter. Kerry has been spat at, ridiculed, and pushed onto the ground, not only by the boys, but indeed some of the girls in her class. It's not just taunting, Helen – it's downright bullying, and it breaks my heart to admit that it goes on in my school at all, but especially at that young age. Didn't she show you the marks on her arms?"

For one long moment, Helen felt as though she was eavesdropping on someone else's conversation. Spat at? Pushed over? Marks on her arms? Why hadn't Kerry said anything?

More importantly why hadn't *she* noticed?

But Helen didn't have to dig too deep to find the answer. How *would* she have noticed? She'd been so self-absorbed, so wrapped up in herself and Paul these last few months that she hadn't even noticed Kerry growing out of her clothes!

"Ms Jackson?"

"Sorry – what?" Helen was so absorbed in her own thoughts, she had almost forgotten the headmistress was still there.

"Look, I know this is coming as a bit of a shock to you, and we would have told you sooner but –"

"Kerry didn't want you to," Helen finished for her, shaking her head sadly. "Kerry didn't want to upset me, did she?"

"Actually," the headmistress began, a strange expression on her face, "that's not quite right. Your daughter didn't want you to be *angry* with her. She said – and these are Kerry's words – 'Mummy says I can't talk properly because I don't practise enough. If you tell Mummy about the bold boys then she'll know I'm not practising, and she'll be very mad.'"

"Oh, God!" Helen's felt a massive knot in her chest. Her hand flew to her mouth and the tears were streaming down her cheeks before she even realised they were there.

What had she done? What had she done to her child? Why hadn't she come in to see Mrs Clancy sooner? Why keep putting it off and putting it off like her daughter's welfare was some kind of nuisance? God, was there no end to her selfishness?

Helen could just imagine Kerry, embarrassed and ashamed, begging the teachers not to tell her because she thought that she would be angry with her for stuttering – that she would say the taunts were all her own doing because she couldn't speak properly. What sort of a mother was she that she could inflict that kind of emotional damage on her own child?

"Helen, try not to upset yourself over this," Mrs Clancy looked genuinely perturbed. "I understand how you must be feeling, but please remember that Kerry is barely four years old. Children that age have great imaginations. None of the teachers here, or indeed myself, would have taken any notice of such claims. We don't believe for a second that you would inflict blame on Kerry for her problems. And as far as I'm aware, a stutter is a physiological and *not* a psychological problem. However, Kerry's lack of self-confidence in this regard is bound to affect her progress. I think this is where the parents come in. I should add that we've already spoken to the culprits' parents, and will take whatever action is necessary against these bullies but –"

Helen shook her head. "It's *my* fault this is happening, not Kerry's and not the other children's . . . I haven't been helping her enough. I haven't done the exercises her therapist suggested in ages. In fact," she paled as the realisation hit her, "I haven't even brought her to see the speech therapist since . . . oh, what have I done?" She buried her head in her hands, shame enveloping her.

Mrs Clancy was silent for a moment.

"Helen, I'm unaware of your own personal circumstances, but from what I can gather you're not married?"

Helen nodded wordlessly.

"There's no denying that bringing up a child on your own is difficult, particularly for a working mother. You yourself will admit that, I'm sure."

When Helen didn't answer, Mrs Clancy got up and walked around the table, putting a comforting hand on the younger woman's shoulder. "Helen, please don't upset yourself any longer with this. I'm sure you've tried your best for Kerry but maybe you two now have a few things to sort out between you."

A *few* things? Helen had never before experienced anything like the raw guilt that was coursing through her just then. It was like molten lava, burning her insides and destroying her own inflated self-worth. Was there anyone she *hadn't* hurt these last few years in her innate desire to satisfy herself, to make up for the rejection and loss she had felt since Jamie's departure?

After a few moments, Helen stood up, and resolutely shook hands with Mrs Clancy.

She'd go home now and talk to Kerry about the bullying and the stuttering, maybe try and boost her daughter's self-confidence and actually behave like a good mother, a *decent* mother for once.

As she drove towards home, Helen pictured her daughter's sunny smiling face, but soon after the image was replaced by an ugly vision of Kerry being taunted by her classmates. At this, Helen felt an overwhelming urge to catch those little bastards and slap them hard, inflict on them some of the suffering that her daughter had endured. She'd catch the little pricks and bang their bullying heads together and she'd certainly have a thing or two to say to the parents, she'd –

Helen's head snapped up. She pulled over and stopped the car, suddenly feeling like St Paul on the road to Damascus. Was this it? she asked herself, hands shaking with adrenaline. This almost primeval urge to protect – *maternal* urge to protect. Was this the feeling that had so eluded her for all those years?

Helen shook her head sadly. She still didn't know.

All Helen knew then was that she had a lot of making up to do.

Chapter 32

"Will you have something to drink, Chloe?" Nicola asked. "Coffee, tea, a glass of wine maybe?"

"Coffee, please." Chloe looked nervously around the room. "Um – you have a very nice house," she said without enthusiasm.

Nicola felt sorry for her. It was really annoying the way Dan had turned up at the same time like that. She hadn't expected him to arrive until at least an hour later and she had intended to spend some time with Chloe first – to prepare her before he arrived. But Chloe had been late and Dan had been way too early so . . .

Now the poor girl looked as though she couldn't wait to get out of here.

"Do you need help? I could make the coffee if you like," Dan piped up meaningfully.

Nicola let him follow her into the kitchen.

"What are you trying to do to me, Nic?" he hissed, when he was sure Chloe was out of earshot.

Nicola checked the percolator and turned to face him.

"I'm not trying to do anything to you, Dan – in fact, I think I'm doing you a favour."

"A favour? You've got to be joking!"

"No, I'm not. Chloe's been curious about me for a long time now – I'm just setting her mind at ease."

"Are you sure that's all it is, Nic? Are you sure you're not enjoying this just a little bit too?"

"Enjoying it?" Nicola looked at him. "What exactly is there to enjoy about this, Dan?"

"Well, why did you invite us here today then – both of us?"

"I didn't intend for the two you to arrive together. I told you not to come until seven because I wanted some time alone with Chloe first to –"

"Dish the dirt?"

"No, you bastard – to explain! To explain what you couldn't – to let her know that I'm no threat to her as far as you're concerned! Something you should have done from the very beginning!"

"Look, I know that," Dan ran a hand through his hair, "but I just didn't know what to tell her . . . I was afraid."

Nicola shook her head. "When I met you that day in Bray, I thought that you had changed – matured, copped onto yourself, even. But you're still terrified by this, aren't you? Even though you no longer have anything to do with me, you're still afraid, aren't you?"

"It's not that, Nic . . . I don't . . . I just couldn't –"

"You couldn't deal with it, Dan," Nicola finished for him. "You couldn't deal with it then, and you can't deal with it now. That's fair enough. But what I can't understand is why you didn't tell Chloe."

Dan looked like a scolded child. "Look, you're right. I know you're right. It's just I didn't want to admit that . . . oh, I just didn't know how she'd see it, maybe she'd blame me, maybe she wouldn't understand what it was like for me."

"Oh, for goodness sake, Dan. It isn't all about you!" Her voice shook as she spoke. "Do you think I enjoyed bringing Chloe here today? Now don't get me wrong. I'm not jealous of her or anything like that, but do you think it was easy for me being on show like this?"

"Look, I know it must be strange for you seeing me with someone else –"

"Whoa!" Nicola made a 'hands off' gesture with her palms. "Don't think it's anything to do with you. Whatever you and I had is long gone, over and done with. You're just a little blip on the horizon as far as I'm concerned, and the reason I'm doing this is because I want you out of my life for once and for all!"

"Nicola –"

"Look, you have no idea how hard it was for me to come back here and start again on my own," she interjected, annoyed that she was forced to drill this into his thick head, frustrated that she had to explain anything. "And I think I'm doing OK – I mean I *was* doing OK until all this started. I can go anywhere I want to go. I have my own house, a job I love – a man I love very much and who loves *me*. I don't need to rely on anyone, Dan, least of all you."

"I know, and it's brilliant –"

"Don't patronise me!" Nicola's eyes flashed. "You've done that once too often."

Dan looked suitably chastened and for a moment, neither one said anything.

Nicola glanced towards the living-room and her tone softened. "Look, can you just forget about yourself for once, and tell the girl the truth?"

He sighed. "I will. I promise. And I'm sorry, Nic. I didn't really consider your side of it. I was angry with Chloe when she spoke to Carolyn but I still didn't explain anything. I thought the fact that I was so annoyed with her would be enough to make her give in." He scratched his nose. "I suppose I just didn't figure how all of this would affect you."

Nicola shook her head. "Same old story," she said. "All you, you, you."

"You're right," Dan wouldn't meet her eyes, "but I promise I'll tell her everything."

"Good." Nicola folded her arms across her chest but there was a flicker of amusement in her eyes. He looked genuinely sorry.

"Now in spite of my big spiel about independence, will you get that tray for me?" she asked easily.

"Sure," Dan picked up the tray that Nicola had filled with coffee and cake and went back towards the living-room. Then he stopped, frowning. "Where's that whining noise coming from?" he asked, his gaze moving around the room.

Nicola smiled mischievously. "I wasn't sure whether or not Chloe liked dogs."

Dan wrinkled his forehead. "She loves them, I think –"

"She does? Great." Nicola opened the utility-room door, and Barney bounded forward, tongue out and bottom-half wagging. He stopped short when he saw Dan, and Nicola noticed the hairs at the back of his neck rise slightly at the sight of this particular visitor. Nice judge of character, Barn, she thought, smiling to herself.

"Oh!" Dan looked clearly uncomfortable, and Nicola allowed herself a little grin as she made her way back to the living-room. Her ex was petrified of dogs – always had been.

Barney followed immediately behind Nicola, spied yet another visitor and raced across to Chloe, sniffing her ankles speculatively.

"Oh, he's fabulous!" The younger woman forgot her discomfort for a second, and appreciatively stroked Barney's glossy coat. The dog responded by nosing her palm and nudging himself against her legs, tail wagging all the time.

"I don't know what I'd do without him," Nicola said with a smile, pleased that Chloe no longer looked quite so uptight. "Chloe, will you have a muffin or a slice of gateau, maybe?"

"I won't, thanks," Chloe was demure.

"Watching your weight for the wedding, I suppose," Nicola said pleasantly. "I'd imagine you're really looking forward to it."

It was obvious Chloe didn't know how to answer that. All of a sudden, Nicola felt guilty. She hadn't meant for this to be uncomfortable for Chloe – she was the innocent party here and her fiancé was the one who deserved teaching a lesson.

Just then Dan's mobile shrilled and, in his haste to answer, the phone fell out of his pocket and slid away from him on the wooden floor. Barney jumped up and immediately retrieved the phone with his mouth, offering it to a surprised and more than a little nervous-looking Dan.

Chloe looked at Nicola in astonishment. "How clever!" she exclaimed, the arrival of Barney setting her more at ease, as Nicola suspected it might. Barney never failed to impress people with his antics.

Nicola grimaced. "Dan doesn't seem to think so," she laughed, watching her ex distastefully wipe the handset with his handkerchief before answering the call.

Dan spoke hurriedly into the telephone. "Can't someone else handle it?" Nicola heard him say to whoever was on the other end. "Well, look I'm in the middle of something here." He gave an apologetic shake of his head as he retreated to the kitchen, and Nicola wasn't sure if the look was intended for herself, or his fiancé.

Seizing the chance to speak frankly to Chloe, she turned to her.

"Look, I'm sorry for surprising you like this. I didn't mean for you and Dan to arrive here together. I had hoped you and I would get a chance to chat a little first beforehand."

Chloe nervously cradled the coffee mug in her hand. "I'm the one that should be sorry," she said, not meeting Nicola's eyes. "I shouldn't have gone behind your back like that . . . if I had known –"

"Look, it's OK, really it is. I know Dan hasn't been exactly forthcoming."

Chloe, clearly troubled, shook her head. "I had no idea."

"How could you? Look, I can understand your curiosity about me, especially with my being away for so long and then turning up like this – just before your wedding and everything. But you must realise that I didn't come back to Ireland to win Dan back." She gave a short laugh. "There was never any question of that. I'm with someone else now, someone I love very much."

There was a pause. "I did wonder why Dan was so anxious to see you," Chloe said, "and why he was so hesitant to discuss the details of your break-up. When it comes to you he can be quite, quite –" she searched for the right word.

"Defensive?" Nicola offered.

Chloe nodded. "I think I felt threatened."

"I can imagine." Nicola reached down, and scratched Barney behind the ears. "But Dan's not defensive about *me* – he's defensive about his own behaviour. Still, now that we've met, do you still feel that way? Threatened, I mean."

Chloe shook her head, obviously finding it all terribly unnerving. "To be honest, Nicola, I don't know how to feel. I certainly didn't expect you to be so . . . well, so nice." She gave a rueful smile. "I'm sorry, I don't suppose I'm handling this very well."

"It's OK." Nicola smiled.

Dan came back into the room and looked from one woman to the other.

"That was the office," he said flatly. "There's a problem at work – Temple Architects are threatening to move their account. They called and left messages for John four times this week and he hasn't returned any of them. I've tried

John's mobile and I can only get his message-minder." He shook his head. "Now I'll have to go and try and sweet-talk Harry Temple into keeping his precious firm with us. I'm getting sick of this."

Nicola knew an excuse to leave when she heard one.

"You're going – now?" Chloe asked, the relief in her voice almost palpable. "Well, I'd better be going too." She stood up. "Nicola, it was nice to meet you. Thanks for the coffee."

"You're very welcome. It was great to meet you too."

"Um, you should come and see us sometime."

Nicola tried to keep her expression neutral. "I will – sometime."

"Right."

Dan looked at his watch. "Sorry we have to rush off like this, Nic, but we'll talk soon, yeah?"

"Sure."

Chloe and Dan headed towards the hallway and let themselves out, Barney accompanying them to the door.

From her sitting-room window, Nicola watched the two retreat to their cars. Chloe walked slowly beside Dan, and Nicola didn't need to be an expert in lip-reading to make out what the younger woman might be saying to her fiancé.

"Jesus, Dan," Chloe was whispering, her expression shocked and confused. "Why the hell didn't you tell me?"

Chapter 33

Dan walked closely beside her. "Look, just get in the car and follow me down to the village. We'll talk about it then."

Chloe said nothing. She reversed out of Nicola's driveway as if in a daze, and as she did, Dan saw her cast a questioning glance at the Ford Focus parked outside the house.

Dan drove off ahead and moments later, both vehicles stopped in the carpark of a local pub. His expression unreadable, Dan got in alongside Chloe.

"I'm sorry," he said simply. "I just didn't know how to tell you."

"But how could you – how could you keep something like that from me, Dan? How could you go on for so long without saying anything?"

"I –"

Before he could answer, she went on. "That dog – Nicola's

dog – he's one of those . . . one of *those* dogs, isn't he? Like a guide dog except –"

"An assistance dog." Dan clarified. "Yes, he is."

Chloe shook her head. "But what happened to her? She hasn't always been that way, has she?"

"No," Dan answered sadly, "she hasn't always been that way."

The dog had been quite a shock for him. While keenly aware that over the last few years Nicola had all but resumed her independence, he had been unprepared for the dog's role in that. He recalled the way Barney – as she called it – had instantly retrieved his mobile phone when it fell on the floor, and how the dog had closed the front door after he and Chloe left the house. Apparently, these assistance dogs could do great things altogether, like switch on and off lights, and load or unload washing-machines. Dan supposed he was a useful guard dog too – able to warn Nicola in advance of any impending danger.

"But why didn't you tell me?" Chloe asked again.

Dan dropped his gaze to the dashboard. "I'm sorry. But as time went by it was getting harder and harder to say anything. I just didn't know what you'd think of me and –"

"What happened?" Chloe asked again.

"I just didn't know how to bring it up, Chloe. You have to understand –"

"Dan, just *tell* me!"

He could hear the desperation in her voice. This was it, he thought with growing unease. The moment he'd been dreading since Nicola came back.

Before speaking, Dan cleared his throat. "Well, Nicola

and I had been through a lot, as you know, with the miscarriage and, of course, the thing with Ken Harris."

Chloe nodded, waiting for him to continue.

"But we got over it – in fact we got over it faster – and possibly easier – than either of us had anticipated. We loved one another a lot, Chloe, and we were both equally determined to get through it, equally committed to making the marriage work." He swallowed. "Of course, it wasn't that easy for me to forgive Nicola for going near Harris, but yet I could understand why it happened. I suppose, for a while, Nicola and I were unconsciously avoiding – not just one another – but what had happened to us. We'd never really spoken about the miscarriage, never really shared our grief. After the Ken thing, I think we both realised what we had been doing, and that we were letting our marriage slip away from us."

He knew Chloe wasn't comfortable hearing this, but yet there was a strange sense of relief in getting the words out.

"After we admitted to one another how we were really feeling, and how fragile things had become, we both decided that although the marriage was weak, we still loved one another deeply and there was plenty to fight for. So, we set about doing just that. We spoke about moving out of our apartment in Bray, and buying a house of our own. We knew that, if our marriage was to survive, we'd have to make a fresh start."

A new house was to signify a new beginning, a new chapter in their life together.

"For a while, it was terrific. Nicola left Metamorph and got another job in a hotel leisure centre – I suppose to

430

reassure me that she wouldn't be seeing Ken Harris again, but I knew he wasn't a problem. All that mattered to me was that I'd got Nicola back – the *old* Nicola back."

He saw Chloe flinch slightly at this.

"I'm sorry, Chloe. I suppose this is part of the reason I didn't want to tell you. This kind of thing isn't easy for you to hear."

"Don't worry about what I think," Chloe said quietly. "Just go on."

Dan exhaled. "Right. Well, as I said, the old Nicola was back and – believe me – this turned out to be a bit of a mixed blessing!" He laughed, remembering. "Nicola is full of unbelievable energy – always flitting off here, there and everywhere. She has absolutely no patience and sometimes you can't get her to sit still in the same place for more than a few seconds!" He paused, realising that he was speaking about it in the present tense. "Anyway, she made an absolute mission out of the house-hunting – it was a big thing for her and I suppose it was something to work towards, something to aim for. I have to admit that I enjoyed it, too – the two of us would take off on our bikes on Saturday and Sunday afternoons to look at show-houses."

"Bikes?"

Dan suspected Chloe was finding it hard to picture him on a bicycle. Dan *adored* his car.

"Yeah, Nicola wasn't a great fan of traffic – she had a touch of the old road rage." He smiled, almost affectionately, but then his expression became subdued. "But just when everything was started to fall into place for us, just when we were starting to get back on track and things were going well – almost *too* well . . ."his voice trailed off, sadly. "We had come through so much together – my parents, the miscarriage, Ken . . . we had come through it all, Chloe, and by then we were convinced that the two of us could survive anything."

And they *had* been convinced, Dan thought. It didn't matter what else life threw at them, they had each been convinced that they loved one another enough, that their marriage was strong enough to survive *anything*.

He laughed, a short bitter laugh. "But, it's true what they say – if you want to give God a good laugh, tell him about your plans."

"Nicola ended up in some kind of accident." Chloe stated flatly.

Dan nodded. "On her bike. She was out cycling up near Glendalough on her afternoon off, and a tourist who didn't know the road rounded a corner and ploughed into her – the bastard was lucky he didn't kill her!"

Chloe shook her head sadly.

"I couldn't believe it, Chloe. I just couldn't believe it. After everything we'd been through, after everything we'd fought for, something like that had to happen – why?"

"I'm so sorry, Dan."

"The ambulance brought Nicola to Loughlinstown, and from there they sent her on to St Vincent's. They set her up in traction but it wasn't long before they came back with a full diagnosis. She'd damaged a section of her spine that couldn't ever be renewed. While, she was OK as far as the waist, they were doubtful that she'd ever regain the use of her legs."

"The poor thing, what must it have been like for her?"

Dan struggled to speak. This was the part he hated, the part he dreaded telling her. What would she think of him?

"However bad it was, I made it ten times worse," he said hoarsely, a huge lump rising in his throat. "I got such a shock when they told us. I couldn't handle it, Chloe, and for a long time I wouldn't believe it. I couldn't believe it. After everything . . . I kept expecting someone to tell me that it had all been a sick joke – a candid-camera type thing. I just couldn't handle it." Dan shook his head sadly, as if still trying to convince himself.

"What?" Chloe looked at him. "What are you talking about, Dan? Nicola was the one affected, not you. What do you mean *you* couldn't handle it?"

It was seconds before the realisation hit her. Despite having met Nicola, Chloe still hadn't understood. She hadn't understood why he had gone to such lengths to hide it all from her. But now Chloe knew that it wasn't so much his wife's disability Dan had been hiding; it was his own reaction to it.

Dan was ashamed and so he should be.

"Oh – my – God," she said, pronouncing each word slowly as she said it. "You left her, didn't you, Dan? You left Nicola to deal with it all on her own."

Dan said nothing but he didn't need to. His shamefaced expression said it all.

Chapter 34

A few days later, Laura was rifling through a sheaf of invoices trying to get to grips with her latest VAT declaration.

"What do you think?" she asked Eamonn, who was lazing on the floor beside her desk. "Would gift boxes be considered Purchases For Resale, or Purchases *Not* For Resale?"

The cat yawned, obviously not caring one way or the other.

"They'd have to be 'For Resale', wouldn't they? Because they're part of the overall product . . . yet I don't actually sell them on to people so . . ."

Laura kneaded her forehead impatiently. She'd been at this all afternoon and she still couldn't make head nor tail of it.

Not that there was any bloody point, Laura thought. The Crafts Exhibition hadn't been the great success she had imagined. Yes, she had given out plenty of cards and, yes, there had been loads lots of compliments thrown about, but still there was nothing concrete – not even the *possibility* of something concrete.

Laura just wasn't selling enough to justify her existence as a jewellery designer. If anything she was losing money, what with all the stock she had to buy and all the packaging and boxes and all the unseen expenses, like phone and electricity and heating and everything! It was just too much.

Laura had to admit to herself that maybe they had been right; Helen, her mother, all the doubters had been right. It just wasn't possible; this kind of life just wasn't feasible, not for someone like Laura anyway. They had been right from the very beginning. She didn't have the tenacity, the confidence, the belief in herself to really make a go of this.

Laura had finally begun to realise that she just didn't have the killer instinct.

"And that isn't exactly something you can fake, or something you can work at, is it, Eamonn?" she asked, feeling more than a little concerned that lately all she seemed to do was talk nonsense to the cat.

She got up to make herself a cup of coffee and, hopefully, clear her head. On the fridge, Laura caught sight of a wedding snapshot Maureen had taken of herself and Neil at the altar. Laura studied Neil's earnest expression, the one he had spent ages practising especially for the day. "I can't show off the gap in my teeth," he had insisted weeks beforehand. But by the time the photographer had arranged and rearranged them all for the photographs, Laura knew the gap in his teeth was well and truly forgotten. She was pleased. At least in their professional wedding photographs,

Neil would look like *her* Neil and not the stiff, uncomfortable Neil in this one.

How would Neil feel when she told him she was about to give up what once had been her dream? That she was going back to the rat-race, where she would be once again a square peg trying to fit into a round hole?

Just then, Laura heard the doorbell ring. She went out to answer it and nearly dropped her coffee mug when she saw who was standing outside.

"Hello, Laura," Helen said nervously, "can I come in?"

"Of course." Laura was shocked at the sight of her. Helen looked as though she hadn't slept in days. Her eyes were bloodshot, her face was pale and she was dressed in a baggy T-shirt and track-suit bottoms – *track-suit bottoms*!

"Do you want a coffee? I was just making one."

"Would you mind?" Helen looked unsure and, Laura thought, nervous. Now this was certainly odd – Helen in track-suit bottoms and *nervous*!

"Come on through." Laura walked ahead of her into the kitchen. She looked at the clock. Almost two in the afternoon. Why wasn't Helen at work?

"Why aren't you at work?" she asked.

"I took a few days off," Helen said quietly. "I needed some time – to think."

"Oh."

Helen took a deep breath. "Laura, I came here today, not to ask for your forgiveness or understanding, or anything, but just to say that I am truly, deeply, sorry for what I did."

"That's OK, Helen."

"Not just for the Neil thing, although that was bad

436

enough, and to this day I still don't really know why I did it . . . I mean I *do* know – I just wanted to fuck things up for you, like things were fucked up for me. I suppose I've always been that bit envious of you and –"

"Envious – of me?" Laura interjected, surprised.

"Well, yes." Helen said. "You just seem to sail through life taking each day as it comes, no worries, a wonderful husband, a fantastic home – everything!"

Laura stared at her. She had thought Helen had come here to apologise, to make amends for her behaviour. She certainly hadn't expected Helen to come up with a pathetic excuse like that! *Envious*, my backside!

"And this," Helen made a broad sweeping gesture towards Laura's workshop. "You took a risk and forged a decent career for yourself by following your dream. How many of us have the courage to do that?"

"You're trying to be funny, aren't you?" Laura said. "You, Helen Jackson, with the designer clothes and the designer apartment and the – the designer *life* – you expect me to believe that you are envious of *me*!"

"Well, of course! Why wouldn't I be? You have everything I want – everything I've ever wanted. I'm not saying that you don't deserve it, of course you do, but everything always seemed to come so easily for you!"

"Easily?" Laura parroted, her eyes out on disbelieving stalks. "You think things have come easily for me! Me, who all these years has sat and watched you bag all the best men, the best jobs – even the best exam results, for goodness sake! Why would *you* be envious of *me* when you were the one who got eight bloody honours in your bloody Leaving Cert!"

The two women faced one another and, for one brief moment, a tension-filled hush descended on the room.

Eventually, Helen raised an amused eyebrow. "Eight honours?" she said, biting back a grin.

Laura immediately felt a bubble of laughter rise up within her. "Oh God," she giggled, her eyes dancing with humour, "I can't believe I just said that – I can't believe that I brought up the bloody Leaving Cert results!"

Helen was laughing too. "I'm sorry, I'm sorry for laughing at you. I know what you mean – it's just . . . God, you should have seen your face! 'You got eight honours in your bloody Leaving Cert, Helen!' Honestly, Laura, you should have seen your face!"

They laughed again, and, as they sat down to drink their coffee, Laura reflected that no matter what had happened between them – no matter how remote and flimsy their relationship had been over the past few years – she and Helen would always have a bond, an odd, bizarre, and often fragile bond of friendship, but a bond nonetheless.

Helen was her oldest friend. Yes, they had let things slip over the last few years and yes, Helen had many times put that friendship at risk, but could Laura honestly admit that she hadn't done the same? Hadn't she made the same mistake of believing Helen's circumstances to be perfect, believing that her friend was the type of person she herself really wanted to be? And hadn't she too envied her for that, envied her poise, her confidence, her looks – even her life? Laura remembered all the times she had sat here in this house, and in her office, feeling self-conscious about her abilities, her appearance and her situation, wishing that she possessed even an ounce of Helen's vibrancy. And then, Helen would arrive in the door all poised, gorgeous, and oozing self-assurance, making her feel even more insignificant.

Laura couldn't kid herself that she hadn't felt bitter towards Helen at times – secretly bitter that her friend looked better than her, that she was more capable, more assured. There were even times when Laura resented Helen just for who she was.

But wasn't that only natural between friends – between women, even, Laura thought, that no matter how much they pretend to be supportive, sympathetic and compassionate, now and again they just want one another to fail? Not through jealousy, she thought, but because through comparing our own successes to other women's failures, we tend to feel that bit better – that bit *smugger* about ourselves. Laura knew that she had many times been guilty of just that where Helen was concerned.

"I'm sorry," Helen said again, her expression growing serious. "I came here today to tell you that, and to tell you that if you want me out of your life then I'll understand completely."

"I don't want you out of my life, Helen," Laura said. "We've both been stupid. We've both been childish. OK, maybe I didn't try and steal your boyfriend but . . ." She trailed off when she saw Helen wince. "Look, I know you weren't thinking straight – you were hurting. And I suppose, if we're being honest, at the time I felt that bit superior to you – for once."

"Superior?"

"Yes. There you were, abandoned, a single mother, struggling to come to terms with losing everything you held dear, and there *I* was madly in love with a man who I knew loved me back, and didn't want to lose me." She gave a little laugh. "In a way you did me a favour, because when Neil confessed what had happened and was so cut up about it, I knew his feelings for me were real. If anything, it brought us closer and it made our feelings stronger. Meanwhile you were left with no one. So, yes, I felt that little bit superior."

Helen looked at her. "Bloody hell – we're not exactly candidates for a remake of *Thelma and Louise*, are we?"

Laura shrugged. "You and I know both know that it doesn't always happen that way. We don't *all* go around sobbing on one another's shoulders and hugging like they do in the movies. Real friendship isn't just about the soppy bits; it's warts and all."

"I wonder if Nicola feels that way – about me, anyway?" Helen said pensively.

Laura smiled. "Now, Nicola is a different kettle of fish altogether. You can't keep that one down."

"I didn't help though, did I? After the accident . . . I mean, I rarely even visited her in hospital and when Dan left she really needed her friends around her and –"

"Helen, Nicola's fine. She didn't need help from anyone – she never has. That girl decided from day one that she was going to get through it, and she did."

Helen nodded. "Where does she get it from, Laura? I don't know if I could have dealt with it – actually I do know – I *couldn't* have dealt with it!"

"Helen, none of us know how we'll deal with what life throws at us. All we do is get on with it, same as Nicola did." She paused, smiling. "God, aren't I being terribly philosophical today! But no, Nicola isn't mad at you, Helen – neither of us are.

Helen gave her a sideways glance. "You're sure? I don't think I've ever heard you talk to me like you did the other night, you know – it was a bit scary, actually. But you really made me think."

"Good," Laura smiled, but then her tone grew serious. "Still, I suspect you had a lot of thinking to do."

"Yes. But not just about myself."

"Kerry?"

Helen nodded over the rim of her coffee mug. "I shouldn't have tried to deny her like I did."

"Did you tell Paul eventually?"

Helen shook her head. "I just told him I didn't think we were 'going anywhere.'" She made quotation marks in the air with her fingers.

"Really?"

"There was no point, Laura. Anyway, he was a bit of a dope."

Laura bit back a grin. "If you say so."

"Admit it!"

"OK – maybe the American accent was a bit over the top for a culchie from County Cork."

Helen chuckled "It got to me after a while too."

"Oh well, I'm sure you'll find someone eventually."

"Laura, at this stage, I'm not too bothered." She gave a watery smile.

"So tell us, how *is* Kerry?"

"Well, that's another thing," Helen's expression darkened. "I found out the other day that she's being bullied at school," she admitted guiltily.

"Well, I wasn't sure, but I suspected as much. She hates school, Helen, in the same way that she hated playschool. I'm sure she finds it hard to make friends and her confidence is shot because of her stutter."

"I know. But I'll have to try and help her with that, and with her confidence too, I suppose."

Laura smiled. "Kerry'll be pleased. She adores you, you know."

"I've made a mess of that too, haven't I?" Helen looked pained.

"Helen, you have to start somewhere."

"I know." She took a deep breath. "Anyway, what about you? Did the exhibition go well the other day?"

Laura shook her head sadly. "Ah, I think I'm wasting my time, Helen. I'll never be successful at this."

"What do you mean?"

"I think you were right from the very beginning. I'm just not cut out for this kind of life."

"Laura, that was just me being a jealous cow. Look, I might not have shown it, but I was always behind you. Please don't tell me you're thinking of giving up on this. After everything you've achieved already, surely you have to give it a chance – make a real go of it."

"Easy for you to say."

"Absolutely," Helen agreed vehemently. "I don't have the same attachment to my work as you do, nor a clue how it must feel to create something from nothing, show it to the world and let them decide whether or not it's worth anything. I suspect it isn't easy. But success? Laura, I don't think you should get bogged down in all that kind of thing. Why can't you just be proud of what you're doing?"

To her surprise, Laura felt tears in her eyes. "Because I don't know if it *is* something to be proud of, Helen. I mean, my parents, Cathy, everyone in Glengarrah – they all think I'm nuts. They think that I'm only playing at being in business!"

"Well, stuff them!" Helen said. "Stuff all of them! Who cares what they think? As long as you know that you're doing your best, then what does it matter? And I'm very proud of you, Nicola's proud, Neil is – we're *all* behind you. What more do you . . . oh, I get it – it's your mother, isn't it?"

Laura nodded. "I know it's stupid. I mean, I'm nearly thirty years of age but I just want my mother to be proud of me, to say 'Fair play to you, Laura, for taking a chance'. I don't know why I want it so much but I do."

"But that's only natural. Don't we all want the people close to us to be proud of what we're doing? And do you think that Maureen *isn't* proud of you?"

Laura looked at her. "I don't just think it."

Helen sighed. "God, Laura, I really don't know what to say to you, but you should try not to worry about what other people think of you. It's pointless – believe me I know all about Glengarrah, and how narrow-minded and unforgiving the place can be. And if your mother is impossible to please, then she's impossible to please. If she's unwilling to lend you her support then you'd be better off just forgetting about her." Helen put down her coffee mug. "Look Laura," she smiled, "if we're being philosophical, I might as well add my two cents. Other people's opinions don't matter, as long as *you* feel that what you're doing is important and you're enjoying it.

You may or may not be successful in other people's eyes, but the very fact that you followed your dream, the very fact that you took the chance – means you *have* been successful and it's all been worthwhile – to you." She sat back and grimaced. "Did that make *any* sense?"

Laura laughed, but she knew what her friend was saying. "Sometimes I wish I had half of your resilience," she began, then stopped when she saw Helen grin. "Shit," she said sheepishly, "there we go again."

"Look, as I said, I really don't think you should let what other people think affect your decisions. Then again, if you *really* think this business is a mistake – if the whole thing is now beginning to get you down – then maybe you and Neil should think seriously about what you're going to do. There's no point in breaking your heart trying to keep going for the sake of it."

"I know," Laura swished the remaining liquid around the bottom of her coffee mug, "but I think this month's accounts will be making the decision for me."

She heard the phone ring in her office and at this Helen got up from her chair. "I'd better let you get on with things," she said. "I have to meet Kerry's teachers again today – see if we can come up with something that will put a stop to this bullying."

"I hope it works out," Laura said, on her way back to her workshop. "Let me know if I can do anything." She got to the phone just before the answering machine clicked on. "Laura Connolly Design – good afternoon?"

Helen mouthed a silent goodbye, and slipped quietly out the front door.

"Laura Fanning?" enquired an efficient British voice.

"Speaking." It wasn't a business call, then, Laura deduced, not when the caller was using her maiden name.

"Can you hold for a call, please?"

"Sure."

Laura listened expectantly to 'Candle in the Wind' as she waited for the call to be picked up.

Then another – Irish – voice came on the line. "Laura?"

"Yes, hello."

"Hi, it's Amanda Verveen here. We met recently."

Amanda Verveen? The *Irish fashion designer* Amanda Verveen? What? Laura had *never* met her!

"I'm sorry, I – are you sure you have the right number?"

The other woman gave a little laugh. "Well, I'm pretty sure – you do handcrafted jewellery, right?"

"Well, yes." Laura's thoughts were going a mile a minute. How on earth would someone like Amanda Verveen have heard about her jewellery? She wouldn't have been at the Crafts Exhibition. International fashion designers with customers the likes of Halle Berry and Catherine Zeta Jones wouldn't be attending lowly crafts exhibitions. She'd be mobbed! And didn't Nicole Kidman wear an Amanda Verveen dress at last year's Golden Globes?

Laura wrinkled her nose. This was obviously some kind of joke.

Despite her misgivings, her heart kept racing.

"You really don't remember me?" Amanda asked.

"I'm sorry, I really don't."

"I was there the day you and your bridesmaids were at Brid Cassidy's for your final fitting. Brid's a good friend of mine. We were at college together."

Brid? Then it hit her. Brid's assistant. Well, Laura had presumed she was her assistant – she had no idea that 'Amanda' was actually *The* Amanda Verveen. Laura could pinpoint any of Amanda's designs in seconds, but had never known what the woman actually looked like. Unbelievable! But what . . . what did she want with Laura?

"Well, I know you're probably very busy, but I was hoping you might consider doing some work for me."

For a long moment, Laura couldn't move. This *had* to be a joke, a dream – something!

"Work?" was all she could say.

Amanda laughed again. "Yes, I'm sorry but did I catch you at a bad time?"

Laura quickly recollected herself. Was this was really happening? She'd better cop herself on and at least try to sound someway professional instead of carrying on like some awestruck gobshite. Even if it *was* just a joke . . .

"No, no, you're fine. It's just . . .well, I'm a little overwhelmed, to be honest."

"Well, that makes two of us then, because I was completely overwhelmed by your work that day."

"Really?" Laura could feel the beginnings of tears in her eyes. Was this was really happening? Then she sat up straight in her chair. For goodness sake stop sounding so bloody pathetic, she admonished herself. "Well, thank you – thank you very much," she said, in the calmest voice she could muster.

"You're welcome." Amanda sounded all business. "Now, I was wondering, could you pop over to the Pembroke Street office sometime soon? I'm in London at the moment, but

I'll be back in Dublin later this week. The thing is, next season I'm doing something with a heavy ethnic influence while at same time keeping my gothic signature, and I'd love to incorporate some of your jewellery. I know this might be a little last-minute for you but . . ."

Next season? Was she talking about next season's *collection*? London, Milan, Paris?

"No, no, it's not last-minute at all. I'd be delighted – I'd –"

Amanda went on, talking a mile a minute. "The thing is, Laura, I was hoping we could vary the materials to suit the fabric. Would you or your staff have any problems working with soft metal instead of silver? And it would be great if we could use, well, not quite ivory, but possibly something equally primitive – wood or stone, perhaps?"

Laura felt her mouth moving, but it was as though someone else was uttering the words. "Well, I've already worked with those materials, Amanda. In fact I've already come up with a few ideas incorporating variations of black metal and stone and I think they might work well. I'd have to take a look at your own concepts of course, but I could pop over maybe Thursday or Friday?"

"Terrific! I'll give you the number for Jan – he's my personal assistant and he'll give you all the details and arrange the appointment. Now, I'm sorry I can't chat for longer. I've a meeting with Harvey Nicks which should have taken place . . . oh, about half an hour ago!"

If anyone had been watching, they would have been convinced by Laura's terrified expression that she was being given the worst news of her life.

"No problem."

"But we'll talk soon?" Amanda trilled.

"Yes, thanks for the call."

"Great. I'm really looking forward to meeting you again, Laura. I feel that you and I have a very similar approach to contemporary design and I think we'll work well together. Bye!"

Amanda disconnected, and Laura sat staring at the receiver for seemed like an age, unable to think, not sure what to *feel*. Amanda Verveen, award-winning and highly revered international fashion designer, wanted to work with her – with *her*, dull uninteresting, Laura Fanning from Glengarrah.

She had to be dreaming. This couldn't be real.

Laura picked up the handset again, and with trembling hands dialled Neil's work number.

"Hey, hon, how are you?" Neil asked cheerfully.

It was then that it hit her. Hearing him on the other end, hearing her husband's voice like that, brought Laura out of her awestruck trance.

Laura bawled into the phone. "I did it, Neil!" she cried. "I finally did it!"

Chapter 35

Nicola awoke to the sound of the telephone ringing in her ears. A quick glance at the clock told her that it was six thirty in the morning. She groaned. This meant that someone had called in sick at Motiv8, and she would need to arrange cover or do the job herself. As it turned out, the culprit was Sally, so there would be no one to cover reception until the next shift started at two that afternoon.

It took every amount of willpower Nicola had to drag herself out of the bed. She had had a restless night, waking in fits and starts and had just begun to drift off to sleep again when duty called.

Her car had begun to give her trouble. The hand controls, particularly the brakes, weren't as responsive as they should be and Nicola wasn't prepared to take any chances with it. The garage was due to collect it sometime this week, although judging from past experiences, it was unlikely she would get it back for some time. As she wasn't an ideal candidate for a courtesy car, Nicola knew that she would be relying on taxis until at least the following week. Ken should have been back last night from his few days in Galway, and no doubt would be tired after it all, so she wouldn't dream of calling on him at this hour for a lift. She hated that, not having the independence to drive where she felt like, whenever she felt like it. And it wasn't all that easy to get a wheelchair-access taxi at early hours of the morning, which is why she arrived at the centre a lot later than she'd hoped. Not to mention the fact that she had to use her manual chair instead of her new power-wheelchair, the one she had laughingly referred to as 'her new wheels' that time Laura had called to tell her about her plans to go into business. God, that seemed like years ago, back long before all the hullabaloo with Dan and his new fiancée. She was glad that was all over and done with now and that Dan was *finally* out of her life.

Poor old Chloe – she had got such a shock when she arrived at the house. Although by now Nicola was well used to that. Most people's reactions to her and her wheelchair generally swung somewhere between discomfort and terror. Nicola let it wash over her now, but it hadn't always been that easy.

Switching on her PC, she gave a little smile and recalled how difficult it had been to get used to that in the beginning, to get used to people's attitudes. But, she thought wryly, she had a headstart on most, because the very first person to panic had been Dan.

* * *

At first, Nicola had been relieved that she was still alive, her specialist assuring her that she had been very lucky. "With the speed you were hit and particularly the weight of your fall, it's a miracle that you didn't do more damage," he had said. "It could have been a lot worse."

It was true, and at the time it sounded reasonable. Nicola knew that there would be a lot of hardship and struggle ahead, particularly when she wasn't used to being inactive but, she believed, she was ready for it.

Throughout the three months she had spent lying on her back in the hospital, she had plenty time to think about how she was going to approach her disability. She could lie there crying and feeling sorry for herself, and the loss of her previous way of life (as she did on many occasions) or she could make the best of it. For Nicola there was no choice to make. Of course she would get on with it. Of course she would make the best of it. She was only twenty-six, there was no question of her giving in and as far as she was concerned she had only lost the use of her legs, not the use of her life.

For a time, this was enough to keep her going. Yes, she was flat on her back in hospital – but she was still alive.

Inevitably, there were times – particularly throughout her difficult rehabilitation – that Nicola didn't feel quite so upbeat about her future, but what could she do? There was no changing her situation, there was no going back to normal, so there was no point being miserable about it. Oh, she had her moments – boy, did she have her moments, days, nights, even *weeks* whereby she'd lash out at the driver, lash out at the useless doctors and the even more useless nurses! But what was the point? She couldn't turn back the clock; she couldn't change her situation.

Nicola recalled how lost, how desolate she had felt immediately after her miscarriage, and how she had all but withdrawn from day-to-day life, consumed by her sorrow. She was determined never to let that happen again.

But Dan was a different story. She could see the change in him; she could sense the fear and despair every time he came to visit her. He brushed it off, protesting that he was worried about the insurance and the hospital bills, but Nicola knew it was something more. Dan was losing faith

Immediately after the accident, he had tried his best to pretend that it was OK, that *they* would be OK, but Nicola could see it in his eyes that he didn't believe it himself.

And soon she found that Dan's sullen visits and stilted conversation were beginning to wear down her early optimism.

When she was finally released from the Rehabilitation Hospital, she went to stay with her mother – the reasoning being that she couldn't possibly stay in a three-storey apartment block, not when she could barely use her new wheelchair. And at the time she needed full-time care, something that Dan wasn't able to provide and something Carmel Peters had insisted upon.

Nicola shook her head, remembering those first few weeks in the chair. That was definitely the lowest point on her road to recovery – to normality. She had regained a lot of strength by then as a result of her rehab, but her arms tired easily while trying to manoeuvre from place to place, and her bedsores stung desperately – all the things doctors had warned her about, but still she hadn't expected. Because she was trying so hard and progressing little, Nicola became easily frustrated and hated the fact that she couldn't do anything for herself – her mother doing all the simple things, carrying her, bathing her, getting her in and out of bed.

At that stage Nicola thought she would lose her mind. Yes, she was lucky to be alive, but what kind of a life was this?

Still, Dan visited every day, but Nicola knew by then that they had already grown apart. They were uneasy around one another, Dan trying hard not to say the wrong thing; Nicola becoming easily annoyed by what he did say. She was sick of his self-pity, his lack of support, his glum appearance. Nicola needed positives, she needed her husband to reassure her that she would be okay, that he would be there for her, that of course everything would be fine. But there was never any talk of what might happen in the future, of where they would live, or what they would do when eventually Nicola regained her independence.

Still, she knew that her attitude at the time was partly the problem. In the early wheelchair days (as she called them), she was often tired, short-tempered and at times – despite all her best intentions – self-pitying. Nothing Dan said or did was enough for her. She was pushing him away, but she couldn't help herself.

One particular day, Dan called to see her after work. He was tired and harassed-looking, and simply because he didn't greet her with a kiss Nicola accused him of being selfish.

Something in Dan snapped.

"Did you ever," he asked, pronouncing his words slowly

and clearly, "ever once think about how all of this might be affecting me?"

"You!" Nicola laughed resentfully. "You're not the one sitting here day after day unable to do anything for yourself, relying on other people to do the simplest things for you. No, you're off living the high life, gallivanting here there and everywhere – with God knows who else!" She didn't know where the outburst had come from but she couldn't help herself.

"Living the high life?" Dan had croaked. "How could you even say something like that? I know how hard it is for you, love, I can only imagine – but it's hard for me too. I don't know what to say to you any more – I don't know how to help. You seem to resent the fact that I'm not here with you, yet you know you couldn't cope on your own in the apartment."

"If you really wanted to, you could take time off work to look after me." Nicola knew she was being petulant but she couldn't think of anything else to say to him. She didn't really want that, she would have hated Dan having to do everything for her and she longed for the day she would be strong enough to look after herself. But, at the time, that day seemed very far away.

"Take time off work? Nicola, do you have any idea how much money we owe the hospital?" Although their health insurance covered most of the hospital bills, it didn't cover the cost of her rehabilitation. "We still don't know the outcome of the insurance with that driver – it could take years to sort out, if ever. I might have to sell out my share of the company to drum up the cash!"

"Money! Insurance! Do you think any of those things

matter to me at this very moment, Dan? Do you think I give one stuff how much we owe the hospital?"

Dan ran a hand through his hair. "Nicola, I don't think I can go on like this," he said eventually. "It's been months, and I still don't know what you want me to do, what you want me to say! Of course it's hard for you, I know that, but it's bloody hard for me too! I never expected things to turn out like this!"

Nicola's heart galloped with fear – a new fear. "What does that mean, Dan?"

"It means . . ." he said, his voice almost a whisper, "it means that I don't know what to do. Our life has been turned upside down by this. I don't know how we're supposed to get out of it. I can't see an end to it. You're coping as best you can, I know that, but there's nothing in the information booklets telling *me* how to cope." He looked at her, his eyes filled with desperation. "Can you tell me? Can somebody please tell me what I'm supposed to do to stop myself feeling like this?"

"What are you saying?"

"I don't know. I just think that – that maybe we should spend some time apart."

"What?" she whispered, stunned.

"I don't see any other way," Dan said quietly. "Maybe you might be able to come to terms with this easier if I wasn't around so much. Nicola, sometimes you look at me like you hate me. I don't know how to respond to that. I'm not made of stone."

"Well, poor you," she said, her voice hardening, "poor, poor Dan. What the hell did you expect? That as soon as I got the chair I'd be back to normal and buzzing cheerfully around the place, playing the part of the happy little wife that you want me to be?" She was crying now, warm tears racing down both cheeks. "Well, what about *you*? What happened to 'for better or worse', Dan – didn't you say those words once, didn't you promise to be there in both *sickness* and in health? *You* did and I did – so what happened? "

"I didn't know," Dan said finally, tears glistening in his eyes. "I just didn't know it would be so hard."

And that was the end.

Nicola stayed on with her mother and Dan's visits became less frequent until eventually he stopped coming altogether. When he did come there was very little to say, the resentment and hurt between them too strong to overcome.

Their eventual separation was an epiphany for Nicola. One morning shortly afterwards, she woke up and felt a sense of unbelievable clarity, as if her mind had been purged of some huge, negative tumour. Although hurt deeply by Dan's rejection of her, Nicola decided to regain control of her life and in order to do this, she knew she needed time away – from everything.

She took up an early offer made by her mother's sister Ellen to spend some time with her in the UK. Her aunt lived near Fulham and was insistent that coming to stay for a while would be the best thing for Nicola. "It'll do you good to get away," Ellen, a jolly fifty-five-year-old had said, "and I'm sure your mother will be delighted to get rid of you!"

That was what Nicola loved about living with Ellen. There was no sitting around and feeling sorry for herself where her aunt was concerned. They talked a lot, slow easy conversations about life, love – and Dan.

Nicola had (a little unfairly she realised now) left for London without telling him. For months she had heard nothing, until one morning Ellen handed her a letter with a Bray postmark. In the letter Dan tried to explain how he had been feeling, and about how sorry he was that they couldn't make it work. The letter had a kind of cleansing effect on her, and Nicola sensed it was his way of saying that it was over – over for good. It had been odd at the time, but strangely liberating.

Was it just them, she wondered, or was there a breaking point in every marriage – a point from which there was no going back, no matter how strong the relationship might be? She and Dan had overcome a lot together, but maybe there was only so much a marriage could take.

A week later she contacted a solicitor.

Of course, Nicola thought now, getting over Dan and coming to terms with life in a wheelchair was only the beginning and she'd been totally unprepared for the reaction she got from the outside world. It was as though she was no longer a person, but rather a *disabled* person. The qualifier was, of course, inevitable, but brought with it connotations that she had never expected. When she had become used to the wheelchair, and had begun going out and about on her own, she had been unprepared for people's attitudes. People treated her sometimes like she had lost not just the use of her legs but also the use of her brain, like Miss Reporter Fidelma that time at work: *'I have to ask – isn't it unusual for someone like yourself to be involved in this type of industry?'* She had seen the slight discomfort in people's eyes at Laura's wedding, when as bridesmaid she wheeled up the aisle ahead of the bride. In fairness, she wouldn't have dreamed of turning Laura down and the bridal designer had done a wonderful job with the dress but it still felt strange.

At times, other people's attitudes were soul-destroying, but at other times they could be quite comical. It wasn't something she thought she would ever get used to, but eventually she had learned not to let people's attitudes bother her.

It wasn't always easy getting around in the chair in public either, and in the early days she often misjudged her manoeuvres and bashed into chairs and tables, knocking over drinks and condiments. It was frustrating but still she knew she just had to take these things in her stride.

It was difficult too to get to grips with the things that were so straightforward for able-bodied people but tricky for her, things like mounting and descending kerbs, opening doors – and as for steps, forget about it! Escalators were a total no-no, which is why she had to pick and choose where she shopped.

Certainly things had improved over the last few years, with various Equality Acts making civil architects and county-council planners more aware of disability issues, but Nicola could count on both hands the number of times she had tried to enter a building via a wheelchair ramp, and then discovered that the entrance door opened outwards – a very difficult prospect! There were now many premises that included wheelchair-parking facilities, but it was pretty obvious that these were often included only as a gesture, and without any real thought – spaces the same dimensions as regular parking spaces. How could anyone have enough room to get in and out of the car with a wheelchair in one of those?

Not to mention the morons who parked too close alongside genuine disabled facilities, ensuring that wheelchair users could barely open the driver's door – let alone manoeuvre into the car. Of course, Nicola thought smiling, this is where the huge mother and child spaces worked a treat – being a harassed mother with a buggy obviously considered by carpark planners as being a lot more of a hardship than being disabled! And leave it all to those upstanding citizens who believed leaving their hazard lights on conferred some excuse as to why their cars were parked in a space reserved for the less able.

Nevertheless, being able to drive at all was a huge bonus for her. It hadn't been easy learning to use the hand-controls, and initially getting herself in and out of the car was a real challenge.

Still, all in all, Nicola couldn't really complain. Yes, it was a huge blow at the beginning and yes, it was a massive change in lifestyle but she had eventually come to see it as just that – a change in lifestyle. There was very little she *couldn't* do. Sure, she had to put a lot more thought into getting from place to place and occasionally she missed being so active – missed her bike rides into the mountains and sometimes silly things like boogeying on the dance-floor when she went out clubbing.

But once she had learned to use it properly, the chair simply became an extension of herself. She had a great job, great friends, her own fully wheelchair-customised house, and of course, she had Barney to keep an eye on her.

Not to mention the wonderful Ken Harris. Nicola smiled. After Dan, falling in love again was the last thing she'd expected.

* * *

Her car had been on the blink *again*, and she'd been waiting for a taxi home from work. The same day, Nicola remembered, she had been in a right strop. Because the car was out of action, she was using the manual as opposed to her trusty power-wheelchair, and she hated the manual chair.

"Waiting for anyone in particular?" Ken had enquired, briefcase in hand as he passed through reception.

Nicola was sitting just inside the centre's front porch. "My lift home," she answered, keeping one eye on the Motiv8 entrance.

"The car giving you problems again?" he asked. "You should have told me earlier. I could have organised a lift for you."

She waved it away. "It's fine. Anyway, I think he's here now."

Ken followed her gaze. "Ah, I don't think so."

The approaching taxi *was* meant for Nicola, but the dispatcher had neglected to mention that the lift was for a disabled passenger. The taxi driver looked apologetically at his saloon Ford Mondeo into which there wasn't a hope of fitting even a collapsed buggy, let alone a manual wheelchair.

"Sorry, love," he said out of the wound-down window.

"I'll ring dispatch and get them to send the right car out to you straightway."

"It's fine," Ken informed him. "I'll give her a lift. It's on my way."

"You sure, bud?" The taxi-man looked from one to the other.

"It's fine," said Ken quickly just as Nicola opened her mouth to protest. "Thanks anyway."

When the man drove off, Nicola glared at Ken. "I can organise my own lift home, thank you very much."

"Oh, don't be so bloody defensive," he said easily, closing the door behind them. "You need a lift home, and I told you that I'm going that way."

"To Stepaside?"

"Yes, but I need to drop something off in Terenure beforehand."

She stopped moving. "I knew it! You're putting yourself out just because I'm stuck and –"

Ken rolled his eyes. "Will you stop your bloody gabbing for once and just say thank you?"

Nicola hadn't expected that. "OK then, thanks," she said, feeling like a bold child.

They reached his car. "Now, do you need any help, or would it be too dangerous for my health to offer?" he said, disengaging the central locking.

Nicola hid a smile. Was she really that touchy?

"I'll be fine," she answered, carefully manoeuvring herself out of her wheelchair and onto the passenger seat. Before she knew it, Ken had expertly collapsed the chair and was storing it in the boot of his roomy Citroen Picasso.

Nicola stared at him, surprised at his ease.

"What?" he asked, seeing her questioning look.

"If I didn't know better, I'd say you've done that before."

He shrugged. "Maybe you don't know better."

Nicola stared straight ahead, not knowing how to answer that.

Ken grinned. "Nothing to say, Nicola? That's not like you."

"Well, what do you want me to say?" she said huffily. Whatever it was about Ken he always seemed to bring out her petulant side. Sometimes it drove her absolutely mad and now was one of those times.

After a moment Ken spoke. "OK then, if you must know, my dad's a C4 quad."

"Really?" Nicola couldn't hide her surprise. She had come across many quadriplegics throughout her rehabilitation. C4 was the one of the most difficult, the worst kind of injury.

"Yes, really. Car accident. He's been in a wheelchair since I was twelve years old."

"I didn't know."

Ken shrugged again. "There's a lot about me you don't know."

That was certainly true. But thinking about it, Ken's easy-going attitude to her now made a lot more sense. He always treated her the same way he had since before her accident. That was why she had accepted the job here in the first place. It was like Ken didn't even *see* her disability. And why would he, Nicola thought, if he had been brought up not to?

"So is he completely paralysed or – ?"

"Arms and legs. He can move his neck and shoulders and has feeling in just one of his fingers. But he's OK."

Nicola suddenly felt ashamed. Here she was feeling sorry for herself and considering herself immobile because her *car* was out of action.

"So does he live with you or –?" Nicola wondered why she was suddenly having trouble finishing her sentences. She wanted to know more, but didn't want to appear nosey.

"Nah, he's at home with my mum." He smiled. "She's great with him but, as you can imagine, it's not always easy. He has a nurse coming in a few days a week to keep an eye on him, and I often take him out and about at weekends, just to get him away from the house." Ken flashed her a sideways grin. "So in case you ever wondered why I drive a space wagon instead of a flashy Beamer, now you know."

They drove in easy silence towards Terenure and Nicola waited patiently while Ken dropped something off nearby. Afterwards, they headed towards Stepaside, getting behind a line of stationary traffic on the way.

"This is completely out of your way, Ken. You really didn't have to," Nicola said, willing the traffic to move. Ken would be all hours getting home.

"It's not a problem."

"Yes, but I could have waited for the taxi and you could be home by now."

He looked at her. "Nicola, did it ever cross your silly little mind that I might actually *want* to drop you home?"

"What do you mean?"

Ken tapped the steering wheel, while the car remained

stationary. "We've known each other – what – nearly five, six years now?"

"Hmm."

"And in all that time, we've never once done anything together outside of work. So I'm bringing you home because I consider myself an old friend – and I want to have a gawk at your house."

Nicola's face broke into a wide smile. "You want to see my house?"

"Well, Jason McAteer will be Ireland soccer manager by the time I get an invitation from *you*, so I thought I might as well invite myself."

Nicola pondered this. Ken was right. They had known one another for a long time, even longer than Nicola had known Dan. While they got on fantastically well in their working relationship, that was where it had always ended. There was usually little opportunity for socialising at Motiv8 because of the odd shifts and long hours. She hadn't really thought about it before, but there was no reason why she and Ken shouldn't be friendly outside work. They were pretty close inside so why not otherwise?

"OK," she said cheerfully as the traffic moved off again, "I'd be happy to give you the grand tour and, if you behave yourself, I just might make you dinner."

Ken grinned across at her. "Now that," he said, "is an invitation I can't refuse."

Barney was always delighted with new visitors – but seemed completely enthralled with Ken. The feeling was obviously mutual, Nicola thought, smiling at them both. Barney jumped up on his hind legs and Ken dropped to the floor to tickle him, the dog eagerly licking Ken's ears.

"Hey, he's great!" Ken enthused. "Aren't you, boy? Yeah!" Ken began to chase him from one end of the room to the other, Barney thrilled with the attention.

"Make yourself at home, why don't you?" Nicola said wryly.

Recalling her earlier promise of making dinner, she went into the kitchen to check the gastronomic contents of the fridge-freezer. Blast it! One shrivelled carrot, two onions, a half-used pepper and a six-pack of outdated Petit Filous. Not even Jamie Oliver could get excited over that lot, she thought, throwing the yoghurts and parsnips into the bin. And not a Marks frozen dinner in sight.

"Nice place," Ken commented from behind, "obviously custom-built."

She followed his gaze. "Yes. The Wheelchair Association were a great help in finding contractors and they did a great job with it. I used to love cooking, but these days I don't cook anything particularly elaborate. It's not worth all the effort for one, but it's great to know that if I want to, I can."

"So you eat out a lot?"

She gave a short laugh. "No, I *order* out a lot."

"Oh. Well, look, I know you said you'd make dinner, but don't go putting yourself out on my account. A Chinese or an Indian would do me."

Nicola grimaced and nodded towards the contents of the fridge. "I'm afraid it'll have to."

She phoned for a takeaway and while they waited in the living-room she and Ken talked easily about work, family and the *Lord of the Rings* trilogy.

"I loved it," Ken said. "Saw it five times."

"What?"

"Yep, an absolute masterpiece – the best film I've ever seen."

"Well, it was good, but I wouldn't go that far."

"OK, what's the best film you've ever seen?"

Nicola thought about it for a minute. "*Planet of the Apes*," she said.

"Really?"

"Yeah, it was great – why are you looking at me like that?"

"Because I wouldn't have pegged you as the sci-fi type," he said, sitting back comfortably on her couch.

"Oh, and what would you have pegged me for?"

Ken's eyes twinkled. "Probably the *Pretty Woman* or *Dirty Dancing* type."

"*What?*"

Ken guffawed. "Well, all the girlies go for those kind of films, don't they?" he teased. "You know, all 'this happy ever after' stuff."

"Not this girlie." Nicola feigned insult.

He laughed again. "No, probably not."

"Well, what's that supposed to mean?"

Ken held his hands up in surrender. "Nothing, nothing – Jeez, sorry I said anything!"

Nicola laughed. Despite herself she was really enjoying their banter. It seemed weird being like this – with Ken of all people.

Just then, the sound of Barney barking in the hallway indicated the arrival of their Chinese takeaway. While Ken answered the door to the deliveryman, Nicola went into the kitchen and hovered by the open fridge, debating whether or not to open a bottle of wine. They couldn't, not when Ken was driving. Anyway, it wasn't as though he'd be staying long. It was only a lift home after all.

For some reason she felt vaguely disappointed. It had been ages since she'd had someone other than the girls around for dinner. OK, so it wasn't dinner in the strictest sense but she was really enjoying the company.

"I'll have a glass if you're having one," Ken said easily, as if reading her mind. He was busily opening doors, and locating plates and cutlery as if he did it on a regular basis. To her surprise, Nicola found that she didn't really mind. Ken had such an easy-going way about him that it wasn't too out of place to see him rummaging around in her kitchen. It was a strange feeling.

"Are you sure? What about your driving?"

"I'll have one or two glasses and –" he paused looking at his watch, "sure, by the time *EastEnders* is over, I'll be grand again!"

Nicola tried to bite back a smile. "You are *not* watching *EastEnders* on my television."

"Ah, come on. I can't miss it – it's really good at the moment."

Nicola positioned herself across from him at the kitchen table. "Ken, it's the same storyline over and over again. He hates her, and she hates him, yet they end up having a raging affair, and then *her* husband, who hates him even more, gets revenge with the other guy's wife, and they all end up fighting in that pub."

"Exactly! It's great!" Ken stuck a forkful of fried rice into his mouth. "Really true to life."

Nicola laughed and shook her head.

They ate in comfortable silence for a while, until Ken eventually spoke.

"You know, it's nice to see you having a laugh, Nicola."

She looked at him, surprised. "What do you mean?" Was she that strait-laced at work? Nicola didn't think so.

"Well, if you don't mind my saying so, you haven't been yourself lately." When she didn't answer, he continued, watching her warily. "Is it Dan?"

Her fork paused in mid-air. "What makes you think that?"

"Come on, Nicola. As I said, we've known each other for a long time now. When you came to work with us first you were great, very positive, full of enthusiasm, not a bother on you. But lately, you've gotten quite touchy, spiky even. The last time I saw you like that," he reddened slightly, "well, you and Dan were going through a tough time. I just wondered if he'd been – I don't know – hassling you or anything."

Nicola was faintly touched. The way he said it, it was almost as though Ken was being protective of her. She slid pieces of green pepper around her plate. "Well, the divorce is due to come through shortly, and I suppose I'm feeling it a little."

"Well, that's understandable, of course, but . . ." Ken was hesitant.

"What?"

"Look, tell me to mind my own business if you like, but you're doing just fine without him. I mean, look at you – you're completely independent, you live alone, you drive yourself wherever you want to go and, of course," he added grinning, "you've got a top job."

"I know all that but . . ." Nicola gave him a watery smile, "that's all well and good, but that's exactly it."

"Sorry?"

"That's it. What you just said, my life in a nutshell. Sure I have a great life, considering, and I value my independence above everything else but – that's it."

"I don't follow."

"I mean, I know I have my friends and my family are great but . . ."

"Ah." Ken seemed to understand. "The divorce is making you wonder where you'll go from here."

"Yes." It was weird discussing something like this with him, and not with Laura or her mother – but he was so easy to talk to.

"I didn't really care about anything like that before," she explained. "When I was in London, I spent most of my time concentrating on getting my life back. When I came back, I was determined to prove to myself that I could live pretty much the way I had before the injury – well, within reason anyway!" she added with an easy smile. "But I'm not even thirty, my friends are only beginning to settle down, and I'm getting *divorced*."

Ken sat back. "You're wondering if this means you're on your own from now on?"

"Well, yes. And I'm thinking things now that I've never really had to think about before – things I've never had *time* to consider, really."

"Like?"

"Well, I don't think I need to spell it out that I'm hardly the ideal person to go out on the town with, so how *am* I supposed to find someone else? Where do I start?"

Ken looked at her. "You think that no one would be interested in you because of your disability?"

Nicola nodded and waited. Waited for him to tell her that *of course* people would be interested in her, that *of course* she wouldn't spend the rest of her life on her own, not when she was so young, and with so much to offer and –

"You're probably right," he said, putting a forkful of food in his mouth.

"What?"

"Well, let's be truthful about it," Ken continued. "Say you go out on the town with the girls on a Saturday night, and you all go off to a club. Now, not wishing to point out the obvious but no matter how fabulous you are, you aren't exactly going to be fighting them off with a stick."

Nicola looked at him, shocked and hurt in equal measures. What was he trying to do? Make her feel worse!

"I see it with Dad all the time," he added. "When he's out and about, people see his disability, and that's all they see. Nicola, if you go out at night to a pub or a nightclub, the fact is that most guys won't even consider you as a potential date," he paused, "despite the fact that you are *extremely* cute."

Nicola suspected the compliment was an attempt to boost her spirits and she gave a slight smile.

"But most people don't look beyond that – they can't look beyond it. People are afraid of what they don't know. And let's be honest, most people – inevitably the ones you wouldn't want to be with anyway – don't need the hassle."

"Hassle?"

"Yeah. Before my dad got injured he was like yourself

– had an extremely active life. He used to go rock-climbing, hill walking, the odd bit of golf, and he and Mum were part of a huge social circle. But when he got injured –"

"People change," Nicola knew the feeling well.

"It's not that people change; it's that *you've* changed, and they don't know how to handle that. They're afraid of it, and I suppose most people really don't want to entertain that side of their personality. They're possibly a little ashamed of themselves."

Nicola nodded. She had had this conversation before with her mother. "The time will come when you have to start 'putting yourself about'," her mother had said, refreshingly ignorant of the connotations of *that* particular expression. Putting herself about indeed! At the time, Nicola hadn't paid much heed to it. But sitting here now and listening to it from a male perspective, Nicola felt rather dispirited.

Ken seemed to sense her mood change. "Hey, don't look like that."

"Like what?"

He shook his head. "Look, I'm not trying to make you feel bad. All I'm saying is that if you're hoping to find someone new, it certainly won't happen in anywhere as shallow as a bar or a nightclub. God, it's hard enough for able-bodied people to do that!" He laughed out loud. "When I think of the fortune I've spent buying drinks for all those good-time girls . . ."

Nicola raised a tiny smile. "I really can't see you having problems with finding someone."

"You'd be surprised," he said, looking right at her.

Nicola's heart skipped a beat and she quickly looked away.

"Oh, let's not talk about this any more!" she announced suddenly. "Anyway, even if I *did* find someone, why would he be bothered with me? It's not as though I could re-enact the Karma Sutra with him!" Humour, she thought, the best form of defence.

Ken laughed. "There are ways, you know! I mean, where did my two younger sisters come from, then?" he said, eyes twinkling.

She laughed, the discussion no longer quite so disheartening. "Can we change the subject now, please?"

But Ken wasn't giving up. "You really think that you have nothing to offer a guy?"

She shrugged. "I don't know. But even *you* have to admit, I am at a bit of a disadvantage – not to mention a whole lot of hard work."

Ken looked at directly at her, his expression unreadable. "Do you know something, Nicola?" he said then. "You have absolutely no idea how wrong you are."

* * *

Thinking back on it now, Nicola smiled. She should have realised it then, she supposed – if not long before – that Ken had feelings for her, had *always* had feelings for her. Things had happened very quickly after that. Ken began spending more and more time at her place, and soon had confessed his interest in her, and his feelings that day in his office when Dan walked in. It was wonderful at the time and it had been wonderful ever since. Ken was honest, loving and gentle and she knew instinctively that he would never let her down as Dan had.

Nicola checked the time at the corner of her computer

screen. It was almost eight – Ken should definitely be in by now. She picked up the handset and dialled his extension, eager to find out how things went with the partners. No answer.

"Jack – did you see Ken come in yet?" she asked, checking with reception. "I thought he was back today."

"He was back yesterday evening actually – he called in last night before closing. But he's taken a day off today – didn't he tell you?

She frowned. "Right . . . well, not to worry – how are you doing? Do you need any help down there?"

"Thanks but it's very quiet so far – I'll give you a shout if I need you."

"OK." Nicola replaced the handset. Day off? Ken was so wrapped up in this place he hardly ever took days off – hell, he rarely even took *sick* days! Oh, well, he was the boss, after all, Nicola thought affectionately, dialling his home number and wondering if, despite the last few months' encouraging figures, things hadn't gone as well in Galway as he'd expected.

A groggy-sounding Ken answered on the second ring. "Hello?"

"Hi! You never told me you were planning on mitching off today! How was the meeting?"

There was a brief silence.

"Ken?"

"Why would I bother to tell you?" he answered brusquely. "You certainly don't tell *me* everything."

Nicola was taken aback. Ken sounded weird. "What?"

"Look, I can't talk to you right now, okay? See you later." With that he hung up, leaving Nicola staring open-mouthed at the receiver. What was the matter with him? Then she realised that it was just gone eight in the morning and he'd had a tough few days in Galway. If Ken needed a day off then he probably didn't appreciate her interrupting his precious lie-in! She'd leave it a while and ring him again later, and, in the meantime, she'd input the wages and arrange next week's roster.

But on her second attempt at conversation, Ken was equally grouchy.

"What's the matter with you today?" she asked easily. It really wasn't like Ken to be in bad form like this. "Didn't things go well in Galway?"

"What's the matter?" he repeated. "What's the matter? I'll tell you what the matter is, Nicola! The matter *is* that I can't quite figure out how you managed to lead me on – so easily and for so bloody long!"

"What? What do you mean, Ken?" she asked in shock.

"I mean, when were you going to tell me? That's *if* you were going to bother telling me at all!"

"What? Ken . . . I really don't –" She was frightened now.

"What was the point, Nicola? Why spend all that bloody time with me, leading me to believe that we were going somewhere, that we had a future together, when you never had any intention – why bother?"

His voice sounded strange, like he'd been drinking or something. "Ken –"

"I mean, what's the bloody attraction? Do you like being messed around – is that it? That you just can't resist wankers – that bastards like him are just too damn attractive, is it?"

Now Nicola was really confused. "Bastards like who?"

"Don't play the innocent with me! Like Hunt, who do you think?"

"Dan? But I haven't seen Dan in ages," Immediately, Nicola was thrown off-guard. Stupidly, she hadn't told Ken about her plans to invite Dan and Chloe to her house. It was a spur of the moment decision as it was, and she just didn't think he'd agree with her interfering like that – and he certainly wouldn't agree with the idea of her inviting Dan anywhere near her!

"I saw it, Nicola!" Ken said stonily, and Nicola's blood ran cold. "I saw the two of you together! I can't believe you would lie to me about it!"

Nicola was wrong-footed now. But how could he have seen? What would he have seen? Oh, shit, why hadn't she told him about it beforehand? Now, it seemed he'd found out somehow. "Look, love, I don't know why I didn't tell you before but, the thing is, the other night I invited –"

"I've no bloody interest in hearing about it, Nicola. Just forget it. Forget the whole bloody thing. I thought the two of us had something, but all along you were just waiting, just hoping he would come back to you. Despite all your bullshit about wishing I had been the one you married. You're full of it, Nicola, and I don't know why I was so bloody stupid in the first place. After all, you went straight back to him the last time, didn't you?"

What? Was he talking about her going back to Dan that first time? "But . . . he was my husband at the time and I didn't know that you –" Nicola wasn't sure how the conversation had suddenly turned to her going back to *anyone*, let alone Dan.

"Ah, forget it – I've wasted enough of my time on you already. Go back to Hunt, and good luck to you. God knows the two of you deserve one another."

With that Ken disconnected.

Nicola stared unseeingly at her desk, her mind reeling. This was unreal. Ken must have *seen* Dan come to the house the other night. But he'd told her he wouldn't see her on Monday evening as he was going to Galway early the next morning, so how would he have seen . . . ?

Shit, shit shit, she thought despondently. Why had she lied about it? Obviously he had seen something the other night but hadn't seen enough to know that Dan wasn't her only visitor. Now, it looked as though she was keeping the visit a secret from him – she'd be bloody annoyed herself, if he'd done the same. She'd have to talk to him, have to make him understand the situation from her point of view.

But if Ken wouldn't talk to her, if he wouldn't let her explain, then what was she going to do?

Chapter 36

Days later and after a highly enjoyable meeting with Amanda Verveen, Laura was still walking on air.

Amanda had loved her designs and once Laura had seen samples of her collection, she knew instantly that she could rise to the occasion and produce jewellery that would be simply outstanding.

"It's won't be exactly ready-to-wear," Amanda had said, indicating a missing breast panel that would have the models spilling out all over the place, "but when has that ever mattered? The main thing is that we use your jewellery to completely transform the look."

From what Laura could gather from Jan, Amanda's assistant, and Amanda herself, most of the catwalk fashion terminology meant little, and she wasn't going to start describing her work as Jan had, namely "raw, wild and totally apocalyptic!". She'd like to see how many pairs of earrings she'd sell if she put *that* on her business cards, but nevertheless she had a definite feel for the look they wanted to convey. Even after that one meeting, Laura felt that she and Amanda were very much on the same wavelength. She didn't know if Amanda wanted to work with her on a regular basis, and at that stage she didn't care. By early spring of next year her work would be appearing on catwalks in London, Milan and Paris, something that she could never in a million years have anticipated.

Not long after the initial phone call from Amanda, Laura had called in on Brid at the boutique. She knew instantly from the bridal designer's pleased expression that she had known about the call.

"I hope you didn't mind my giving her your number," Brid began, slightly apologetic. "I wasn't sure how busy you were, but since that day she was going on and on at me –"

"Are you mad?" Laura cried, enveloping her in a huge hug. "I couldn't be more grateful to you. I had no idea who she was!"

"Amanda keeps a low profile on purpose," Brid said. "She thinks it makes her that much more mysterious – like her clothes." She laughed. "It's her image, and to be honest, I find it all a little bit pretentious – but that's why I chose to design wedding dresses instead of haute couture."

Neil had been over the moon. "I knew it would happen for you," he had said, the evening of Amanda's call, when he had arrived home with a massive bunch of roses and a bottle of champagne. "OK, I didn't quite imagine it this way but – wow!" He lifted her up and swung her around. "My wife a catwalk designer!"

"Ah not quite," Laura corrected him. "I'm just providing the decoration."

"Still, you wouldn't know what this might lead to. Mention Amanda Verveen – whoever she is," he added, not being overly familiar with the fashion world, "in the same sentence as Laura Connolly Design, and the business could take off altogether!"

"I hope so," Laura said, almost afraid to believe it.

The girls had been completely taken aback, Helen in particular.

"I have to hand it to you, Laura. Even when the rest of us – well, me in particular," she added slightly shamefaced, "thought you should pack it in, you kept on going. And of course, some of us didn't make it easy for you."

Nicola too had been delighted by her news but, for some reason, Laura sensed over the phone that her friend's mind wasn't quite focused.

"Ken's gone," Nicola had said worriedly.

"Gone?"

Nicola filled her in on the situation, and the details of her last conversation with Ken. "I tried going over to his house, but when I got there he was out. Then I found out from Sally that he's taken a few days' holidays from the Centre. I was mortified – I mean, it was pretty obvious to her that we were rowing – especially since he had dropped his key for my house into the Centre!"

"Look, he probably just needs a little time to cool down, that's all."

"I really hope so," Nicola said, sounding worried.

Laura wasn't unduly concerned. Things might be a little up in the air now, but Ken and Nicola would sort it out. She was sure of it. Still, trust good old Dan Hunt to be right in the middle of things – again.

"I'm so thrilled for you, though," Nicola said, brightening a little. "I still can't believe my best friend is going to be a famous jewellery designer!"

"Ah, let's not go mad with ourselves just yet," Laura had said, although secretly she was enjoying the attention and excitement.

She hadn't yet said a word to her parents. She wasn't ready to, not until she had met with Amanda and finally convinced herself that yes, this was real – this was actually going to happen. Laura would never live it down if she told her family, and then the entire thing fell through. But after the meeting with Amanda, she knew that this was definitely going to happen, and that Amanda was just as excited about working with *her*.

She and Neil were travelling down to Glengarrah that afternoon to tell them in person. Laura couldn't wait for her mother's reaction, partly because she wanted to prove her wrong, to let her know that her eldest daughter did have talent, that people did want her designs, but mostly because she wanted her mother, and indeed Joe, to share her happiness. How much better did it get than this? One of her daughters being asked to design jewellery for an international designer! Maureen would undoubtedly get great mileage out of that. They wouldn't be able to shut her up down at the flower club. Now it was safe, her mother didn't have to worry about failure any more – Laura's dreams had come true.

* * *

Later that evening, Neil parked the car outside the cottage and he and Laura made their way round towards the back door.

"What are *you* doing here?" Maureen looked as though she had just caught an intruder in her kitchen.

"Hi, Mam," Laura ignored her mother's typically unfriendly greeting, having long since got used to it.

"Just in time for dinner, I hope?" Neil looked longingly at the pots simmering on the stove.

"And Neil too – what's going on, Laura?"

Laura grinned from ear to ear as did Neil.

"Well, I have some good news," she began, looking from her mother to Joe, who was sitting quietly at the kitchen table, waiting for his dinner.

Maureen dropped her tea towel. "You're pregnant!" she wailed happily. "Oh thank God, thank God!"

Laura's face fell. Thank God? Was Maureen doing decades of the rosary, hoping that her eldest daughter would fall pregnant?

"Oh, this is the best thing that could have happened!"

Laura couldn't remember ever seeing her mother so excited about anything.

"You'll definitely have to give up those business notions of yours, now that you'll have another mouth to feed!"

Instantly, the mood changed.

"I'm not pregnant, Mam," she said shortly, her earlier enthusiasm totally deflated.

How selfish could the woman get? She *knew* Laura and Neil weren't planning to have children until the business got off the ground. What was wrong with her mother?

Why was it always what *she* thought was good for Laura? Why didn't she care about what Laura actually wanted?

Laura felt sick. She didn't want to tell her mother her news now; all the good had been taken out of it.

"Laura's not pregnant," Neil said, when Laura didn't speak, "but she has some great news about the business."

Laura saw Maureen actually roll her eyes to heaven. Her mother didn't even bother trying to hide it.

That was it. Laura had had enough.

"I was *going* to tell you my good news, Mam," she began, her tone cold. "I was *going* to tell you that a famous fashion designer has asked me to provide jewellery for her new collection – a collection that will be shown all over the world, in all the magazines, on television and in the newspapers. I was *going* to tell you that I – little old useless me with all my notions and talk – have finally begun living my dream, have finally succeeded in doing everything I've always wanted to do. I was *going* to tell you that somebody – somebody *important* – had enough faith in me, and my work, to take a chance on me. But judging by the look on your face, I don't think I'll bother."

Laura had never spoken to her mother like that before. In fact, she didn't think that Maureen had ever *let* her speak for that length of time without some interruption or smart comment.

Maureen looked stunned and Joe looked nervous, as if caught in the eye of a storm.

The silence in the small kitchen was almost potent.

Neil spoke quickly to fill the void. "Maureen, I can understand how you got the wrong end of the stick there and no, Laura isn't pregnant, but didn't you hear her

news? The fashion designer is called Amanda Verveen."
He shrugged, as if in exasperation. "I know, I haven't heard
of her either, but apparently she's very popular. She's Irish
too – I think she won something on *The Late Late Show* a
few years ago – anyway, she wants Laura to work with
her – isn't it brilliant?"

Maureen slumped down on one of the kitchen chairs.

"What is *wrong* with you, Laura?" she said, flabbergasted.
"What are you trying to prove?"

"To *prove*?"

"With all this jewellery business?"

"Maureen, did you not hear –"

"Leave it, Neil!" Maureen interjected. "To be perfectly
honest, you're the cause of all her problems. Laura was
perfectly happy in her office job before you came along
and starting putting ideas in her head!"

"But I wasn't happy, Mam. You know I wasn't happy!"
Laura's eyes flashed wildly. "Why do you think I spent all
those years in Art College – for *fun*? Why do you think I
spent every bit of spare time I had designing and making
things – doing what I really love?"

"But you had a good job . . ." her mother said sorrowfully.

"But I wasn't fucking happy!" Laura roared. "Didn't
you hear me? Don't you *ever* hear me?"

Neil looked at his wife. For as long as he'd known her,
he had ever heard Laura utter a single swearword. She
wouldn't even say 'feck'.

"My being happy doesn't matter to you though, does
it? It's what makes *you* happy that's important, isn't it?
As long as you can say that Laura is doing well and has a
great job in Dublin – never mind that she hates it so much

she feels as though a piece of her is dying with every passing day – as long as you can say that Laura is doing what she's *supposed* to be doing, then *you're* happy! Well, do you know something?" Laura put a hand on her hip. "I couldn't give a shit what makes you happy any more. I've spent most of my life *trying* to make you happy, *struggling* to make you proud of me, and all I've being doing is making myself miserable because it'll never fucking work! *Nothing* will please you. I'm not Cathy! I'm not happy to marry a local, have twenty kids and sit around doing nothing but gossip about everyone else while life passes me by. I want a life – *my* kind of life. And from now on, I'm going to get it! To hell with what you think, Mam, because I just don't give a shit any more!"

Without another glance at either her mother or her father, Laura raced out of the room, the door slamming deafeningly behind her.

Stone-faced and unmoved, Maureen lifted her chin into the air. "A piece of her dying every day," she repeated sarcastically. "Did you ever hear such rubbish in all your life?" Then she sniffed. "Well, Joe, after all we've done for her, at least now we know what she thinks of us."

Neil shook his head sadly from the doorway.

"You're a very silly woman, Maureen Fanning," he said, "because you really have no idea what you've lost."

* * *

Later that evening, sitting at her own kitchen table, Laura was inconsolable. "I can't believe it, Neil," she said, tears streaming down her cheeks as he held both of her hands in his. "I can't believe she reacted like that. Doesn't she care? Does she take some kind of sick pleasure in making me feel like shit, screwing up my confidence, making me feel unworthy?"

Neil looked worried. Laura had been saying things like this all the way back in the car. This could be far, far worse than it looked and could degenerate into an all-out break with her family, something he didn't think Laura could handle. For all her problems with her mother, Laura loved the woman deeply – for reasons Neil couldn't quite understand. His own mother had been thrilled for Laura – in fact, the news had given her a real boost this week. Pamela adored Laura and knew all about Maureen's reservations, but couldn't understand them. Then again, Neil's mother came from a long line of business people, her father a self-employed cabinetmaker and her husband and sons in the travel business. To Pamela, enterprise was something to be celebrated and not ridiculed in the way that Maureen did.

At this stage, Neil too had had enough of the Fannings. They had upset and taken advantage of his wife for long enough, and their wedding day, which was supposed to have been a quiet reserved affair, had been almost ruined by the carry-on of Maureen's family who had made absolute fools of themselves falling around on the dance-floor, and annoying other guests with their over-the-top drunkenness. Neil had been raging over that and was fully intending to take Maureen to task, but for Laura's sake and indeed Pamela's, he hadn't wanted to make a fuss and so eventually said nothing.

No, Neil was sick to the teeth of Laura's family, which is why – when he went to answer the ringing doorbell –

he wasn't at all happy to see Joe Fanning standing apologetically in his doorway.

"I wonder if I might have a word with Laura?" Joe said, in his usual nervous manner. "I'm on my own," he added, seeing Neil glance behind him toward the car.

Neil stood back and let him pass. "She's very upset, Joe – what happened back there wasn't fair to her."

"I know that, lad, and believe me I've tried to talk to Maureen, but she's a very stubborn woman."

Slight understatement, Neil thought to himself.

"Dad!" Laura looked up in surprise, but then her expression hardened. "If she's here I don't want to speak to her."

"She's not here, love. I came on my own."

"Oh." Her dad never usually got involved in this kind of thing. Arguments made him very uncomfortable. Laura wondered if he had taken it upon himself to ask her to 'go back and apologise'. Well, he could forget that, for a start.

Joe cleared his throat and looked at Neil. "I wonder if we could have a little chat, Laura, just the two of us?"

Neil's expression was wary. "Laura?"

She waved him away. "It's fine, Neil – I've never had an argument with Dad in my entire life, and I'm not going to start now." She gave her father a gentle smile as Neil went into the living-room and closed the door behind him.

"How is she?" Laura asked, wiping her tear-stained face with the sleeve of her jumper.

Joe gave out a low laugh. "Do you know something, Laura. Only yourself would ask a question like that. Anyone else wouldn't give a damn."

"I never wanted to upset her." Now that her father was here in front of her, Laura felt guilty for behaving the way she did. All the way back in the car, she was feeling glad she had said the things she said, but now she wasn't so sure.

"Well, I don't agree with the language, but maybe your mother needed to hear some of the things you said – she mightn't have wanted to hear them, but hear them she should."

"I don't understand . . ." Her father always backed her mother, even at her most unreasonable, *especially* at her most unreasonable.

Joe pulled out a chair and sat down. "Laura, I've been working in the factory now for what, nearly thirty years?"

Laura looked at him. "Well, yes, since I was born . . ."

"And remember I told you I used to work at that local newspaper, *The Herald*?" He gave a wave of his hand. "Ah, it's long gone now. It went not long before you were born."

Laura wondered where this was going. She knew her dad had worked at the paper, supposedly fixing the machinery and things like that.

"Well, there's something about me back then that myself and your mother never told yourself and Cathy. I was a writer at that paper, Laura. I used to do a weekly article."

A writer? Her father? Was he having her on?

"You wrote for *The Herald*?"

"Not just for the paper." Joe took a deep breath and looked away, as if embarrassed by what he was about to say next. "I wrote other things too, Laura – novels, short stories – that kind of thing."

"Novels?" Laura wondered when exactly she had turned into a parrot. But she was hearing all of this for the very first time. Her father wasn't a novelist; he was just an ordinary Joe Soap – a factory worker. She didn't think he had even finished school!

"When I met your mother she was all for it – she'd read some of my stuff and was very supportive. Back then, we were sure that eventually someone important would read them and maybe publish one or two of them. We used to get a right kick out of talking about it." He smiled at the memory. "We'd be famous, your mother would say, like Brendan Behan, John B Keane and all them fellas." He looked away. "Ah, but they were only pipe-dreams, Laura – I was never all that good."

"Have you still got them?" she asked, intrigued as to what her father, *her* father might have written in his younger days.

"Ah, I think your mother might have tidied them away somewhere but it doesn't matter now."

"So what happened?" Laura probed when Joe didn't continue. "You didn't just give up, did you?"

"Well, times were hard back then, as you know. There were factories closing down, a lot of unemployment and the country was going through a very black period. I married your mother, and for a long time we lived on our dreams, well that and the fact that I did a bit of writing part-time at the paper. Because I had a typewriter some of the local businesses would get me to do a bit of work for them too."

"But you were waiting for a break with your stories?"

Joe nodded. "It was all I wanted, Laura. I was consumed

by it, so consumed that I didn't worry too much about putting clothes on our backs or food on the table. I used to lock myself away for hours on end working on my baby, my masterpiece."

"And Mam?"

"Eventually your mother began to resent me for it and sure, who could blame her? Nothing was happening. It seemed that the rejection letters were piling up at the same rate as the bills. Then the paper went bust, and to all intents and purposes I was unemployed – but as half the village knew about my writing and my bits on the side typing – I didn't qualify for the dole. They were all a little wary of me too." He sighed deeply. "Laura, you know Glengarrah as well as I do. The worst thing anyone can do in that village is try to be different or stand out in any way. As someone who didn't make a 'normal living', I was a bit of an outcast." His voice wavered a little. "Your mother, who of course was born and bred in Glengarrah found this –disapproval, if you like, very hard to tolerate. So, when I was let go from the paper, Maureen got a bit of work in the factory, but after a while she couldn't continue, being around the smell of the sausages made her sick and –"

Then the realisation hit her. "She was pregnant," Laura finished, "with me."

Joe nodded. "Things were tight but I was still hell-bent on realising my dream, and keeping up with the writing. But one day your mother made me put a stop to it for good."

"What happened?"

"We were badly off, Laura, badly off in the old-fashioned sense, not like nowadays when badly off means you can't afford a second holiday or to change your car every year – badly off in the sense that we could barely feed ourselves. So one day, your mother swallowed whatever bit of pride she had left and went to the Kellys asking for help."

To the Kellys? The Kellys who never had two pennies to rub together? Laura couldn't imagine it.

"It was a small victory for Joan Kelly. She'd been telling Maureen for years that I was only a 'layabout who had notions about himself' and that no good would ever come of my 'scribbling'. It seemed to Joan then that she'd been proved right. She gave her a few bits to keep her going for a little while, but it was probably the worst thing your mother ever did, because they never let her forget their generosity. I'm sure you know as well as I do that by now Joan's charity has been repaid many times over."

Laura tried to put herself in her mother's shoes. Firstly, she couldn't get a handle on how her parents had been that badly off. But Glengarrah was a small village with nothing much going for it back then other than farming or the factories in Carlow. And her parents weren't farmers. She could only imagine the shame her mother felt then, how damaged her pride must have been.

Laura shook her head. "So that's why she's always so concerned about what everyone thinks of her, of *us*."

"And why she was so worried about you going the same way as I did. She saw it in you quicker than I did. Laura, if you weren't drawing pictures you'd be making things out of toilet rolls and bits of paper. You've been artistic since the day you were born. Maureen was terrified."

"So she tried to stifle me, to make me go another direction . . ."

"She gave in to the college thing – thinking that maybe then you might get it out of your system – and for a while you did. And you started what these non-artistic types call 'a proper job'." He winked. "But I was secretly pleased for you, love, when you started up your business. Of course, I worried too. I worried about how you'd manage – what with you being so mild-mannered and that – but I never said anything to support you and that was a mistake. I should have. I should have stood up to Maureen, and made her see that she had to let you go your own way. Things are different now. Young people are more confident. There are greater opportunities and you have so much talent." Then he laughed. "Still, you've more of your mother in you than I thought, love. You went your own way, anyway."

Laura sat back. She had never ever considered that her parents might have had their own hopes and dreams, dreams that were eventually smothered by circumstance. And yet, how could she *not* have known?

When Laura thought about it now, it had always been her father helping her and Cathy with homework – never her mother. He had always been the one with all the answers to the general-knowledge questions on the quiz programmes, the one with the balanced opinions and the open-minded outlook – Joe being one of the few in Glengarrah openly spurning gossip or idle talk.

Laura had never really given it a second thought; she thought that her father knew things because he read so many books and newspapers. In fact, her father was *always* reading. Just then, Laura had a brief memory flash of her father scribbling things in a notebook, things he

491

found interesting or things he wanted to remember. But she had never thought twice about why that might be.

Now Laura would have given a lot to read some of her father's writing. He might have been brilliant!

"Look, I didn't come here to make you feel guilty," Joe said, seeing Laura's torn expression, "and I hope you don't think that your arrival was the reason for my giving up the writing. We were mad for a baby, and when you came along it was better than anything. No, I just wasn't good enough and over time I came to accept that. Anyway, there were more important things in life. I had to look after my family and I did."

"But haven't you ever pursued your writing since? OK, I know it wouldn't have been possible when Cathy and I were around, but the house is very quiet now. Couldn't you try again?"

Joe's eyes twinkled. "Ah, I do a bit now and again, when your mother's not around," he said. "I enjoy it as much as I've always had, but I doubt it's any good."

"Dad – I'd love to take a look at what you've written! Will you let me read it?"

Joe shrugged. "Why not? But it's more of a hobby for me these days, love, not something I could do on a regular basis, so don't get any ideas. And we don't want your poor mother losing her mind altogether!" he added, laughing.

Laura looked at him, thinking she had never heard her father speak so much, so *easily* all at once. Then again, when did he ever get the chance – Maureen more than made up for the both of them!

Joe continued. "Look, I suppose I just want you to maybe try and see things the way your mother sees them.

She's nervous of things like that, Laura, nervous and untrusting of anything she can't understand – anything she can't control. Because of what happened with me, Maureen craves stability, and I suppose she couldn't really understand why you would throw caution to the winds and give up a good job like you did. And let's face it, love, sometimes the worst thing an 'ordinary' Irish person can do is actually *be* successful and have everyone else believe that *they* think they're better than them."

He gave a wry smile, and Laura thought she understood exactly what he meant. A sense of innate inferiority was at the root of Maureen's problem and why she worried so much about Laura 'running away with her notions'.

"I was so hurtful though, Dad, and I tried so hard to make her understand how important it was to me, and why I had to do it. But she's impossible to talk to and she treats me like I'm a child . . . " she trailed off exasperated. "Oh, I don't suppose we'll change her now."

"No, we definitely can't do that," Joe laughed softly. "In a way, I suppose she *does* still see you as child. But, Laura, what I'm trying to say is that you shouldn't make the mistake I did, and let the bedgrudgers or Maureen affect your choices. Your mother can't help herself, and in fairness I don't think she realises that she *is* hurting you."

"I know," Laura said, and for a long while she and her father sat in silence, lost in their thoughts.

"Look, pet, it's late and I'd better head back," Joe said eventually. He stood up and then reached across and patted Laura lightly on the hand. "I'll tell your mother you'll give her a ring tomorrow, maybe?"

"I'll ring her first thing." Knowing what she knew

now, Laura was anxious to make it up with her mother but she needed to mull things over a bit first. "Thanks, Dad, thanks for everything."

Giving him a quick hug at the doorway, Laura closed the door behind her father, and went back into the kitchen. She'd tell Neil all about it, but first she needed a coffee.

Despite everything, she felt a little better now that she understood her mother's reasons for being so hard on her all these years. She had thought it was because she wasn't good enough, but that wasn't it – she had been *too* good and that had terrified her mother.

Her mother's lack of trust, lack of belief still hurt, but in spite of everything, maybe it was understandable. And as her father had said, Maureen had been raised in a different age – an age where people raised their families, went to work on a weekday and Mass on a Sunday, and were perfectly happy about it. Her mother couldn't comprehend ambition and dreams and crazy things like that, because she had seen it all go wrong for Joe. And maybe, Laura realised, maybe she too had inherited some of her mother's sense of acute inferiority – something the Catholic Church had drummed into most women of her generation, and something that this one was doing its best to discard.

But it was always there, wasn't it? That old-fashioned sense of guilt. Finally, Laura had dared to dream, and to realise her ambitions, and then, when something good *did* happen, she worried that she didn't deserve it. After Amanda Verveen's call her first thought was that it couldn't possibly be happening to her, that she just wasn't worthy –

despite the fact that she'd worked as hard as she possibly could to attain it.

She smiled inwardly. Catholic guilt she could deal with. But for the moment, she resolved to talk to her mother, firstly to apologise for the argument, and then have it out with her about the business. OK, so it might take a while, and Maureen was still a stubborn old witch, but maybe over time, and with Joe's help, she might be won over. And Laura was going to make her parents really proud of her.

Both of them.

She smiled warmly and shook her head as she waited for the kettle to boil. Her father – a writer! These days, life never failed to surprise her.

Chapter 37

Nicola looked up. "Hi," she said softly, her heart quickening.

"Hi." Ken stood in her office doorway, stony-faced and tired-looking.

"Did you enjoy your few days off?"

He wouldn't meet her eyes. "Yes, thanks."

"Well, did you go away somewhere or . . ."

Ken ignored the question. "Nicola, I just wondered if there were any problems here while I was away?" he asked curtly. "Anything you couldn't deal with?"

"No, nothing." He sounded so cold, so distant, she thought. Why was he doing this?

She sat forward, her body taut with anxiety. "Ken, come in and close the door, please. We need to –"

"No," he interjected, his tone brisk and offhand and still he wouldn't meet her eyes "I don't think we have anything to say to one another. As far as I'm concerned, it's over and done with."

"What?" She barely heard her own voice. "But, why? Why won't you listen, give me a chance to –"

"Look, Nicola, I know I gave you back your key but I wondered if I might have permission to get some things from your house? My golf-clubs are still there – I should have taken them before but I wasn't thinking."

Her *permission*? Who did he think he was talking to – the Queen? "Well, of course you can – do you want to call round later and maybe –"

"I need to go now, if that's okay."

"Sure." Wounded by his curt and dismissive manner, Nicola reached into her handbag and tossed the keys at him.

"Thanks."

"But can we not . . ." She trailed off in mid-sentence, realising he had already left the room.

Nicola moved to the window and, looking down at the carpark below, she saw Ken approach his car, his expression rather amused as he got in and drove off. What the hell . . .? What was so fucking funny? Was he enjoying taunting her like this? All of sudden, Nicola felt a burst of annoyance. Okay, so he *thought* he saw something that night and she made a mistake in lying to him, but the very least he could do is give her a chance to explain. But no, he had just taken what he wanted from it and gone off sulking like a spoiled child. Never mind that he might have taken things up wrong, never mind that Nicola would never *dream* of going back to Dan – no, Ken had decided that he had seen something damning and that was that. Well, stuff him!

Nicola moved back behind her desk. Who the hell did he think he was, speaking to her like that and going off in a strop, letting no one know where he might be going? Here she was, these past few days, worrying and fretting over him, wondering how he might be feeling and what he might be thinking. Well, stuff him – a second time! If he wouldn't give her a chance to explain then that was his bloody tough! 'Permission to get my things' indeed! Well, it was about bloody time he did call and collect his *things* – those awkward bloody golf-clubs and squash-racquets and gym-gear that had been cluttering up *her* house! And he could take his blasted *Lord of the Rings* DVD box-set with him too, and his shagging Grisham books and his Playstation 2 and . . .

Nicola slumped miserably on her desk. Was that it? Was it really over? She couldn't imagine being without Ken – he was such a huge part of her life now. He *was* her life now. What would she do without him?

Nicola didn't get much of a chance to wonder as just then her extension buzzed and Sally put through a call from one of the gym-equipment suppliers. She groaned inwardly as the rep on the other end tried to explain why seven of the ten treadmills they currently supplied to the centre would need to be taken away for servicing.

"But can't you do it here?" Nicola asked impatiently, but her heart wasn't in it. At this stage, they could take the bloody swimming-pool out of the place for all she cared!

A long, highly volatile conversation later, Nicola rang off, tired and frustrated. She kneaded her forehead, hoping to massage away the beginnings of what would undoubtedly be the mother of all headaches.

With growing irritation, she turned to her PC only to

discover that while she was on the telephone, her hard drive had crashed and the database information she had spent the whole bloody *morning* inputting and didn't save, had gleefully toddled off into PC Never-Never Land! Grrr! Nicola resisted the urge to throw the whole bloody lot out the shagging window.

Could *anything* else go wrong for her today?

"Nicola," Kelly announced breathlessly from the doorway just then, "Mrs Murphy-Ryan's kids have just –"

"*Aaaaaah!*" Nicola yelled, putting her hands over her ears. "*Please* don't say any more, Kelly – I don't think I can take it!"

Slowly, the pool attendant stepped backwards. "O – K," she said, obviously taken aback. "I'll get someone else to talk to them."

"Thank you!" Nicola exhaled relief.

She got back to work but her mind wasn't focused and she had covered very little ground before Ken reappeared in her office, and, without even looking at Nicola, casually dropped the keys on her desk, before turning to leave. This indifferent gesture, along with his blatant, unashamed rudeness was just about enough for her.

"*Hold on there. Just one second, you!*" she said, in a tone that brooked no messing about.

"What?" Ken answered innocently but, most annoyingly, she could see him trying not to smile. He *was* enjoying this, the bastard!

"What? *What?*" she mimicked, doubly annoyed. "Ken Harris, I don't know who the hell you think you are, but if you think you can treat *me* like a piece of dog – dog – *meat*, then you've got another think coming! How dare you carry on like this – sulking and grouching like a spoilt child and making it plain to all and sundry that you're annoyed with me! How dare you take off for days on your own – refusing to listen or speak to me when you know damn well that I've done nothing wrong! Not to mention embarrass me here at work by not telling me you're going!"

"You've really done nothing wrong, then?" Ken said, in a tone that Nicola could only describe as brazen.

"Yes! I mean – no!" She shook her head. "I mean, I haven't done anything wrong and yet you're treating me like I'm responsible for a breakout of bloody chicken-pox or something! Ken, I'm sick of it! You won't listen to me, you won't even *look* at me – who the hell do you think you are?"

"Fine, I believe you," Ken said and shrugged indolently, a gesture that *really* set her off.

She could feel her heartbeat quickening, her pulse racing, her irritation rising as, saying nothing more, he headed for the door again.

"Don't turn your back on me!" she shouted at him, desperately trying to resist throwing something at the annoying, infuriating, *exasperating* – idiot! "Hey, I'm talking to you . . . what? What the hell is *he* doing here?" Nicola watched in astonishment as Barney sauntered casually through her office door, his tail wagging enthusiastically as he sniffed the floor beneath him.

"Well, would you look at that?" Ken said nonchalantly, his eyes wide and innocent-looking. "He must have sneaked into the back of the car while I was at your house, and came back here with me."

"*Sneaked* into the back of the car? For goodness sake, Ken, he's a fully-grown Labrador – how could you not have noticed him?" What was the matter with him? Of all the stupid . . .

"I don't know. I suppose I wasn't thinking. Anyway, he'll be fine with you now, won't he?"

Nicola harrumphed, now *really* frustrated. "This is a leisure centre, Ken Harris – you can't have dogs in . . ." Barney ambled to Nicola's side and she reached down to pat him on the head. "Sorry, Barn, as much as I'd love it, you can't stay here." She glared at Ken. "And silly Ken here will have to drive you home . . . now what have you found for burying *this* time . . . oh!"

Nicola's heart leapt as Barney dropped whatever he had been carrying in his mouth out onto her lap. She stared in disbelief at the small, navy, velvet . . . was it?

She looked up and saw Ken watching her, his expression now no longer sullen. Instead it was . . . expectant.

"Well done, Barney!" he said, and then to Nicola, "We've been practising that trick for a while."

"Ken?" she said breathlessly, almost afraid to ask. "Is this . . . is this what I think it is?"

"Well, why don't you open it and see?" he asked, coming closer.

Barney flopped down on the floor and put his head on his paws, his dark eyes rising upwards with curiosity as his mistress opened the – admittedly sticky – velvet box to find an unusual and stunningly beautiful, ornate diamond ring.

Nicola's hand flew to her mouth and, for a long moment, she was unable to think – let alone *say* anything. Was this really . . .?

"Well?" Ken urged gently, his eyes full of emotion. "Will you?"

Nicola looked from the ring, to Barney, to Ken and then back again to the ring. At this the Labrador groaned loudly, apparently frustrated by her lack of response.

"I'm just so shocked . . . I don't know what to . . ." She looked at him, still unsure that this was actually happening. "But I thought you wanted to break up with me – you were so angry with me . . ."

"I was being an idiot. Immediately after I saw Dan at your house I was annoyed and angry with you. Then afterwards when you denied you'd seen him, I thought –"

"Oh, Ken." She knew she was stupid to deny it on the phone then, but he had put her on the spot and she hadn't been thinking straight. And she really had no idea he would have seen Dan at the house. But afterwards, he wouldn't *let* her explain.

"So, what changed your mind?" Nicola asked him.

"Well, I went off and sulked for a while, deciding that I wasn't going to speak to you until I was good and ready. To be honest, I was also a little bit afraid that you *had* gone back to Hunt. Then I met Helen in town at the weekend and she told me what had happened, how you were just getting the thick bastard to come clean with his poor girlfriend."

"But I could have told you that, if you had let me."

"I know, and I was being an idiot. I'm sorry, Nicola. I should have given you the chance to explain, but, as I said, I was also terrified that you'd tell me you *were* going back to Hunt. I was willing to delay that possibility for as long as I could."

"But then why . . . today?"

Ken shrugged easily, his eyes twinkling "Well, after days of not speaking, and then stupidly giving you your key back, I had no other way of getting Barney here." He shrugged. "And I figured we might as well get our first decent argument over and done with," he said mischievously. "You're really great to watch when you're angry. Your face kinda gets screwed up and your eyes are –"

"Ken Harris! You don't mean to tell me that you came in here today and set out to make me mad on purpose!"

He shrugged again. "As I said, I couldn't think of any other way to get your house key off you. But bringing Barney here to the office wasn't in the original plan. I had planned to ask you before now . . . actually, I had planned to ask you that night."

Nicola sat back, shocked. Now she really understood why he was so angry, why he had reacted so badly to seeing Dan at the house. But arranging all this and Barney too . . . Tears sprang to her eyes. Was this really happening?

"Look, you haven't answered yet, and you seem a little confused, so just in case you haven't yet got the picture, I suppose I'd better make myself clear." Ken crouched down beside her and took both of her hands in his. "Nicola, I love you and I want to spend the rest of my life with you. Will you marry me?"

Nicola looked at Ken, looked at his kind, uncomplicated face, his expressive, honest brown eyes and didn't have to think too hard about the answer.

"Yes! Yes, Ken . . . of *course*, I'd love to marry you!" Nicola threw her arms around him and kissed him hungrily.

Barney watched them both for a moment, and then, realising they would be busy for some time, gave a loud groan and rolled over onto his back.

Chapter 38

It was a glorious afternoon, the air was cold and crisp, and there was barely a cloud in the sky.

Helen wrapped her scarf tightly around her neck, and savoured the sharp breeze on her cheeks and the sun in her face. Talking these long walks with Kerry had become a habit of hers lately and, not for the first time, Helen wondered why she hadn't done this before. Just ahead of her, she heard Kerry call happily after the newest member of the family – a white and tan floppy-eared beagle called Fuzzy.

Kerry was a different child these days, Helen thought, watching her daughter racing along in the grass. While she had made no major inroads with her speech problems in general, Helen could see it in her eyes that she was becoming that little bit more confident, especially around her mother. Kerry hardly stuttered at all in front of Helen now, sensing her support, and the fact that she wouldn't be annoyed if Kerry didn't speak properly.

The taunts at school hadn't stopped, but the physical side of the bullying had – Mrs Clancy had taken steps to give the culprits little excuse as possible for jeering, by moving them to another class and away from Kerry. In the meantime, Kerry had made a friend, a tiny little thing called Fiona, who – according to Mrs Clancy – had also been given a hard time in class because of the fact that she was adopted, and sometimes had to wear glasses. If it weren't so serious, Helen would have laughed. Who would have thought that the daughter of self-assured, confident Helen Jackson would end up as one of the class nerds?

But apparently, Fiona was anything but nerdy – rather a tough little cookie who had one day stood up to one of her tormentors, a bulky brat called Dean. Arms folded and chin out, Fiona had informed Dean that at least *her* mammy had chosen her 'aspecially' out of lots of other babies, but like it or not poor Dean's mammy was *stuck* with him. Apparently, it worked, as that same evening Dean was heard asking his mammy in panicked tones, whether or not she 'wanted to give him back and swap him for someone better'.

Some of Fiona's daring had begun to rub off on Kerry, Mrs Clancy having told her that only the other day Kerry had an answer for a brat that made fun of her by imitating her stutter.

"If you call that a s-s-stutter," she said, "I think I'll h-h-have to give you l-l-l-lessons." The young fella, surprised by her humour and bravado, began to view Kerry through changed eyes.

But the change in her daughter, Helen believed, was mainly due to the change in their mother/daughter relationship. These days, Helen not only spoke to her daughter, she actually *listened* to her. Helen had to admit that Kerry was quite good fun, and she had lately begun to see her more as a person, rather than an inconvenience. She was bright, quick-witted and easily amused. Helen now regretted the years she had missed with Kerry as a result of her self-absorption. She could have done her child serious damage. After all, look at Laura's situation, where the desire to please and make her mother proud of her had resulted in her friend's unbelievable lack of confidence and self-belief.

Helen felt a familiar hole in the depths of her stomach when she thought about the part that she too had played in damaging Laura's self-belief. Who would have blamed her for feeling inadequate and lowly beside Helen? But Laura had begun coming to terms with her mother now, and this new contract she had to design for Amanda Verveen – well, that was just incredible! This time round, Helen was genuinely thrilled for her friend, and it was certainly a much better feeling than the jealousy and envy she had felt that time she tried to seduce Neil.

Amazingly, Laura was still sticking by her – was still calling Helen a friend. She had berated Helen for blaming herself for Kerry's situation, suggesting that perhaps this might have been the best thing that could have happened.

"Think of it as not quite a wake-up call," Laura had said, "but more of a gentle nudge out of a daydream."

Helen knew what she meant. There was still time to make amends where Kerry was concerned.

As for everything else, Helen wasn't so sure. She was going to stay out of Laura's hair for a while, and let her friend decide whether or not the friendship was worth continuing. Helen hoped it would continue because, over the last few months, she had come to finally appreciate that Laura was, and always had been, one of her greatest friends – stalwart and supportive, if only in the background. She had had a chat with Nicola too, apologising for her behaviour immediately after the accident.

"Helen, give yourself a break – it was years ago!" Nicola had said, astonished, and not in the least bit bothered about it. There was little that could bother Nicola these days, Helen thought smiling, now that she had her forthcoming wedding to plan. News of her engagement to Ken, despite their little tiff, wasn't in the least bit surprising and Helen was delighted that for once, she had actually played a small part in *sorting out* the lovelife of one of her friends.

She raced after Kerry and the ever-hyper Fuzzy. He wasn't quite a pup, but he was easily as silly and playful as any young dog Helen had ever come across. There he was barking and racing after birds that he hadn't a hope in hell of catching, Kerry trying her best to keep up with him.

"Look, Mummy, F-F-F–" Kerry struggled, and Helen wondered again if she had made a mistake calling the dog something that was difficult for her to pronounce, but her speech therapist had advised that this could be most beneficial. That way, Kerry couldn't avoid difficult consonants. So, when one day Helen brought the young dog home from the local animal shelter, and had declared he already had a name, Kerry had no choice but to work on her f's and z's.

"Fuzzy w-w-wants to play in the match!" she cried, pointing happily to where the dog was now hijacking the football from a game of soccer already in full swing.

"Fuzzy, come here!" Helen ordered, mortified. The game wasn't exactly a kick-around – both teams were in full gear and there were plenty of spectators.

The dog continued wrestling the ball from the corner-forward, acting as though Helen wasn't even there.

"I'm so, so sorry." Helen was all apologies to the other players as, lead in hand, she ran out onto the pitch.

"Fuzzy, come *here*!" she repeated in a tone that this time had the desired effect on her daughter's errant pet. Fuzzy dropped the ball and – with what Helen could have sworn was one last mournful look towards goal – allowed her to lead him away to the sidelines. Kerry stood there, hand over her mouth, tittering.

"Bad dog, Fuzzy!" Kerry said with no conviction whatsoever, while at the same time reaching down and tickling him under the ears.

A spectator standing immediately beside them looked on in amusement.

"That dog might play for Ireland, yet!" he said, and Kerry giggled.

Helen, embarrassed and more than a little out of breath from running, stood quietly for a moment and watched the play continue. The game, judging by the age of the players, was an Under-15's match of some kind – possibly a Sunday league game. Both teams seemed pretty good. The passing was quick and accurate, and the play flowed easily from one half of the pitch to the other.

One player in particular though caught her eye. He

seemed to be playing just above midfield in a sort of floating role – and when necessary, tracked back to defend – but in the few minutes Helen had seen him play, she knew he was something special. At that moment he won the ball in his own penalty area, and raced up along the wing, fast as lightning. The spectators rippled with excitement as, easily stepping past three defenders, he moved towards goal. Because he was so far wide, Helen was sure he was about to cross the ball to his forward-moving teammate – but no – this kid checked his man, did a little shimmy and within seconds of striking it, the ball was in the back of the net. The crowd roared with applause, Helen included. It was one of the most skilful and spectacular goals she had ever seen.

Kerry too, clapped her hands excitedly. "He's good, Mommy," she shouted over the crowd, "like M-M-Michael Owen."

"Well, it's a long time since we've seen Michael Owen do anything like that," Helen said with a wry smile, "but he *is* very good."

"Spoken like two women who know their football, I think." Kerry looked up at the man standing beside them and smiled shyly, amused – and more than a little pleased – to be referred to as 'a woman'.

Helen smiled at this. "My daughter certainly knows her stuff," she said easily to him. "She's been following Michael Owen since she was barely out of nappies, haven't you, hon?" Then she turned slightly towards him and dropped her voice conspiratorially. "Although I can't say I'm pleased that my four-year-old is not only already having crushes – but crushes on millionaire footballers."

The man laughed, a slow easy laugh. "Well, you never know," he said. "She could end up marrying your man yet – stranger things have happened, I'm sure."

"Will you stop!" Helen feigned horror. "Anyway, I only have myself to blame for getting her into football in the first place. Don't tell me I've created a monster!"

It was new, and very unusual for Helen to be chatting simply without being flirty with a male stranger like this – but she thought she knew exactly why. For once, it wasn't all about whether or not he was a potential boyfriend, or even whether he was checking her out. Helen was finished with that kind of thing. From now on, if it happened, it happened, but Helen had made a promise to herself that Kerry was the most important thing in her life. Men could come second.

Which is why she and Kerry found themselves chatting easily to this other man, who eventually introduced himself as Cormac. He was tall and wiry and, as Nicola would say, 'certainly no oil painting'. But he had striking green eyes, eyes that sparkled when he laughed and somehow instinctively made you warm to him. That was how Helen felt anyway, but Kerry must have felt the same way as, normally shy, she was now chatting merrily to him with little sign of her stutter.

"I wouldn't worry about that kind of thing anyway," he said to Helen, referring to her earlier remark about Kerry's crush on Michael Owen. "My wife had a life-long crush on Gary Lineker."

"Had?" Helen laughed. "So, why did she go off him? Oh, let me guess, it was the ears, right – she finally noticed the ears?"

Cormac shook his head. "No, she died," he answered simply.

Helen was horrified she had been so flippant. "I'm so sorry," she said. "I didn't mean to —"

"Sure, how would you know?" he said, waving her away with a wry grin. "Anyway, I was the one who brought it up." He gave a tiny smile, as if remembering. "Yeah, she was mad about him — thought he was the greatest goal-scorer ever. I hadn't the heart to tell her he hardly ever made a goal in his life."

Helen smiled. "Best goal-*poacher*, maybe."

Cormac looked at her with new respect. "You *do* know your stuff."

"Don't look so surprised!"

"Well, I am — most women's eyes glaze over at that kind of talk, and there's no way they would stand here watching the game for as long as you did."

"Some people would call that a sexist comment," she said, feigning affront, but at the same time trying to bite back a smile.

"Sexist it might be, but it's true."

Helen looked back towards the pitch. "That young lad, the winger — he's terrific."

"Greg?" he said in a tone that suggested the lad was local. "He certainly is. And," he bent down towards Kerry, "if you promise you won't tell anyone, I'll tell you a secret about Greg — well, you can tell your mommy if you like, but that's all."

Helen smiled, watching Kerry's eyes widen as Cormac whispered in her ear. Then Kerry motioned for Helen to bend down, and when she did she said, "He's goin to play in Pwemiership, Mommy!"

"Ooooh!" Helen said breathlessly, then she fixed Cormac with a questioning look. "Is that true?"

"True as I'm standing here. Newcastle signed him right after his first trial."

"Wow, although I can't say I'm surprised he's been scouted. When he is going over?"

"After this season ends – June possibly."

"Will he settle there, do you think?" Helen knew that a lot of Irish footballers sometimes had problems being away from home so young.

"Oh, I'd be almost positive of it," he said knowledgably, as the referee blew for full time.

"So, how do you know so much about him – is he a friend of yours or something?" Helen asked over the applause, and then watched astonished as match-winning Greg began to approach them.

Cormac was smiling. "Actually – he's my son," he replied proudly.

Chapter 39

On a cold afternoon in January, and dressed in full snow-queen regalia, Chloe prepared to walk up the aisle of St Anthony's Church.

Her father, dressed handsomely in top-hat and tails stood back to let the photographer get some shots of the bride on her own.

"Such a shame we don't have the snow," the photographer was saying and if Chloe didn't know better she'd have sworn there was mockery behind his words.

She turned slightly to the side and gave him a beaming smile. At least, it was supposed to be a beaming smile. Chloe wondered if the lens would pick up on her nervousness, capturing it on film forever. Yet it didn't feel quite the same as nervousness, she decided, it was more like . . . like uncertainty.

Why was she feeling like this? Chloe wasn't quite sure. She had been looking forward to this day for so long, and despite all the setbacks and the chopping and changing, her wedding day was finally happening.

Why then, did she not feel what she was supposed to feel – elation, excitement, anticipation? Where were all of those feelings?

Chloe followed the bridesmaids inside. Now, standing at the back of church with her mother with Lynne fussing over the hem of her cloak, she felt . . . unsure.

What the hell was wrong with her?

Just then, Lynne looked up at her and smiled. Chloe wondered if she was just imagining the faint look of anxiety on her friend's face. Was Lynne feeling uncertain too? Had she made a mistake confiding in her? But what else could she do?

After her meeting with Nicola, Chloe hadn't known what to make of her fiancé's behaviour towards his ex-wife. She knew that there were two sides to every story but Dan had all but admitted that he had abandoned his wife when she needed him most.

"What's to say that he wouldn't do the same to you?" Lynne had said. "What's to say that he wouldn't go running at the first sign of trouble?"

But Dan hadn't gone running though, had he? He had just admitted that he couldn't continue with the way things were.

"I just couldn't cope with it, Chlo," he had said. "There was no point in pretending otherwise. It wouldn't have done Nicola any good in the long run."

It was true that Nicola seemed to have got on just fine without him but then, she hadn't had much of a choice, had she?

"It's not so much his leaving her that should worry you, but the fact that he had no intention of telling you about it *is* a problem," Lynne had said.

Or had she?

No, Chloe thought, Lynne *hadn't* said that, it was the little voice inside herself that had said it.

The little voice that at this very moment was doing its best to make Chloe feel incredibly nervous.

The opening bars of the bridal march began. This was it. Chloe felt a sudden rush of adrenaline – or was it panic? She exhaled deeply, and flinched when her father touched her elbow.

"This is us, darling," he whispered, entwining Chloe's right arm in his left.

As she followed her bridesmaids up the aisle, Chloe's gaze travelled past the rows of smiling guests and flashing cameras and settled at the top of the church. She didn't see the elaborate flower arrangements, she didn't hear the harpist – she didn't even care how she looked. Somehow Chloe thought she would be blown away by all the romance and excitement of it all, blown away by being a princess for a day.

But Chloe didn't feel like that at all.

If anything, she felt as though all of this was very, very wrong.

She looked up and saw Dan standing with his back to the congregation, stiffly awaiting his new bride's arrival.

Chloe exhaled, resisting the urge to quite literally shake the uncertainty out of her head. She loved Dan. Surely that was all that mattered? And everything that had happened in the past was simply that – the past.

They were getting closer now and Chloe's heart was knocking hard against her ribs, pounding in her chest. Suddenly, white spots appeared before her eyes and she felt her throat close over and her mouth go . . .

Then the bridesmaids stopped walking, and Lynne turned around to take the bridal bouquet for the duration of the ceremony.

Dan was smiling.

Her father was smiling.

The priest was smiling.

Then . . .

Chloe looked up. What was *wrong* with her? *Nobody* knew what the future held, did they? Nobody could be a hundred per cent certain. Could any bride on the day, what with all the fuss, pomp and spectacle – really, *honestly* say that they were absolutely certain?

Chloe thought about it.

Could anybody *ever* be absolutely certain?

The bride moved forward to take her place before the altar.

Probably not.

Epilogue

London Fashion Week

Laura was walking on air. She was still waiting for the alarm-clock to ring, for Neil to call her name and wake her out of sleep, anything that would finally convince her that all of this was just a dream.

But months later, that still hadn't happened.

Now she was sitting directly in front of the catwalk, waiting to view Amanda Verveen's long-awaited Collection. It hadn't been easy, and Amanda could be one temperamental battle-axe, but despite all the late nights designing and altering – in her own opinion – some of the most spectacular jewellery she had ever produced, Laura had enjoyed every second.

On one side of her Neil sat proudly. On the other side . . .

"Wouldn't you think with all the money the likes of your woman makes, that she'd be able to afford a watch, Laura? I make it well gone half four. Honestly, you'd think we've nothing better to be doing after coming all the way over to London and –"

Joe patted his wife's hand. "Sure, we're in no rush, are we, Maureen? And if I were you I'd stop looking at your watch, and start smiling for that photographer." He winked at Laura. "He probably wants a photo of us for *The Clarion*."

"*The Clarion*? And who'll see us in that? Joe Fanning, if you've ever seen anyone in Glengarrah reading a copy of that hoity-toity muck, I'll give you twenty euro!"

Laura couldn't help but smile. There was no changing her mother – that was for sure. But they had had it out, and although she hadn't come round completely, Laura knew that perhaps in her own way Maureen was behind her. She was still a little afraid, in the same way Laura supposed that she herself had been afraid that this whole thing with Amanda Verveen wasn't real, that it was a big mistake and that someone would eventually tell her so.

She looked at her father. Since learning of Joe's love of writing, Laura had bought him a second-hand word processor and had tentatively showed him how to use it. She didn't know if her father would ever get the hang of the machine, or indeed rediscover his passion for writing but she wasn't going to push it. If Joe had a story to tell, it would come out in its own good time. Maureen didn't have much to say about the subject either way, which Laura took as a very good sign.

She looked at her own watch and scanned the room. No sign of the others yet. Laura really hoped that they would make it here in time. She couldn't imagine Helen missing something like this. London Fashion week? Helen would be in her element.

Laura smiled. Helen was in her element all the time

these days. She had been spending more and more time with Cormac Doyle, and although she was still maintaining they were 'just good friends' Laura thought that they were perfect together. In fact, she couldn't think of anyone more perfect for Helen. He was mature, easy-going, adored children and had an up-and-coming footballer for a son! Helen and Cormac's son, Greg, got on famously – Greg regarding Helen with intense awe as being the first woman he had ever met who 'really understood football'. And most important of all, Kerry adored them both. Lately, she and Helen had made a lot more time for one another as mother and daughter, and the results were satisfying.

Laura was thrilled for Helen. Her friend had finally found exactly what she was looking for, and just when she wasn't looking for it. Kerry was like a different child these days.

Laura felt a tap on her shoulder from behind. She looked around and smiled.

"Missus, can I please have your autograph?" Ken teased, and Laura shushed him away as Nicola reached across and hugged her.

"Nic, I'm sorry I couldn't get you or Helen seats up front but . . ." Laura gestured across the way, "those ladies are kind of hard to shift."

Nicola followed Laura's gaze around the catwalk. "Oh my God, I must be seeing things," she gasped, putting her hand to her mouth.

"Either that or Kate and Gwyneth have doubles," Ken added.

"And is that *Madonna* over there?" Nicola couldn't hide her awe.

Maureen sat forward and peered over the top of her glasses. "Is that who that blondie one is?" she said. "Well, I really feel like giving her a piece of my mind over that song she had out a few years ago – making a mockery of Our Lady, she was. I think I might go over now before the show starts."

Laura looked petrified. "Don't mind them, Mam," she said as calmly as she could. "It's not really Madonna. She just looks like her."

Maureen sat back. "Well, that's a pity all the same."

"They're not half as good-looking close up though, are they, mate?" Neil said to Ken, his gaze firmly fixed on one of the Corr sisters, who were also seated in the front row.

"Not half – ouch!" Nicola gave him a dig in the ribs.

"Where's Helen?" she asked Laura. "I think the show's about to start."

Sure enough, the lights dimmed and the music boomed from the speakers. Laura sat forward in her seat and felt a rush of excitement like never before. Then a thought struck her. What if at the last minute Amanda decided to leave the jewellery out altogether, that it wasn't good enough? Her throat felt dry. But surely she wouldn't do that, not after all the work . . .

"Ladies and gentleman – the Amanda Verveen Collection!" The announcer's voice boomed around the room, and soon the first model appeared on the catwalk.

Laura couldn't bring herself to look as she felt Neil give her hand a little squeeze. Then she raised her eyes, and for a split second, Laura couldn't see – she couldn't focus on the girl, never mind what she was wearing. There were just too many tears.

Alongside her, Laura heard her father whisper. "This is your moment, pet. Savour it."

She looked up just in time to see the first model do a little pirouette on the bottom of the catwalk. The girl turned back, and as she did, the lights caught the choker around her neck. *Her* choker. For one long moment, Laura couldn't breathe.

It was the same for the next two – even three girls, until finally Laura began to relax and enjoy herself. There was simply no describing the feeling of unqualified pride and achievement she felt in all of this. Laura knew that even if nothing ever came of this – if she never had another commission again – it wouldn't matter. This, today, was all she ever dreamed about and so much more.

From behind, she felt someone give her a shoulder a little squeeze. "Sorry we're late," Helen whispered.

Laura smiled up at her. Her friend looked beautiful and, in the style stakes, easily matched any of the celebrities in the room – if not on the catwalk.

She was dressed in slim fitting trousers and a sparkling fitted bustier, to which she had added one of Laura's vintage-style pendants. Helen had been insistent Laura make her one for ages, Laura never knowing what it was for. Now she knew it was Helen's way of showing her some support today. Either that or Helen as usual wanted to be one step ahead of the fashion posse. She found that either scenario was equally satisfying.

Laura sat back and savoured the rest of the show, and it seemed no time at all until Amanda Verveen, all glamorous and smiling, stepped out to greet her adoring public. The room thundered with rapturous applause, and a few people began to stand up one by one until Amanda was given a complete standing ovation.

Laura clapped madly, proud to have been a tiny part of it all and delighted for the designer. Then, somehow in the darkness, she caught Amanda's eye, and all of a sudden Laura was hauled up on the catwalk with her, and her name was being called from somewhere in the background, and she could see Neil and Nicola and Helen and her mum and dad all smiling and applauding her.

Laura thought then that she would surely burst with joy.

Eventually, Amanda stepped back inside, the lights brightened, and the show was over almost as quickly as it had begun. Laura rejoined her still-clapping family and friends. Afterwards she was unable to keep the smile from her face.

"It was brilliant!" Nicola enthused, reaching upwards to give her a hug. "You are brilliant!"

"Thank you." Laura wiped tears from her eyes.

"You certainly are."

She looked up to see a smiling Pamela standing beside her. "Pamela! I didn't know you'd be here!"

"And miss my favourite daughter-in-law's big moment?" Pamela hugged her. "You must be joking!"

Laura was thrilled to see Pamela look so well. She had recently completed her chemotherapy, and according to her latest scan, was in remission. Her hair hadn't yet grown back but there was colour in her face and she had put on a little weight since the last time Laura had seen her.

"She was always brilliant at that kind of thing, wasn't

she, Joe?" Maureen piped up. "But I have to admit that everything looks a lot nicer under all those lights."

Pamela gave her daughter-in-law a conspiratorial wink. "I think that might be your mother's way of saying congratulations," she whispered.

Laura smiled.

"Right," Neil put an arm around her. "I think my wife deserves a little celebration after all that," he said, "so I'm taking you all out to dinner – just give me a second and I'll tell Dad where we're going." He went across to where his father and Joe were sitting together, laughing over something.

Laura stood back for a moment and savoured the scene around her. Her mother was in deep conversation with Pamela, telling her how she and Joe had always known Laura was that little bit different. "It was hard to tell what Laura had going on in her head most of the time, you see, because she always had some quare notions. Still, we knew she'd go down the right road eventually."

Still seated in the second row, Helen was flanked by a very dapper-looking Cormac (Helen had obviously done a quick job on his wardrobe) and was conversing happily with Ken, who Laura noticed could hardly take his eyes off Nicola. These days they were busy making plans for their wedding, and Laura didn't think she had ever seen Nicola so happy.

She shook her head. The three of them had come a long way since this time last year and despite everything, had each found exactly what she was looking for – albeit in ways they hadn't expected.

Just then, Nicola looked up and caught Laura's eye.

"I'm so proud of you," she said, moving towards her. "It was fantastic, and you really deserve it."

"Did you not hear?" Laura cocked her head toward her mother, but there was a smile in her voice. "*I* didn't do anything – it was the lights!"

"No – really," Nicola said, "you should be very proud of yourself."

"I am."

The two women were silent for a moment.

"Nic, I never asked . . . did you –" Laura began.

"Go to the wedding?" She shook her head. "You didn't really think I would, did you?"

Laura didn't know what to say. She thought Dan had had a terrible cheek ringing up and inviting Nicola and Ken to the wedding in the first place. "Seeing as we're all friends now," he had said, apparently.

"Although I must admit, I was very tempted," Nicola continued, a smile playing about her lips, "but I think poor Chloe would have enough to worry about without me turning up and putting her off!"

"Would *you*?" Laura asked. "Go ahead with marrying Dan after what you'd learned about him – if you were Chloe, I mean?"

"I'm not really the right one to ask!" Nicola laughed easily. "But no, I don't think I would."

"Me neither."

"What are you two gabbing about?" Helen appeared alongside them, her face lively and eyes sparkling. Since meeting Cormac she was positively glowing. Same old Helen.

"We're talking about weddings actually," Laura said.

"Oh, and Nicola, now that I think of it – it completely went out of my head to give you Debbie's number. Remind me again when we get home."

"Who's Debbie?" Helen asked.

"Amazing Days – Laura's stationery designer."

"Oh, God, don't!" Helen's eyes widened. "Knowing my luck, *you'd* end up with bloody Jamie's!"

The girls laughed, but surreptitiously, Laura caught Nicola's eye. Not once, in all the years since Jamie left, had Helen ever joked about him like that. This was progress indeed.

"Does Kerry mind staying with Cormac's sister while you're away?" Nicola asked.

"Mind? She couldn't wait for us to leave. Any excuse to spend time with Greg. She adores him, and strangely enough, the feeling's mutual. I didn't think big macho footballers like him would get a kick out of playing with Barbie dolls, but there you go."

The three girls laughed again.

"Listen, I must get my coat," Laura said, catching Neil's eye. "I'll see you later at the restaurant, OK?"

"Sure."

As she left Laura heard Nicola trying to wheedle information out of Helen about her and Cormac. "You must know he's mad about you," Nicola was saying.

"Do you really think so?" For once, Helen was bashful.

Laura was on her way back to her seat when she was waylaid by Amanda.

"Laura, fantastic show, wasn't it? I've been getting such a reaction from your jewellery. People just adore your work!"

"I think it went well."

"Went well! Nobody even noticed the clothes! It was your day, darling, your success!" And with that Amanda was off again, having spied someone else to fuss over. Laura shook her head, smiling. She had worked with the woman just long enough to know that while Amanda was a fantastic designer, she was invariably false and you couldn't believe a word that came out of her mouth.

"You're Laura?" an Irish male voice piped up from behind her. "The jewellery designer for the show?"

"Yes."

Whoever he was, Laura thought, he certainly belonged here. Dressed head to toe in what was undoubtedly Jean Paul Gaultier, the guy screamed fashion victim.

"Pleased to meet you," he said extending a hand. "I've been trying to find you since the show finished."

"And you are?" Laura asked, wondering why a camp guy like this could possibly be interested in handcrafted jewellery.

He flashed her a beaming smile. "You don't know me," he said, "but you might know my girls."

"Your girls?"

"Yes!" he smiled giddily at her. "You know, they just *adore* the whole gothic thing, and the fact that you're Irish – well, that's just great! You know it's so difficult for me to find hip Irish jewellery – all those Celtic crosses and Ogham stones are so passé these days!"

"O – K." Laura began to slowly back away. This guy seemed a bit of a nutter.

"Anyway," he went on, "Ms Connolly, I really don't want to delay you as I'm sure you're very busy, but it would be really great if your people could give us a call some time soon. We'd love to have you do something especially for us – the girls were delirious about the stuff you designed for Amanda's show."

"Us?"

"Well, yes." Mr Trendy stood still, puzzled by Laura's apathetic reaction, and then instantly seemed to recollect himself. "Oh gosh!" he exclaimed. "I still haven't introduced myself, have I? I'm a fashion stylist, Ms Connolly," he said, handing her his card with a beaming smile. "Fashion stylist to The Corrs!"

Laura's mouth dropped open.

THE END

Never Say Never

Melissa Hill

Sometimes hopes and dreams don't go according to plan – sometimes, real life gets in the way.

On a mild May evening, a group of friends on the verge of graduating speculate on what the future holds. Will Leah be a chef? Robin an accountant? And Olivia the one who holds it all together? The one thing they know is that they'll always be friends – no matter what – but they make a pact to meet up in years, just in case fate intervenes.

Years later it's clear that life has not gone according to plan. Why is Robin in New York determined never to go back to Dublin? Why is Olivia grieving? And why does Leah feel so left out as she heads towards the big three-o?

When Robin is forced to return, they all find themselves face to face with the past – suddenly nothing can ever be the same again. And they start to realize that sometimes it's best never to say never . . .

'An absolute joy from start to finish' *Irish Independent*

arrow books

The Nanny

Melissa Nathan

It'll take more than a spoonful of sugar to sort this lot out ...

When Jo Green takes a nannying job in London to escape her small-town routine, complicated family and perfect-on-paper boyfriend Shaun, culture shock doesn't even begin to describe it ...

Dick and Vanessa Fitzgerald are the most incompatible pair since Tom and Jerry, and their children – glittery warrior pixie Cassandra, bloodthirsty Zak and shy little Tallulah – are downright mystifying. Suddenly village life seems terribly appealing.

Then, just as Jo's getting the hang of their designer lifestyle, the Fitzgeralds acquire a new lodger and suddenly she's sharing her nanny flat with the distractingly good-looking but inexplicably moody Josh. So when Shaun turns up, things get even trickier ...

'One to gobble up in one sitting'
Company

'Hugely enjoyable'
heat

arrow books

The Waitress

Melissa Nathan

Katie Simmonds wants to be an educational psychologist. Last week she wanted to be a teacher, and the week before that a film director. Katie isn't short of ambitions, but none of her ambitions are to be a waitress. Unfortunately, Katie Simmonds is a waitress.

Hassled by customers, badly paid and stuck with the boss from hell, Katie's life isn't turning out as she'd planned. And a career choice isn't the only commitment she has problems with. But just when she thinks things can't get any worse, the café where she works is taken over by the last man in the world she wants to see again.

Maybe Katie's been waiting at tables – and waiting for Mr Right – for far too long ...

'Highly entertaining'
heat

'You'll find this very moreish'
Daily Mirror

arrow books

Restoring Grace

Katie Fforde

Ellie Summers' life is unravelling. Finding herself pregnant – and her sexy but idle boyfriend Rick less than enthusiastic about parenthood – she needs a plan. Fast.

Grace Soudley's life has been coming apart at the seams – her only real security is the beautiful yet crumbling old house she was left by her godmother. But unless she can find a fortune, Luckenham House will disintergrate around her.

When Ellie and Grace meet, the two very different women suddenly find they can help each other out. Ellie needs a place to stay; Grace needs a lodger. Both of them need a friend. But then disconcertingly engaging Flynn Cormack arrives on the scene, apparently determined to help. And when Grace discovers some beautiful painted panels hidden behind the tattered dining-room curtains, the whole business of restoration starts to get serious ...

'A heart-warming tale of female friendship, fizzing with Fforde's distinctive brand of humour'
Sunday Express

arrow books

THE POWER OF READING

Visit the Random House website and get connected with information on all our books and authors

EXTRACTS from our recently published books and selected backlist titles

COMPETITIONS AND PRIZE DRAWS Win signed books, audiobooks and more

AUTHOR EVENTS Find out which of our authors are on tour and where you can meet them

LATEST NEWS on bestsellers, awards and new publications

MINISITES with exclusive special features dedicated to our authors and their titles

READING GROUPS Reading guides, special features and all the information you need for your reading group

LISTEN to extracts from the latest audiobook publications

WATCH video clips of interviews and readings with our authors

RANDOM HOUSE INFORMATION including advice for writers, job vacancies and all your general queries answered

Come home to Random House

www.rbooks.co.uk